THE REVEAL

OTHER TITLES BY MEGAN CRANE

Edge of Obsession

Make You Burn

Devil's Honor

THE REVEAL

MEGAN CRANE

Montlake

This is a work of fiction. Names, characters, organizations, places, events, and incidents are either products of the author's imagination or are used fictitiously. Otherwise, any resemblance to actual persons, living or dead, is purely coincidental.

Published by Montlake, Seattle
www.apub.com

EU product safety contact:
Amazon Media EU S. à r.l.
38, avenue John F. Kennedy, L-1855 Luxembourg
amazonpublishing-gpsr@amazon.com

ISBN-13: 9781662531538 (paperback)
ISBN-13: 9781662531521 (digital)

Cover illustration and design by Story Wrappers

Printed in the United States of America

For Louise, because we miss our girl

1.

There are zombies in the trash again.

Twice already this morning and it isn't even light yet.

I punch my pillow and stop pretending I'm asleep. Who sleeps these days? That's a luxury I barely recall. I wake up from something resembling bad sleep every morning with a headache, my skull like an egg with a tender shell that's threatening to crack open. Thank you, terrible nightmares that plague me all night long, starring hideous creatures who call themselves "dark goddesses" while committing unspeakable acts upon my person.

So really, the zombies outside feel like a delightful escape from my own head.

I get up, scrub the not-enough sleep from my eyes, and mutter the same thing to myself I do every time I live to see another morning. "Monsters are real, and they will eat you without a second thought. Act accordingly."

A happy little mantra for life three years into the Reveal, because this is actually what "lucky" looks like.

What it *feels* like is complete shit, but you get used to that. Or you die.

I shrug into my usual uniform, strategically left on the floor last night by yours truly. Makes it easier to access, should something attack. Cargo pants to carry the necessities, like extra ammo, because no one goes anywhere without extra ammo. And whatever T-shirt I remembered to wash, because it's still hot at the end of September here in Southern Oregon. I strap on my knives and stick one in each boot. Then I move to the windows we boarded up three years ago, even up here under the eaves. I do a quick check to make sure nothing is loose, because monsters are crafty and relentless, the creepy fucks, and a loose board might as well be an invitation.

Through one of the old bullet holes, I look out into the yard behind my grandmother's house. It's littered with an old van my parents claimed they were remodeling but never did and four other broke-down cars no one ever claimed in my hearing. There's something that looks like farm equipment, though no one in my family has ever farmed anything. Everything is covered in the weeds that no one's cut in three years, because who has time to care about *lawns*. My gaze lingers on the remains of the vegetable garden that something dug up the last time I tried planting—leaving claw marks the size of my torso.

That ended my fantasies of freshly grown vegetables at our house.

"Cans over claws," I mutter, because I talk to myself now. A lot.

Maybe I always did, but back in the before time, I hid it better.

I reach for the BB gun my granddad used to shoot raccoons and pigeons out back when I was a kid. I'd love to see an adorable little raccoon, as a palate cleanser, but no. It's zombies.

But at least it's better than my nightmares. And my headache is beginning to ease its tight grip on my temples as I look outside, like real monsters are better than the ones in my mind.

I see them out there in the predawn light, snuffling and thrashing and moaning around in the trash enclosure. The lock on that gate never holds no matter what I try, so I always have to run them off myself. Zombies are harmless enough, relatively speaking. They want dead things, spoiled things. Not brains. Not blood or living flesh. Mind you, they move slow enough that you could turn into dinner—fully dead and spoiled—before they decide to shuffle on.

I don't like that I've become an unwilling expert on this subject. But there are a lot of other things I like a lot less these days, so I don't dwell on it.

Or I *try* not to dwell on it.

I load the gun without thinking about it, then I fire. *Pop pop pop* and the zombies do their slow-motion scatter, heaving themselves across the overgrown yard. I fire off a few more shots just to be sure, but they shamble away into the trees right as the sun comes up, sending golden light to dance through the lingering wildfire smoke.

It's pretty. The oranges and the reds remind me of the kinds of things Augie used to paint—

But thinking about my twin brother hurts, so I shove it aside. I put the BB gun back on the shelf by the window and leave the attic, running down the narrow stairs that lead to the rest of the house. I can already hear my grandmother muttering to herself. She likes to sit by her window and play with her spooky oracle cards every morning, but I know that in a minute or two she'll start shouting for me.

If she remembers me today. If not, she still shouts, but she doesn't use my name.

More stuff I try not to dwell on.

I check all the possible entrances and exits to my attic room to make sure they're secure. I do the same on the second floor, taking in the way the sunlight creeps around the edges of the boarded-up windows, beams of light shooting into the three bedrooms that line the hall. It's the only thanks I'll get for scouring them of any remnant of my parents, my brother, and Gran's crafting room, which was filled with way too many unnerving little items I wish I didn't know were there all along, *that near* to where I sleep—or try to sleep through the dark things in my head, anyway.

I try to look at the house like a stranger would as I head down the main stairs, to get a full sense of all the changes I've made. I've spent the past two weeks cleaning the hell out of it so it will match the cottages I've overhauled out front. It's not just the past three years of panic and hunkering down that were packed into this place, it's the lifetimes that came before. There were fingerprints all over this house my great-grandfather built with his own hands, and I wiped them all off myself.

Besides, cleaning out the rooms means I have better vantage points over the handful of cottages that are scattered out in front of the house along the edge of the big, wide yard that keeps the woods at bay. They were built at various times by various relatives of mine and have served many purposes over the years. It's taken me a long time to clean them out and turn them into rustic little dwellings, working on them in what few spare moments I could find.

Something I never would have done if I didn't think it was necessary.

Welcome to life after the end of the world, at least the one I knew. There are no *good* choices. Only bad ones, worse ones, and deadly ones.

I make it to the ground floor and pause by my grandmother's door, but she's deep into her muttering. My headache is still kicking in my temples, and the muttering doesn't help. So I walk through the living room and the old formal dining room, big and echoey around me now. It's hard to get used to. I haven't heard the floorboards squeak like this since I was small. That's how long it's been since anyone hauled all the crap out of here.

Some of it I packed away in the sheds out back, working fast in whatever sunlight there was. Some of it I burned in the firepit with all the monster bones. Some of it I couldn't bear to get rid of, so I used it to furnish the cottages. The rest I found places for upstairs in the now airy, empty bedrooms. I touch the medallion around my neck that I took from Augie's room, the one he never took off until he did, and hate that I still want to feel connected to him.

I know he doesn't want that. He's proved that enough times.

He doesn't want anything but the vampire blood that keeps him high, somewhere down by the river with the rest of them. Those lost souls who lived through the first catastrophic rush of the Reveal, then decided that a living death was better than figuring out how to go on.

Not that I had a choice about that, either.

I go into the kitchen through the metal door I installed—with a locking system that would make a feudal lord jealous and will more importantly keep the rest of the house inaccessible to any tenants—and make the bitter coffee I like because it tastes like my feelings. And usually helps clear out my morning headaches, too. I doctor Gran's with that powdered creamer that might be the only thing she truly loves. She's already squawking by the time I make it through her door, and she doesn't stop when she sees me. She points down at her cards instead.

I hate those cards. Old, weathered, long-used cards that my grandmother has always claimed let her *see*. Whatever that means. They're dark colored—or they were, once, long ago—with strange symbols on the backs and even stranger drawings on each card's face. Looking at them always makes me feel funny, like I'm standing on some high cliff and might topple off at any moment.

But there's no telling Gran that. She says the cards are a *sacred family heirloom* that I will appreciate *in time*.

I don't have the heart to tell her that like most of our family heirlooms, all of which I've cleaned out of this rickety old house, they're junk.

"You have a reckoning coming, Winter," she tells me loudly, squinting at me, and I feel the usual relief that today is another day she remembers my name, because those are getting scarce.

Reckonings can bite me like everything else that tries.

I set her coffee down. "Before or after I get you to the bathroom, Gran?"

She sniffs, but she lets me help her up. Then we take care of her usual morning routine. I don't mention that she seems more fragile or that she can walk fewer and fewer steps each day. I tell myself I'm protecting her, but I know better. As long as she can get herself from the bed to the chair, we can both pretend she's independent.

Some days I'm not sure which one of us is doing more of that pretending.

I settle her in her chair again when we come back so she can slurp her coffee. I make her bed because she complains if I don't.

"Remember what I told you," I say, though I don't expect her to. Her memory took off right around when my parents did. That was maybe a month before the Reveal, and it was a blessing, in its own way. For a while, Augie and I told her they were on their way back from the store.

Now she thinks *he* is.

I wish I didn't know better myself.

She frowns at me suspiciously, a little gnarled root of a woman in a chair that dwarfs her. Her frail little ankles stick out from beneath her nightgown because she likes slippers, not socks, and I find the sight of them heartbreaking, the way I always do.

"I remember," she says, the way she always does.

"We're going to have some new people around," I tell her in this weird, cheerful voice I only use in her room. Neither one of us buys it, but I can't stop. "I'm finally renting out the cottages. It's going to be fun."

She scowls at me, clearly not remembering that it was initially her idea that we open up the cottages to neighbors in need after the monsters started burning people out of their homes. "My mother always said that only a dire house takes in strangers."

I want to tell her that the house is dire as is. That it was so dire that cleaning it out made me feel as close to actual tears as I think I've ever been, and I'm the stern twin. That was what Augie always called me. I was the stern one and he was the sensitive one, but that's another dire thing, because now he's too sensitive to live and I'm so stern it might kill me.

I don't tell her that.

I want to tell her about my meeting with Franklin Hendry, the local mortgage broker who is my father's age and once dated my mother when they were kids—according to him, and she's not around to confirm or deny—at the bank at the end of last month. I want to share with her how dire *that* was. It's the end of the world in real time, but Franklin Hendry's out here ruining what few lives remain. I could tell her that it never occurred to me that anyone would come for the bills when there hasn't been an internet or cell phone service in years, or even any way out of this valley.

But Franklin Hendry was not devoured by the werewolves who cluster in the hills around the still-standing historic town of Jacksonville and no longer wait for full moons to change shapes. He was not exsanguinated with sneering contempt by the vampires who came out of the shadows and never went back in. He apparently avoided whatever that horrible clawed thing is that tore up my vegetable garden.

Some monsters are human, and this one has given me a deadline. I have until Halloween to pay off the back mortgage or Franklin Hendry is throwing us out.

I don't tell Gran that it's not me I'm worried about. It's her. I'd love to tell Franklin Hendry to go fuck himself, but I can still pretend there are things I might outrun, given enough of a head start. She can hardly walk.

Taking in a few tenants is the least of all these evils. If I could find my manager at the drive-through coffee hut on the road that heads south, toward Ashland, I would officially ask for more hours and a raise, but no one's seen poor Doug in months. Someone stocks the place, though. And I get an envelope of cash every Friday. That's the only reason I still show up. That and because I like a routine that feels normal when nothing else does, or ever will be.

Also, it turns out monsters like caffeine, like anyone else.

I don't tell Gran any of this. "It's a new adventure," I say instead, *brightly*. "When I was a little girl, you always told me that being afraid of new adventures was my cross to bear."

Gran frowns at me in that censorious way she never used to, but it's better not to think about the past. The good memories are harder to deal with. At least I know I survived the scary shit when the Reveal hit. It's not a happy ending, but it's something.

"I would never say something like that to my own daughter." She huffs at me. "I raised you better than to tell such lies, Lilianne."

I lean over and kiss her on her soft, wrinkly cheek. I stack her books and those battered, spooky old cards on the table beside her. I don't tell her I'm not my mother.

"Besides," Gran says in that dark, knowing way she does sometimes, "you never had the gift. It would be cruel to taunt you."

Sometimes my grandmother creeps me out more than the monsters roaming the valley—and the world—but I try not to let that get to me. Just like I try not to think about all that weird shit she had in her craft room. Knobby old roots and alarming figurines that looked a little too much like the shapes and symbols on her cards, no thank you.

"It's light out," I mutter. "I'll be back in a couple of hours. Blow the horn if you need help."

I give her the usual song and dance as I place the air horn on the table, within reach. I don't know if she'll remember to blow it. I don't know if the neighbors will come running the way they claimed they would. I don't even know if the Petersons made it through the night last night, or over the past week, because I haven't actually seen them in a while.

But when everything is uncertain, it's like nothing is. I act like what I want to be true is a fact. Because what else can you do?

Then I slip outside, making sure all the bolts and gates are shut tight behind me. I keep my weapons primed and ready as I head for my truck, scanning the yard for any incoming threats. I also look at the three cottages tucked into the edges of the woods, all of them "rustic," certainly, but a lot nicer than they used to be. Not something that can be said about much else these days.

I don't exactly hold my breath, but I don't really exhale fully until I'm in the driver's seat, the engine's running, and everything's locked. Better yet, until nothing blocks my exit out of our drive and onto the road that leads into town.

I used to love this drive. It winds through the woods, cutting its way down a neighborhood tucked into a hillside, into the main part of Jacksonville. Jacksonville itself is a perfectly preserved Western town that looks like Old West cowboys should come swaggering out through the doors of the old saloon, though these days, if they did, you'd have to accept that they were vampires. Growing up, it was filled with cute boutiques, festivals, restaurants, and a trolley that took tourists into the Applegate Valley wine country outside town.

But now the Applegate is overrun with monsters. Vampires feasted on the big megachurch out that way, gobbling up most of the parishioners one bloody Sunday. No one knows what happened to the wineries. I've heard rumors that there are human settlements way out by the lakes, where the California border lies and the gulches are easier to defend, but no one knows that for sure.

Jacksonville fared better. It was designated the only human-safe space in the valley about eighteen months ago by the powers that be in this valley, most of them monsters. Supposedly, we can walk around free of fear and don't have to worry about getting eaten. Or being dragged off to be someone's plaything in sick games I'd rather not think about too closely.

At first, no one believed we could ever be safe. Then we all got a little too comfortable with it. Every now and then, there's a monster who forgets the rules, and we all get vigilant again for a few days. The truth is, life is much shorter and more brutal than it used to be. We always come back out in the open.

This morning there are already people walking around, basking in the illusion of all that safety.

I slow the truck when I hit the main street, because I see Samuel Ruiz on the corner. Samuel is a few years older than me. He was a football player in high school and went on to play for the Ducks, which people cared about back then. Now he's basically the mayor and the entire city council of Jacksonville.

"Nice to see you out and about, Winter," he says into my window when I roll to a stop beside him. His voice is low and *perfect*, and his eyes are still green. Still so ridiculously *green*.

That's his way of saying, *Nice you're not dead.* And maybe more than that, I like to think. Maybe he's also saying *he's glad* I'm not dead.

"I'm going to do a few hours at the coffee hut," I say, stupidly, because I'm sure he knows where I'm going. There aren't that many people. We know each other's routines because knowing them means we also notice when you get dead.

He still has that same football body, I can't help but note. I'm not dead, not yet. And neither is he. He looks at me in that piercing way he has, then shifts that gaze to sweep for monsters and nod hello to other humans. Like a normal person would.

Like I should, but I don't.

"Jenny tells me you're taking in renters," he says, and then all that *green* is on me again. "Be careful. You don't want to wake up with a monster under your roof."

"Will the monster pay the rent money on time?" I ask, and he actually laughs, and I don't think about much else all morning.

Not even when a pair of hungry-looking vampires take advantage of the smoke that's filled the valley over the course of the morning, turning everything a choking gray. They don't have to worry about bursting into flame in the sunshine when the smoke strangles it, so they come at the window of the coffee stand and only back off when I turn the holy water squirt gun on them—the best thing ever found in the ruins of the local church by one of my coworkers, and left here to keep the vampires in line.

I watch them run and jump into a very nice Escalade they likely took after feeding on the poor driver—whoever he was—then peel out.

Then I think about Samuel some more. And more specifically, that day in the first year after the Reveal when Jacksonville's remaining humans actually crept out and met up for the first time. He'd organized that. He'd been the one to get everyone thinking about community again, instead of just hiding away by themselves. Then later he'd walked me home, up the hill to say hello to Gran, and he stayed.

I remember his mouth on mine in the dark of the crowded living room, piled high with crap and fortifications. I remember his body pressing me down, and how I'd wound myself around him like I was clinging to him for life.

It had been a dark, hot rush, and sometimes I think I dreamed it.

I hate dreams—they're why I prefer nightmares. Nightmares let you know where you are, that being some or other version of hell, and usually come in with a killer headache to make sure you're paying attention. Dreams pretend you could be somewhere else.

I especially hate dreams that were never talked about and never happened again, though I still catch him looking sometimes. Like today.

I tell myself he was definitely looking *today*.

At midday I go home, because the Jenny he mentioned is his sister and she runs the paper, because we have a paper again now. There's power—no one has ever explained how—but no internet, no TV, no radio. All of that blew up. Or someone ate it, who knows. Jenny's been collecting news for the past couple of years and passing it out all over the valley in the armored truck she got from one of the banks that didn't make it.

That's how I advertised for renters right here in the human safety zone.

I get home, I check on Gran and get her settled again, and then right on time, at twelve thirty, when I advertised that I'd talk to any cottage-rental hopefuls, there's a knock on the front door.

I open the door, but not the metal gate, and stand there with my guns drawn, the way I'd greet anyone.

But this isn't anyone.

This is a girl my own age.

A girl I recognize.

A girl I haven't thought about in a long time, because she was one of the few who got out. Back then, it wasn't monsters that kept people in the valley—it was not having money or sufficient imagination, take your pick. People hit ceilings in a place like this and stay put. And often wither. My parents are a prime example of that kind of surrendered life.

Maddox Hemming had never seemed like the college type. Too . . . physical. Slinking around with her wild hair, covered in tattoos, she was always followed by a pack of boys who couldn't seem to decide if she was one of them or their queen. I'd assumed she was having the sort of glorious adolescence *I* certainly wasn't.

That was a long time ago. Now it's three years past the Reveal, and I see the truth about Maddox isn't that she's secretly an academic, despite her defection to her fancy East Coast school.

Maybe she's that too.

But the important thing about Maddox Hemming is that she's a werewolf.

And, I now realize with a kind of horror mixed through with something that's not exactly *admiration*, always was one.

Because these days I know what a werewolf looks like in its human form—another gift of the Reveal. The way they hold themselves. That wild hair. And eyes that gleam gold when the light hits them just right.

She smirks at me. That's when I realize I've cocked both guns.

"Damn, Winter," she drawls, like this is a casual conversation in the bathroom of the old high school that someone burned down last year. Like she isn't a monster. Like I'm not pointing weapons at her face that she must know I'm fully prepared to fire. "That's an aggressive way to interview a potential renter. No wonder you have space to spare."

2.

I don't know how to respond to the idea of Maddox Hemming as a potential housemate, but I also don't have time to worry about it, because all I can hear is growling.

The kind of growling that makes every hair on my body feel like it's trying to crawl off and take cover.

It takes me a minute to understand that's not just inside me, a little hysteria to meet the moment, though if it were, that would be surprising. Given everything else that's happened, what's a werewolf at the door? Even if it's *this* werewolf, who won prom queen in a write-in campaign but was too cool to actually attend?

The growling gets louder, though, and it's not coming from Maddox, who crosses her arms and leans back against the porch rail like this is an easy, casual moment, with growling wolves and the smoke getting thick.

"Ignore them," she advises me. "I wish I could."

I take my eyes off her then, which maybe isn't the smartest thing in the world. But I don't lower my guns. There are different levels of *not smart* on this side of the Reveal. And I like my chances at close range.

That's when I see them, shapes in the smoke out there where the yard turns into tangled knots of madrone trees and tall pines. The wind shifts, so the smoke does too, and the shapes become men in leather jackets, jeans, and motorcycle boots. A pack of them, and I would know them for werewolves even if I didn't know them by name. More or less.

They are the type of men that everyone could tell were feral before we knew how to identify wolves at a glance.

"My cousins," Maddox confirms, without turning around. "They're not real big on the idea of me moving this close to humans."

I shift my gaze back to her. "You have fangs. And claws. And, you know, superhuman strength and speed. According to all known reports."

She laughs at that, and I feel the strangest sense of dizziness, because it's like falling through time. Back before all the monsters and loss and terror. Back to high school, when I would hear that same laugh down a hallway and see a glimpse of Maddox as she glided by, more effortless and powerful than a teenage girl ought to be.

If someone had told me she was a werewolf then, even though it was years before all the monsters would reveal themselves, I would have believed it.

"Historically speaking," she tells me when she stops laughing, "humans are pretty good at coming up with new and ingenious ways to hunt us down. We take a dim view of that and generally prefer to stick together."

"If you move into one of the cottages, what I'll want to hunt down is your rent money." I hold her gaze for a moment, noticing how strange and compelling her eyes are. Were they always this unusual? I'm not sure I ever dared look at her directly before. But I'm looking now, and her gaze is like smoky quartz, though it feels silly and overwrought to describe anything so poetically in days like these. But that's what they're like. Smoky and dark. I force a little smile. "And a hefty pet deposit."

I don't lower the guns as I say that, either.

Maddox looks back at me for a long moment, kicked back there against the post like she can't personally hear her cousins growling behind her. Then, slowly, her mouth curves into a smile.

"Cute," she says. She inclines her head. "I don't blame you."

We stay like that for a moment, taking each other's measure, I think.

It must go on too long because one of her brows hikes up. "Are you going to show me what you have available?"

This is the moment of truth. She knows it. I know it.

But I also know Maddox. Or I know *of* her, anyway. She went off to college, and not here in Oregon. She went all the way to the East Coast. That makes her different enough from most of the kids we went to high school with, including me, even before we got to the monster situation.

In some places, going to college after high school used to be a given. An expectation, even. But here it was just one possible choice among many and, given that it was the one that cost the most money, not the choice that most people took. I certainly didn't. Yet Maddox not only made that choice but took herself far, far away after she made it. And I would have heard about it if she'd been involved in a killing spree while she was off studying in one of those cities I've only ever seen on TV. It would have been the talk of the valley.

As far as I know, she also never killed anyone in high school, despite the great many fools we went to high school with. Besides, it's not that werewolves aren't scary—they're fucking terrifying, actually—but they don't attack without provocation. Generally.

They also don't tend to play with their food. This goes in the plus column.

"Okay," I say after I do this math a time or two, second-guess it, and then do it again. "Sure. You can look around. See if you're a good fit."

She looks like she wants to laugh at that, too, but she doesn't. Instead, bonelessly, she shifts off the porch rail and looks back over her shoulder. "I'm going to look around. You're not."

Maddox says that quietly, as if she's talking to people standing right beside her, though it's clearly not directed at me. I make a note that werewolf hearing is as good as people claim it is, because there's an immediate chorus of growls at that. I don't have to speak wolf to get that they don't like it.

She only waves a dismissive hand at them. "You want to keep guard, keep guard. But keep it at a respectable distance."

Her gaze is back on me. She lifts a brow again, like she's waiting but possibly getting a little impatient.

And so, second-guessing myself all over again like it's my only true vocation, I tuck one of my guns into its holster and undo the locks on the gated door. Then I push it open, step out, and basically present myself on a plate to a werewolf.

I keep the other gun trained on her.

"Why do you want to rent a place anyway?" I ask as she glides down the steps to the yard, smooth and inevitable, enough so that I have to question what I think the gun is going to do if she comes for me—but that's not a helpful line of thought. "Not that I know your life, but I always thought your family liked to stay close."

I wave the gun in the direction of the line of cottages, off to the left. The other werewolves are clustered at the mouth of the drive toward town, so if they start for me, I'll have a few moments to react—but I like those odds. I keep an eye on them as Maddox saunters past me toward the first of the cottages and takes her time looking around.

She looks like she's admiring nature, nothing more, but I doubt it. I imagine she's calculating the position of each cottage and how defensible they all are, the way I would be.

I should be used to looking impossible things in the face by now.

Her being here, wandering about the yard I cleaned up myself, shouldn't even register.

She shoves her hands into the pockets of her jeans as she walks, her hair as long and wild as always, not one shade but all the shades. Today she's wearing a cropped tank top that shows off her mysterious tattoos and the sort of physique that would require a human to commit to nothing but brutal aesthetics forever but I think is just standard werewolf athleticism. It comes with killer abs and a belly ring, apparently.

"Diplomatic," she murmurs, right when I'm about to forget I asked a question. "My family does stick together. Kind of like a pack."

The last thing I need to do is insult a fucking *werewolf* while standing this close to her. If she decides to attack, I won't have any moments or odds. I'll just be dead. "I didn't mean—"

"Settle down." Her laugh is throaty. "I'm not looking for a snack, and anyway, you're not wrong. The family in general likes to keep it close, but I got used to living on my own."

"Right." I'm still holding the gun on her, though it's beginning to seem foolish here in the middle of a perfectly pleasant conversation. But I don't lower it. "How was that? The whole East Coast college thing?"

Her expression changes and she looks away, but not before I see . . . something there on her face. On someone else, I'd be tempted to call it sadness.

But when she looks back, she smiles. "It's not a bad thing to go someplace where no one's ever heard of you. I liked it."

It's my turn to smile. "I can't even imagine. Not Lilianne Bishop's daughter? Not Augie's twin? Not Sarah's granddaughter? How would I even exist?"

Maddox nods. "You get it."

I tell myself that it's just leftover high school stuff that has me feeling a little silly after that, like my insides are carbonated, because the coolest girl in high school approved of something I said.

This strikes me as a really great way to get eaten.

I order myself to snap out of it as we reach the first cottage. "There's a kitchen and laundry in the main house," I tell her. "But other than that, the house is off limits."

I don't explain why. The fact of me being human and snackable is why. It doesn't need stating.

Then again, if her other wolf senses are as good as I suspect her hearing is, she probably doesn't need any explanation. She can likely scent my wariness as easily as she can smell my grandmother in her room from across the yard.

Or maybe she knows all about me the way I know all about her, because monsters or not, Jacksonville is a tiny little mountain town in a valley that has always been fairly isolated. The population was just under three thousand people before the Reveal. I don't think anyone knows what it is now, only that it's smaller.

Much, much smaller.

At the door to the cottage, I motion for her to go in before me. I think I see a glint in those compelling eyes of hers, but she doesn't argue. She lilts her way onto the front step with that same light, easy athleticism that reminds me—in a jarring sort of way—that I've known this woman for most of my life. Maybe not for the past seven years or so, but before that, I would know her at a glance even if I saw her in a crowd.

It feels like a strange sort of intimacy. I've had precious little of that the past three years.

I wait outside, my back to a tall tree and my eyes on the growling men across the yard, as Maddox goes in and out of the three cottages. They're all minimally furnished, with beds and dressers, and rugs to take the cold out of the wood floors. The largest one sits a little bit farther back into the woods, giving the illusion of privacy. I made it nice, but to me, it will always be the shack my parents moved into when they wanted my grandmother out of their business. That led nowhere good. Augie followed their lead after high school, moving into one of the smaller cottages with similar results.

Maddox takes her time exploring, then comes back to find me by the tree. "I'll take the big one, if it's available."

"It is."

"Look at that," Maddox says with a smile. "We're practically roommates."

I think about that as I take her around to the back of the house and sit at the kitchen table—gun still between us and pointed at her—to hammer out the details. Was she being nice? Or was that a threat? If a person happens to be a supernatural being with excessive agility, speed, and even more athleticism than she has in her human form, she could very easily use her proximity to the house to find a way into it.

Augie and I climbed out onto the roof above the front porch and then down to the ground more than once during high school—and then back in again. It wasn't *easy*, but it was doable. And we were not werewolves.

I think about what Samuel said, about not letting monsters live here, but that's easy for him to say. No one's chasing him and his sister for mortgage money, which we might all know is just an extortion racket—but everyone in the valley also knows Franklin Hendry is a bully. A mean one.

I name an extravagant rent-and-wolf-deposit figure, or at least it seems extravagant to me, but Maddox only shrugs. "Sounds great. When can I move in?"

I assume this shell-shocked feeling will fade. It better. I need to be more scared of her than awed. "As soon as you want."

"I'll be in by tonight." She stands up from the kitchen table, then digs into one of her pockets and pulls out a very thick wad of cash. "This is half the security deposit. I'll be back with the rest of the deposit and all of my shit. Can't wait for girl talk, roomie."

"That sounds vaguely threatening, actually." I'm proud that I dare to say that to her.

"What? I can braid hair." But she laughs at that as she turns and saunters on out of the house.

And it takes me a long few moments to recognize that I'm still sitting there where she left me. At the kitchen table, still holding a gun in front of me.

A gun that didn't seem to concern her at all.

But beggars can't be choosers, especially not in times like these. I pocket the cash after counting it out to find that it is, in fact, exactly half of the security deposit.

Then I make my way out of the locked-tight kitchen to the front door to secure the gate from the inside. Out in the yard, I see Maddox and those men. Her cousins. *Wolves*, just like her.

But what they look like—what they've always looked like—is bikers. The dangerous, Harley-Davidson-riding, *Sons of Anarchy*–type outlaw bikers, that is. There are symbols on the leather they wear, but they're not in English. Maybe they never were. They're the kind of men that encourage you not to make direct eye contact, because even when they were passing as human, they were still predators.

Maddox, meanwhile, weaves through them with total unconcern.

No wonder she found high school entertaining, if this was her homelife.

I stand there watching as they walk back into the trees. When I finally hear the sound of their motorcycles firing up, it's far enough away that I get the impression they parked down at the bottom of the drive.

It feels a lot like they walked up to get the lay of the land without alerting anyone to their presence. Something that wouldn't have occurred to me three years ago, but I think a lot more about defense strategies now.

When the earsplitting sound of their Harleys is gone, I take the opportunity to walk out into the yard and look around. I don't see any lurking monsters, which is good. But looks can be deceiving. I'm hoping that the presence—and, I can only hope, lingering scent—of that many werewolves in the front yard will keep all the rest of the tooth-and-claw crowd at bay.

I examine the front of the house and the yard, then the cottages, and not with the usual surge of nostalgia and emotion. Because right now it doesn't matter that this is my childhood home. That it has its own tangled little history, plunked down here in the Jacksonville hills. Right now I'm looking for access points and weaknesses in my perimeter.

It will obviously be no trouble at all for werewolves to hop right up onto the roof of the porch of the main house and go inside, should they decide they want to. That means they can also get up on the actual roof, giving them access to me in the attic, so that means it's time to install some more iron gates over the windows.

Probably should have thought of that before I put an ad in the paper, but in my defense, I thought humans would be the ones moving in here. I thought we'd unite against the monsters, if necessary—but just in case the humans were untrustworthy too, I'd blocked access to the house from the kitchen.

I remind myself that Maddox could have killed me at any moment during the house tour. She didn't. Not to mention, there's no reason I can think of that the local werewolf pack would want to go to such lengths to station one of their own here.

Besides, she gave me money. I need money. So that kind of answers any questions right there.

I go back inside, close the heavy gate but not the door, and check on Gran. Thankfully, she's deep into her afternoon nap. She mutters a little as I look at her, and I wonder what she dreams of. Or if she has nightmares like me. But if she can recall her dreams when she wakes, she never remembers them long enough to tell me.

I ease her bedroom door shut behind me and lock it again, just in case anyone else drops by. The ad said I would be entertaining candidates from 12:30 to 3:00 p.m. I expected that no one would come. When Gran came up with the idea to make room for renters in the cottages, it was to help people. But that was a long time ago, when we thought folks would band together and take care of each other. We learned better.

Franklin Hendry made the rental idea a necessity, though, so here we are.

As I'm thinking that, I hear a vehicle approaching. My first, wild thought is that it's the werewolves, coming back to tell me it was all a joke and it's snack time after all—

But they wouldn't come up the drive, which is half washed-out and not something I'm in a hurry to fix, in an SUV.

Particularly not the gleaming, scratchless, *shiny* Land Rover that pulls up in the yard outside and parks next to my poor old beat-down truck. I'm so dazzled that it takes me a minute to recognize that someone's climbing out of the driver's side and alighting on the dead grass of the yard.

My second thought is that this woman is much too *expensive* to be looking for housing. She looks upper crust, whatever that means. Almost otherworldly, because everything about her looks smooth and soft and *cared for* in a way I would have found alien even before the Reveal. She's wearing a *dress*, first of all, instead of the more utilitarian clothes that suit this postapocalypse. A silk dress, if I'm not mistaken, not that I'm a fabric expert. Her hair is long, thick, and glossy brown, and her bangs expertly frame her face. When she slides her oversize sunglasses down her nose to look toward the house, her eyes are luminous, a shade darker than her hair.

She looks as if a harmful ray of light has never dared touch her glowing skin. The smoke seems to clear a path around her, and the yellow tinge the wildfires leave in the sky doesn't make her look the least bit jaundiced. Not like the rest of us.

But she doesn't cross toward the house. She doesn't check out the cottages, either. Instead, she frowns. She shoves her sunglasses back into place and looks back down the drive, toward the trees, where the smoke seems heavier and thicker.

I feel the urge to shiver, but I don't. I pull out my second gun and am thankful I'm safe behind the gate.

The woman by the Land Rover cocks her head slightly to one side, and the trees seem to shake, but I have to be imagining that. I make myself breathe.

And then, oddly enough, a girl who looks about my own age walks out of the forest and into the yard.

She and the woman look at each other, and I swear there's some kind of . . . ripple of recognition between them. Or maybe the smoke seems to move. It's weird, and it leaves me winded, but they don't speak.

Both of them walk to the front door, though to me it seems as if there's some kind of humming electricity all around them. Or maybe an incoming storm, as rare as those are before October.

"Do you two know each other?" I ask when they draw close.

"I just know the vibe," says the girl, and I can see the piercing in her tongue as she rolls her eyes. "Fancy car, fancy clothes, fancy life. Not like the rest of us."

It's true that she doesn't look like she possesses any of those things. She has a stocking hat jammed on her head, with black hair braided messily beneath. She's wearing a faded old Pixies T-shirt, baggy cargo pants, and is covered in tattoos. There's even one wrapped around her neck, like a background canvas for all the other piercings I can see on her face.

The beautiful woman sighs. I hear Gran's wind chimes move in the old oak tree, though I can't feel any breeze. "I'm looking for a private cottage to call my own," she says to me, as if the other girl never spoke. "Are any left?"

I catch the girl looking at her with such animosity that it's hard to imagine there isn't at least *some* personal feeling behind it. Then again, it could be the silk and the smooth skin, like she's spent the past three years in a spa.

But I stop worrying about their interpersonal dynamics, because I'm too busy trying to scan them for signs. That they might shift into something scary. That they are some kind of monster I can't identify on sight. I check the smoky sky behind them, and that's the trouble. They could be vampires. Especially the fancy one.

Substitute "crypt" for "spa" and she makes sense.

Despite some initial hopes that the vampires who turned up after the Reveal would sparkle and long to keep taking high school classes as their main form of entertainment, that has not proven to be the case. They're mostly just vicious and terrifying as they rampage at will, but true to most myths, they can't go out in the sun.

How lucky for them that the weather here is either cloudy or smoky almost all year round.

I open the gate. Meaning, I throw the locks. Then do nothing else.

I step back, my guns in my hands because bullets slow anything down—at least enough for me to get the wooden stakes—and wait.

Understanding flashes in the woman's gaze. She opens the gate and steps inside, no invitation required. Not a vampire. This doesn't mean she's not deadly, but she's not *that* kind of monster. These days, everything is a process of elimination.

Both of us glance back at the stocking-hat-headed girl. She sneers as the gate slams shut in front of her, then flings it open herself and walks on through.

"No bloodsucking dickheads, apparently." She glares at both of us, but mostly the fancy woman beside her. "I would have lost that bet."

The woman—who, now that she's closer, also looks vaguely the same age as me, though she's so well kempt that it's impossible to tell—sighs again. "Not the first bet you've lost, I imagine."

I want to laugh, but that seems unwise. I shoo them back outside again and let the gate slam shut behind us. Then I give them what I guess is now my landlady spiel. "I'll be armed at all times," I tell them. "You can only be visibly armed when I'm comfortable with you, and that will be unlikely. You are allowed in the back of the house, meaning the kitchen and the laundry room. If I catch you in any off-limits areas, immediate eviction. Whether you break curfew or not is your business, but if you think you can get around that by bringing unvetted guests back here, think again. You and they will be forcibly evicted. By me. In daylight."

"That sounds eminently reasonable," says the first woman, and her voice is so . . . melodious that I wonder if it was really wind chimes I thought I'd heard before. Something in me even seems to shift at the sound of it, and that's annoying. Also alarming. I grip my guns a little tighter.

"I'm Savi Wynn," she says, and smiling graciously, she extends her hand.

"We don't need to shake hands," I tell her, because it's never a good idea to touch something if you don't know what it is. "Nice to meet you."

"I'm Briar," says the sneering girl. Still sneering. Then she pauses and we both look at her. "Briar Monroe."

I don't know that I believe that's actually her name. Then again, the thing about life-altering events like the Reveal is that people end up different on the other side. Assuming this is the other side. Maybe it's not the worst thing in the world to take on a new identity. Forge a new path. Do whatever you can with what little time you have left.

And anyway, there's no court I can go complain to if it turns out they both made up their identities.

All I have is my gut, and it's gotten me this far. I go with that as I take both of them out to the cottages and watch as they register the two that are left.

I expect them to get into a scrap over who gets which cottage, particularly because one of them is little more than a shed and held what I dearly hope was just old farming-type implements. If not, it's highly likely that one of my ancestors had a taste for the odd serial killing. I don't like to go in there, and not only because it's tiny. But Briar seems drawn to the place. She goes inside and closes the door, and I can hear her clomping around like she's measuring the space with her feet.

Savi and I are out in the yard, our backs against different trees, while the smoke dances between us. For some reason it makes me think about my latest nightmare, smoky and scary, but I shut that down fast.

"I like this one," Briar says when she opens the door and peers out. She glares, but not at me. "If that's all the same to you, Your Majesty."

"I think this is a very happy place," Savi says. This time directly to me.

I can't help but laugh at that. "You don't have to flatter me. There's nothing happy about this place. There never was, even before the Reveal. But the cottages are yours if you can pay."

Savi smiles in that way of hers that I find surprisingly mysterious. And possibly aristocratic. "Money is no problem. Safe accommodation, on the other hand, is of paramount importance."

The way she says that makes me wonder who she's running from if she wants to hide out from them on a hill in the woods. I don't ask.

"About that," I say as Briar drifts back out into the yard. "How do you feel about werewolves?"

Briar snorts. "Which side of their teeth am I on?"

I shrug. "She's someone I went to high school with. Didn't realize she was a werewolf then, of course, but she is. She took the other cottage. Says she wants a little distance from the pack."

"And you believe her?" Savi asks.

It didn't occur to me *not* to believe her, and that's interesting. I file that away.

"I didn't shoot her. Yet."

Once again, Savi and Briar look at each other in a way that seems to spark with an energy I can't quite understand. It doesn't feel personal, or romantic. Just heavy and clearly obvious to them—and I decide that letting on that I notice it is a bad play, so I keep that to myself.

"I'm fine with it as long as she keeps her fangs to herself," Briar mutters. "Theoretically. I don't really like dogs."

"I do have some concerns about the full moon," Savi chimes in. "As long as we all reach an agreement of acceptable behavior, I'm not opposed. Necessarily."

"Great," I say, like that was a full-throated agreement, and wave them toward the house with my gun. "It's like we're a happy family already."

And after they leave, having signed my makeshift lease agreements and ponied up some cash, I go and check on Gran again. I'm happy to see she's still snoring and decide that the smart move is not to sit around with this much cash on hand.

There are at least three people who know that I have piles of cash on me right now. That's three too many, and more, it's asking for an ambush.

I fire up the truck and head back down the hill into town.

It's crowded again, and I can't help but find that comforting. Like *normal* might be a possibility again someday. If I squint, maybe having to pay the mortgage is almost normal too? But I can't quite get there. I wave a hand at folks I recognize and then park my truck in front of the bank. I grit my teeth and go inside, feeling more resentful with every step.

This place is part museum, part bank, because that's how this town rolls. And no one works here except Franklin Hendry himself, that asshole.

"Come to cry uncle, Winter?" he asks, his smarmy voice filling the airless room, ricocheting in and out of the pioneer exhibit in the window.

I find it more satisfying than it should be to march up to his massive desk, look him in the eye, and slam that pile of cash down in front of his jowly face.

"I'll need a written receipt for this portion of the mortgage payment," I tell him. "Just to keep us both honest."

He squints up at me in that same way he always does. Patronizing. Condescending. *Pitying.* The dick.

"It's like trying to plug up a leak with chewing gum, Winter," he says sorrowfully.

I wish for a moment that I had a pair of fangs at my disposal, but I don't.

"A written receipt, please," I say, and I hope it sounds like I think he's a liar and a cheat, because I do.

I keep standing there, refusing to give him the satisfaction of sitting down, or looking cowed, or doing anything but staring back at him impassively as he takes his sweet time counting the bills. He licks his finger between each one, which disgusts me. I'm not sure if it's because he keeps fondling the filthy money itself, or if it's simply that fleshy *slurp* he takes off his finger each time.

Both, I decide. This is a man who's gotten fat and rich while the world lies in ruins around him. He's gross.

He pulls out an enormous ledger and ostentatiously marks the amount I gave him in it. Then he swivels it around so I can see how much I have left to go.

I already know. It's a lot.

"You might want to face reality sooner rather than later," he tells me. "There's no shame in it. You're just a young girl, and these aren't even your debts."

"I don't need to be given permission to fail by the guy personifying predatory lending, thanks." I do not call him "Mr. Hendry," as he's repeatedly requested. I think it's a gift that I don't call him the colorful names my father liked to use when talking about him.

He shakes his head at me as if I am a great disappointment to him—not a surprise—and detaches the receipt part of the page to hand it to me. "I can't say that I appreciate your attitude, Winter. I've been nothing but accommodating. And you are only extending the agony. Losing that house is inevitable, I'm afraid."

"Maybe you missed the part where monsters rose from the dark shadows, ripped the world apart, and left us nothing but trouble, ruin, and imminent death." I laugh. "You or I could be torn apart by zombies at any moment, but sure, let's talk about the inevitability of defaulting on a mortgage payment when I'm pretty sure there are no *real* financial institutions left."

We stare at each other, maybe both contemplating the injustice of this—but we both also know there's not much I can do about it. Who is there to complain to? Franklin Hendry doesn't scare me in and of himself, but I know he has his goons on hand to take care of the people he considers squatters. I can't have them roughing up Gran the way they did the family that lived in a fifth wheel that Franklin had his eye on last fall. He claimed they owed him money, they refused to pay, and next thing you know they're all beat into little more than bruises. No one's seen the father since.

Franklin has his own crew of monsters. They just happen to be human.

If it were just me, I'd tell him to go fuck himself and take my chances with his minions, but it's not just me.

We both know he's got me.

"Halloween, Winter," he says softly.

I feel sick to my stomach, because there's nothing I can do. Because I feel helpless, and I hate feeling helpless. Not that anyone *likes* it, but it reminds me of too many things, only some of them monster related.

Watching my parents get worse and worse before finally taking off. Watching Augie follow that same path, telling lie after lie until it was easier, somehow, for him to simply disappear.

This almost feels worse, because Franklin Hendry doesn't *have* to do this. He's not *compelled* by forces outside his control to be a dick. He *wants* to bully people he thinks are weak and have no recourse.

I just have to come up with more money.

I turn and storm back out of the historic bank onto Jacksonville's pretty main street and run straight into Samuel.

Straight into him so that he catches me by my elbows and I nearly collide with his chest.

I wish I did.

"Oh," I say, suddenly feeling the polar opposite of sickened. "Hi. I just—"

"Did you really rent out outbuildings on your property to *actual monsters*, Winter?" Samuel demands, scowling down into my face. His green eyes are *blazing*. This is more exhilarating than he means it to be, I'm sure. "Is this some kind of death wish? Because you don't have to go to all the trouble of putting out ads for monsters, you know. You can just go down to the river, show a vampire your neck, and let it feed. Problem solved."

3.

“The jury is out on two of them as to whether or not they’re monsters,” I reply almost automatically, not sure if I’m confused or simply taken aback, but his hands are still gripping my elbows and that’s hard to think past. Also, I’ve never seen him angry before. Certainly not at *me*. “The other one is Maddox Hemming.”

Samuel knows exactly who Maddox Hemming is, I can see that immediately. Because everyone knows who Maddox Hemming is. He lets go to step back, and normally I would consider that one of the greatest losses of all time. But instead, I fold my arms over my chest and frown right back at him because . . . what is this?

“Maddox Hemming is a werewolf,” Samuel tells me, very distinctly and slowly, as if I’m an idiot.

“Thank you,” I reply. Stiffly. “I’m aware.”

“Winter. You can’t live that close to a werewolf.” He shakes his head as if I’ve disappointed him, and unlike the disappointment of crooked and creepy old bankers, this lands. It feels like a punch in the solar plexus. I’m not sure I know *how much* I rely on his good opinion of me until this moment. “For any number of reasons, but mostly because she’ll slaughter you in your sleep.”

“How did you even hear about my tenant situation?” I ask him, because there’s the usual small-town grapevine that none of us can ever escape entirely, but this feels extreme. “This literally all happened in the past few hours.”

"News travels fast when you do stupid shit," Samuel says darkly.

"Luckily, I'm not doing any stupid shit," I reply, stung. "I live in Jacksonville, Samuel. Supposedly a safe zone. We can either choose to believe that or not."

"One way to keep it safe is not to shack up with *fucking werewolves*."

"Of the monster attacks in the past three years that violated the safe-zone boundaries, none of them were perpetrated by werewolves," I remind him. Maybe a little tensely. "You know that as well as I do."

Because we go to all the same meetings. We read the same paper his sister puts out. Or maybe *I* go to *his* meetings, something that I find sits on me wrong, all of a sudden.

I don't like it. "Is there anything else, Samuel? Any more character assassinations? Want to call me an idiot a few more times?"

He blows out a breath, though he doesn't apologize. "I don't think you should do this," he tells me gruffly. "It's not safe."

I'm touched by his concern. Really, I am. Later, after I barricade myself in my bedroom and put new iron gates on my windows to deter the werewolves I refuse to admit I'm *slightly* concerned about, I'm sure I'll trot that out and cuddle up with it. As I try to sleep through another long night of nightmares about some scary, powerful creature with snakes in her face.

Right now, all I can do is laugh. "Samuel. Look around. What the hell is safe anymore?"

I'm still asking myself that when I get back up to the house—after getting extra keys made for the back door and the cottages and taking a trip to the scrapyard, where I avoid another clutch of zombies and find some good pieces of usable iron—to find my three new housemates standing in the yard.

It looks like they're all about to throw down and get in a fistfight.

This seems deeply unwise for many reasons, but the main one is that there's a line of dangerous men and Harleys to one side.

"Finally," Maddox drawls when I get out of the truck, my favorite gun already in my hand. "This is getting very boring."

She certainly looks bored, but then, she always does.

"Which one of you told all of Jacksonville that I'm taking on a werewolf as a boarder?" I ask as I make sure to lock my own truck. "Just out of curiosity."

"Oh, that was me," Maddox confesses with a grin, all boneless there against the side of her vehicle. "You know how it is. Mrs. Bosko always hated my guts, but she *loves* you. It was petty, but it had to be done."

"Mrs. Bosko lives two doors down." I shake my head. "She's never going to sleep again."

Maddox grins wider. "I did say it was petty."

This is another reason I don't think Maddox is planning to feast on my bones while I sleep. It's too small-town here. Maybe the wolf pack wouldn't care if she ate me, but everyone else will gossip about it forever after, and if she's still upset that Mrs. Bosko—our sixth-grade teacher—doesn't like her, she's small-town too.

This I find comforting. Almost feels like old times—the before times, when a person's behavior in preschool could haunt them for a lifetime.

"Maybe you don't see the pack of werewolves right there," Briar interjects from where she's standing back near her cottage. "I thought you said *one* werewolf."

Savi, still in silk, looks unperturbed. But this seems like deliberate provocation to me.

Maddox shrugs. "I keep telling her to ignore them. They're not a *pack*, they're just my cousins. And, this time, as a bonus, one of my brothers."

She glances over at the extraordinarily scary and dangerous-looking men standing there like they're getting ready to wade into war, arms folded, with stony glares moving from Maddox to each of my other two housemates, and now to me.

Having never drawn the attention of the local werewolves, I can't say that this thrills me either.

"They *really* don't want me moving in here," Maddox tells me lazily. "They prefer to keep the home fires burning the way they always have. Very traditional, apparently, for a bunch of dudes who take pride in calling themselves outlaws."

This inspires a low sort of communal rumble. It takes me a moment to realize it's all those scary men growling again.

Now only Maddox seems unperturbed, but I think she might be faking.

"He's gonna kick your ass," says one man, who I recognize, with a shock, as her brother Liam. The last time I saw him was in high school. He was a senior when I was a freshman, and I'd thought he was dangerous then. Now it's hard to find that boy's face behind the beard and the tats and what looks like pure fury aimed straight at his sister. "And you'll have it coming."

"Don't listen to him," Maddox tells me. "I don't." She looks slightly less boneless, I notice, and maybe that's her version of alarm. "Can we move in?"

It's not like I haven't thought about this from every angle, despite what Samuel seems to think. I had a lot of time to think about it while I cleaned out the cottages to make room for the new tenants and then the house, too, to make room for vantage points. The truth is, everyone and everything is dangerous in its own way. If there were only humans here, it's not like I could trust them either. Everyone's out for themselves.

Maybe that was always true, but it's only after the Reveal that those things became a lot starker and more likely to involve someone dying.

Opening up our property is risky no matter what I do.

But not opening it up means handing over these acres my ancestors tamed to revolting Franklin Hendry without a fight.

And deep beneath all the reasons that can't happen is this one: There's a part of me that thinks that some member of this family has to stay in this house in case the ones we lost find their way back. My mom and dad. Augie.

There's almost something about inviting a werewolf here myself that feels like some small measure of control in the middle of all the rest of this shit that I can't seem to do anything about.

"Welcome home," I tell the three of them.

Then I give each one of them a key to their particular cottage and stand back with an eye on the werewolves in the yard as my life changes once again.

Briar rushes inside her shed with nothing more than a beat-up duffel bag slung over her shoulder. She looks around furtively, then barricades herself inside. I can hear her throw the bolt from the porch, across a decent span of grass and dirt.

Savi unloads a collection of bags, all of them pristine-looking in matching white hardshell, and zipped up tight. There's no clue as to what might be in them. Books? Clothes? Weapons? The secret to looking so *unruffled* all the time? She brings them out of her gleaming SUV two at a time and carries them across the yard to her cottage as if they are weightless, because she never seems to break a sweat.

Maddox takes her time, unloading that big old Ford Explorer she drove up here and appearing to lollygag while doing it. I immediately understand that she's doing this to irritate her family—because the more they grumble, the slower she goes.

I can't help but find it amusing that even werewolves have family drama.

But when I step inside to leave them to their games and settling in, I can hear Gran muttering. It's true that I don't think Maddox is here to hurt me, but I can't say the same for her relatives, so I lock the gate and the front door tight behind me. I do the same with the door to her room once I'm inside.

I help Gran out of bed and into her chair. Once she's settled, she eyes me, cannily enough that I am tempted to imagine that she's all there this afternoon.

"Who is on my land?" she asks.

The way she asks this reminds me—sharply—of years ago when Augie and I would run around, get into all kinds of trouble, and then have to explain ourselves to our stern grandmother when we came back home. Gran was never the pushover our mother was.

Gran liked consequences. She was never afraid of delivering them. Mom just liked getting high.

"I told you earlier that we'd be getting tenants today," I say, cheerfully, because she sometimes responds to cheerful. "I'll be honest with you, Gran. I thought it would take a while. Not everyone wants a very simply furnished room in a rustic little cottage. But I got three takers within an hour."

It seems more unbelievable to me when I say it out loud, but it doesn't have to be *believable*. It just has to pay the mortgage and keep Gran in one piece and without bruises. Nothing else matters.

"Winter." I can't help it. Every time she says my name, it makes me want to dance around a little bit. Or cry. Because every time she says it, I worry that it's the last time. That she'll never know me again. "You need to be more careful."

"Careful of what?"

Gran looks at me in that way again, as if she can see straight into me, down deep into my bones. "Can't you feel it? She is stirring."

"You don't have to worry about the new housemates," I tell her, ignoring the *she is stirring* part. My grandmother never had what I would call a sunny personality. No one would mistake her for Pollyanna on even her best day, but the dark prophecies she likes to mutter are a whole new level. I'm convinced they're the reason why my nightmares are so intense, especially when she starts talking about the *Goddess of Filth*, as she's been doing all summer. I try to think of it as Gran Radio, and I do my best to change the frequency. "They seem nice enough. But we don't have to be friends with them. They just live here now. They *pay* to live here. That's all."

"Every lock can be opened with the right key," Gran mutters, and reaches for her cards. This is her way of dismissing me.

I leave her to her intense shuffling, trying not to look directly at the dark cards with all the golden figures and symbols that always seem *sticky*, like they're trying to pull me in. I back out of the room, lock it tight, then peer out the barred windows to find that most of the moving in has been done. The cottage doors are all shut up tight with lights visible behind the boarded-up windows. The motorcycles are gone too. Standing there in the old dining room, with everything quiet around me, I can *feel* that our home, our land, isn't ours any longer.

Or isn't *only* ours.

It's tempting to imagine that I can *feel* the tenants the way I would feel bruises on my own body, but I try not to indulge in flights of fancy. Too much of that and I'll turn into Gran.

I make my way into the kitchen and stand there, not sure what to do with myself. If I close my eyes—which I don't, because I'm too aware that someone could walk in on me and take advantage of that weakness—it could be almost any day from my childhood. Back when the house was always full of people, slamming in and out, some living out in those very same cottages—under decidedly less cute circumstances. Back when my grandfather was alive and my parents lived up in the front bedroom, and Augie was always deliberately stomping up and down the stairs, making as much noise as possible because he thought it was funny.

If I take out each one of the people I've lost and look at them separately, it doesn't make me feel the same sense of grief. Because all of them were complicated losses. Some so enormously so that I'm not sure I'll ever untangle my impressions of them, or my feelings about the way I lost them. Maybe that's what grief is.

Old men like my grandfather, at least, are supposed to die. It's the natural order of things, no matter that our whole family never quite recovered from it. The other losses were crueler.

Like the twin who was once so much a part of my life, of me, that it was like we were one person, and now he's just . . . out there. Hopefully alive, but alone.

Leaving me equally alone here.

Sometimes I have the deeply unworthy thought that it would be easier if he was actually dead. Even though that's my worst fear. And even though it breaks my heart to imagine it, at least then it would be over. I would know where he is.

I hear a faint noise at the back door and look over to find Savi standing there. I make myself smile.

"Are you settling in okay?" I ask her.

Because that seems like the kind of thing a landlord-type person *would* ask.

She smiles at me and seems almost to . . . float into the room that would be bright and sunny and happy if the windows weren't mostly boarded up. And if there wasn't so much smoke outside.

"This is such a lovely, historic house," she says, but she says it the way people say things when they don't have any idea what to say. It's oddly endearing. Like she doesn't know how to do this either. "Has it always been in your family?"

"Every generation adds on to it." I wave a hand toward the place where the kitchen juts out from the original part of the house, because it was once a porch. You can see where my grandfather connected them. "It's like a collaboration with ghosts."

Savi pauses at the windows that look out over the backyard, squinting through the little slits between the boards. "I suppose collaborating with ghosts is preferable to fighting them off."

I want to follow that up, but I figure that attempts at intimacy might kill us both. I can come up with some theories as to why an upscale woman like Savi might flee wherever she came from to hide out in a place like this. None of them are pretty.

I move over to the refrigerator instead and open the door. "I divided this up so that everyone has space," I say, waving my hand at the interior shelves. "So we don't have to worry about sharing things or taking other people's things by accident. You can claim a space now if you want."

I have the impression that Savi doesn't really know what to do with this information. As if she's never shared anything in her life.

She smiles at me. "How thoughtful."

I excuse myself and leave her there, because I don't know how to interact with strange people living in the house. No matter how much money they pay me. Left to my own devices, I will be awkward and direct, and no one wants that in a landlady.

No one wants that at all, come to think of it. Augie was the charming one.

Besides, there's only so much daylight left.

I spend it hauling all the iron I got at the scrapyard up to the attic and pretend I don't notice Briar's door open a crack each time I go out to my truck, as if she's peeking out but doesn't want to be seen.

We didn't sign up to be friends. I don't need to pay any attention to what anyone here is doing as long as it doesn't bother me or anyone else—and someone watching me walk in and out of the house doesn't bother me.

The threshold for that is significantly different than it was three years ago.

So is everything else. I never considered myself particularly good with my hands back then. That's another gift of necessity. There are no other hands to do the job, so mine had to learn. The good news is, I don't care if the results of my handiwork are pretty.

I fix the iron bars across my windows, leaving spaces so I can still shoot. Anything that tries to come inside will have to work for it. I don't try to convince myself that a few bars could keep whole werewolves out if they want in, but it might slow them down a bit. Just long enough for me to get a weapon. That's all I need.

I hope.

It's getting dark as I finish, but I jog down the stairs toward Gran's room, once again a little too keenly aware of the fact it's not just the two of us any longer. I expect them all to come bursting into the kitchen, or to hear them in there, but everything is quiet.

I find Gran still in her chair but, more surprisingly, still awake.

"Are you hungry?" I ask her, not that it matters. She will sometimes say no and eat her dinner anyway.

"Not like *she* is," Gran tells me, and nods toward the window.

I hear a crow squawk and wonder if she's made a little friend. A little, creepy, carrion-eating friend.

I help her up, get her neatened up, and then we shuffle out to the kitchen together. I take the precaution of barring the back door, just to keep us safe from any tenant incursions. I seat her at the little table there, and she looks up at me balefully. "My home has been ransacked."

I blink, then remember that she's still resistant to the fact I cleared out all the crap in this place. She hasn't met the tenants yet. Those complaints are yet to come.

"We just cleaned up a little," I reply, keeping my voice as cheerful as possible.

I put together a supper for her of easily digestible things, which is simple enough because such things tend to come in cans, and cans are where it's at these days. Supply chains ruptured almost immediately. Since then, there have been all kinds of enterprising black-market options, but the trouble is, the black market costs money. Or higher-level bartering that I'm not prepared to enter into with the people involved.

Not everyone is Samuel Ruiz, determined to build community. Some people out here think that communities are pointless, and it's better to thin out the herd so as not to have to compete for resources. Those are the kinds of people that Franklin Hendry uses to do his dirty work.

I would rather live on BPAs and sodium. I sit down with Gran and watch as she sullenly eats a slice of canned peach.

She frowns at me. "You should eat, Lilianne. You're going to need your strength."

"I'm already strong." I don't correct her. I don't tell her I'm not my mother. Sometimes I wonder if it's not just that she's confused these days but filled with wishful thinking.

Wishful thinking I understand.

After she eats, I clean up, unbar the back door, then take her in for her nightly routine. I run her a bath and tend to her nails, hands, and feet. She reads her books for a while and tries to get me to look at her cards with her. I decline. Then I tuck her into bed.

I don't know if she likes my company. I don't know if she likes anything. But these are the sorts of questions it's better not to ask, so I never do.

We are who we've got. That's all there is to it.

Once she's asleep, I secure her door, check all the locks and windows, and then head back up the stairs. It's dark outside, but from the second floor I can see lights around all the doors and the boards on the windows in that line of cottages out there. For a moment, I'm sure I can hear the creaking of floorboards as they move around, like each cottage is a tattletale.

Up in my attic, under the eaves, I take a shower and find myself overly aware of how *short* my hair is.

I used to have long hair. When Augie and I were young, we were both pretty shaggy. We were also a gleaming bright blond, but I cut all mine off not long after my parents disappeared.

I'm sure there's no emotional through line there.

These days it's more gold than white-blond, and there's some red in there too, and the only reason I'm even thinking about something so random now is because of all the *hair* on display, thanks to my new tenants.

Maybe Samuel would like me more if I had long, silky hair like Savi. Or Maddox's wild waves that flow everywhere like they have a mind of their own. Or even that long, thick black hair stuck under Briar's hat.

This is the girliest line of thought I've had in years.

I'm not sure I like it. The main reason to not have long hair, after all, is because it can be grabbed.

And Samuel thinks I'm an idiot.

Since I'm back to thinking about Samuel, I take that to bed with me. Not the idiot part. I glide over that, daydreaming about the way his hands wrapped around my elbows instead.

Though as I daydream off into sleep, he's moving closer the way he did that one night, and this time, it isn't rushed and quiet—

When I jolt awake sometime later, something's wrong.

My head is pounding. My stomach is in a knot.

She is stirring! a voice that's a lot creepier than my grandmother's echoes inside my head. I feel something slick and upsetting move through me, and I think about a ruined face and claws where hands should be, rearing like a dead thing from a grave and lurching toward me—

But whatever *that* is, it's not the issue. Not now. I glance at the clock and see that it's three in the morning, which is not a time anything mortal and consumable needs to be up and about. It's feeding time out there.

That's when I hear the noise again, the one that must have woken me up.

I'm up and moving before I can process what's happening, strapping on my weapons and taking to the stairs. It's only when I reach the second floor that I realize what I'm hearing is a pounding sound.

Not any old pounding sound.

Someone is hammering something—maybe a fist, maybe a battering ram, it's hard to tell—against the front door.

I have my guns in my hands as I go down to the first floor, not bothering to turn on any lights. It's the middle of the night. People with good intentions don't go out in the middle of the night, because too many nasty things *only* go out then.

I go down to the door, slide open the peephole, and stick the muzzle of my gun through it.

I peer out around it, and I can make out the dimensions of a man.

A very, very, *very* large man.

"If I were you, asshole," comes a deep, rough growl of a voice, "I would rethink pointing that fucking gun in my face."

I do rethink. I release the safety and chamber a round.

I see a faint movement in my peripheral vision and risk a glance to see Maddox coming across the yard. Fast. I take a split second to note that she and I are not the same. Because I sleep in my clothes. She apparently sleeps in tiny baby-doll pajamas like she doesn't have a care in the world what might come busting through her windows or pounding at her door.

Or in this case, my door.

Must be nice, I think, but I turn my attention back to the stranger on my doorstep.

"You have three seconds to get the fuck away from my door," I tell him. "And two of those seconds are gone."

"It's okay," Maddox calls as she comes up beside the porch. "He's my . . . I knew he was going to show up. It's fine. He's not here to hurt anyone."

"Don't fucking count on it, you little shit," comes that deep voice from the other side of the door. But he doesn't look at her. He's glaring at my gun.

I stare at Maddox as she comes up on the porch, putting herself well within this man's reach. She stares back at me, and I swear there is something almost . . . beseeching in her gaze. Or maybe it's the middle of the night and this was the plan all along, to roust me out of bed.

I think of that terrible voice inside me. That ruined face. But I blink it away. And I don't know why, if there was a slaughter planned, Maddox would roll up to it in those pajamas.

I pull the gun back inside. Maddox smiles gratefully.

I realize I'm holding my breath, because this does not, in fact, feel *fine*.

And then the huge man on my doorstep steps back. Just enough that I can see him beneath the porch light, and I freeze.

Because I know him, too.

Everyone knows him. Back in the day, they whispered about him because he was the leader of that biker gang. The outlaw element that hunkered down here in the hills, where they could do as they pleased and no one bothered them.

That was scary enough.

Tonight, though, it's more obvious who and what he is.

Ty Ceridwen. Alpha wolf of the werewolf pack.

Here.

At my house.

4.

The huge werewolf pays me no mind, but that's not exactly a comfort.

He moves so fast it makes my breath catch in my throat—so fast that I only realize he's moved in the strangled second afterward, when I'm still standing there at the door and he's pressing Maddox up against the far porch post.

By her neck.

I struggle to get a panicked breath in. I fight to unlock the heavy door.

"Don't worry," Maddox squeaks out, her remarkable eyes aimed my way, which is really something given the giant hand on her neck. "I'm fine."

"Bold statement, babe," the werewolf alpha growls.

Only then does the lock on the door open, making it frighteningly clear to me exactly how fast he moves. How vastly different he is from me, and by extension, how different Maddox is too.

It makes me feel fragile, and I hate *fragile*. It's the gateway drug to an unpleasant end.

It's also scary when I don't have time for *scary*. There's only living through the moment and hoping I get another one, repeat and reload. The gun is heavy in my hand.

But when I twitch a little, like I might lift it, Maddox shakes her head. Just slightly.

Just enough to keep me from it.

"Am I losing my fucking mind?" Ty Ceridwen growls, but it sounds more like a curse than a question. The same Ty Ceridwen I heard once burned down an entire cartel operation in the woods during Oregon's illegal weed farm days, then dared them to come for him, and this was before we all knew he was a werewolf. Among other myths and legends that I am pretty sure, now, are all true. "Tell me I did not come home to hear from your own fucking brother that you ran off and shacked up with prey."

"You don't like it when I tell you that you've lost your fucking mind," Maddox replies.

And her tone is so . . .

My eyes widen. I realize with a start that she's not scared. She seems whatever the opposite of intimidated is, standing back against the post as if it was her idea to go there in the first place.

I watch one of Ty's massive thumbs move down the length of her throat, then up again, and I have no choice but to conclude it's a kind of temper-fueled caress.

And that she . . . doesn't hate it.

"Pack your shit," he growls at her.

I have to think that a normal person would be terrified by this. Instead, Maddox tilts her head back so he can grab more of her throat in that giant hand of his.

"I can't," she tells him, and she doesn't sound the slightest bit sorry about it. "It's not that I don't want to, except . . . I don't really want to."

"There comes a point, and you know it, when we are going to be out of choices," Ty says in a low voice that seems to reverberate through the night outside, and even in me, like one of those asshole Harley engines that splits the sky in half. "And when I say *we*, babe, I mean you."

"You're fully aware of what happens if you go there," she says as she shrugs, but there's something different in her gaze. Something harder.

It's obvious to me that this is an old argument.

"You let me know when you're tired of playing your little fucking games, Maddox," Ty grits out, and I don't know how she manages to simply gaze back at him the way she does. I can feel my knees beneath me like water, and worry they might splash me right over, when he starts talking in that gravelly way of his again. "When you feel like stepping up to what you should've done years ago. I'm not the only one you have to answer to."

"I know exactly what I'm doing," she replies, and there's more steel in her voice than I'm used to, because she's normally so lazy and disinterested, light and easy.

I don't see either one of them move, but suddenly their mouths are fused together, and I find myself looking away, feeling embarrassed. But also frozen to the spot. I don't know what to do with myself—and then I hear what sounds like a low bit of laughter, again in that deep register that seems to shiver straight through me to threaten my already precarious knees.

I only realize it's stopped when he's moving again and is looming right in front of me. Right there on the other side of the locked gate that seems pretty damn flimsy just now. It's possible I swallow my own tongue. But I do have the good sense not to point my gun in his face the way every single screaming cell in my body demands that I do.

And fast.

"Good impulse control," he bites out at me.

It was one thing to look at him through the door. It was another thing to see the back of his head from across the porch—this whole, huge alpha werewolf leader of all he surveys and can hold with his claws.

Staring up at Ty Ceridwen and finding myself the focus of his attention is like staring up the steep side of a very tall mountain. I can feel sheer, shaking terror coil tight inside me—

But I'm also not blind. I've never had occasion to look at him too closely before, but it's unavoidable now. Knowing that he is a wolf—*the* wolf—means his features make sense, but it doesn't make him any more easily palatable.

He has long dirty-blond hair currently twisted back out of his way, though parts of it hang down in the front. His beard is slightly darker, and it's hard to tell if it simply grows that way or if he trims it to look *just* rough-edged enough. He's huge, and seems bigger up close. Easily six foot five, though I might be underestimating that, and like a wall of muscle. A tank. Everything about him is big and bold, and he's staring down at me as if he's imagining frying me up in a pan and eating me like a midnight snack.

"You better be worth it," he says to me.

"I don't know that I'm worth anything," I say, alarmed.

He scowls at me, then looks back at Maddox. "I want a detailed map, babe," he tells her. "A point-by-point analysis of the road ahead. You get me? Or I'm taking it out of your ass."

She seems remarkably unconcerned with a threat that would probably have me tossing up my dinner in the nearest toilet. All *she* does is shrug, still standing there against the porch post with his fingerprints on her throat and a look of complete ease.

"When don't you?" she asks.

He laughs again, like a reckoning, and then he's gone.

It's not that he disappears in a puff of smoke, though that would be alarming enough. It's that when he moves, he goes so fast that my brain can't quite make sense of it.

Once again, there's the slamming grate long after he's disappeared, and there's nothing outside but the smell of the wildfires in the distance. And, now and then, the sound of the critters either too brave or too foolish to keep quiet in the dark.

But when I stop scanning the dark in disbelief that anything can move *that fast*, Maddox is still standing there.

"So," I say, drawing out the syllable.

She looks away, letting out a rueful noise that isn't quite a laugh. "Yeah. *So.*"

And somehow we end up sitting out on the back steps after it turns out we both think that sugar is the only thing that can get us through this moment. I don't let her walk through the house to get there, and it makes me feel like an asshole, but she doesn't seem to care. Besides, she gets to the back door quicker than I do. We make mugs of contraband hot chocolate, which is so hard to find these days that I hide it from my own grandmother and would normally share with no one.

Then again, this is the werewolf who lives here now, and I think I feel something like shell-shocked.

Part of that is because we take those mugs and . . . sit outside.

"I don't go out in the dark if I can avoid it," I say quietly as we hang out there on the back steps. "I'm not sure why I let you talk me into doing it now. Maybe this is an elaborate plan to get me set upon by monsters, after all."

"I am a monster," Maddox says serenely from beside me. "And anyway, you're safe. First of all, there are only a few things that actually scare me, and none of them are likely to be lurking around in your vegetable garden." She takes a sip of her hot chocolate and makes a little humming noise of approval. "Second, and probably more important where you're concerned, I live here now. That means this whole house, this whole property, probably the whole hill, is protected. All of Jacksonville, really."

"Jacksonville is already protected." I frown at her. "That was the deal. A safe zone for humans."

"Sure." She's not looking at me. She's studying her bare feet as she flexes them on the step below. "But now, if something happens up here, Ty will take it as a personal attack on him. There aren't a lot of folks who want that."

I take that in. I think about that massive hand on her throat and the way she keeps putting her free hand up to touch the fingerprints that I can still see like stains on her neck.

She does not look like she's touching them because they hurt.

I clear my throat and wonder what Ty Ceridwen's "protection" might cost me. "So you and Ty, then."

We're sitting so close that it's almost tempting to forget both that she's a *werewolf* and that she was *that* Maddox Hemming in high school.

Maybe I have forgotten, because I'm not pointing my gun at her. Maybe because I'm not, she leans in, pressing her shoulder to mine. For some reason she doesn't scare me when I think she should.

Maybe I'm just pathologically desensitized.

"Me and Ty," she says, and again, there's that rueful sound. "How much do you actually know about werewolves?"

I wrap my hands around my mug. It's cooler out here than I expected, but I wasn't kidding. I don't go out much at night. I forgot that even when the days are warm this late in September, the nights get cold, and fast. The mug feels good in my palms.

"Let's see. Full moons. Jagged teeth. You walk around like humans until you decide to tear faces off. Silver bullets. That one werewolf in London who got a song. You know, all the usual stuff."

"Just say you know nothing, then," Maddox says with a laugh. "First, there are two different kinds of werewolves. There are the blood and there are the bitten. *Blood* is what I am. And what Ty is. When you talk about the pack, that's what you're talking about. *Blood.*" I think for a moment I can see the moon in her eyes, but she keeps talking, and I don't see any sudden, hairy transformations out here on this step. "The *bitten* are foot soldiers, at best. They're entirely slaves to the moon. We're not. *Affected*, yes. But if we have to, we can hold back the shift. Critical difference." She punctuates that with a sip of her drink. "Another critical difference, pack leaders win that position through combat. Bloody. Brutal. Probably as bad as you imagine, and worse. But the mate of a pack leader is preordained."

"What do you mean by preordained?"

"I mean full-on fated mates, Winter. Straight up."

"Oh." I try to digest that. "Okay. You're fated to be his mate, but you don't want to be. He does want you to be his mate, though, so he doesn't like you're hiding out here, somehow escaping that destiny."

"Close." Maddox's smile is looking lazy again. "Of course I want to be his mate. Did you look at him?" She laughs at whatever expression I have on my face. "I like power. I like a male who can wield it. And

I really like the fact that I've been promised to the *Rix* of the Western Wolves since before I was born. I've always been his. I don't have a problem with that."

"But instead of living with him in . . . What was that word? Rick's?"

"Rix," she says, a subtle correction. "It basically means 'king' in the old language." She waves that away. "I have every intention of taking my place beside him, but the thing is, I want to do it my way."

In the midst of all these things that don't make sense and that I should probably not be just accepting so easily, this tracks the most. Maddox Hemming, doing it her way. Whether that's not going to prom despite the fact she was named prom queen, randomly championing the kids in high school who everyone treated terribly, or even this. Showing up at my house. Moving away from whatever her situation is because she feels like it. Maddox all the way.

Maybe she sees my appreciation of that on my face, because she nods. "Mates of the Rix don't go to college. And don't really stay in high school half the time. Their job is to support their man, keep him calm when necessary, and fire him up when needed." She is looking at her feet again. "But there's a meekness there, if you see what I'm saying. It's *assumed.* And I don't like it."

"Well," I say, frowning out into the dark, where there are definitely no zombies tonight, because who would dare defy Maddox in anything? "One thing I think we can all agree on is that you've never been meek."

She taps her mug to mine. "There's a ritual. It can only be performed during a full moon, and once it happens, he and I are bound together. Permanently. He wanted that done years ago. But I want him to make it clear that it's me, specifically, that he wants. Not just whatever woman could have come along to take this role. I've been holding him off, and as you saw tonight, he doesn't like it."

"He did not like it at all." I study the tree line, wondering what's out there, watching us. "So you're refusing to get intimate with him until he—"

"I didn't say *that*." Maddox lets out a low laugh. "Tonight might be the first time in as long as I can remember that we've been in the same room together and *haven't* fucked. Intimacy isn't the issue." She laughs again. "There's no doubt at all that I'm his mate, Winter. The whole pack knew before I was born. Everyone can sense it, like a change in the wind. *That's* not the issue. The issue is, I want him to see me as a whole person first. And only then as his mate."

I sit with that for a minute. Maybe a lot of minutes. The smoke isn't as thick at night, and I can stare up at the stars. I can't remember the last time I simply sat here, beneath them, without keeping watch over my perimeter—or running for my life.

It's been more than three years. I know that.

"Your brother is on his side of things," I say, remembering that scene in the yard earlier. "And I'm betting all your cousins are too."

"They are, because they're assholes," Maddox says, but cheerfully, as if assholery is only to be expected. "They want power. Once Ty claims me, their status changes in the pack. Me refusing to submit to the ritual puts that off, and they're pissed. They've been pissed. They would probably all stop talking to me to really show me how pissed they are, but then how would they use me once I take my fated role?" Her laugh this time has an edge. "Such a conundrum."

"If I'm following this, and I'm probably not, what you're telling me is that you defied your entire culture to stay in school, to not be the prom queen, and to go off to college."

"Proms are really dumb," Maddox says with a roll of her eyes. "And you know, werewolves live a long time. There's a movement within the pack, to be more . . ." She pauses, as if she's trying to translate it into words I'll understand. "Instinct based is how I'd put it. 'Let the wolf lead,' they say. That's fine, but we don't live in a world that's only wolves, and sometimes it makes sense to take in other perspectives. That was how I pitched it to Ty, and that's why he let me go to college. Because he could have said no. Half the pack thought he should have. He's mad about that, too."

I try not to look at her then. "How long have you been actually with him?"

Her laughter floats up again. "I can't tell you. You humans are so prudish about the most natural things. Remember, you and I are not the same species. I was never as young as you were. Not in anything but years."

I'm still thinking about that later, tossing and turning in my bed upstairs, because I can't keep myself from thinking about the scene I witnessed right there on the front porch. I saw the way they looked at each other. I don't know why I ever imagined that they *weren't* having sex constantly. They practically *exude* sex.

I also think about the fact that I could barely meet Ty Ceridwen's gaze. Every single thing inside me screamed at me to look away, and I did.

Yet I watched her stare right at him.

I sleep, but it's not better. That dark bitch is waiting for me, her breath full of decay.

You will submit to me too, she tells me. *It's what you're made for.*

When I wake up in the morning, my throat feels raw, as if I was screaming. My skull feels like it might split open. I think I hear a telltale shuffling out in the woods. But if the zombies are circling when I heave myself out of bed, they don't come near enough for me to see them, much less shoot them.

Maybe what Maddox told me is true. Maybe her being here offers protection after all.

The house is quiet all around me as I pad down the stairs, though I pause briefly when I reach the windows in the front room. I can hear a faint sound of chanting out in the yard. My first thought is it's something evil, coming to try out some vile spells—but then I see the light from Savi's windows. Meditation, I think then, because she has that overly yoga-ed look. Two things I should probably look into, but that sounds like the sort of stuff people do when they're concerned about their longevity.

That's not an issue of mine.

I go through the usual routine with Gran's and my coffee, and even let her tell me a little too much about her cards, until I remind her that we both need to eat our breakfast.

I don't like to stop her from talking about the things that interest her, but I've always had an aversion to those damned cards. There was never any telling her that when she was fully herself. Now that she's not, why would I be so cruel?

I head for the kitchen to make us some food but stop short in the front hall.

There's a piece of paper wedged beneath the flap of metal that covers the peephole. I drift closer, my adrenaline already sounding the alarm. Gingerly, I shift the peephole to one side, and whatever it is falls away. I can hear it flutter to the ground outside.

I wait there a moment, counting. *One, one thousand. Two, one thousand.*

Only then do I take the risk of putting my eye to the peephole, a quick look first to make sure nothing is standing *right there*. Then, when I see only the porch with nothing scary looming, I take a second, longer look.

When I'm reasonably sure that no one's lurking about, I ease open the heavy inner door and frown down at the folded piece of paper that someone stuck on it. Deliberately.

I nudge it with my foot, but nothing blows up, turns into a snake, or does any of the other horrible things that I can imagine only too well.

I bend down to pick it up, but I don't look at it. I look around instead, keeping an eye out for anything out of the ordinary. Anything that might indicate someone is watching me pick this up, which will be a good indication that I shouldn't.

But there's nothing.

Just the usual sound of morning birds in the trees, that chanting that sometimes sounds like a song, and a little bit of clear daylight because it's early morning and the smoke hasn't settled in yet.

Back inside the house, I lock everything up and then unfold the paper, though I quickly realize it isn't paper. It's heavy card stock.

I have a message for you, the card reads, written out in a bold, thick hand. *Please come to Archangel MMA at sunset.*

And below that is a signature. *Ariel Skinner.*

A lot of things press into my head at once, making the headache I thought I'd gotten rid of threaten again, because everything I'm thinking is nuts. I know what Archangel MMA is. It's the old mixed martial arts school that's been there as long as anyone can remember, down where Main Street meets the river, where every kid I know took at least one martial arts class over the years. It was called Spartan Arts when I was a kid. It was a karate school before then.

As for Ariel Skinner . . . I know that name too.

Everybody knows that name. I've never seen him in person, which is likely part of why I'm still alive, because Ariel Skinner is the king of the vampires.

Apparently of all the vampires, or so I've heard, but particularly the ones in this valley. Samuel has actually met him and claims that it was his negotiation tactics that brought the likes of Ty Ceridwen and Ariel Skinner to the table and got them to agree to let us humans live in relative peace in Jacksonville.

I can't think of a single reason why the king of the fucking vampires would be sending me card-stock messages through my doorway.

I toss it aside when I get into the kitchen and set about making myself more coffee. Even more bitter than usual.

I'm not hungry, but I make Gran her eggs and toast and sit with her for a while, and when I come back into the kitchen with her dishes, Maddox is coming in the back door. We smile at each other, but as she crosses the threshold, she stops dead.

Like she's slammed straight into a wall.

"What's wrong?" I ask her, my gaze racing around the room. I press my back against the locked metal door behind me.

Then I look at Maddox and watch her eyes go gold.

I am suddenly, terrifyingly aware that she isn't a girl I know who sometimes turns into a cute little monster—she's a wolf.

Who only pretends to be human when it suits her.

Maddox inhales, deep. Then she peers at me with those molten eyes, and I find I'm holding my breath. "Why the fuck do I smell vampire blood?"

5.

I assume this means the card is written in blood, which is gross and creepy if not immediately deadly, but when I pick it up off the counter and hand it over to Maddox—it's more like I throw it—she takes in a deep breath. Then she shakes her head.

"He touched it. But no, that's ink."

"You can smell him?" I rub at my face. "And by 'him,' you don't really mean . . . ?"

She looks at me, her eyes somewhere between that ferocious gold and her usual gray-brown. "An invitation from a king is a summons. You know that, right?"

"What it sounds like is a trap," I counter, because events might be spiraling beyond my control, but *I* am still the boss of *me*. Though that gross and awful voice from my nightmare seems to swell in me again. *It's what you're made for.* I repress a shudder and keep going. "The kind of trap that I walk into and then die. Do you know how I've stayed alive through all of this, Maddox? By not walking into traps."

"Fair." She frowns at the card, and then goes over and helps herself to some coffee. She doses it with a hefty pour of what looks like real cream. She must have brought it with her. That means werewolves must have access to cows—but I order myself to focus on what she's telling me about the larger, fanged issue at hand. "But you need to think carefully about the consequences of disobeying a man like Ariel Skinner. Because there will be consequences. Either he will send you a . . . more imperative message"—she takes a draw of her coffee, leaving me to imagine what *more imperative* means to a *vampire*—"or he will send someone to deliver the message in person." Maddox looks at me then, and I don't like the images in my head. "Or worse, to collect you and deliver you to him. You don't want those things to happen."

She is correct. I don't.

But. "You can't possibly be suggesting that I, a very mortal and breakable human, traipse off to the horrors of downtown Medford—in the teeming, terrible dark—to see what a scary-ass vampire wants to say to me."

"If Ariel Skinner wanted to kill you, he would just kill you," Maddox tells me, and I think she's trying to be kind. I *think* that's what her expression means, and maybe that would feel sweeter if I wasn't envisioning being torn apart by monsters on Main Street in Medford five seconds after the sun sets.

"No truer words have ever been spoken," says Savi, and we both look up to find her at the back door. She smiles as if she forgot that we could *look* at her like this. "Ariel is no joke."

Maddox surprises me by nodding her head toward the card that's now sitting on the counter again, as if she wants Savi to get a load of it. As if she thinks Savi will have some insight that I don't. Savi exchanges a long look with Maddox that I can't read—I can't say I like that, either—and then she goes over and peers at it.

She doesn't touch it. She wrinkles up her nose as she reads it, then shakes her head.

"I don't like it." She looks at me. "You must go, of course. But you're going to have to be very careful."

I laugh, but not because I think anything is funny. "I'm not going. I don't know why you think that I would?"

"He's not a butcher, not like some." Savi says this thoughtfully, but she's looking over at Maddox, not me, like they're *conferring*.

It's weird. If the situation didn't involve my inevitable bloody and painful death, I would be much more interested in why the werewolf is so chummy with the fancy-pants lady from fancy-pants Ashland, the southernmost town in the valley that people who fled the Bay Area in California flock to the most.

Or they did. Now there is no fleeing from San Francisco. I'm not sure anyone's made it out of California since the Reveal.

I wasn't surprised to see Ashland as Savi's previous address.

"Really, he's entirely civilized," Savi is saying, while Maddox nods. "That has its own issues, of course."

"He *is* very reasonable." Maddox shrugs. "That's why he's the king."

Savi stares at the coffee machine as if she doesn't understand how it functions. Or as if, maybe, she doesn't know what coffee is. "That and the fact that he is an ancient."

When she looks back my way, I must be staring at her in befuddlement, because she smiles again. "Rumor has it he was born a Spartan."

I blink. "Meaning he was raised to enjoy minimal furnishings?"

I expect her to laugh, but she doesn't. "A Spartan. From the Peloponnese." Savi studies me and adds, "In Greece."

That is probably a dig at me and what she assumes is my education, but I can't really focus on that. "You mean like . . . *This is Sparta.*"

And I mimic the old movie's iconic kick into the pit.

Their expressions are solemn. They both nod.

I decide that really, it feels better to lean back against the sink, where I keep meaning to wash Gran's dishes. That or my knees might give way beneath me.

"How do you know about all this stuff?" I think to ask Savi, because that's better than thinking too much about Sparta. In the Peloponnese. In ancient fucking Greece.

Maddox directs her attention to her coffee.

"I make it my business to know things like that," Savi tells me in her lovely, cultured voice. "If there's a king in the mix, you can bet that there are subjects. And I prefer to be an informed one."

I hear a sound a lot like a snort, but when I look over, Maddox is coughing. "Wrong pipe," she mutters, and pounds on her own chest.

"I know who he is," I tell Savi. And also Maddox, who coughs again—pointedly, I think—and looks like she's trying too hard to appear innocent. Which, obviously, has the opposite effect.

"Do you have any idea why Ariel would want to talk to you?" Savi asks.

"None whatever," I reply, and the crushing anxiety about all this is making me feel something akin to giddy. I laugh. "I make it a personal policy to spend as little time around vampires as possible."

"Solid plan." Maddox raises her mug in my direction. "The good news is that this particular vampire doesn't need to summon random human girls to feast on. I'm not even sure if he bothers to feast on humans any longer. He's next level."

I stare at her. "How is that good news?"

There is a thudding sound, and then Briar slams her way in through the back door, looking assaulted by the sight of us.

"Why did I smell fresh werewolf in the yard?" she demands in a surly tone. She glares at Maddox. "Did you bring one of your dogs here?"

Maddox only bares her teeth in reply.

This could be a moment for me to tell everyone that *yes*, speaking of local kings, Ty Ceridwen was here last night *and* will likely be here again, given his relationship with Maddox. But I don't.

I don't know why I don't.

I'd like to think it's because Maddox and I are friends now. Or getting there, after last night and the hot chocolate.

But a part of me worries it's because of who she is. Not the werewolf part. I can't really process the *wolf* of it all. I mean the other part. The high school part, where I was like every other kid there, sitting around daydreaming that I could one day be as cool as she already was.

This makes me so unhappy with myself that all I can think to do is make myself an overly big breakfast. My feelings on toast.

Maybe what I'm really worried about is that it will be my last.

But I don't eat it. It's like I can't. I slide it directly into the trash.

Maddox and Briar clear out. I can hear them muttering at each other as they walk outside, and it does not sound like anything leading to hot chocolate. Savi stays behind, looking as effortlessly perfect as she did before.

She is not in baby-doll pajamas or even the sweats and flannel and ubiquitous beanie Briar appeared in. I'm tempted to think that she's fully dressed for her day, but I suspect that the hoodie and drawstring trouser set she's wearing is made of the finest cashmere and, more, is what she considers lounging attire.

"There are certain precautions you should take," she tells me, and something about her direct gaze makes me want to sit a little straighter at the table with the remnants of my feelings on plates before me. "The fact that he chose to summon you to him indicates that at the very least there's the expectation of a conversation. That could be interpreted as good."

"Meaning he won't kill me on sight."

"He could do that anywhere." Savi says this more matter-of-factly than Maddox did, and oddly, it's more comforting. "Or have one of his many minions do it. What's more interesting is how you came to attract his notice."

"Yes." My voice sounds faint. I tell myself it's the not eating, but I'm still not hungry. "Very interesting."

"You don't know why?"

I sigh. "I really don't."

Savi frowns. "I would warn you against being armed. It will be tempting, but there's no possible way that you will be able to fight him. I think going before him unarmed is more of a power move."

"And you think . . ." My throat is dry. I take a long pull from my coffee—and I should probably stop drinking so much of it when I'm already jittery, but I know I won't. There are only so many pleasures left. "You think I should be making power moves on a vampire king?"

"Creatures of power respect only power," she tells me, so frankly that something about it seems to trickle down inside me, setting off alarms as it goes.

Once again, it makes me wonder who she is. What she's running from. Yet I get the feeling that if I ask her, she not only won't tell me, she'll stop helping me, too. And yes, as forthright and breathtaking as her advice feels to me, I do believe she's trying to help me.

I'm self-serving enough to keep the questions to myself.

"You know where the MMA school is," she says after a moment, and it's not a question.

"Everyone knows where the MMA school is."

"Don't go in the front door." This part is clearly a warning, and she holds my gaze until I nod to indicate I understand.

"Um. Why not?"

"It's too exposed. And you will have to navigate too many unfortunate souls and other monsters, who may not have gotten the message that Ariel himself wants to talk to you. If you go around back, there's a hidden entrance there, down an alley. No one would dare be in the alley without Ariel's permission, so it's safe. Even for you. That's how you should access the school."

I think about this woman, who is almost certainly the only person who has ever worn cashmere under this roof, taking mixed martial arts lessons. Is that her secret? She's badass in disguise?

I don't ask her. That's my power move. I blow out a breath instead. "I guess we've all decided that I'm actually going to the MMA school, then."

Savi takes a sip of the coffee she's had in her hands for some time, and I watch her struggle not to look horrified. For some reason this entertains me a lot more than maybe it should. Or maybe it's easier to focus on that than . . . all the other things I should be concentrating on.

"It seems you have come to the attention of a great many powerful creatures," she says after a moment. "This is a reality that comes with some significant downsides, I suppose you might say."

I want to ask her what she means by that. I don't. There's something about the way she looks at me that makes it clear she knows perfectly well who visited us last night. But there's no way she could have seen Ty on the front porch unless she was out on the steps of her cottage and therefore visible to me at the door. That has to mean she's a monster too.

Trouble is, I have no idea what kind.

"I don't want to be the focus of anyone's attention," I tell her quietly. "I want to live what's left of my life right here in the woods and be left alone while I do it."

Her expression grips me then. An old, deep sadness, maybe, overlaying a kind of hard recognition.

"No one asks a sacrificial lamb what she might have liked to do with her life," Savi says after a moment, and not exactly bitterly. Not *exactly.* "They light the fire, chant out their incantations, perform their rituals, and bury her in the swamp of their dirty little religions."

I'm pretty sure I see her chest move, like she's breathing too hard.

In my head I can almost see chants around a fire, a scream in the dark—

No, thank you. My own nightmares are bad enough. I rub at my temple as if it aches again.

I force a smile. "If this is a pep talk about trotting off to the vampire's lair to get ritualistically exsanguinated or even, you know, just plain old killed, I think we've veered off track."

Savi collects herself. She sets her nearly untouched coffee back on the countertop with a decisive *click.*

"You can't put yourself back in the dark of oblivion," she says after a moment. "He knows who you are. Too many others know who you are. Oblivion is not an option. All you can do is try your best not to get burned in the light."

I decide later, while neatening up in Gran's room, that she probably really did consider that a pep talk. That makes me feel kind of sad for the both of us.

"Your mouth is drooping, child," Gran says from the depths of her chair. "What can be so terrible?"

I don't know who she thinks I am today, but that's all right. "Sometimes," I tell her quietly as I restack her books so she can reach them from her chair, "I think too much is expected of us. Specifically, women."

To my surprise, my grandmother chuckles. "What's the alternative?" she asks, and then laughs all the more.

I laugh too, because this kind of hilarity from her is unusual.

That afternoon, during a happily boring shift at my job, it occurs to me that Gran was throwing some serious shade at my grandfather. Possibly my father and my brother, too. I remember my grandfather as a tough, fair sort of man who was baffled by his children and their choices. My father was never good enough for my mother, in my grandfather's opinion.

I love them both, but I can't disagree.

It's just that before today, Gran never really seemed to take a side in all that.

Augie once dared to yell at her about it.

But the last thing I need to be doing while scanning the customers and the surrounding parking lot for monsters is lose myself in old, unhappy memories.

Augie had been mad at me that same night. *You think that you're winning points by saying nothing, don't you? You think you're really* doing something, *but all you're actually doing is sticking your head in the sand.*

Not everything I feel needs to be broadcast to the entire fucking world, I snapped at him.

I relive that a lot.

I ask myself, often, if that was the moment he decided to stop fighting the darkness in him. Oh, I have other moments to choose from, but I remember that one so clearly. The look on his face, like I had stabbed him. A kind of dawning understanding, like he didn't know me at all.

I think about that expression all the time.

It wakes me up in the middle of the night sometimes, with a damp spot on my pillow.

But when a very rude blast from a truck horn slaps me back into the coffee stand and the line of angry, not-entirely-human customers comes back into focus, I'm grateful.

Pathetically grateful to think about nothing but coffee drinks until it's time to go home.

6.

On the drive home through the late-afternoon smoke, I also think about Ariel Skinner.

He looms over everything, much heavier than the smoke. I've never laid eyes on him, but I remember women talking about him years ago. *Ruinous,* I heard one of them call him, but with a certain widening of the eyes as she huddled with her girlfriends at one of the many coffee shops we used to have here.

I used to wonder what that meant. Now I *really* wonder. What was ruinous back then? We all know the various ways sadistic or even nonsadistic vampires can *ruin* people. Anyone who lived through the first few weeks of the Reveal knows this, very likely against their will. But how did vampires—much less their king—do it back when people would have thought he was human?

The kids I know who took classes at his school refer to him, still, as "Master Skinner." I always thought that was a weird martial arts thing. Now I think about Ty Ceridwen's hand around Maddox's neck and wonder if it's more than that.

I take the road that bypasses California Street, Jacksonville's main drag, because I don't want to run into anyone I know. It's likely that Samuel has shared his feelings about my new tenants with the entire town, and the idea of tending to all that potential hysteria on top of a summons from the vampire king is . . . overwhelming.

I can easily imagine someone like the perpetually tutting Candace Wei, proprietress of one of the town's wine-country inns in the before times, demanding to know how she should sleep knowing that the monsters are not only roaming the darkness but tucked up on my grandmother's land.

I do not need to school poor Candace Wei on real problems, mostly because I would *love* to do exactly that.

Though I'm sure her take on Ariel Skinner would be interesting. There aren't many people in this valley, living or dead or undecided, that she doesn't know. And none she doesn't have an opinion on.

As I head up the hill and into the woods, I decide I'm *definitely* not going to Archangel MMA tonight. By the time I park, look around, and make a run for the front door, I'm back to thinking I should.

I spend the rest of the afternoon vacillating back and forth.

And also accidentally tracking what the tenants are doing. I don't mean to. I'm still not used to anyone being here but me and Gran, so every time I catch a glimpse of someone else on the property, I automatically pay attention. I think they call that a trauma response.

Briar leaves not long after I get back. I see her out the window, walking with her head low as she goes straight down the drive. This makes her either very brave or extraordinarily foolish. No one I know would risk being out in the open in the woods—up on the hill where no one can see a monster violating Jacksonville's safe zone—without the temporary safety of a vehicle made of steel all around them. Too much fragile flesh and easily crunched bone on display when you're walking, to my mind.

Later, I see Savi's gleaming vehicle as it drives away because I am *still* working on a particularly annoying latch on one of the living room windows. It won't catch as securely as I want it to, so I'm wrestling with it. I frown at her taillights, because it's weird that all the rest of the vehicles here are covered in ash from the fires. Hers is the only one that ash doesn't seem to like.

I'm up in my attic rooms when I see Maddox through one of the windows I've decided needs more boards over it before another nightfall. She comes out of the woods, clearly walking back from the path that winds its way into the trail system that used to be one of the selling points of this area. These days, I don't know many people who go out for a hike, or an evening in the outdoor amphitheater that used to throw summer concerts, because it's too tempting to the things that live in the forest.

We're already bait. Why throw ourselves directly at the predators?

Werewolves have no reason to worry about such things. Maddox looks like she's been for a run. I stare down at her, and it takes a few moments for my brain to filter through *why* I find what she's wearing so extraordinary. It's that she's dressed the way girls used to dress—*before.* Cute little running shorts and a sports bra, because back then, no one had to worry about toting around weapons and first aid kits.

The fact that I, personally, would never be caught dead in booty shorts and a sports bra—or out on a run, for that matter—doesn't keep me from feeling a wild pang of jealousy. Or nostalgia. I'm not sure which it is, but I order myself to get over it as I finish up with the window.

When I'm done, I gather up the dirty clothes that are starting to look like a carpet on my bedroom floor and head down to the laundry room off the kitchen.

I meet up with Maddox as she swings in through the back door. She smiles, stepping aside as I move past her with my arms full.

"Have a nice run?" I ask her.

"Run?" She blinks. Then her smile widens. "Yes. It was an excellent run."

She says that so strangely that I look after her as she goes to rummage in the fridge and see what looks a whole lot like more fingerprints on the backs of her thighs.

Oh, I think.

And then I have a lot of trouble sorting out my darks and lights in the laundry room because I keep thinking about Ty Ceridwen's hand on

Maddox's throat, which was the thing he felt was okay to do *in public*, and how little she seemed to mind.

But it all kind of shifts around, and I'm suddenly thinking about Ariel Skinner instead, only it's *my* throat and *his* hand with his face in shadow but all the blood in me moving wild like honey—

Only this, too, leads to more waffling on my part. Because I certainly don't need to have weird fantasies about fucking *vampires*. Aren't nightmares about slithery powers that want to gulp me down gross enough? Isn't it bad enough that I had to make direct eye contact with the werewolf alpha? Why do I have to meet all the terrible things that live in this valley? Much less convince myself that the ones not in my head are *hot*. There must be a word for people who decide to lust after the things that will almost certainly kill them. It's clearly pathological.

What I can't get past is the distinct feeling that none of this should be happening. Not to me. Samuel is the person who's made himself visible to all the various monster factions. He's the one who bravely put that target on his back and is the voice of humans in this valley.

I'm a goddamn barista, for fuck's sake.

I decide, definitively, that I'm doing absolutely nothing tonight as I sit down to dinner with Gran in the kitchen about an hour before sunset. I wanted to feed her in her room, but she insisted that she could not bear it.

And believe me, once her mind is made up, there's no changing it.

But I make sure I'm heavily armed, all the same.

I tense a little when Savi walks in the room, because there's no telling how Gran is going to react. I wait as Gran looks up from her dinner—a selection of her favorite canned delicacies—and blinks, no doubt as taken aback at the sight of such elegance and sophistication in our family kitchen as I am.

"You," she says.

Savi looks at her and inclines her head. "Me," she agrees.

"It's like you two know each other," I say, and laugh.

Neither of them joins in, and I find myself thinking about the ashless vehicle and the fact that it's always a little bit cold when Savi ventures near. I thought it was just me reacting to the novelty of more people around, but I don't have to fight off the urge to shiver when it's Maddox, do I?

"The cards are filled with portents," Gran says confidingly, but not to me. It's like she's decided that Savi will know what she's talking about. "Death and destruction are the least of it."

"Death and destruction are always the least of it," Savi replies in a tone that suggests that this is a perfectly normal and reasonable conversation. "Dying is a lovely oblivion, if you do it right. Destruction is merely the road map there. It's the living that hurts."

"There are worse things." Gran taps her fork against the inside rim of her bowl, then points it at Savi. "Like the hunger."

"If you're hungry, Gran," I interject, keeping my voice calm as I can, "you could just eat your dinner. Instead of wallowing in all these dark prophecies."

Out of the corner of my eye, I see Savi flinch at that. As if I've startled her.

But when I look over at her, she is simply unpacking various items of food from a tote bag and placing them on one of the empty shelves in the refrigerator. Not that I'm spying, but I am interested to see that all of it is vegetarian. Vegan, I'm pretty sure. Alternative milks. Leafy greens. Green juices, indeterminate pastes, and other such things that I would have told you were impossible to get this side of the Reveal, even if I'd wanted them.

What I can't decide is if Savi is some kind of monster I've never heard of before, or if she's the kind of monster I've always known about. Like one of those insufferable doctors' wives who spent their pre-Reveal lives holding court in their giant Italianate houses up in the east Medford hills, sending their children to private schools and summer camps out of state and acting as if their cheating, scrubs-in-public husbands were actual deities.

My intuition tells me that Savi is running from something, and being alive in the world tells me that the thing that women mostly run from is men. Any old human man, as we all know, can become a monster far too easily and without provocation.

But since I don't know, and her stuff could be trauma based, I don't ask.

After dinner, I get Gran ready for bed, even though she grumbles that it's early.

"I suppose you have big nighttime plans again," she says sharply as I settle her in the bed. "I keep hoping you'll change, Lilianne." Her gaze gets sad as she looks at me, and it makes everything in me clench. Even though I know she's not talking to *me*. Just the ghost of my mom. "You keep promising and you keep breaking your promises. If you can't do it for yourself, or for me, what about those babies? Don't they deserve more?"

"They do," I whisper.

I bend down and press a kiss to her forehead, feeling a kind of trembling deep inside because she is so papery now, so insubstantial, when in all my memories of her she could have taken down a mountain with her bare hands.

And likely did every day of the week before lunch.

When I go out of the room and lock her door behind me, I'm still shaky.

I go into the laundry room and fold clothes, vaguely thinking that it might be time for a snack, or possibly it's time to walk the perimeter of the property before dusk to see if anything's lying in wait—then nearly jump five feet in the air when I turn back toward the kitchen.

Because Briar is standing there, silently. Over by the counter next to the stove.

And somehow I know that she's been watching me for a lot longer than I want to imagine. My temples throb a little bit, like *knowing* something I shouldn't be able to is painful.

"What the hell are you doing?" I yelp. "Lurking around is a great way to get shot."

She only stares at me, and I think for a moment that she's wearing the exact same clothes as yesterday, but then I recognize that the T-shirt is different. The Dead Kennedys. I guess it's nice that she's thematically consistent.

"I know that werewolf was roaming around the property last night," she says.

"Okay." But if she already knows, why is she confronting me about it?

"You said there were rules." Her mouth shifts into that sneer. "Or are there only rules if you don't happen to be the pretty little werewolf princess who lets everybody kiss her ass from the Cascades to the Coastal Range?"

Meaning the entire valley.

"You have a specific complaint, Briar?" I ask.

"You know what they say." That sneer deepens and her eyes flash darkly. "Lie down with dogs, get up with fleas. Now imagine if it's werewolves. You won't get up at all."

"I don't think that's the thing they say."

She mutters something at me that sounds a lot like "Go fuck yourself," but I'm too surprised to ask for clarification, or even to take offense. Then she darts for the back door, slamming her way out so hard that the glasses in the cabinets rattle.

I find all my new tenants confusing, but Briar most of all. Not least because she is still wearing that cap pulled down over her ears when it's really not that cold outside.

I jog upstairs to my room and tell myself I'm going to have a lovely evening in. Perhaps mend my clothes, because it's so easy to tear them to shreds while shooting at things, hiding in the underbrush, and vaulting in and out of the coffee stand when monsters decide that the trash run is an invitation to attack. Perhaps read a book.

Perhaps stare at the ceiling and succumb to existential despair, like you do.

But instead, I think of how it felt last night to sit out on the step behind the house, head tipped back and all the stars there before me. Of how magical it was to do something that I once took entirely for granted.

If Ariel Skinner wanted to kill you, Maddox said, *he would just kill you.*

This time, when I think it, it actually does feel comforting.

Maybe that's why I find myself leaving the house as the sun drips toward the Coastal Range, reds and oranges mingling with the smoke into something spectacular.

Jaw-dropping. In another life, I would have hiked up to the scenic overview on the Britt trails and watched the sky turn into art.

I only wish I had nothing to do tonight but sit and watch the sun go down.

Once I'm locked up tight in the car and driving down the hill, however, my head is full of lore. About the vampire king who I've had no particular reason to think about with any specificity before now. He was just another element of this new world of ours. Nothing to do with me.

I can't even remember who first told me that, turns out, there'd been vampires living among us all along.

As I drive through town, I see Samuel engaged in conversation with a few other neighbors outside the local saloon. Normally, I would slow the truck down and make sure that there was at least a little eye contact with him, but I don't tonight.

Maybe I don't want to have another conversation with him if he's only going to yell at me about my tenant situation. Maybe I'm enough of a disappointment already, even if it's secondhand, my grandmother thinking that she was talking to my mom.

Maybe, I think as I take the road out of the safe zone of Jacksonville, a wide curve past fields gone to seed, *you should concentrate on the fact that you're now driving unprotected to what is almost certainly your death.*

That feels like a bit of a wake-up call, and the truth is, I need it. I need to pay attention to this insane thing I'm doing. I scan the road, making sure that my weapons are within reach, and happy that I attached more steel to the bumpers only recently to discourage swarming attacks.

For a few moments, as I drive through the sunset, I can almost forget . . . everything. There's just the glow of the setting sun, making the valley look as beautiful as I remember it being all throughout my childhood. The Rogue Valley is shaped like a lazy rainbow and stretches from the north side of the Siskiyou Mountains on the California border to the north and the west, following tributaries of the Rogue River until it meets up with the river itself. The Applegate Valley nestles in close beside it to the west, with Jacksonville as the linchpin between the two—the place where gold was discovered in 1850. The Cascades sit to the east, the Coastal Range to the west, and the passes farther north along the interstate are dramatic enough to make the valley itself feel completely isolated. Especially in bad weather.

Ashland is in the hills near the California border, the southernmost town in the valley, once famous for the local university and a Shakespeare festival. Grants Pass is north and west, and inaccessible these days. Medford was always the biggest town in the valley, with the mall, the big movie theater, all the hospitals, and a whole lot of people.

But thinking about *people* brings me back to reality with a thud, because there are a lot fewer of those around these days.

I blow out a breath as I drive farther into Medford proper, past the rubble of old apartment buildings that the monsters turned into buffets. Then I brace myself as I take the turn that will lead me into central, downtown Medford.

I don't come here much anymore, not even in daylight. Back before, Medford was a relentlessly pragmatic sort of town, filled with the big-box stores and the fast-food establishments and sprinkled through with various attempts to bring a little burst of new ideas and brighter lights to the place. These attempts never quite took.

Now there's not much left but ruins. Humans don't live in Medford, unless they've been taken by the shadows and the streets. The ones that didn't succumb were eaten years ago. The safe zone for humans is

Jacksonville, though I know there are human enclaves down in Ashland, and there are always whispers of others in harder-to-reach places.

I take a longer route than I need to, despite the debris in the street and too many eyes in the dark recesses of the squat, low buildings. I can't help myself. It's like a physical compulsion to drive around the perimeter of Hawthorne Park, situated at the end of Main Street, right there on the river, where drug addicts used to congregate. There were always homeless initiatives, drug outreach attempts, and all the rest. Addicts are still here, though now they're after a different drug.

I drive slower than I probably should, scanning the faces.

Always desperate to see Augie and relieved when I don't. All those gaunt, ruined faces. All those wild, pleading eyes.

The route I take goes past the front of the martial arts school, propped up there across from the park on the other side of the bridge. I drive past it, seeing lights on inside, and then take Savi's advice and go around the back.

It's dangerous to drive here. The roads in downtown Medford are covered in garbage, and there's no question that half the shit I navigate around is a deliberate trap. I make certain not to catch the eye of any of the shuffling blood addicts on the street who come out as the sun goes down to hunt their next fix. There's no telling what they might do.

But it's the things that don't show themselves that worry me more.

Around the back of the building, I drive up as close to the back of Archangel MMA as the parking lot allows. I find the alley and can see, way down at the other end of it, the very small sign that still says Spartan Arts, like a relic from a different world.

I park, then I sit there with my heart so loud in my chest that I'm surprised it doesn't bring every vampire in Medford running.

I know I can't stay where I am. The longer I sit here, the more likely I am to draw attention to myself.

I hate doing it—it actually *hurts*—but I peel off my weapons and conceal them in the truck's door pockets and beneath the seats. Then I sit there, feeling completely naked, before I force myself to open the door, crawl out, and then . . . not sprint all the way down the alley to that far door.

Running invites a chase.

I walk slowly into the mouth of the alley. I don't look back, even though all my senses are tingling and I'm as certain as I can be that I'm being watched.

I keep the same slow, careful pace even though my skin is crawling. I feel a little lightheaded from trying so hard to keep my breath even. I have to force myself to keep that pace as I go from the parking lot into the darkness of the alley.

I have to let it swallow me up, and it feels like dying.

Immediately, I regret every single decision I made today that led to this.

Not just today. Clearly, letting random people move onto the family land was a huge mistake, because they must have something to do with all this unwanted attention. I didn't have any before they turned up, did I? Unless you count Franklin Hendry.

But there's nothing I can do about it now.

The alley is so dark that it aches, maybe because the bricks on either side of me seem to heave a lot closer than they should. There's a faint hint of something coppery in the air, cutting through the smoke, and I choose not to ask myself what that might be.

What it *must* be in vampire territory.

I break out in a cold sweat, and I'm furious with myself. The last thing I want to do is walk into a vampire den sweating like this, heart racing, like I'm offering myself up as a one-girl experience for whatever lurks within.

But what I can't have is vampires appearing at my grandmother's door. That's the truth I keep coming back to, and it's what got me in the truck to drive out here. It spooked me enough to find Briar lurking around in the kitchen like that. What if she's more dangerous than she seems, even if she's not a vampire? What if she got to Gran?

I have to do this. I have to do it and hope that I make myself amenable enough to this vampire king and give him whatever he wants so I can make it back home.

After I die what feels like a thousand times, I finally reach the door at the end of the alley. The eyes I can feel on my back are more like daggers now, but I don't dare turn around. I test the big steel door with significant dents in it, expecting it to be locked, but it swings open easily.

I'm honestly not sure if that's better or worse.

I walk inside and freeze, because I'm out of the alley and I like that steel at my back, but I'm not sure where I find myself is any better.

I'm in a large, empty room that sprawls the length and width of the building. There's a bit of light coming in from the windows, which have steel bars over them just like mine do at home. Well. These are nicer than mine. Probably not sourced from scrapyards.

I can see the river below, glinting in what little sunlight is left, and it makes me feel like I'm spinning again. The river looks too normal, and yet here I am in a martial arts school that's actually a vampire stronghold—

But that feels a little too much like hysteria. I pinch the inside of my wrist, hard, until I gulp in more air. I force myself to take stock of where I am, especially as my eyes adjust.

There appears to be nothing in the room where I'm standing. What looks like some exercise equipment. A series of doors, all shut tight, against the far wall.

It's empty, but I don't feel alone.

As I stand there with my back against the steel door, I suddenly hear what sounds like a muffled command and then a great sound of stamping up above. If I cringe a little as I look up, expecting a vampire horde to descend upon me through the ceiling, well. There's no one around to see me.

I swallow, though my throat is dry. The light is gloomy now, but I can see the only staircase across the cavernous room, and I make my way to the lowest step.

Then I slowly, reluctantly, begin to climb.

The noise gets louder, but it's rhythmic and strange. I want to run away more than I've ever wanted to do anything, but I don't. I remind myself that I *can't*.

Ariel Skinner not only knows who I am, he knows where I live.

I pass the landing and order myself to keep going when I pause. I take the second flight, admittedly more slowly, and when I get to the top I emerge into something I don't understand at all.

The first thing I see is a throng of astonishingly good-looking people, dancing.

No, not dancing, I immediately revise in my head.

What they're doing looks violent. And dangerous. They're all doing the same thing, they're just doing it at an incredible speed.

An arm in the air, a complicated exchange of arms and feet. A stamp. A kick.

Like they're mapping out fighting styles in the air.

I look past them to the single man standing before them, arms crossed and legs wide, and I know at once it's him.

Ariel Skinner. King of the vampires.

The first thing I notice about him is his stillness.

It feels like an intense invitation.

Like a hand around my throat, but worse. *More*, somehow.

The second thing is the great *wallop* of his presence when he looks right at me.

I don't know how else to process it. I feel it like a blow. Like the very *fact* of him slams into me and sends me staggering back, and I realize that it really does when I have to reach out and grab the railing beside me to stay on my feet.

I jerk my eyes away from his, and it feels harder than it ought to. I look instead at the wide expanse of the mirror behind him.

But the only thing reflected is me.

In the mirror, I'm all alone. In this actual room, however, there must be thirty vampires performing for their king, and he is scarier than all of them.

"Scary" isn't the right word.

I can feel everything inside me shifting. Changing. *Humming.*

Like he's some kind of tuning fork and my body is responding despite my best efforts.

It doesn't help that he is, by far, the most beautiful man I've ever seen. *Ruinous* seems like a vast understatement. He is almost too beautiful to look at directly.

Last night the werewolf alpha was a study in brawn. Brute force, muscled accordingly and riotously.

But this man is something else entirely. There's all that lean muscle, honed to perfection. If the werewolf was a hammer, Ariel is a knife. The kind assassins use, long and sharp and so deadly it feels like blood just to *look.* His hair is black and closely cropped. He has a fierce nose and a cruel mouth, though looking at it makes everything inside of me go soft.

Soft and hot, and I don't understand it at all.

He has his arms crossed over a chest marked in wicked-looking scars, and I can see the hint of a dark-inked tattoo that loops over one shoulder and comes around again at the opposite hip.

I don't have to see the rest of it in the nonexistent reflection. I know, somehow, that it's some kind of dragon. That he is fire.

I feel as if I'm running. As if I'm trapped in that alley with terrible nightmares coming in hot on my heels.

But I can't look away. His gaze is like quicksilver, a searing alchemy that I can feel roll all through me like he's turning me into something new.

I blink. I pull in a breath. I watch as the lines of spinning and kicking suddenly . . . stop.

Like a screech, though there is no sound.

Well.

There is one sound.

My pounding, wildfire, disastrously mortal heart.

Every single one of the vampires turns to stare right at me, but the only stare I *feel* is his.

Wrapped all around me like his tattoo.

"Hi," I say brightly. Foolishly. "I'm Winter Bishop. You summoned me?"

7.

The vampire king lifts a hand in a manner that should appear languid but . . . doesn't. He waves it, just slightly, but I stand straighter at the sight of it. Like it's a command wired straight through me.

It must be, because all the other vampires disappear.

I look around for puffs of smoke, or hints that they simply moved really fast, the way Ty did last night, but there's nothing to see. They're just gone.

"Vampire tricks," says the king.

I find myself thinking about his name. Ariel. Like an angel.

But paired with *Skinner*. Which I suppose is self-explanatory, really.

My own skin prickles with warning. Then *blares* with alarm as it really settles in on me that I am standing all alone in this huge room, all mirrors and high white ceilings above polished wood floors, with this valley's apex predator.

He doesn't move, but that almost makes it worse.

My body knows exactly what he is, and I wait a strangled breath or two for it to decide if flight or freeze is the better option here—*fight* being laughably out of the question—but something else happens. At first, I think it's catastrophic, a disastrous explosion of heat from the very depths of me, but it doesn't make me keel over.

It just makes me too hot and too uncomfortably *aware* of that heat in all the worst places.

All the most humiliating places.

He stays where he is, across that polished floor, with nothing of him in the glass at his back. I've never laid eyes on him before, I wish I never had, and yet I know two things immediately.

One, if he crooked one of those fingers at me, I would go to him. Without question. I can feel a hard pulse of soft heat between my legs at the very idea, and it shocks me. I'm not the sensitive twin. I'm not *sensitive.* I don't *feel* things, and even if I do every now and again, it's not like *this.*

Even that night with Samuel wasn't *this.* It was a rush. It was exciting.

What it was not was this . . . *catastrophic longing* that I can feel pulse in my fingertips and the tops of my ears.

Two—and worse—he knows.

Ariel Skinner, king of all the vampires, knows exactly what effect he's having on me.

I can see it in the way his eyes gleam.

I can feel the way that reverberates inside of me.

"You are not what I expected," he says.

His voice washes over me, and it feels like singing. As if the sound of it is inside me, a chorus of the most beautiful sounds—

I frown at him. "Are you doing that? Stop doing that."

Ariel's head tilts slightly to one side. "What do you mean?"

I wave my hand near my head. "The voice thing. It's annoying."

"My apologies," he murmurs, sardonically enough that it, too, feels like an unnecessary caress. "I would hate to be *annoying.*"

If that's his normal voice, it's not really better. It licks all around me like fire this time.

And by the time I manage to process that, or at least survive it, he's right here in front of my face.

I didn't see him move, either.

"Is that tiring?" I ask. "Popping around like that. Does it take extra energy? It looks like it would be exhausting."

I'm babbling. Something I'm not sure I've done in years. In fact, the last time I can remember the urge was that night Samuel walked me home.

This is significantly more overwhelming.

Because *he* is something close to unfathomable.

Up close, I notice other things about the vampire king. Maybe I'm grasping for a handhold in the middle of the cyclone happening inside me. Maybe I'm desperate to humanize him when it's clear that nothing about him is the least bit human.

I have no idea how he passed as one before.

There's all of that astonishing male beauty, an immediate shock to the system. He's perfect. Even the scars that I can see etched into his chest seem to gleam as golden as the rest of him, and if that's not enough, he smells good.

I can see sweat on his body, but he doesn't smell like a gross, sweaty man. There's a hint of something like the sea. I don't know how I know that's what it is, having never been to the sea myself. When have I ever had the time to drive six hours round trip just to say I went to the coast? But I know it all the same. Mixed in with that is something that reminds me of rosemary. Maybe the slightest hint of eucalyptus, and beneath that, something warmer I can't identify.

In my whole life, I have never had the slightest urge to move toward a sweating man and *press my face into his armpit.* Yet I realize with a shock that, right now, that's exactly what I want to do.

I want more than just to smell him, though. I want to nuzzle my face into him, and maybe lick him, too, so that I can—

What the fuck.

I frown at him. "You sent me a message. A handwritten message, delivered—not at all ominously—to my front door."

Ariel is standing a little too close to me. Not in a threatening way. Or, anyway, it's not immediately life threatening. Still, he shifts back a bit, and I can't decide if I feel relieved or . . . something perilously close to *regretful.*

I don't like either one.

His arms are folded, emphasizing all the muscles in those arms, his wide chest, and below. I can see the place where those indentations over his hips dip below the flowing pants he's wearing. I think they have a name. The pants, not the indentations. What is it that martial artists wear? *Gi pants,* I think.

I'm not sure why it seems critical that I remember.

His feet are bare. I tell myself that a barefoot, half-naked man wandering around in a place of business should not be getting to me like this. I should find it all a bit strange and sad, and what I should not do is keep taking in too-deep breaths of that scent of his.

But every time I do, I can feel it everywhere inside of me, like a violent, seductive tide.

As if, at the slightest provocation or maybe no provocation at all, I'm going to fling myself at this man and do whatever I need to do if only he'll—

I blink again.

"Are you doing that too?"

He allows a small, disastrous curve of that deliciously cruel mouth. "I think that you simply find me attractive."

"So you *are* doing it."

"My great curse is that mine is a mesmerizing beauty," he tells me in that same sardonic tone. He lifts a sculpted shoulder. "It is a burden."

"That's going to have to be a *no, thank you* from me," I say, and cross my own arms. Defiantly. I remember myself a moment later and swallow, though that's tough when my throat is so dry. "Your Majesty."

He really smiles at that, completely transforming that hard mouth of his into something so sensual that it seems to pour all over me, molten and gold.

I feel an ache inside of me yawn open, so wide and so fast it almost feels like an illness, but I know it's not. I only wish it was.

More than that, I know that he's not doing it.

This time, it's all me. It's a *roar.* It's *ruinous.*

It's all heat and longing, need and wonder, and a new sort of terror takes me over.

Because it's one thing for a vampire to play games with me. That's what vampires do. It's something else entirely for me to actually find this . . .

But the word I want to use to describe this is too scary. Too revealing.

I shove it back down, deep inside, and do my best to bury it with all the other things I refuse to feel.

"I'm surprised you came down to the school tonight," Ariel says, still wearing a hint of that smile on his face. "It's very dangerous for humans at night."

"I was given to understand that an invitation from a vampire king is actually a direct summons." I have to clear my throat and am certain that makes me look weak—then I remember that no matter what I do, I *am* weak. "And that it would be foolish to ignore it."

"Excellent advice." He moves away then, and I feel it. As if this whole time I've been clenched in a fist—his fist—and he's finally opened his palm.

I can feel a low, wild sort of throb deep between my legs. I can feel it in different parts of my body, too. My breasts feel heavy. My nipples hurt.

I'm sweating again, but I'm not afraid. Or not afraid of dying. More afraid that I might die before I get to taste—

I frown at his back as he walks across the floor, but now I can't tell. Did he do that? Or did I?

How is it possible to hunger for another being like this? So quickly and so overwhelmingly, with parts of my body I didn't know could feel this way?

Even when I know he's evil.

I blink a few times, then focus on that tattoo that winds its way over the perfect surface of his back. But it's not the dragon I'm expecting.

It's a phoenix.

There's an unpleasant sort of jarring sensation deep inside of me, and for a moment I truly believe I'm about to throw up. There's a ringing in my ears and a sharp, sickening horror in my gut.

Because it looks a lot like another tattoo I know. Two tattoos, in fact.

The ones that Augie and I got on our eighteenth birthday. Matching phoenixes that look a lot like this vampire's boldly drawn, sweeping rendition, dark feathers and all. Mine is more delicate, a splash of bold lines on the right side of my abdomen. Augie's is on the left side of his.

Two firebirds in a pod, he said back then.

His medallion is around my neck, and it feels like it's burning my skin. The fact that we have basically the same tattoo as this vampire king makes my head hurt. I feel hungover and drunk at the same time.

I watch as he walks to a desk I didn't even notice over in one corner, surrounded by a high counter. Behind it are the sort of prosaic things you might expect in any martial arts studio. Even knowing nothing about martial arts myself, I can see that there are pants like the ones Ariel is wearing hanging on the wall. What looks like duffel bags, marked with the gym's branding. Various fighting things like gloves and helmets, though I'm not sure what immortal killers want training equipment for.

He walks behind the counter and rummages around, then shrugs on a T-shirt.

That doesn't really help. Something about this man in a black T-shirt with ARCHANGEL stamped on one pec makes him that much more . . . dangerous-looking. I wish I could say I mean that in the sense of the supernatural abilities and general vampirism.

But I'm afraid what I really mean is to *me*. Personally.

Looking at him makes me feel like I've never seen a real man before in my entire life.

I grit my teeth, and when that doesn't snap me out of it, I bite my own tongue.

That sucks. I wince a bit. But when I look at him again, that high tide of hunger inside me ebbs. Just a little.

I think of Gran's words about *hunger*, and shudder. The tide ebbs even further.

"Did you invite me down here for some martial arts lessons?" I ask into the pressing silence. "Because I love the idea of turning myself into John Wick, but there's enough random violence in my life already, I think."

"It never ceases to amaze me," he says quietly, though I can hear him perfectly. Like he's speaking directly into my ear. "The commitment that fragile, mortal creatures have to pretending they do not fear death."

"Do we fear death more or less than you immortal creatures?" I ask, without pausing to question whether or not it's prudent to get philosophical with a fucking *vampire*. "It seems to me that when you live a millennia or two, you might want to protect your extremely long life even more than those of us who are lucky to get fifty short years." I'm aware I'm talking too much again, but I can't seem to stop it as he stalks toward me. "I never understood all those stories about immortal creatures who were always so *deeply bored* by the *endless grind* of living. Is that what it's like? Is eternity really that boring? Or is it maybe that *you're* boring?" I catch myself there, though it's not soon enough. "Meaning the universal *you*, of course."

His silver eyes glitter. "I never said I was bored."

One of the biggest problems with life post the Reveal are moments like this. I know the reality is that I'm standing here talking to an ancient vampire. I know who Ariel is. I have a sense that I would know who he was even if I didn't know his name. He has power all over him, as if it blares out of his skin, and if I listen, I can hear another spate of that *singing*.

There's a chorus everywhere he goes, proclaiming who he is in a way that makes my bones tremble.

But part of me still can't believe it. Part of me keeps waiting to wake up.

Some people, I'm well aware, feel these things so keenly that they crack. It happened more often in the beginning. Faced with evidence that monsters were in no way located beneath the bed or in dismissible nightmares but were *everywhere*, a great many good people simply couldn't take it onboard. Their brains couldn't handle it.

I don't know what it says about me that mine could. Well enough to survive this long, anyway.

Jury's out on whether or not I'm going to survive Ariel Skinner.

To be honest, I'm not even sure I want to, because surviving this moment means that I'll actually have to live with what I've discovered here tonight.

That given the faintest opportunity, I would welcome the chance to succumb to that vampire magic I've heard whispered about. That thing they do that makes perfectly rational people strip off their clothes, lose themselves in the vampire sex that everyone claims is better than Ecstasy, and leaves the poor humans who indulge in it mere shells of their former selves. Ruined for anything else, ever after.

I've never understood the appeal.

Until now.

"Are you staring at my pulse?" I ask, possibly with some hysteria, as he comes even closer. "Right there in my neck?"

I clap my hand over it. But he only smiles.

"I don't have to stare at it," Ariel tells me in that low, commanding tone of his that washes through me and makes everything *simmer*. "Your pulse is so loud they can hear it down the street."

I don't like that at all.

Now that he said it, I can feel my own pulse too, and it feels brash and showy. Like it's attacking my own palm. Yet somehow, I can also envision his mouth taking the place of my hand, as he presses it over that same insistent throb—

I feel as if the phoenix inked into my skin is throbbing the same way.

He's closer now. Intensely, impossibly close.

Ruinous not only makes sense to me now, it feels like an understatement. A comical understatement.

I find myself lost somewhere between his silver eyes and the darkness of his hair. That Spartan profile, his golden skin, and that perfect, beautiful, deliciously cruel mouth.

I am hot and wet. I am shivery all over.

"Winter," he says, and my name in his mouth makes me clench hard and maybe even whimper, hopefully not out loud. His gaze holds me still. I wouldn't be at all surprised if I was floating off the ground, held tight in his grip. "I brought you here to talk about your brother. Your twin, is that right?"

8.

I feel as if I've been forcibly hurled into a vat of ice water. I feel myself shake with the impact, and I jolt back away from him.

The desire inside me doesn't shift at all, however, and I hate myself for that.

Augie's medallion is starting to feel more like a brand, disfiguring me where I stand.

"What do you mean?" I demand, my voice a little too close to a yelp. "What happened to my brother? What did you do to him?"

Ariel only watches me with that stillness that I can still feel like a shudder of heat straight through me, like gasoline on a fire when so much of me has gone terribly, horribly cold.

"Do you not know how your brother spends his time?" he asks me, quietly, so quietly, that silver gaze of his moving over me as if he's looking for clues. Context.

Weakness, I assure myself. *He's looking for* weakness *so he can tear you up in more ways than one.*

Vampires are famous for the sick games they play.

Because they work.

I never got that before tonight. *They work.*

I feel a flush of deep shame. It rolls through me, vicious and mean, and I back away from him like that might help. It doesn't. I stagger a little as I go, and when my calves come up against the line of benches behind me, I sit down. Heavily.

That I'm used to the flavor of this particular shame doesn't make it any easier or more pliable. That I know it well doesn't make it sit in me like soft cotton instead of the usual thick, heavy concrete.

It brings back far too many memories, all of them connected to life before the Reveal, which wasn't exactly the paradise I sometimes like to pretend it was. Maybe there were no monsters like Ariel, but there were monsters all the same.

Heroin. Fentanyl. Meth.

The scumbag dealers who sold it.

The addicts who let those monsters eat them whole.

Just to name a few.

In many ways, my mother's promises were worse than all of those. That *this time* she learned a lesson. That *this time* she meant it. *This time*, for sure, she was *definitely* done. *This time* she was *absolutely* getting back on her feet.

I know more than anyone should about how to talk to the thing that's killing the person you love, right there in their own body. While you watch, helpless.

Just like I know the searing shame of having to talk about it with anyone else.

"I'm sure there are a lot of things about what my brother does that I don't want to know," I manage to say, and it feels like my own bones want to shake themselves free of my flesh. "But you're asking me if I know the broad strokes? Yes. Sadly, I do."

"His addiction has progressed," the vampire king tells me with what sounds like cool disinterest. How I wish I could share it—but when it comes to the addicts in my family, I've never been any good at distance or disinterest.

I try to push back from the wash of shame and from what lurks beneath it—that absolute terror that I've lost Augie forever to unspeakable circumstances and terrible choices I can't accept.

I try to push back enough that I have access to my brain again.

Because beyond all these unwelcome *feelings* and horrifying *needs*, what I can't figure out is what a whole entire *king* wants with me. Somehow I doubt he's brought me down here so we can stage an intervention with my brother. Out of the goodness of his unbeating heart.

I think I would have heard if he was the undead Jesus with fangs, ministering to the lost and lonely on the streets of Medford, Oregon.

He looks like nobody's savior as he watches me, clearly entirely too aware of my reactions no matter how I try to hide them. "The problem with the kind of progression I mean is that sooner or later, there is no longer any way to afford the habit."

Like this is another Franklin Hendry situation and we're going to mince around, talking in euphemisms like he's not the giant dick in this scenario.

It's even more offensive now that it's Augie he's discussing instead of a mortgage payment.

"If only there was a way that the king of all the vampires could do something about the robust black market of vampire blood," I throw out at him acidly.

Stupidly.

Not that I don't mean it. But it's not a smart power move by any stretch of the imagination, and I know it.

When those quicksilver eyes find mine, I swallow hard.

"I'm sorry," I say, though I'm not. But there's no point in antagonizing a creature so dangerous, especially not when he's holding Augie over my head. When I don't even know what state my brother is in, or where he is. "I'm sure you know what it's like to want to help a family member who doesn't want helping."

"The last of my blood relations died so long ago that even their graves have been rendered unto dust," he replies with a matter-of-factness that reminds me, with a kind of slap, that he really is an immortal creature who's been around forever. Or twenty-five hundred-odd years. Six of one, half dozen of another.

"Note to self," I retort, because apparently I am making suicidal foolhardiness my entire personality. "Stop trying to relate to the scary vampire."

Ariel's gaze on mine is entirely too steady. It makes me flush, everywhere. It makes me think I might cry. It makes me want to throw myself at him—and I'm not sure if I mean to fight him or fuck him, both of which would likely lead directly to my painful death.

I have no idea what's wrong with me. What this man—this impossibly ancient *vampire*—is bringing out in me.

"I am finding this conversation baffling," he tells me, and he sounds almost as if he's musing out loud. I have never heard of a vampire who *muses*. Maybe this is that *civilized* thing Savi was talking about. He *analyzes* his prey. How sophisticated and terrifying and . . . oddly hot. "Usually when I have conversations with mortals, one of two things happens. They froth about until they exhaust themselves, too overcome to make any sense at all. Or they fling themselves upon me, swept away by my . . ." His silver eyes are far too knowing. Far too bright. ". . . charm."

"Do you get off on that?" I demand. I don't even know where a question like that came from.

But I have no time to track it as everything between us . . . *shifts*.

There's nothing but that searing heat.

It's so hot it makes my eyes water.

He tilts his head to one side. It feels like some kind of accelerant washing over me, and then the match strikes. It's the way his mouth moves again, curling in one corner.

"I beg your pardon, Winter. Are you interested in how I get off?"

I can't breathe. Once again, I can't decide if he's doing this to me or if I'm doing it to myself.

Or even if I care about such a pointless difference when it's happening just the same.

"I want to know why you're trying to come on to me while you're also bringing up my brother's challenges," I manage to get out, though none of my systems seem to be operating at the moment. Everything is haywire. I am lost somewhere in this conflagration. "Talk about things that aren't hot."

"Are you sure?" His voice isn't that song inside me, but it's a low, curling lick of impossible heat. And I understand immediately that he knows it. He's *doing it* deliberately. "Because you seem overheated to me."

"Is he dead?" I grit out.

And I hate the storm inside me. It shouldn't be possible. I shouldn't be this worried about Augie while simultaneously bright hot and wild with this impossible hunger.

Especially not for a fucking vampire.

"No," he replies.

It takes a long time for that word to penetrate. For it to make sense. For it to actually turn into understanding.

Augie is not dead. Ariel Skinner, King Vampire, did not call me here to pick up my brother's body.

Something I have been expecting that I will have to do for years now.

I feel the same rush of relief and anguish, shame and fury, that I've felt before, and more than once. That time Augie came home and I found him rifling through Gran's things. The time I saw him on the street, he caught my gaze, and then pretended he didn't know who I was.

Always happy that he's not dead. Always furious that this is how he chooses to live.

Always so damned hurt that he abandoned me.

I blow out a long, shaky breath. "So you didn't call me here to identify his body. You probably could have led with that up front."

"You seem to have a lot of confidence that I won't kill you for your impertinence," Ariel says almost absently.

But I can see the way he's looking at me. There is nothing absent about it.

It is all a terrible alchemy and it hurts, and yet there's a worryingly large part of me that just wants *more.*

"If you want to kill me," I say, letting out a sound that's awfully close to a laugh, "you could do it at any time. It doesn't matter what happens today. It doesn't matter what I do. You're not just any old run-of-the-mill vampire, are you? You're the king. Everything that lives here in this valley does so because you allow it, right?"

He looks at me as if I don't make sense. As if he's trying to puzzle me out and not quite managing it, but now that I'm through the sickening punch of relief that Augie's not dead, I'm on to the other side of that.

That being all the other things Augie could be that would have this particular vampire looking for me.

All the other things that could happen. All of them dark and desperate.

Then, a distant second, all the things that could happen to *me.*

Right here. Right now. Thanks entirely to this pitiless, beautiful creature who is watching me so closely.

I take a breath so ragged it feels as if it leaves marks behind.

Ariel steps back, and while that doesn't exactly break the spell, it makes it . . . shimmer, somehow. Enough so that this power of his, like a hand wrapped around my throat, recedes.

Just enough so I can breathe.

Just enough so I understand that I miss it. Immediately.

"Come with me," he tells me.

I'm not foolish enough to argue with him. Foolishness doesn't enter into it, because that implies a choice. And I don't pretend to have one. He moves across the polished wood floor, and I follow him. I can't help but sneak looks in the mirror to make sure I still can't see anything but me marching across an empty room.

I can't.

It's disorienting.

I focus instead on the sculpted expanse of his muscled back. And the hints of that phoenix I can see peek out here and there when the way he moves makes his hem or collar shift.

I feel the phoenix on the side of my body pulse like it, too, wants to burn.

I tell myself that's psychosomatic at best, but I burn all the same.

In the corner of the great room, he directs me to the steps that lead up to a loft that looks out over the whole of the space and all those dizzying mirrors. But he doesn't stop there. He keeps going, leading me to the far corner, where a spiral staircase rises up toward the ceiling.

He does not look back to see if I'm following him. He simply walks, as if my obedience is a foregone conclusion. And that might rankle, but I follow him around and around the spiral to nowhere anyway.

It doesn't occur to me to do anything but what he wants.

I tell myself that's just King 101.

We climb and climb, and at the top he comes to a small landing and pushes through the door that waits there.

I have no other choice, so I hit the landing and promptly follow him into the dark.

"Your eyes will adjust in a moment," comes Ariel's voice, as if he's part of the darkness.

Because he is.

I feel it like a deep, wild shudder, and there's more of me than I'd like to admit that wants nothing more than to melt into the darkness. Especially if he's a part of it.

But slowly my eyes adjust, and I realize that we're standing out on the roof of the MMA school.

My breath leaves me in a rush as I make out the stars above and the low moon just starting to rise in the distance. And it's not that I forget that I'm in the presence of a vampire, but I can't keep myself from drifting over to the edge of the roof, where I can look out over the dark remains of Medford's city center.

There are very few lights out there, and it would be foolish indeed to confuse any of them for a beacon. In the early days after the Reveal, there were tales of mooncussers, of a sort, who would roam the dark nights, setting up beacons to draw in the terrified masses looking for shelter, then slaughter them for what goods they carried with them.

Or eat them, depending on the story.

It's yet one more reason why anyone with a modicum of common sense stays locked up inside from dusk to dawn.

Yet here I am, standing up above this town we lost three years ago to the monsters, somehow aching like I've lost a limb. It wasn't that I spent so much time down here. There were always grumblings about the homeless populations that crowded the riverbanks and spilled out into the streets, waxing and waning with various city ordinances. There was always the suggestion of violence here, thanks to the businesses that only opened by day and closed up tight at night. The graffiti no one could seem to keep at bay. The clusters of the homeless and the addicted rising up like zombies come nightfall, or after the police rousted them out of their hiding spots along the river.

I didn't spend a lot of time here, but it was still mine. It was still home.

There is no reason to suppose that it will ever be safe to walk the streets again, and it's just one more tide of grief washing over me, washing through me, and never quite leaving me clean. I turn back around and face the king of the vampires, who is closer to me than I thought he was.

"You shouldn't sneak up on people," I mutter at him, frowning.

"Maybe you missed the part where I'm a vampire. Sneaking up on people is part of the fun." He studies me. "Lurking is in the job description."

"Just so long as we've established that you do, in fact, find all the rampaging and murdering fun. To clarify our positions."

"Tell me," he says after a moment, "have you killed any monsters since the Reveal?"

I take a moment to make certain I'm keenly aware of how fragile I am. How breakable. How decidedly weaponless.

Maybe he's brought me here to act as judge and jury. Maybe this is monster justice.

I swallow, though my throat is dry. "I have."

"So we are all murderers, then. You and me alike."

There's that intensity in his gaze. And that power of his that feels stretched out all around me, but not pressing in on me. Not anymore.

I pull in a breath. "I've never really thought of it that way. But yes, I suppose. I think you'll find it's difficult to live in peace with things that want to kill you. That consider you not just prey, but a snack."

"Says a representative of a species who has no trouble using wooden stakes or silver bullets to knock out sentient beings a little bit higher up the food chain."

"Well," I say after a long, breathless moment, "I hope we can all agree that zombies need killing. If you can kill something that's already dead. Please don't tell me that there's a zombie rights movement too."

"I prefer not to cast stones on members of the living dead," Ariel replies in that low hum of a voice. "It would be a bit hypocritical, would it not?"

"Maybe the zombies have it better. After all, they don't know that they were once alive."

To my astonishment, he laughs. It's a low, quiet thing, sounding faintly like music, or maybe that's simply how my body interprets it.

And how it tries to sing along.

"It is very difficult to surprise me," Ariel tells me. "And you've done it more tonight than anyone else has. In a long, long time."

"Gold star for me."

But I look away from the curious intensity on his face. I look up, and there they are. All the stars I didn't know I would miss like this. The whole Milky Way itself, a bright, hot mess shining on down from so far away. Looking at this planet that, on the surface, probably still looks green and blue, spinning lushly about our sun.

Instead of black the way it is down here on the ground, washed over with blood.

I was always about the sunshine. I never would've guessed how much I'd come to miss dark. The night.

The stars.

I could tell him that I've seen the stars more recently than since the Reveal, but I don't. It feels too intimate.

A feeling I should not be having around Ariel Skinner, King of the Damned. I shouldn't be having any feelings at all. So I concentrate on the feelings I'll allow myself. "Are you going to tell me about my brother? Or did you bring me up here to toss me off the side of this building so I can die like everyone else?"

"I don't have to throw people off the sides of buildings to kill them," he says, as if I'm being amusing.

On purpose.

That makes my temper kick in, and that's a good thing. I need a little anger. I need . . . *something*. Anything that feels like a weapon in a situation like this.

"You said that Augie is alive. Is he hurt?"

"His demons are bigger than he is," Ariel says. "You can call that hurt if you like."

"Let me see if I have this straight. You came to my door. You left a summons. I answered that summons, and you told me that . . . what? He owes you money? So does that mean you think I owe you too if he can't pay you?"

"Something like that," Ariel says, and I choose not to think too closely about the way he's looking at me. Or the way he said that, like he means something else entirely.

Maybe I can't let myself think about it, because that feels like surrender.

"This is very surprising," I say instead. "I was told you were very civilized. I didn't realize they meant not only civilized for a vampire, but for the average Mob boss, too."

"I've never cared much for Italian food." Ariel drifts over, and for a creature who as far as I know can turn into a bat, suck my blood, and transform into something horrible before my very eyes, he is remarkably . . . physical. I try to tell myself that this response I'm having to him is false, that he's doing it, that it's part of that mesmerizing thing vampires like so much, but I can't quite convince myself.

Because beautiful is beautiful. And believe me, these days, no one takes beautiful for granted.

"I don't have any money," I tell him flat out. "And any money I do have is already being extorted from me, so you're going to have to get in line."

I get the sense that he doesn't like that much, but when I glance at him, his expression is unreadable. So I don't know if he's against the extortion part or the fact that I don't have the thing he wants.

"Money would be easy," he says. "This is not about money at all."

I want to be relieved. I'm not.

"Your brother is in a precarious state," he tells me. "I think perhaps I can help him. If you help me."

I've vowed to myself a thousand times that I'm done with Augie, but who am I kidding? He's my twin. Literally the other half of me. And if he's addicted to vampire blood like so many people are these days, there's a silver lining there. It means he's off the other stuff. The human stuff. I don't know what it takes to detox from blood, but maybe it's different.

And maybe pigs will start flying around in Jacksonville.

Either way, this is still my only brother we're talking about. I've never been able to convince him to save himself. But Ariel isn't asking for that. He's asking me to step in and do something that might save Augie whether Augie himself wants it or not.

And unlike well-meaning pastors and counselors over the years, Ariel has the power to compel Augie to do it.

I can't help but feel like this is an opportunity.

I don't have it in me to refuse. I can't.

"I'll do anything," I say recklessly. "Please don't hurt him."

"Addicts hurt themselves," Ariel tells me, and there's something stern and old and knowing in his voice that I recognize. But I don't want to recognize it. It feels too much like truth. "Over and over again."

"You don't have to tell me what addicts do."

Those eyes of his gleam, but I can't tell if it's with approval or warning.

"I'll do anything," I say again. "What exactly do you want?"

He doesn't answer that. And it's in the pause that I can feel his power surge. As if I've sacrificed myself right here on this rooftop. Given myself away, bared my neck, and let him bite down, deep and hard—

I don't know where the image comes from, or why it seems to shatter its way through me, and not in a bad way. I've never fantasized about a vampire bite in my life.

Then again, I've never met Ariel before.

When he comes to stand beside me to look out over the city, I'm sure he can hear the racket my heart makes. But there's nothing I can do about it. Just like there's nothing I can do about the fact that his closeness sets everything in me alight.

It's a scalding heat, everywhere, pooling between my legs and making me want to press my thighs together—

But I don't.

On the off chance that he can't tell what's happening to me, I don't want to give him the CliffsNotes version.

"What do you think the Reveal is?" he asks after a moment, when I'm beginning to think this much access to starshine might intoxicate me. I feel dizzy and fragile again.

It's probably not the stars, I admit to myself.

"What kind of question is that?" I rub at my face. "It's in the name. All the monsters were revealed. *Boom.* The end of the world as we know it. Though I suppose it's more the dawn of the world for you."

"It's really just the same world." Ariel shrugs. "For good or ill. It's only the rules that have changed."

"That's a highly sanitized version of a global slaughter," I point out. "Or anyway, I assume it was global. It took, what? A week to lose the internet, live television, radio, and all the rest of it. Pretty much any long-range communication device. But before then, it was pretty clear that there was a feeding frenzy, and we were on the menu."

"But you survived." He says that like it's meaningful instead of just dumb luck. And given how these years have been, maybe not *luck* at all. "Even your brother, despite giving every indication of having an overdeveloped death wish, remains alive. And nominally human."

I feel, deeply, that he wants me to jump on that. And ask him what he means by *nominally*.

So I don't. I let that day three years ago flood back into me, all that dawning horror and sadness, the beginning of all this grief that has nowhere to go.

And the innocuous way it started—for me anyway.

"It was a Tuesday," I tell him, this vampire king who could have caused the whole thing, for all I know. Who certainly doesn't *care* what happened, because why would he? I certainly can't trust that he's asking this for any reason but his own, whatever that might be. I even laugh a little. "Just a random fucking Tuesday that no one would ever have remembered if it hadn't all started that day."

9.

I'm not sure I mean to speak out loud.

But there I am, speaking with my whole voice on a topic I don't think I've ever discussed. Not in any depth. What's the point of describing a bomb to everyone else in the same bomb shelter?

I'm not looking at the vampire beside me. Instead, I'm staring out at the dark streets of Medford, down toward the intersection of Main Street and Riverside, where there used to be a bento food cart that always smelled delicious—far better than it looked. There's an old neon sign above what used to be a decidedly down-market strip club that always looked sticky from the outside. In the years before the Reveal, there had been more new restaurants and other such attempts to bring life and light to the streets. All in vain, now.

Ariel doesn't say a word, though I can feel his power humming all around me. He doesn't speak, and somehow that makes it easier for me to keep going.

"It was just a Tuesday," I say again. Just a random, pointless, boring day in the middle of an unremarkable and otherwise unmemorable week. "Augie was home, which was getting rarer in those days, though we were all not quite talking about it. But I'd called out of my shift at the coffee stand that morning because Augie had come back in the middle of the night, and I didn't want him waking up disoriented with my grandmother at home."

I was afraid he would wake up in one of his rages, and I couldn't in good conscience leave Gran to deal with that alone. Mostly because she has always been the one most likely to pull out the shotgun in moments of stress, and our family was jacked enough already.

Gran had been more mobile then. She didn't require all the tending to, not yet. Maybe, looking back, it should have been clear that things were slipping. But I didn't know that then. I didn't realize things *could* slip the way they would shortly thereafter.

I'd slept in past my usual predawn wake-up time, and when I went downstairs, I found Gran watching TV in the study on the first floor, which was odd for her in the morning. I frowned at the sight, but she didn't move or seem to notice that I'd come downstairs. Also weird.

I went into the kitchen and made myself espresso in my stovetop percolator like a European, because working at the coffee stand has ruined me for drip coffee. And I think about those moments a lot, even now. Standing in the kitchen when the windows were still glass. Letting the morning light stream in and dance all over me like that wouldn't be a luxury within days. Waiting for the espresso to be ready and sighing a little as the rich, earthy scent filled the room. Taking my first sip gratefully, sighing again as I stared out back toward what must have been a kicking garden back then, because Gran could always grow a plant or a flower seemingly at will.

I try to think back to what was on my mind on such a run-of-the-mill day. What was filling up my head. What I thought was important before the world changed.

I can remember every detail of what I did in the kitchen in those last few moments of normalcy, but I never have been able to recall what I was actually thinking about. Augie, probably. Whatever sad social life I didn't really have going on.

At some point—a few minutes later? An hour? I'll never know—I padded into the study to see why my grandmother was glued to the television set on a Tuesday morning when she had been known to unplug the TV on weekends to force us kids outside.

But somewhere between the doorway and the seat I took on the couch beside her, I forgot anything I might have said.

I don't know which images I saw first. They all jumble together in my head. The explosions in far-off cities and the creatures celebrating them in force, though I thought, at first, that there was something wrong with my eyes. The CN Tower in flames with what I thought were people in ghoulish masks dancing around. Big Ben, swarming with those horrible bug things I prefer to believe stay on that side of the Atlantic, because the alternative is too horrible to accept. Gruesome scenes from everywhere, but the horror of the actual destruction of cities on television—like too many action movies except *real*, though at first it didn't *seem* real—faded as I came to realize what was doing the attacking.

Then, of course, came the real horror.

And it came in stages.

Disbelief was first. It couldn't be real. It was some Hollywood thing. I remember initially feeling angry and removed, furious that a joke like this could be played on so many people.

But that faded into a kind of numbness as image after image, with less and less commentary from newspeople, showed the hideous truth.

Monsters were real. And they weren't hiding any longer.

At some point, Augie woke up too, and whether he was detoxing or not, what I remember is him sitting silently on that couch with Gran and me. For hours.

The three of us in a silence marred only by the disgusting, grisly scenes unfolding on the screen before us, sometimes staring at each other, sometimes weeping quietly, sometimes frozen still.

Maybe it was days. Time flattened out and never recovered.

There are things that stand out to me. That deep rejection of what I was seeing. My instant, bedrock conviction that it had to be a cut of some movie. A marketing experiment that some film studio was doing, like that Orson Welles thing from back in the day.

Though even as I kept thinking that, I knew better. I knew it wasn't fake.

Death in the movies is a whole lot prettier.

We all have images in our heads now that we'll never get out. It's why some folks lose it altogether and opt in to whatever opiates they can find, and as much as I hate it, I get it.

It had to be the first night, though it's hard to remember how time moved then. I remember that it was dark, or maybe it simply got gloomy enough in that room. Maybe the power had gone out by then, because it was off for months once it went.

Then again, it could have been the bright light of day. What I know for sure is that the three of us were sitting there, silent. Stricken. But together in a way we hadn't been in a long, long time.

And then, together, we heard the wolves begin to howl.

It was the first time in my life I learned that "bloodcurdling" wasn't just a thing people said, because I felt it.

It's here, Gran said in a raspy whisper. *It's not just the cities. It's happening here, too.*

"We were lucky," I tell Ariel now. "The people who were out doing errands and living their lives—very few of them made it. There were bodies in the streets. Augie and I went down at some point. It could have been days later, maybe a week, and we saw them. Then learned a valuable lesson about leaving the house without enough weapons. The hard way."

It's difficult to remember now that there was a time when I didn't know how to fight. That I was ever foolish enough to drive into an unknown situation without numerous weapons at my disposal.

Once things changed, everything changed. And fast.

That particular day, a pack of wraiths swarmed the truck while we were still reeling from the piles of dead everywhere, and all Augie and I had going for us was that we were raised *just* rural enough. Our dad had taken us hunting since we were small. We knew our way around guns. Augie had taken the shotgun with him when we left the house, and that was all we had to work with, so we made it work.

He shot. I drove.

We didn't speak.

We didn't have to. I could feel his terror. He could feel mine, mixed in with that hollow despair.

But neither one of us could bear the thought of not making it back to Gran.

"It wasn't long after that the monsters started roaming the hills at night," I tell Ariel. "And I know that by the time they made it to our house, we'd boarded up all the windows and installed metal gates on all of them. For those long, terrible first months, all three of us huddled together down in the basement because we figured we were more likely to make it through the night if there were heavy metal doors between us and the roving bands of nightmares everywhere."

"It would certainly offer a bit of a buffer," he says. Very politely, since I doubt very much *he* would have any trouble getting in—or, more likely, forcing us out so as not to have to deal with that pesky invitation issue.

I try not to think about what it would be like to stagger out of a burning house to face down my impending beautiful death in the form of this creature.

I think about it anyway. Until it makes me quiver, though I do my best to hide it.

"As far as I know, it was a feeding frenzy," I tell him, trying to sound serious and not like I'm imagining his fangs on me. *In* me. "A free-for-all. Power was out. Internet was out. We had a hand-crank radio for camping that lasted the longest, but even that was eventually nothing but static. After a while, there were fewer attacks in the night. They used to come and try to tear off the windows and scratch up the house, but they stopped. I don't really know why."

"I can tell you why." Ariel gazes down at me, his silver eyes bright and unreadable. "But you seem remarkably incurious as to why it happened in the first place. Do you not wonder why that Tuesday of all Tuesdays?"

It's tempting to feel chided, but I don't.

Or more accurately, I won't.

"One thing I've learned is not to wonder about things that can't be changed." It's my turn to shrug, and I make it operatic. "What's the point? Maybe there's a monster union and that was your version of a strike? Maybe it was the monster revolution? I don't know. All I know is, I went from leading a fairly uneventful life in rural Oregon to being prey in the course of one terrible day. Who cares why it happened if it's not going to stop?"

He turns slightly, and once again I'm too aware of him. I'm too aware of *me*. It's as if the borders of my own body want to blur into him. As if I want to hasten the process and simply melt against him. Into him. Everything in me is certain that if I touch him, I'll burst into flames, when everything I've ever heard about vampires is that they're cold.

But if Ariel's cold, he doesn't feel like it to me.

All I can seem to feel in his presence is *fire*.

"Seven thousand years ago, there was a historic planetary and celestial alignment," Ariel tells me. "Humans love to elevate their sciences above all else, but nothing in the universe is so simple. Seven thousand years ago, that alignment heralded the birth of what I suppose you would call a goddess. In human terms."

"A goddess," I repeat, and it's a struggle to keep myself from thinking about all that dark goddess shit that stalks me through my nightmares. And the Goddess of Filth that Gran keeps muttering about. I feel the hint of a headache bloom in one temple. But I do my best to sound skeptical. "Naturally. Because along with all the monsters, there have to be gods and goddesses too."

"Gods and goddesses are simply the monsters that can be bribed." Ariel says that with a certainty that tells me that no matter what I might want to disbelieve, *he* thinks what he's saying is true. Meaning, it probably is. "The monsters who can demand human participation in their affairs. After all, the stock tastes so much better if it thinks it's responsible for its own bloody sacrifice."

A kind of dark thrill sweeps through me at that. Or maybe it's fear. If so, it's not the sort of fear that I can understand. It's not the sort of fear that makes me want to run, screaming.

Unless it's to him.

Which really should also terrify me, yet doesn't. Not the way it should.

"Who was this goddess?" I ask instead, trying to sound whatever the opposite of incurious is. Or maybe because I want to be scared of the right thing. "Why do you know about her and an *alignment* anyway?"

"Death goddesses tend to leave a trail of carnage in their wakes," Ariel says, and this time it's his matter-of-factness that makes me fight to repress a shiver. Because I've seen carnage, but somehow, the way he's *not* describing hers makes me think it's worse. "This particular goddess was called Vinča. Over the course of some centuries, she hacked her way through the better part of what is now Europe, making a name for herself and developing a rabid cult in the process. Over time, her bloodlust became unmanageable and she was neutralized."

I try to imagine what he's talking about, behind the cool, emotionless way he's telling it to me. I think of my nightmares, and the horrible bird that sometimes chases me, sometimes stares, and sometimes pecks its way into my flesh. "How do you *neutralize* a god?"

"Carefully," Ariel replies.

So dryly that I can't think of anything else to ask him, so I nod. I hope it looks like the understanding I certainly don't feel.

"The same set of celestial events took place three years ago," he tells me after a moment. "The best way to describe it is like the opening of a lock. Once this lock was opened, certain restraints disappeared. It is something that the creatures you call monsters had been waiting for.

For a very long time, and some more than others. But crucially, it is the first in a series of foretold events."

"Foretold events," I repeat. "Like . . . Nostradamus?"

"The trouble with prophecies and visions is that they are so often the province of madmen and drug addicts." Ariel makes a dismissive sound, deep in his throat. "I can't tell you the number of times the rambling of some mad fool was held to be a great prophecy, only to repeatedly not come true. This particular planetary alignment, however, did in fact occur. You could argue that's simply science. But to the Kind, it was the first step toward a very particular fate."

I don't know which part of what he said I should focus on first. *"The Kind?"*

He pauses, and I can't read the look he sends my way. Did he not mean to say that? "A generic term. For your monsters."

The Kind, I think. Kindness is not what I associate with the creatures he's talking about. Though I know that's not quite the meaning intended.

"So what's the prophecy?" I ask.

"As I said, this particular prophecy is a series of steps." I get the impression that he's studying me again. Looking for something on my face, in my eyes, though I can't tell what. "Certain things will happen, and if they do, they are keys to a set of locks. Once all of those locks are open, a much bigger event will occur."

"Thank you. That's very illuminating."

"It is just about time for the second of these locks to be thrown open." There's no mistaking it now. He's watching me intently. I just can't figure out why.

"But you're the king. Surely, you have all the keys."

Ariel does not smile. Not exactly. But that power hums in the cool dark all around us, and the way he looks at me feels like he would smile, if he could. Maybe if things were different—but then, if they were, I wouldn't be standing here. "If only it were that simple."

I turn toward him, and we're so close. The air all around us is cool, and I can see pinpricks of light in the distance. Fires in the hills.

Moonlight up higher. Small fires or flashlights deep in the shadows in the city streets. Even the odd flickers of electricity here and there by people who clearly don't fear attracting the nightwalking *Kind* to their doors.

But there's nothing as electric as whatever this is that blazes between the two of us.

This thing that shouldn't exist.

I feel doomed. But in that doom, somehow, there's a certain elation that I can't make any sense of, because it's impossible.

It's a shivery kind of ache in every part of me, a desperate pulse.

"I've never been much for prophets," I tell him, not entirely surprised to find that my voice has dropped to a whisper. "Seems like anyone with a little creativity can warble on about the end of days. Sooner or later, they'll be right."

I still can't read that look on his impossibly perfect face. It's something like quizzical. Or maybe it's wonder.

But that's nothing next to how it feels when he takes his hand and traces a pattern over my cheekbone. Down the line of my jaw, just shy of my lips.

He is cool to the touch after all, but it's like an ice cube on overheated skin.

My body reacts with a hot, deep flush that there's no possibility of hiding.

It rolls over me and about flattens me. It blooms inside me.

It devours me.

"The Reveal was foretold by many ancient seers." Ariel's voice is so low that at first I think he's whispering dark sex words. Not this same prophetic bullshit. "Over many millennia. But also, more recently, by a local oracle of surprising strength."

I scoff at that, though maybe I just want to move my face in his grasp so I can feel the friction. "What good is an oracle who doesn't tell people what's coming? Who doesn't even try?"

"There is an oracle on every street corner claiming they know the end is nigh," Ariel says softly. "Are you in the habit of listening?"

I'm listening now. And I have never felt anything like the clamor inside of me at the moment. Maybe he's doing it. Maybe I'm doing it.

All I know is it's unbearable, but maybe it's the dark that's doing this to me. Here in the ruins of Medford, where no one can see me. I have a stray thought that all my sins take place in the dark and then are ignored ever after, but that's the only comparison to Samuel I can muster up.

Because Ariel puts the likes of Samuel to shame, something I would have said was impossible. I think about that awful Tuesday when everything changed, forever. He can call it locks or keys and talk about Vinča the death goddess, but none of that is likely to have anything to do with me. It was the end of the world. I know it. I was there. I watched it happen.

But if the whole world is made up of impossible events these days, what's another one?

I hate myself, but not enough, because I tip myself forward and press my mouth to his.

It's a mistake.

It's a miracle.

He's a vampire, and that makes it hotter and crazier, and I don't even think about stopping, because his lips are cool and firm. I feel him smile against my mouth, as if he's made of marble but I've brought him to life.

But then . . . he devours me.

His touch is cool, but his kiss is like fire.

He goes deeper. It gets hotter. He angles his head and his hands take possession of me, easily.

Totally.

There's one hand at the nape of my neck, guiding me, holding me. The other moves down the length of my body, smooths over the curve of my ass, and then lifts me like I'm nothing.

Like I'm made of air.

But he settles me against his body, and I can't seem to help myself. I wrap myself around him, my arms around that strong neck so I can press my breasts against that wall of a chest I saw so much of downstairs. My legs lock tight around his waist and I groan, helplessly, as I come up flush against his thick, hard cock.

I nearly come then and there.

Everything in me is soft, a molten white heat, and I lose myself in it.

In him.

I'm so wet and my clit *aches* as he eats at my mouth like I'm dessert—deeper and deeper. His cock is huge and hard and right where I want it, and I keep having insane and dangerous little flash fantasies.

Every single one of them involves his fangs.

I hate myself, but not nearly enough, because I'm rubbing myself against him. Writhing in his arms while he makes low, encouraging noises in the back of his throat. His big hand holds me and helps me move up and down against him, but even if he wasn't helping I'd be completely unable to stop myself.

His cock is so *big*. Hard, like marble, and I want him deep inside me—now—with a feverish need I've never felt before. He holds me so easily. He kisses me dirty and deep, like his tongue against mine is a filthy sex act all its own, and I am lost to myself.

For the first time in my life, I understand the addictions that nearly everyone else in my family suffers from.

Because this makes *no sense.*

But not one part of me wants to stop.

Not now that I'm wriggling myself up and down, rubbing myself through my clothes and his, getting my clit in contact with that hard, long, enormous cock of his. I imagine us naked, just like this, high up on this roof but safe because he's *him*. I imagine me impaled on his cock, all that cold, hard marble, with his teeth buried deep in my neck—

Oh no, I think.

And then I come in a terrible rush with a scream that might have torn down what buildings remain in downtown Medford if his mouth wasn't still on mine.

I feel something sharp, and I jerk, but that hint of his fangs only makes the orgasm clench harder and roll out longer.

For a long while, there is only that shaking.

And the taste of copper in my mouth.

Until, a thousand years later, he sets me down on my feet and I think very hard about simply diving off the side of the building. That seems infinitely preferable to lifting my gaze to his.

To admitting that this just happened.

He doesn't wait for me to make a decision. He reaches over, tilts my chin up, and then . . . brushes his thumb over my mouth.

I pull my head back and see a smear of blood on his thumb.

And I watch—horrified and something a lot worse than simply *horrified*, something that makes my clit throb with need all over again—as he puts his thumb in his mouth.

Then sucks on it.

"You bit me?" I manage to ask, though I'm not sure how. I feel raggedy. I feel torn apart.

I have no idea who I am or what just happened, or what I'm going to do with the knowledge that I could ever behave like this. That I did.

That, most shamefully, I would do it again in a heartbeat.

I feel shamefully certain he knows this as well as I do.

"I didn't bite you," he says, and has the gall to sound amused. "Trust me when I tell you that you would know if I bit you. This is nothing but a little nick."

"Thank you, that's a great consolation to me. When will full sunlight start burning me? Should I invest in blackout shades and a coffin?"

"You don't have to worry too much about the sun in this valley. Surely, you've noticed."

"That's not really comforting."

"Winter."

And he says my name gently, which sends that same sort of storm of sensation thundering through me, because he's terrifying and somehow tonight I mixed up healthy terror with sex, and I can't get those fantasies out of my head. *Especially* when he says my name.

I can still see how hard he is. And how little he seems to care that I can see it. That cock of his, literally a monster cock, pushing out those soft pants of his like a whole stone ledge.

His gaze seems even more silver than before. "This is real life. There is very little comforting about it. I would expect you to know that already."

"I really wish that you would just kill me and get it over with," I blurt out.

It's not true. I don't have a death wish. I want to live, and I want it with a kind of fierce desperation that I don't even know how to explain, because if I didn't, I wouldn't keep fighting so hard. If I didn't, there are so many ways to simply surrender to death coming for you, relentlessly, from every side.

I try not to think about it too much, because wanting to live in the wake of the Reveal is begging for trouble.

Begging for trouble, like what I'm doing now, seems suicidal.

My words hang between us like a death sentence, and I wait for him to do it. A flash of fangs, a snap of my neck, a push.

There are so very many ways to die.

"What makes you think I want to kill you?" Ariel asks. "You are so shiny and new and mortal. You have death stamped on your forehead the day you're born. Why rush it?"

Then he smiles, wide enough this time that I can actually see his fangs. Not fully extended. Just enough. Maybe they come out when he's turned on.

Something that shouldn't turn *me* on at all.

"Well," I manage to say into the thick silence that follows. "If that's all, maybe you can tell me why you wanted to talk to me about my brother. Do you know where he is?"

He shakes his head. "We'll get to that. But don't you want to know who the oracle is?"

"So I can go slap him upside the head for doing a terrible job at warning everyone?" I ask brightly. "Yes. Yes, I would *love* to know who he is. Complete with a current address, please."

But when his gaze settles on mine, gleaming intently, I go still. I understand that whatever he's about to say is going to wreck my whole world.

Again.

And that's exactly what he does.

10.

I don't know how I make it home.

What I mean is, I stagger away from him in shock, his words like a poison in my blood. I throw myself back down that spiral staircase, not sure how I don't fall and break my neck. My body doesn't feel like mine, and I don't know what to do about that. I feel . . . disfigured by Ariel, by the way he kissed me, by the *nick.*

By the way I came apart of my own volition, rocking myself against his cock the way I did. Like he's one, big, giant sex toy.

Shamelessly. Mindlessly.

No, not mindlessly. That's the worst part. Much as I'd like to blame it on vampire compulsion or whatever magic it is they do, *I* kissed *him.* I started it.

I knew exactly what I was doing.

I make it down the set of stairs on the other side of the polished wood floor, through that dark, empty room, and I don't even look around. There's some part of me that doesn't care if more terrible things leap out from the shadows.

On some level, finally getting eaten alive would be an excellent way to not have to deal with the ramifications not only of my actions here tonight but of what he told me.

But the thing is, I still don't want to die.

And I want to know what's happened to Augie, with the same level of ferocity.

I make it outside again, into that alley, and walk a whole lot slower than I should. As if I'm daring something to come for me.

Yet somehow, I know that nothing will.

Sure enough, nothing does.

I stand next to my truck, holding my breath. I can hear the rush of the river nearby. I can hear shouts in the distance and what sounds like drums. There's a loud *boom* somewhere, and I can see shadows racing away from it on the other side of the river. And then, moments later, more shadows racing toward it.

I gulp in some air and make myself look up. Up high to the roof of the MMA school, where I can see a figure silhouetted against the stars.

That form of his like marble, etched into my own skin like a new tattoo.

Like he's altered the shape of my body with his.

So there's nothing to do but climb into my truck and aim it home.

I barely see the road and all the usual blockades and other issues as I drive. I do it all on dangerous autopilot, out of downtown Medford and into the fields that used to be suburbs. Into Jacksonville, where curfew is in effect and no humans are on the streets. Samuel makes sure of it. But that means it can only be monsters congregating beneath the old neon JVILLE TAVERN sign, so I take the early turn and head up the hill.

Then I'm driving up toward the house, and I'm home, but when I turn off the truck's ignition, I don't go anywhere. I sit there.

I sit there for much too long, trying to figure out what the hell I'm going to *do*.

Or how I'm supposed to feel about all the things I just did. And didn't do.

I'm not sure which is worse. That I didn't manage to get a straight answer from Ariel about where Augie is or what's happened with him or *why* the vampire king knows who he is anyway. Or the fact that I rubbed myself all over that giant marble cock of his, let him not *quite* bite me, and liked it.

More than liked it.

I almost feel like maybe I finally experimented with some of those drugs that everyone else in my family seems to like so much. I feel . . . loopy. Outside myself. Something like *fuzzy*.

I don't normally sit in the truck, not out here in the yard like a target. Certainly not in the dark. I normally don't go out in the dark at all. I *normally* take the curfew Samuel imposed seriously, because it's just common sense. The fewer humans wandering around at night, the more of us make it to morning.

I know that I should move quickly, get myself to safety, lock myself away from the monsters.

Though that feels less imperative than usual when I was just scaling one like a jungle gym.

I sit where I am. I stare up at the house and the lights beckoning from the attic, where I left them on before I took off. I look to the side and see more lights from the three cottages, announcing that there are people at home.

I try to find this comforting. But I'm long past that.

At first, I didn't believe him.

I gaped at him, absolutely certain that what had just happened between us was messing with my head. Making me loopy and strange. Because what he was saying couldn't possibly make any sense.

So he said it again. *The most powerful oracle on this continent lives right here.* He spoke slowly. Deliberately. *You know her. More than know her.*

Stop it, I gritted out.

Sarah Jessup Brown, he said, and the second time wasn't any better.

It was like it caused a short circuit inside me. I can still feel it now, as if something snapped. Or burned straight through. I can feel it fraying inside me.

He only stared at me, those silver eyes making that burning sensation inside of me worse. *Your grandmother, Winter.*

Like I don't know my own grandmother's name.

I still can't believe it.

I start to get out of the truck in the same daze I've been in since he told me, but I catch myself. Slacking off on protocols is a great way to get eaten, and much as I might have wanted to be picked off on the way home, I'm here now. Might as well get some answers before I become someone's midnight snack.

I remember what Maddox said about her presence here keeping the rest of us safe, but I decide it would be foolish to bank on that, monsters being monsters and all. I gather up all my weapons, tucking them back into place, and I let it become something like a meditation. The sound of each gun as I check the chamber, the safety. As I secure them into place and then slide my knives back in my boots.

These little rituals that save us, in the end, by becoming muscle memory when it matters most.

I've been sitting out here long enough for my eyes to fully adjust to the dark of the yard, and as I peer around, I see nothing but the watching, waiting trees and hints of life behind boarded-up windows. I ease the truck door open, close it behind me, and assess the yard once more—this time with my gun in one hand and my keys to the front door's assortment of locks in the other.

I pause briefly there, but only to listen for any sounds in the thick dark around me. There's that chanting sound that I'm beginning to associate with Savi and whatever meditation practice she has that goes along with her veganism and all the rest of it. Very Ashland, really. Other than that, I don't hear anything but the wind through the trees.

I sprint, then. And I don't look back.

Looking back is a great way to get eaten, because it's a waste of time. Something is either on you or it's not—there's no point in worrying about which is which unless and until you have to. I tell myself that I'm verging on the profound as I hit the porch. I work the locks quickly, slide through the outer gate, and bolt up the door once I'm inside the house.

The lights are all off downstairs. I drift through the dining room to put my ear to the metal door separating me from the kitchen, but

I already know that my tenants usually make more noise when they're clattering around in there. I frown at the useless study with its useless TV, the memories of that horrible Tuesday a little too fresh tonight.

I accept that I was expecting an ambush. Probably because that's what Ariel felt like.

It's certainly how the revelation he dropped on me *still* feels.

I blow out a breath, then march myself over to Gran's door. I let myself in and then lock us both inside.

I turn from the door and stop dead, because Gran isn't asleep. She's sitting up straight in her bed and staring right at me.

There are no lights on in the room, only the bright illumination of the waxing moon outside, pouring in through the slits between the bars and the boards.

And all the way here, it wasn't that I *disbelieved* what Ariel told me. It was more that I *couldn't* believe it, and maybe, somewhere inside, I was starting to convince myself that he was wrong. Or that there are some other Sarah Jessup Browns wandering around Jacksonville that I've somehow been unaware of all this time.

We stare at each other, Gran and me. I feel something big and ugly sit on me, and recognize it a moment later. *Betrayed.* I feel *betrayed*, and heavy with it. It feels thick and gnarly in my lungs.

But somehow I know that coughing won't dislodge it.

"I can sense an immortal all over you," Gran says, her lips flattening as she gazes at me. "A vampire, if I'm not mistaken."

I press myself hard against the door at my back. "What the hell do you know about immortals?" I ask her, though my voice barely sounds like mine. "Much less *vampires*, Gran?"

"More than I want to," she replies tartly. "And more than we can discuss in polite company, can we, Winter?"

I should feel ashamed. I'm sure that someday, I will. Because it's clear to me that she somehow knows exactly what happened between Ariel and me on that rooftop, and I don't have any way to process that, since I don't know how to process anything that's happened since I got in the truck to head to Medford tonight.

"Why are you even awake?" I ask instead. "Since when are you up in the middle of the night?"

"The things you don't know about me, your own family, and your own gifts, not to mention what goes on in this house, are too numerous to list," my grandmother tells me, and there's absolutely no trace of the dotty old woman I've been taking care of for years.

I can't decide if it's a relief or a stab to the heart.

She leans over—more nimbly than I expect—and reaches over for her cards. Then she places them on her lap. Decisively. She taps them expectantly and then looks at me, like she thinks I might . . .

"I don't want to mess around with your cards," I say, and I think that I deserve all kinds of applause for not *yelling* that. "You know I don't like them. I never have."

My grandmother only stares at me, pointedly, and I don't have it in me to disobey her. Not even tonight, when it's as if she's transformed into someone else performing the role of the Gran I thought I knew.

I walk over and sink into her usual chair, there beside the bed. I don't often sit here. It's her chair, and I like to keep it sacred for her, since we have so few sacred spaces left.

But tonight, as I sit there with the window beside me with all those slatted iron bars and the moon coming in anyway, it reminds me of something else. A confessional, maybe.

Or, a voice inside me suggests, *more like a drive-through retail window.*

I have an immediate vision of my grandmother and her damned cards sitting at this window, telling futures to whoever might stop by in the dark. While I lie awake upstairs worrying about zombies in the fucking trash, which is at least better than the nightmares that come for me if I fall asleep.

But this can't be true. This can't be happening. This is my *grandmother.*

The window lets in starlight, and a bit of moon, but that's all. It's just a window, or as near as we get to windows in a world that doesn't encourage that many easy entries for the so-called *Kind*. My grandmother is an old woman. She has dementia.

And for all I know, this is a vampire dream I'm having on a rooftop in downtown Medford while Ariel slowly drains the blood out of me.

Maybe that's why I say nothing as my grandmother shuffles and reshuffles her cards, then fans them out in front of her, making little sounds in the back of her throat as if she's having a conversation with the images she sees.

"We have always had the sight in this family," she tells me. "Like it or not. Sometimes they call us witches. Sometimes they call us grifters. But it doesn't matter what they call us. They always come back, and, mother to daughter, down we pass it as the years go by."

"The sight?" I shake my head, which is starting to ache again. "What are you talking about, Gran?"

"You and Augie used to say that I knew what you were going to do before you did it," she reminds me. Her gaze meets mine. "Because I did."

I can't take this in. I don't *want* to take this in. "*The sight?* Really?" I can't bring myself to go fully scathing, but the look she slides my way suggests that I've come close enough. But I keep going. "And you couldn't predict that Mom and Dad would take off?"

She stares at me, with a kind of knowledge in her gaze that I dislike. Intensely. "I did."

Those two small words tear at me. Maybe they tear me apart. I feel something thick inside me, like a sob waiting to flood through me, but I can't let it out. I can't start, because I don't know if I'll stop.

I force a laugh, but it comes out weak and uneasy. "This is ridiculous."

Gran continues to stare at me, like she expects me to ask for details, but I can't. I won't. *I refuse.* Then she sighs, and that same old shame wallops me once again.

"You are hardly the first member of the family to deny the truth, and the sight itself," she says, which shouldn't make the shame heavier, but it does. "Like that vampire, child, it exists whether you believe in it or not. And it is just as fickle."

It strikes me as funny to think of Ariel Skinner as *fickle*, but there's a different sort of tide rising in me now.

"He told me." I frown at her, taking in that beloved face I know so well. The creases in the corners of her eyes and bracketing her mouth that I like to tell myself mean a life of fun. I might not have seen her laugh in a long while, but it's not like there's been much to laugh about. "The vampire king told me that you saw the Reveal coming. That you knew."

The thing about this betrayal, from her, is that it's all-encompassing and woven together, so it's like a whole involved tapestry of a kick to the stomach.

Gran does nothing. She barely reacts. She only watches me, yet there's nothing blank about her gaze. Nothing confused. It's a steady focus, intent and unwavering.

It makes me want to sob, but I don't.

"You knew," I say, and it's worse to say it out loud than it was to sit with on the long, dazed drive home. "You knew, Gran, and you didn't even *try* to save us."

I'm not clear which *us* I mean. Me? Me and Augie? My parents—wherever they are? All the people in the valley? The whole wide world?

Something changes on my grandmother's face, though I can't exactly track it. She looks sadder and wiser, all of a sudden.

"And how would I have explained it to you?" she asks quietly. "How would your senile old grandmother manage to convince you that every scary thing you ever heard of was suddenly free to roam and pillage at will? Do you suppose you would have believed me? Or do you think you might have started investigating options for a nursing home instead?"

If I wasn't sitting down in her chair, I think I would fall over. "Are you actually senile at all? Has this all been an act?"

Looking at her now, it's hard to believe that I could ever have imagined her anything less than sharp as a tack.

"I'm no spring chicken." She considers for a moment. "Some days are cloudier than others. Some days I might forget where in time I am."

"Gran."

"I'm old and I'm tired," she tells me. "I'm not sure what world I'm in, some of the time. But one thing I do know, Winter, is that I need to live until I can pass the torch. I've been waiting for you for a very long time."

"You've been waiting for *me*?" I realize my voice is a little too loud. I lower it. "I've been right here. Doting on you night and day."

She waves her hand. "That's not what I mean. The gift is a tricky thing, like anything else. It can't be forced. It has to be accepted."

"If I had that kind of gift," I tell her in a low voice, "the last few years would have been very, very different."

But my head throbs, as if to contradict me.

Gran's eyes gleam. "You would have shown us how it's done, would you?"

"I don't want your torch," I tell her. "I don't even know what a torch is in this context, and anyway, I'm sick to death of fire."

"Everyone is sick to death of fire, child," my grandmother replies. "But that's no reason to go on burning."

She picks up the cards in her lap and hands them over to me, placing them down before me on the table next to her chair with a decisive little thump.

I stare at the cards, the same pile of them that she always has in her hands or near enough to swipe up at a moment's notice. They are worn, with frayed edges and creases, plus the clear sense of her fingerprints all over them.

If I squint, I think maybe I can *see* those prints on the dark edges. Or pressed into the gold symbols.

"This deck has been handed down in the family for generations," she tells me, and there's a certain ringing in her voice that echoes in me.

Uncomfortably. As if she's calling my bones to attention, these words like some kind of tuning fork. "They like to be handled, as they do enjoy a good preen, but only by the blood. Our blood. The cards don't like being touched by anyone outside the family. They are not simply oracle cards that anyone could pick up in a shop. They are the cards of the oracles that have long been in this family."

I'm finding it hard to breathe. "Discussing a deck of cards like it's sentient is not really going a long way towards convincing me that you're not senile," I tell her. "In case that's a concern."

Gran only sniffs at that.

I shake my head. "I've always had an aversion to them. You know this."

"You loved them when you were little," she says. Almost sadly. "They liked you from the start, the day you came home from the hospital. That's how I knew it was you, Winter. They took such a shine to you." She sighs. "But your mother hated that the gift skipped a generation. So far as she could tell, it was *her* gift and you had no right to it. She punished you anytime you considered picking them up and getting to know them. If they weren't hers, she thought the tradition might as well stop dead."

I want to feel that same sense of bafflement and disbelief again. But I don't. Instead, the things she's telling me are starting to feel like memories. And my temples are kicking at me, not as painfully as they do after a nightmare, but enough to get my attention.

I have a snatch of memory in my head then, as if it burst on the scene with these words. With the spike of a headache. My mother catching me on the stairs with Gran's cards and wrenching my arm so hard as she pulled me away that it still twinges now. I reach over to wrap a hand around that ribbon of pain, like a ghost in my bicep.

Gran nods, like she can see my memories all over my face. "It's my fault. I should have managed Lilianne better. In a thousand ways. But these things are always more clear in hindsight, which has never been my strong suit. Give me a future any day."

I stare down at the cards, scowling at them as if the symbols stamped all over them are jeering at me. Wishing I had the nerve to pick them up and throw them out the window for the zombies to ooze all over. There is no part of me that wants to touch them. I can almost feel my skin crawling. As if something is prickling all over me, poking at me, changing me. I hate it.

"Your mother never liked the futures I told," Gran continues, and she sounds like her old self still, but I can also hear a weariness in her voice. Age showing itself, maybe. Or possibly just the heaviness that is my mother. "She thought I could change them at will and was furious when I couldn't. That's my fault too. I want you to know that my intentions were good, Winter. They were always good, even though things never ended up the way I wanted them to. That was a test and I failed it, again and again."

There's a growing din in my head. My skin feels uncomfortable stretched over my bones.

That prickling and prodding seems to grow more intense with every jarring beat of my heart. The headache is starting to build.

"What test?" I ask. My voice sounds thick and strange, far away and . . . not mine.

Her gaze looks like precious jewels in so little light. Those deep indigo eyes Augie and I got from her, another gift that skipped a generation. The moon slips and slides all over her, capturing her like a kind of cameo, right there in her bed. I have a feeling I'm looking at a memory of her. It feels slippery inside of me, as if I'm looking around time and not through it.

As if I've already lost her, and that notion is far worse than any sense of betrayal I might feel.

Because she's not wrong. She could have spent the Monday before that horrible Tuesday telling me every single thing that was going to happen, and I would have gently suggested she get some sleep. I would have called her doctor in the morning.

There is no possibility that any version of me would have believed any of the things I've learned over the past three years, much less the things I learned only tonight.

"It is a test we must all face, anyone who sees into the wheel of time," Gran says, and she is watching me intently, in a way that makes my bones seem to rearrange themselves inside me. They take up new positions, hold new weight, and I can feel a coming tide of memories—or maybe not memories—hovering somewhere in all of that. "Do you see the future or your own desires? Would you impose upon the future your interpretation of what it should be or let it do what it will? I'll tell you now—if you choose wrong, you pay."

"That's very enticing."

"You pay either way, child." Now she sounds almost kind, and that makes my eyes water. As if she's being gentle with a terrible diagnosis. This is the first moment when I think past the things I feel on a physical level. The first moment I think, *This might be a real thing.* Gran nods. "There's no gift without a price. And only you can decide how much you're willing to pay for the things you see, the way you interpret what you see, and who you tell."

"Who did you tell?" I ask. But my voice is hoarse. Little more than a whisper.

"There is always, always, a reckoning. Anyone who tells you otherwise expects to die before paying it, or intends to take that price out on you."

"What a grim and grisly little gift," I manage to get out.

"They chose you a long time ago, Winter." Gran nods toward the cards. "They've been waiting years and years to speak through you." When I start to argue, she lifts a hand, and I stop. She cocks her head as if she can hear whispers in the moonlight. "It is time to listen, child."

I don't want to listen to anything, but I can't pretend that the cards aren't calling to me. Now that she's made it obvious, it's like she's turned up the volume to its highest level.

When I look down, the deck before me is glowing, pulsing.

The cards know me, I think, and the creepiest part is that I'm *not* weirded out by that thought. Instead, it settles into this new configuration of bones and sinew inside.

Like a key into a lock.

I tell myself it's the dark. I tell myself that my defenses are down because of Ariel. Because of all the things I did that I shouldn't have done, or didn't do at all—but I still can't think about that. About him.

What I can admit, at last, is that I can hear the cards whispering to me.

I think about Augie. I think about Ariel. I think all the way through the mess of these last few years. And back before the Reveal, too. My mom disappearing. My father not long after. So many secrets. So much deep, dark family *ick*.

And all the while, Gran and these cards were part of it.

Seeing things no one else sees. Knowing things no one should know.

Maybe I've had a secret weapon all along, mine if I can be brave enough to accept it. To use it. To learn how to wield it.

And so, at last, I let my hands creep forward until they rest on that dark deck the way I've seen Gran do a thousand times.

I feel something bright and hot shoot through me, filling me up, golden and painful and *right*.

Like I'm meeting myself for the very first time.

I don't need to ask what to do. I just *know*.

I pull a card.

11.

It hits me like a train.

It's a vision, hot and intense, and it takes me over. Or takes me down. I don't have the slightest idea what my own body is doing.

Because I see a body in the woods, mutilated.

I see a great, beaked thing with sharp teeth and a slithering within.

The Goddess of Filth, I understand.

Vinča, I think.

But first—or maybe I'm moving forward and back in the time of this vision, it's not clear—there's a woman surrounded by horror, choking on her own fear and despair. It's sharp. Acrid.

I see sharp blades in high, thin air that smells of pine awash in copper.

I see something like an altar in the wilderness, and I think the word "sacrifice."

I have the use of all my senses. I can smell the thick, fall scent of the green Oregon woods. I can smell rotting things and the rich earth, late hints of flowers, and mossier suggestions of dark hollows. There is a snowstorm coming in—I can smell it on the breeze. I understand that I am high above the ground and know that I'm on a mountain.

I have no sense of myself, and yet it's like I'm standing in the same clearing with the scared woman tied up on an altar. There are figures I can't identify, wearing garments that don't make sense to me—like strange, dark cloaks that make my stomach hurt when I see them—moving in what looks like wild but choreographed movements around a firepit and that altar that sits before it.

I look all around and see nothing but trees. No trails leading to or away from this clearing. There's what looks like far-off lights in the distance, though I can't tell if it's so high up that I'm looking out at a starry night or if it's a tiny burst of light from settlements far below.

I gaze up toward the moon above, quiet and bright. And full.

Then down to the woman, mangled so badly it's difficult to tell that she was ever a woman at all. Only the altar offering she's become is left, flesh carved into signs and sigils.

I breathe out, hard.

And then I slam back into myself. With enough force to leave bruises.

Once again I am sitting in my grandmother's chair, my hands on her cards, and it's disorienting because it feels no less or more real than the forest clearing where I was only just standing. I snatch my hands back from the cards as if they're on fire.

I feel dizzy and a little bit sick. Gran's eyes are on me, too knowing. Too calm, too certain.

"The first journey is always the most unsettling," she tells me.

"The journey?" I repeat weakly. I know exactly what she means. But I don't have it in me to give her the satisfaction of admitting that I believe in this.

I know it's foolish. Childish, even. I think of all the things I've learned to believe in over the past three years, like it or not. This is no different from any of that, and compared to the Reveal, it's fairly benign. Visions of monsters being preferable to actual monsters at the door, teeth bared and claws sharp.

But monsters are things that happened to us. Just like drugs.

This is apparently something I *am*, and I hate it.

Because there were other things I was once, and they were taken from me, one by one. Daughter. Twin. Fully human. Just for a start.

"It can help to talk these things through," Gran says, the moon making her indigo gaze even more intense. "Visions are not always straightforward, and the future loves nothing more than to contradict itself."

"I don't know what that means," I grit out past the nausea that won't let up, radiating from my diaphragm as if that dark, bloody altar is stuck there, making it hard to breathe. And the pounding in my head is worse, making me wonder if I've been having nightmares all this time—or if they were more of this vision shit.

I'm clearly hitting a wall. There are too many things to process, I haven't even begun, and I don't know how to add anything more to that file. Even thinking the word "process" kicks my body back into another wash of all that heat I felt in that MMA school, as if it's bright and new.

It's difficult to imagine that my vampire compulsion—*king vampire* compulsion—extends hours later and across the valley into this room where my grandmother and I are sitting in the dark and the moonlight.

That means that the greatest danger to me right now is *me*.

"I felt something," I tell Gran because I've never been all that great at lying to her. "But if I saw anything, I can't remember what it is."

This is not *entirely* false. I know what I saw. I can still see it, the images like noise in my head—I just don't know what it all *means*.

My grandmother only gazes at me, the same way she used to when she would ask if I happened to know where all her mints went. And I would stand there, mouth sticky with peppermint, and claim I had no idea. Fooling her not at all.

But I don't have it in me to tell her that I can still taste that dark, slippery copper in my own mouth. That there was a *smell* that I don't want to discuss with anyone, ever. "I think that maybe nothing happened. Maybe I'm my mother's daughter after all, and I don't have it. Augie was always the sensitive one anyway."

Gran sighs. Then she waves at me, dismissing me. "By all means, Winter. Go to bed." That she's calling me a liar is barely even subtext at this point. "Perhaps a good night's sleep will refresh your recollection."

I want to argue with her, possibly just for the sake of argument, but instead I stand up obediently. I start to move across the room, but she makes a tutting sort of noise that stops me. I look back at her, and she indicates the deck of cards with a jut of her stubborn chin.

"You have to take the cards. They're yours now." I stare at her, but she doesn't relent. "They won't want to come back to me."

"They are *cards*," I grit out through my teeth. "They don't have feelings."

"If you say so." She doesn't *quite* roll her eyes. "But I do. If the only gift you can accept tonight are these cards, I know that I can trust you, Winter, not to let your old grandmother down. After all, I'm not all here, am I?"

Maybe later I'll sit back and admire how adroitly she locked me into that. I can either claim that she's senile and all of this is false, in which case why wouldn't I take a deck of cards she wants to give me? Or I can admit that all of it is true, tell her what I saw, and accept not only that she's an oracle but I'm apparently one too. In which case I would also have to accept that the cards are mine now. And that they probably do have feelings. Or rather, whatever animates them does.

Just another list of things I don't want to deal with tonight.

I take the easy way out. I go over, scoop up the damn cards I still don't actually like touching, and make a show of tucking them into my shirt so they can rest against my heart.

She looks . . . touched. As if I've done something deeply honorable.

Obviously, that makes me feel like shit.

"I see no one had to tell you to treat them with respect." Gran sounds proud, and that doesn't make me feel any better. "It's like you know."

"I like to keep my hands free, Gran." I growl it out, feeling surly and mean. "My pockets are full of ammo."

I don't stick around for more middle-of-the-night chats and other opportunities to feel selfish and small. I go to the door, let myself out, and lock her back in. Assuming she doesn't have secret keys to go with her secret life, that is.

Out in the hall, I feel like the house is breathing all around me, heavy and close. Not like it's threatening me, but like it's as out of breath as I am.

I climb the stairs, listening as I go, but everything is quiet. I must have been in Gran's room for a long time because when I get to the windows on the second floor, I can see that all the lights are out in the cottages across the yard.

I only really start breathing once I unlock the door to the attic stairs, lock it again behind me, and start the steep climb. Once I'm finally safe in my own space, with no eyes on me from any direction, I find myself just . . . standing there under the eaves. Working on breathing past the collection of overwhelming sensations, feelings, and images storming around inside of me.

I don't know what to do with myself.

The whole night spirals through me, drip-feeding that cataclysmic heat everywhere—but it's mixed up with all the rest of it. That ritual on a mountaintop that something in my bones tells me is close. The nightmares that might not be as simple as nightmares after all. *Death goddesses.* And the truth—or truths—about my grandmother that I'm finding hard to accept.

The fact that, like it or not, all these years have been a lie.

Not just the past three.

I stand in the shower and let it run hot enough to sting, but it doesn't help. I let the water beat into me until I can't tell if I'm flushed inside or out, and then, following an urge I can't pretend to understand, I turn the water to cold.

Ice cold.

For a moment, or maybe for a lot of moments, I can feel the heat of my own body as it's pelted with the sudden chill, and it feels like pressing up against Ariel all over again.

I brace myself against the wall, squeeze my thighs together, and come in a hot, shocking rush that nearly takes my knees out from under me. They're so compromised that I lower myself down into the shallow tub and sit there, cold water pouring all over me, while my body reminds me of its various betrayals.

Over and over again.

And it's like touching those cards rewired my brain, because now I'm remembering what happened on that rooftop in the same high-definition, surround-sound way. Complete with sensory input. Touch and taste and smell, and my god, am I fucked.

I'm out of breath again, shaking inside and out, when I finally climb into bed. I'm sure I'll fall off a cliff into an exhausted sleep immediately, but I don't.

Maybe the headache I already have is warning me that if I do, I'll regret it. That terrible things wait for me there.

I lie there, wide awake with too many things on bright, intense replay, until it's time to get up again.

I have an early shift at the coffee stand, so it's still dark when I roll out of bed, rubbing at my gritty eyes.

I check out the yard the way I always do, dark or light, but not only are there no zombies out there now, there also appears to be no sign of them. It's as if what Maddox said really is true. That this is actually protected land now.

But if Gran is supposed to be some big oracle, why wasn't she protected already?

That makes me think about Franklin Hendry. Does he really want this house? Or does he have a bone to pick with Gran herself? And while it's difficult to imagine so unimaginative a creature as Franklin Hendry believing that a woman with a deck of cards could tell his future, I wonder if she told him his. And he didn't like it, so he figured he'd change it. Through me.

I shake all that off as I get ready for my shift. I strap on my weapons, run my fingers through my hair, and congratulate myself for the ten-thousandth time that I was smart enough to cut it all off.

When I go down to the kitchen, I'm shocked to find Savi already there when the sun isn't so much as an inkling in the sky. There's nothing but faith to suggest it might ever rise again, that's how dark it is out there. And despite the warm days, October is coming in fast, so the house is cold this early in the morning. The kind of cold that, in happier times, made me think of getting cozy by a fire with nothing to worry about except how many pumpkin spice lattes I might drink.

Savi is sitting at the kitchen table, dressed in another matching set that is one more sumptuous example of luxury textiles. Her silky dark hair is piled on top of her head, making her cheekbones look more pronounced and her eyes *even more* intense from beneath her bangs.

She is sipping daintily from a mug, and I can smell from the doorway that it's not coffee. Some kind of tea, I imagine. Or, who knows, a *tincture* of some kind, the sort that you could always find for sale in the Ashland Farmers Market in cloudy brown jars from witchy women dressed in earth tones. It's strange the things you miss.

"I'm delighted to see that you're alive," she says as she regards me.

I blink at that. "Was there that much doubt? Because last night I was under the impression that everyone seemed to think I could just waltz into Archangel MMA without weapons and be fine."

"And you were."

I shoot looks her way as I set about preparing the coffee I'll take in the truck with me. I remember the way she and my grandmother interacted, as if they knew each other. I think about all the things she told me yesterday and the fact that she's not a werewolf. Or a vampire.

But that doesn't mean I know what she is. I just know she's not quite human.

"Exactly how did you come by all this knowledge about the civilized behavior of the local vampire king?" I ask, trying to sound casual, but it's a bit early for that. "Because I've known about him for years, but I certainly couldn't describe his habits to anyone." I clear my throat. "Were you one of his students?"

I'm convinced that's amusement I see in her gaze when I glance over. "All ancient and immortal creatures have something to teach us," she says. "If only about the different costs of longevity. Personally, I like to consider myself someone who is always open to a lesson. And I'm happy that in this case, the lesson was not as grisly as some."

I decide not to tell her that motivational speaking is clearly not her strength. "Me too," I say. I don't share with her that there are some lessons that are worse than dying.

They involve living with what you did. And daydreamed about all night. And would almost certainly do again, no matter what I might try to tell myself—all this while, for all I know, he's got Augie secreted in one of those dark rooms I walked past on the way in.

Maybe the lesson is simple. I'm a terrible person.

"What exactly did he want?" Savi asks, and I recognize that casual tone because I just used it myself. It makes those little alarms ring inside me. I was digging. That means she's digging now. But I still can't figure out what she's digging *for*. "Because if it was to kill you, you would be dead."

"I'm still puzzling out what it is he wanted," I tell her, and it rings true because it is true. "I would describe him as . . . opaque."

I see that gleam of amusement in her gaze again. "Vampires do love a mind game or two." She says this the way I might once have said, offhandedly, *puppies love treats*, or something else so obvious that it hardly requires comment.

"You know so much about him," I say, making myself sound admiring. Or that's what I'm going for. "Or maybe it's vampires on the whole? I guess I was under the impression that anyone who got close to them ends up as dinner."

I'm relieved to finish speaking. I've never been any good at small talk. Or pretending I don't know the things I know.

"I'm a very good listener," Savi tells me. She takes another sip of her drink, and for a moment it's like I can hear that chanting, though her mouth doesn't move. Her smile is almost self-deprecating, but I don't quite believe it. "I listen, I remember. I've learned a lot this way. It's a very underrated talent, I think."

I am not even remotely satisfied by this answer, but I fill up my favorite travel mug and make myself smile at her when I leave. Then I take myself off to the coffee stand, and it feels deeply and surprisingly good to focus on tasks I could do in my sleep. Opening up the stand. Getting everything ready for the morning rush.

And then spending the rush pleasantly unable to think about anything else but coffee drinks.

Coffee drinks and my instant assessment of the customers in each vehicle. Because I have to decide at a glance whether to hand each drink to the drivers or leave them on the shelf because they look like they might chew off my arm.

Something that was always true about feral caffeine addicts in the Pacific Northwest, it has to be said.

There is finally a lull a few hours later. The smoke has settled in hard after the usual ray or two of sunlight. I use the slower periods to clean up inside, deal with the garbage, and then barricade myself inside the stand once more.

At noon, my coworker's car pulls up to the drive-through, which is standard procedure. We like to see each other before we let someone into the stand. Just to make sure that no one is, say, sporting a new set of fangs.

That was an example of a lesson learned the hard way.

I smile and start to say hello, but Birdie Jones—who I've known since we went to kindergarten together and have been friends with since roughly four seconds after we were dropped off at that Montessori school—lifts up her hand to give me the palm.

"I heard a rumor about *you*, Winter Bishop," she says.

I freeze up at the window, wondering how anyone could know what happened with Ariel. *Already.* Was that the whole point of it? Was he filming it?

Do vampires even show up on film? Does that count as a reflection, or is it something else?

And even if he did all those things, where would he show this film? There is no internet these days for revenge pornographers to use.

Focus, I order myself.

"You know what they say about rumors, Birdie," I drawl, with a careless sort of smile that I don't feel. "One day you're spreading them and the next day they're burying you."

"Maddox Hemming," Birdie says. Reverently. "In your house. True or false?"

Samuel really has applied himself to getting the word out, I see. I feel the urge to lie. Or explain. I don't. "Not in my house," I say. "But in one of our little cottages, within sight of my house? True."

Birdie sighs, dropping her hand and getting a wistful look in her eyes. "Maddox Hemming is how I knew I was gay," she tells me dreamily. "It was sixth grade. I knew I wasn't like everyone else, but I didn't know why. All the girls were clustered together at recess talking about boys and bras and who they wanted their first kiss to be with. It was like everyone had a script and I didn't."

"I don't think anyone had a script," I point out. "If they did, it would just have been school. Instead of twelve-plus years of trauma."

Birdie isn't listening to me. "And then one day, in gym class, Maddox Hemming was *running*." She sighs again, and it's deeper this time. "She was just running. In a little pair of shorts. I looked at her and just like that, I came *online*."

"And here I thought you were going to yell at me for living with the werewolves."

"In any other circumstances, I would," Birdie says with a laugh. "But not when it's *Maddox Hemming*. Who *wouldn't* live with Maddox Hemming if they had the chance? I would live with her right now, in fact. Do you have an extra cottage? A spare room?"

I laugh too. "I don't think that Miriam would like that much."

"My wife is a woman of great discernment," Birdie says with a cackle, as if I don't know Miriam, wasn't at their wedding, and don't know all about her wife's so-called *discernment* when it comes to Birdie ogling other women. Though it's true that Maddox is a law unto herself. "She would move us both in."

Birdie's still laughing when she goes and parks her car, then waits for me to open the back door. Once I'm covering the small parking lot with a shotgun, she jumps out and hurries inside, then helps me throw all the locks.

She smiles at me as she goes to make herself a drink to start her shift. "Tell me everything," she says. "Like what *shampoo* does she use?"

"I'm not a stalker, actually? So I don't know?"

"Now I might yell at you," she says, frowning. "I need *details*."

I'm feeling almost normal when I get back in the truck a while later. I wave at Birdie—who yells something about documentation—and head back toward Jacksonville. The smoke is brooding today, moving in sullen clumps along the road as I make my way back toward the Jacksonville town line. In some spots I can almost glimpse a little blue sky. In others, the smoke is so thick I can't see much of the road in front of me.

I almost manage to convince myself that too-hot vampires, cavorting on rooftops with said vampires, and disturbing visions were nothing but a dream.

But as I make my way over the hill that winds its way down from what used to be vineyards into the heart of Jacksonville, a huge, gleaming SUV with ominously tinted windows swings around me as if it means to pass.

It comes out of nowhere. One moment there's nothing but smoke in the rearview window, then they're practically in my back seat.

"Shit," I mutter.

Then I say it again, louder, when the SUV doesn't pass.

It slows, then careens toward the passenger side of my truck.

I assume it's going to run me off the road, so I slam my foot on the brake. They swerve ahead of the truck and end up perpendicular to me.

I assume this is an ambush.

Good thing I'm ready. I reach for the shotgun that rides shotgun, as is right and proper, pointing it out my window as someone in the vehicle before me rolls down its blacked-out windows.

And the only reason I don't shoot is because I recognize them immediately.

First, I realize that they're vampires. Two of them. Second, I realize that I saw them last night at Ariel's studio, performing those disturbing, mesmerizing forms to perfection.

The vampire in the driver's seat bares his teeth at me so I can see his fangs. Long and sharp. The smoke dances all around us, thick like fog on this part of the hill or he wouldn't dare open a window in the first place.

I don't lower my weapon. His companion, a woman, sneers.

"He wants to see you," the first vampire says, and he makes it sound like an insult. "Tonight. Sundown. If I were you, I wouldn't be late."

12.

That night, I storm down to the school at sunset, not sure exactly what I think I'm going to prove. What I know—or feel deeply, anyway—is that I have to make it clear to him that I'm not going to be bullied.

Not by douchey minions who try to run me off the road.

Certainly not without comment.

Ariel is finishing up that class of his again—or maybe it's vampire military training, what do I know—but he makes me wait. He inclines his head and indicates that I should sit down on those benches again, so I do.

Entirely too aware that I'm the only person in the room with a pulse.

I figure everyone else is equally aware. This, by the way, only makes my heart beat faster. Louder.

Like a fucking kettledrum.

"You really have a way with invitations, don't you," I throw at him when he finally makes his way over to me, once the grand room is cleared again. It's not that I'm not appropriately overawed by him, because I am. But since he could kill me at any moment and likely will, why go out in a grovel? I glare at him instead. "First you make it clear you can find me in my home. Then you have your goon squad come for me on the road."

"I'm sorry I can't live up to your family's high standard of gentility," he replies in that offhandedly scathing way of his. I don't miss that this is a roundabout reference to my brother, who hangs over this interaction and this school and me like a dense fog. One of his perfect brows rises. "But to be clear, I'll expect you here every night at sundown, Winter. No need for invitations."

He does not say, *Consider this an order.* But I hear it all the same.

"And if I decline?" I ask, and I have to push the words out. As if they know better than to show themselves.

But Ariel only laughs.

And I'd love nothing more than to say that I see the error of my ways and keep my hands to myself in the presence of a creature so overwhelming and dangerous, who might not be *actively compelling* me but certainly isn't trying all that hard to keep me at arm's length, either. A creature who knows where my brother is when I don't.

But I fail at this. Spectacularly and pretty much immediately.

Because when he finishes laughing, Ariel simply kneels down before me where I sit on the bench, puts his hard hands on my thighs, and bends his head between my legs.

Then bites me, through my clothes—though not through my skin.

I come so hard I think I might have passed out, or at least toppled over, if he wasn't holding me still.

By the time I manage to find my way back into my own body again, he's moved on, peeling off the long-sleeve T-shirt I'm wearing and the cargo pants too. And while I'm still panting and sobbing from that first wild explosion of heat, he settles down between my legs once again. This time there's no barrier between his mouth and all that soft heat that was making my pussy ache, and he licks his way in all over again.

Somewhere in the middle of it all, as he works that stern, cruel, gloriously demanding mouth of his over my clit and sucks just a little too hard—so the sensation sears through me, pleasure and near-pain and too much of both—I open my eyes.

I look down the length of my own body, and I can see the dirty, erotic sight of him crouched over me, those muscled shoulders of his working as he moves my body where he wants it. His grip on my ass is sure, holding me open and digging in just enough to make the sensation that much more intense.

I can see the top of his head and the long line of his perfectly shaped back, with hints of that phoenix covering it. I shudder, hard, because I forgot about the phoenix on my own body. The tattoo I really don't want him to know I have and yet forgot to hide when he stripped off my clothes.

In fact, I actually *helped him* get me naked.

Ariel looks up, and once again it's like he knows what I'm thinking, because his smile comes again, slow. Something like wicked. Then he reaches up a hand and places it directly over my tattoo like a scalding-hot brand.

As if he is linking us without saying a word.

I feel that like another bite, and shudder into it.

He bends himself back to his task, and before I tip my head back and surrender to the storm of it all, the sensation, and the mad fire, I look in the mirror.

And see only me.

Writhing on the edge of another gut punch of that same, impossible ecstasy.

But this doesn't shame me. It makes me come even harder than before, my legs wrapped around his face.

And when I come back to earth, I tell myself that he's doing that vampire thing again. That I have no choice. That I never have.

Though there's something in me that knows I'm a liar.

Still, I assure myself that's the only reason I follow the urging of what feels like another song inside of me as I kneel down before him and finally run my hands up his powerful thighs. I look up at him and find his severe and beautiful face another kind of chorus, lighting me up while his silver eyes gleam.

I reach in and pull out that enormous cock that I only writhed on once and dedicate the next few hours to learning how to take him in my mouth.

Not an easy task when he is so big. And so . . . *resolute.*

I learn other things too. That he tastes like snow and flame, that he is thick and long and hard like marble. And something about the heat he causes in me leaves me trembling on the edge of another orgasm as I play with him, learning what he likes, learning how to move, learning how to tilt my head *just so*.

So I can take even more of him.

Until he finally holds my head between his hands and fucks his way deep into the back of my throat, then pours himself into me with a roar that I'm surprised doesn't shake the building apart.

I learn something then, too. That his come is also cold, and something like addictive. I gulp down every last drop of him while my pussy reacts like I'm the one getting all that attention, clenching up tight into a lush, hot, rolling orgasm that makes me sob around his cock in my mouth.

I'm still shaking and sobbing a little when he picks me up from where I'm kneeling before him. He carries me over behind the counter, where there is a sofa set back against the wall. And he holds me there for a long time, in what I try to tell myself is nothing but a parody of aftercare.

It's like I can't control my own body. It makes me think back to that night with Samuel, that rush in the dark and the fumbling with each other's clothes, tipping back onto the sofa, and then the great hurry toward what I thought was a perfectly satisfying finish.

But that memory is laughable compared to Ariel.

That's something else to grieve. Ariel is stripping everything from me. My clothes are the least of it. My self-respect. Even my fondest memories.

All of them gone in that rush of ice and fire.

"Where's my brother?" I ask him when I can speak again.

He studies me, his silver gaze moving over me with a certain intensity that I can't quite read. "Come back tomorrow" is all he says. "At sunset."

He says this like he thinks we're playing a game. *He* probably is.

As I leave the school later that night, I beat myself up for succumbing to him and that *song* that lives inside me now and for failing, yet again, to find out the things I need to know.

The things that are the reasons I'm putting up with this, I tell myself in the truck as I head home. Self-righteously, even.

As if I imagine I can thwart the fucking vampire king.

Besides, an asshole voice inside me pipes up, *you would have to stop lusting after him to do that. So.*

I clench Augie's medallion in my fist, careen down the dark roads, and loathe myself.

This becomes a nightly pattern.

Every night for a week.

After turning me inside out, Ariel sends me back home without a word about anything but my expected obedience. *Tomorrow, Winter. Sunset.*

He controls this, not me. I'm very clear on that. Ariel is very deliberately keeping me off balance. Yet knowing that doesn't change the experience of trying to pick my way through each evening's minefield.

I try to tell myself that the sex stuff is simply the price I pay for the bits of conversation we have, that I can ponder this way and that once I'm out of his presence. I try to tell myself that this will lead me to Augie, who he claimed wasn't dead, so that's already more information than I had going into this.

But when I'm home, I find myself less eager to look my grandmother in the eye, and not only because of the things she told me. Or the cards she gave me, which I don't want to look at and yet seem to see when I close my eyes. It makes my heart ache and my head hurt—and I already have enough headaches.

Though, these days, when I wake up with horrific images in my head and that piercing, throbbing pain in my temples, I also have a death goddess's name on my tongue. Vinča the terrible. Vinča the foul.

"Vinča the fucking bitch," I mutter to myself while scouring the back garden for zombies, who still don't venture near. "Vinča the giant pain in my ass."

I've decided that self-loathing is just another form of grief.

But I also decide that I have to stop avoiding my life during the day if I'm going to keep doing these nightly meetings with Ariel. For the last few days of September, I work my usual hours at the coffee stand like always—but in less of a daze. I find myself looking forward to this thing in my life that remains entirely straightforward. Working coffee and dealing with customers, both the human and monster variety, requires that I think about nothing else, and I like that.

It's a small daily holiday from all the things I'd rather not think about.

Like my grandmother, who, I am forced to accept, *really is* the powerful oracle the vampire king told me she was. I'm still sifting through my feelings on that. She's also neither as senile as I thought she was all this time nor as consistently shrewd or with-it as she was that first night I came back from meeting Ariel.

On the one hand, it's good to know that she wasn't snowing me completely. She isn't *that much* of a liar.

On the other hand, she wasn't *not* snowing me, either.

This doesn't change the fact that I need to take care of her. That I would and will no matter what. It just means that everything *feels* different.

When I'm at the house, I never can tell which of my tenants I'll encounter. You'd think that I'd develop a sense of their routines, but I don't. Savi is as mysterious as ever, with her chanting. Maddox slouches about, seemingly boneless, but I couldn't tell you what she does with her time.

Briar is a mystery. Sometimes I think she reminds me of someone, though I can't think who. Other times I entertain myself by imagining that her entire cottage is filled with yarn, and she sits inside it knitting herself an endless array of those beanie hats to cover her hair.

But most of the time I'm home, I think of Augie and vow to myself that *next time* I'll *make* Ariel tell me what he'd done with him. Next time I'll *insist*.

Next time I'll do more than betray my own twin with these things I feel for the monster who knows too much about both of us . . . over and over again.

13.

It's the first night of October and suddenly cold outside. It is now a week since I met Ariel, and I am no closer to finding out what happened to Augie than I was on night one. This does not make me happy.

But rather than brood on this privately, as I've been doing, I am sitting in the kitchen before my nightly drive into Medford. I'm watching Briar—in a knit hat, as usual—stomp around the kitchen making dire predictions that we should live it up tonight because tomorrow night is a full moon and Maddox and her friends will eat us all alive in our beds.

"Like a bag of chips, served up to them on a silver fucking platter," she seethes.

I opt not to express my feelings on how unlikely I find it that anyone would serve bags of chips on silver platters, especially to silver-avoidant werewolves. Because I doubt that is an observation that would lead to peace on this property, and as the landlord, I need to consider such things.

Also, Briar speaks so seldomly. I'm fascinated that *this* is what she wants to talk about.

"Maddox and her friends could eat you at any moment of any day or night," Savi replies in her serene way, which only makes Briar fume. Visibly. She is clearly as comforted by this observation as I was when they told me Ariel could kill me at any time yet hadn't, lucky me.

"Why would they wait for a moon rising to lead the way when Maddox already has a key?"

It does occur to me to wonder why Savi is always so sure that a killer who hasn't murdered you *yet* is somehow safer than one who *tries*, but this doesn't feel like the right moment to explore her worldview. Likely because that would come with more questions about who she really is.

"What makes you think you'd be a good meal?" Maddox asks mildly, seeming completely unperturbed by Briar's accusations as she makes herself some dinner. Rare meat she slaps into a frying pan for about three seconds on each side that looks like it might squeak when she bites into it. She smiles at Briar as she slides her steak onto a plate. "Have you showered even once since you've moved in? That's not a personal question, it's just that I take my food prep seriously. That includes washing."

"Besides, I assume that werewolves have better things to do under a full moon," I add, because that seemed reasonable enough to assume. And also because Briar looks murderous. "What with all the myths and legends and whatnot."

And then, suddenly, it becomes another one of those moments when I realize that I've stumbled onto something. All my tenants stare at me, as if waiting for me to say the very obvious next thing—

Except I don't know what that is.

If it weren't for the vampire problem occupying my thoughts, I would probably brood on that more than I have.

"Yes," Maddox says after a moment, carefully returning her attention to her actual dinner. "There's a lot of magic in the moon. Everyone knows that."

For some reason, this makes Briar scoff, then storm out, slamming the back door behind her.

I remember what Maddox said that night on the back stoop about the moon and the ritual she keeps putting off. And I don't realize how much I'm worrying about that until she comes over to the kitchen table with her plate and laughs when she sees the expression on my face.

"Don't worry," she drawls. "He hasn't fucked me into submission yet. Though it has to be said, he does try."

When both Savi and I laugh in the same helpless way, I find myself thinking that it may be a *dire house*, as Gran said once, but it's significantly more entertaining than it used to be when it was packed tight with only our family ghosts.

Which isn't to say that I'm not haunted by them all the same.

Tonight it's already full dark when I make it down that alleyway outside the MMA school, which hasn't gotten any more welcoming. It still feels like eyes and fangs are pointed my way, but I don't react to that. Not anymore.

Not when I have my own, personal interview with the vampire to get through before I make it home again. *If* I make it home again.

I think about that as I let myself into the school, shivering a little from the cold breeze outside with teeth in it, and pause for a moment on the threshold of that dark lower level. Gathering my strength. Getting ready for the chess game I'm about to engage in, for however long he pleases, with no clear winner.

Though it always feels like I lose *something* in the bargain.

Maybe more than I want to admit.

Augie's medallion hangs heavy around my neck, like it agrees.

I know I'm late tonight, and yet I don't hurry as I head up the stairs to find the martial arts studio itself empty. I'm tempted to turn around and leave, but I know better.

Though it's more honest to say that I *could* leave, but I don't. I wander through the dark room, spooky with shadows and sounds of violence from across the river and up on the old freeway overpass that used to be thick with traffic, I-5 being the major artery from California through Washington. I climb the stairs to the loft and then, with only a considering glance for the door that I suspect leads to his apartment, I head for the roof instead.

It's like the night calls to me now. Having hidden from the stars for too long, I can't let myself go back.

I tell myself that, if nothing else, these nights with Ariel mean that I *deserve* a little starshine for my trouble.

I don't wait there long. I stand outside, basking in the stars and the nearly full moon, gearing up for all its glory tomorrow night, until I can feel Ariel's presence behind me on the rooftop.

There's no mistaking that sudden punch of power. I couldn't say if he materialized here, the way I'm pretty sure he can, or if he simply moves that quietly.

I reach up and wrap my hand around Augie's medallion to remind myself why I'm here.

"Do we have to play these games?" I ask him, keeping my eyes on the street far below. I see an ominous fire in the mouth of an alley. I see shadows streaking toward it and away. I hear more noise from the park, angry shouting and then agonized cries, though I know better than to believe either sound. "You don't have to put on this big song and dance. I already told you I'll do whatever you want, and you still haven't taken me to my brother. If you want to fuck me, surely we can just fuck and get it over with."

He comes up behind me, his strong arms wrap around me, and I realize that I know him now.

I know the shape of that perfect body. I know the way he presses against my back. And I can feel the jut of his cock, hard like marble, against my back.

"Winter," he says, his voice low and sardonic, a punishment and reward all its own, "I don't have to fuck you to get you to submit to me."

And then his mouth is on my neck.

As always, I feel the heat in me and the faint graze of his teeth, and though he sometimes bites down slightly—he never pierces me.

Always close, never quite there.

I realize when he laughs that I said that out loud.

His hand moves, coming around the front of my neck to hold me there, as if he's reminding me that he could choke me that easily.

One more thing that should horrify me, but instead turns my whole body to a shuddering, needy mess.

He keeps his mouth on my neck and his hand on my throat, and I can already feel that shuddering move lower and lower inside me. It pulls tighter, gathering strength and fire, until he squeezes, just slightly.

That pressure against my neck is divine and deadly, and then he presses his teeth against my skin almost to the point of breaking—

And then he laughs as I press my legs together around that pulsing, greedy bolt of electricity, and come.

So hard it almost hurts.

He pushes me forward so that I brace myself on the low wall, shocked to find dampness all over my face. I do nothing about it. I don't accept that I'm *crying*. I feel the cool touch of his powerful hands at my hips, then around the front of my body as he tugs my trousers open and then pulls them down my legs. Then he steps between them, kicking my legs farther apart.

I think, *This is it.*

And every lie I told myself on the harrowing drive over tonight—about how all I needed to do was happily submit to whatever game he was playing to get what I need in the end, that being access to my brother—goes up in a puff of smoke.

Because it's true that I want to help Augie. I always want to help Augie. But it's also true, and significantly more true in this moment, that I want this.

The feel of his cock, heavy and cool, as he presses himself between my legs.

Between them so that he can rub himself against my pussy, hitting my clit each time, but he does not angle up and thrust his way inside.

He holds me there, each deliberate movement of his cock banging against me in such a way that I gasp and try to move but find myself anchored in place. He moves one hand back to find its way between my legs from the front and slides his fingers into all my shameful heat, and then there's nothing to do but surrender.

That giant cock is never still. It moves forward or back, creating friction and pressure, and his hand in front presses and pulls and swirls around in all that wetness, teasing and toying with me. With great deliberation and knee-weakening skill.

I'm a mess, and there's nothing I can think to do about it.

My breasts feel heavy and huge. My nipples are in tight points. All my weight is on my hands, and my head hangs low, and surrender tastes like copper in my mouth as I bite the side of my cheek to keep from moaning out this dark and dirty blaze of pleasure and despair to the streets below.

There's nothing for me to do but accept that I'm his toy, to do with as he wishes.

And the scariest part is that I like it.

I like having no control, no responsibility, nothing I *should* do here.

I more than like it.

This time, the orgasm comes in heavy, like I'm being wrung out. Slow, steady—a gradually undulating build of wild sensation that goes on and on and on.

It doesn't stop.

"I can't," I pant out at one point, but he ignores me.

Ariel doesn't say a word, but his hand is implacable and his cock is as stern and cruel as his mouth, and I learn as "I can't" turns into "yes" that he knows my body better than I do.

Another grief to pick apart when I'm alone.

But first is this, and it's still going. No beginning, no end. Coming and coming, a shudder that rises and falls like breath and turns every last part of my body into jelly.

My clit feels enormous, swollen and lush, and he hits it unerringly every time. I can't decide if I want to push into that thrust or move away from it, and that indecision only puts me more firmly into his hands.

It's like a pendulum, back and forth forever, and on every side there's only more sensation, more of that dark greed that has taken me over entirely.

Another thing I learn is that I like that, too.

He growls, and I feel that everywhere, too. It makes my nipples pinch even harder.

My head is hanging down. I don't know if my eyes are open or closed. All I can see are stars either way.

He spears two fingers down onto either side of my clit, holding it there as he slams into it from behind. Once, again, and then something white hot and impossible slams into me.

It wrecks me.

But as it hits, as I shatter in his grip, I feel him pull back and then he floods me. Drenching my lower back, my ass, between my legs.

Then he presses himself against me, as if trying to seal us together.

My breath saws in and out of my lungs. I have no idea how long we stay like that, all that cool come between us, and me in ruins. He pulls me up to a standing position, still pressed against my back, and I feel his mouth on my neck again.

I realize what he's doing is licking my pulse.

It's unbearably erotic. It makes my knees so weak that if he wasn't holding me up I'm sure I would collapse, something that should alarm me more than it does.

He sets me apart from him after a few moments, but I can barely stand.

Ariel turns me around to face him and takes a look at me as I sag back against the wall. I'm sure that the gleam in his eyes is amusement. That I'm entertaining him somehow, and that makes me feel proud—something else that should set off a claxon or two inside me, but doesn't. He reaches down and pulls my pants up, fastening them with great intent and care.

That makes an entirely different part of me shudder.

"I think I need to shower," I manage to say.

Ariel makes a sound that I think is his laughter, low and deep. And rare. "In some centuries, it was considered an honor to bear my mark. Those lucky enough to be anointed would rub it deep into their skin and praise me for bestowing such a gift upon them."

"Um. Thanks?"

I stand up, and it's strange. I can feel where he came all over me, but it doesn't feel cold. Or gross. Or even really the slightest bit sticky. It feels like heat, as if I'm glowing.

I decide not to tell him that.

"Such a graceless age this is," the vampire king says quietly. "No wonder the world crumbles all around us."

"I thought that had more to do with the rise of the monsters." I remember what he told me and correct myself. "Excuse me. I mean *the Kind*."

"Monsters have manners," he tells me. "Even if you don't see that, I assure you, they know how to behave. Our hierarchies demand it."

"What hierarchies?"

"There are always hierarchies, Winter. Humans are sent to your schools to learn this. All creatures have rules, and whether they break them or follow them, those rules still exist."

"Spoken by someone who gets to be king."

"I didn't happen upon that title. I earned it. All monster enclaves are meritocracies. What you wish to hold, you must defend. Might is always right. That's the way of the world, little seer. If you thought otherwise, you've been kidding yourself."

That strikes a spark in me, and happily, for once, it has nothing to do with my insatiable lust for this man and his perfect body.

This time it's temper. Maybe it's that *little seer* business. It makes me think of what Gran said to me about the cards waiting for me. About them no longer wanting her. It makes me wonder if he knew that telling me that Gran was the oracle would trigger . . . whatever that was. Whatever that means.

"I don't need you to tell me how hard life is," I grit out at him. "You're not prey, are you?"

"Do you think you are?" He laughs, and this time it's big and loud and for show. Not that real laugh I heard before. "Do you think it's the luck of the draw that the oracle and her family remain untouched? Why do you think Jacksonville is the safe zone?"

I don't like the way he's looking at me. I don't like the intensity of that silver gaze bearing down on me. "Because that's what Samuel negotiated with you. You and the werewolf king."

"There are three major powers in this valley," Ariel says, and there's something too watchful about his gaze. Too . . . *careful.* "The vampire king, you are lucky enough to know all too well. The werewolf alpha, you've met. But you must not count out the sorceress."

"The sorceress?" I repeat, in disbelief.

Again, he studies me for a moment that stretches on too long.

"Among other things, she controls the weather." He shifts his weight, calling attention to his previous stillness, then crosses his arms over his chest. "Every now and again, to remind me of the part she plays, she allows us a sunny afternoon or two. But mostly, it rains or it's smoky, and we live happily in the gray. At her whim."

"A sorceress," I say again, possibly with less disbelief, because it shouldn't be hard to believe in even more impossible things. Not at this point.

"A refugee from a major sorcerer family." He sounds as close to merry as I've ever heard him. "You won't know these families, but they have wreaked their own brand of havoc since the first sorcerer willed himself into being by an unnatural collusion with certain dark texts in the bowels of the Dark Ages. All the infighting and drama and world-altering nonsense you can imagine, like any other subset of the Kind. Only with more weather events, because they do like a show."

I blow out a breath, suddenly aware of how much more there is to the world of monsters than my own small despairs here in a forgotten valley. "How many kinds of the Kind are there?"

"That is a question that can never be answered." Ariel lifts a shoulder and drops it, though his gaze is unwavering. "There are always more. There is no ceiling. What should concern you are the clans that act as one.

Surely, even humans know that when you band together, your strength is amplified."

"I do know that. That's why Samuel rounded up the humans and had us all—"

"Jacksonville is protected because the oracle lives there," Ariel tells me coolly. I get the distinct impression that he does not want to talk about Samuel, though I can't think why. "It is a bargain your grandmother struck. She is who you should thank, not anyone else. No matter who takes credit."

I frown even harder at that, because that almost sounds as if he's saying—

But he stops me with another crook of his eyebrow and asks the question I've been waiting for since I met him. "Would you like to see your brother?"

14.

I have time to think about how much I really ought to hate myself, and how much I *really do*, as I follow him back down into the building and then out the school's front door onto the street.

I can hear creatures move in the shadows, but none dare come out. Not with Ariel there, looking completely unbothered.

He glances over at the barricade I saw from the roof. "They build that up every week or two, and we take it down. At this point, it's almost becoming a conversation."

"Why do people need a barricade on Main Street?" I ask.

"You know what it's like," he says, almost conversationally, though there's the hint of something like steel in him then. It makes me think of the way he barks out his commands to his minions as they move like one on the school's polished floor. "The less someone has, the more they wish to defend it."

I find that sits on me unpleasantly as I follow him down the center of what was once a fairly busy street, crossing the bridge over the river and circling around until we're deep into Hawthorne Park.

A place I tried to avoid even before the Reveal.

Long ago, the towns in the valley decided to put in a beautiful greenway that follows Bear Creek, an offshoot of the Rogue River, for some twenty miles, connecting Ashland, at the southernmost part of the valley, up to Central Point, near where the tributary meets up with the actual river. In some places, it's probably still beautiful.

But here in the center of Medford, it was never anything but sketchy. There were always throngs of desperate people, in and out of their hiding places in the bushes. I rode a bike this way exactly once before vowing I never would again.

Being out here tonight feels particularly precarious.

Especially since I can still feel that mark he left on me, blazing now. Part of me is worried that it's blistering my skin.

Yet I feel certain I would rather die than indicate I even notice.

Ariel ushers me through the dark with that same stern confidence I already know too well, and all the shadowy figures that I don't want to look at directly move out of his way. Whether because they recognize him or sense who he is, I don't know.

I'm just glad they move.

I hear murmuring, but I don't know what that means either, and I refuse to ask him.

Maybe I'm afraid to ask him.

He leads me down to a path I didn't know existed on the riverbank, separate from the old greenway that meanders along beneath the interstate. And then we walk.

I quickly lose my bearings once I can't see the MMA school in front of us, a landmark sitting high on the other side of the water. Ariel strides ahead of me, and I hate that I have to scurry after him to keep up, so I don't. I walk fast enough not to lose sight of him, but that's all. This path is well worn, but then he takes us on a smaller path that winds around and goes under a bridge, where he stops and waits next to a concrete wall covered in graffiti.

I go and stand next to him, not sure why we stopped. I look up at the bridge above me and realize that we're directly underneath the freeway, though I can't hear any vehicles up above. Someone told me that the freeways are turning back to nature, though I haven't investigated this myself. I like the idea of flowers pushing their way through, grass and trees reclaiming what's theirs. It lets me imagine that everything moves in cycles, and maybe one day I'll recognize this world again. Maybe one day it will feel like mine once more.

The darkness presses in all around us. The river rushes down below.

I comfort myself with the knowledge that if he wanted to kill me, he wouldn't need to take me down to a bridge near the river to do it.

It's actually not that comforting.

When I hear a scraping sound, I jump.

I hate that I display that kind of vulnerability and that Ariel simply puts his hand on my back and that's enough to stop me. Worse, it feels like comfort, and I don't know where to put that. My heart pays no attention, however, and catapults against my ribs like it's trying to claw its way out.

I look around wildly, and then I can't help but stare—possibly with my mouth open—when a slab of painted-over concrete at the base of the bridge . . . *moves.*

It takes me a shockingly long moment or two to understand that I'm looking at some kind of door.

A woman peers out of the opening. She is beautiful, in a harsh and demanding kind of way—all jet-black hair and impossibly smooth skin—that would have made it clear that she's a vampire even if I didn't recognize her as one of the minions who ran me off the road.

"All clear, sire," she says.

Sire, I think, the word landing in me like a hard slap.

I don't know why it hasn't occurred to me that just because I've been viewing my interactions with the vampire king as a series of sexual co-payments toward a dark insurance that might help Augie, it doesn't mean that everyone does. And that to some, like all his vampire minions and apparently the whole of the valley, the fact that he's *the king* isn't hypothetical.

This makes me feel heavy and weak all at once.

There's no time to process it, because his hand is on my back and he's guiding me forward. I can either do as I'm told or turn and run. Screaming.

Shamefully enough, I consider the latter. My mind is spinning out as I try to imagine what it would look like if I really did make a break for it.

But reality asserts itself, as stern and unyielding as that hand on my back.

As that heavy, cold cock against my clit earlier, as hard as the brick wall in front of me.

There's nowhere to go. If I run, he will catch me, in seconds and without much effort. Even if he doesn't, I'm weaponless, out in the dark, and the only way to access my vehicle involves crossing a park full of addicts and monsters, then circling a block in the war zone of downtown Medford. I essentially have nowhere to go.

Not if I want to see Augie. In whatever state he might be in, down beneath the earth in the clutches of *vampires*.

It's impossible to imagine what might be happening or what shape he's in—my mind actually flinches away from such thoughts, and my temples begin to burn again.

The only remedy is to go down into the dark pit, so that's what I do.

After I ease myself in through the opening and start climbing down the ladder that waits there, I make a command decision not to think too closely about where I'm going. Much less make comparisons to the sewers I've seen in movies. The ladder seems to go down and down forever, deep into the earth, where it is already winter, damp and cold.

When I land, I stagger a little, surprised to find ground beneath my feet. I turn and find that cold-faced woman staring right at me.

I glance up at the ladder, but Ariel isn't there.

"The king has important matters to attend to," the woman says, in a tone that I can only describe as surpassingly hostile. "Surely you can't imagine that you, a mere human, should command his attention?"

"I would be delighted to avoid his attention altogether," I shoot back.

This is probably unwise.

She confirms this by baring her teeth at me. They are all fangs, and it's beginning to occur to me that this is part of how vampires communicate. The amount of teeth they show at any given moment indicates the truth of things.

Right now, she's indicating that I should watch myself.

"He used to mark all of his sacrifices," she tells me, and the tone is vicious. It matches the fangs. "It didn't save them. It won't save you."

I stare back at her, and her terrifyingly beautiful face, and have to come to terms with a number of things. Quickly.

One is that I'm standing deep underground in what is clearly a vampire lair.

Two, she and I are discussing his *mark*, which is a very fancy way of saying that when he came all over my body he clearly knew that other people—other vampires, certainly—would be able to sense it. Or smell it. Or whatever it is they do.

And three, that I have to suffer this if I want to see my brother.

I do the only thing I can do. I show her my own teeth in what can only loosely be described as a smile. Fangless though it is.

"Are you going to lead me to Augie?" I ask.

The vampire wheels around and starts walking. This is when I realize that instead of being dropped down some deep, dark well, I'm actually in a tunnel. More critically, there is no hint of any light, and she's not walking slowly as she heads into the maw of darkness before us.

It's very clear that she wants me to feel every possible misgiving, and I do, but I also hustle to keep up with her. Because I decide I don't care if *she* sees me scurrying.

I have only passing, muddied perceptions of this tunnel we're in, because it's so dark and she's moving so swiftly. I'm sure I can feel the walls closing in all around me, but when I reach out a hand to test that, there's no wall within reach. Whether it's my mind playing tricks on me or run-of-the-mill vampire games, it's hard to say.

My mind whirls, trying to fill the darkness, so I quickly establish some rules with myself.

There will be no thinking about Ariel, his mark, or his *sacrifices*.

There will be no unnecessarily snarky remarks to all these things that are probably just waiting for reasons to kill me.

I have to assume, as ever, that if Ariel wanted me dead, he could and would do it himself without taking all this trouble with the nightly visits and the sex and the *marking* and the wandering around riverside paths in the dark of night when surely all good vampires are out exsanguinating the innocent, et cetera.

I imagine that if I say something like that out loud, the vampire who is my unwilling guide will leap at the opportunity to hiss at me and tell me I'm far beneath her king's notice in life and death. So I don't say it.

But deep down, I believe it. And I finally get why Savi thinks it's comforting.

It's been my experience that things that want to kill you only let you live when they want something from you. I still don't quite know what that is, but I'm alive. Despite spending every night in Ariel's company since he first summoned me.

I decide that has to mean something.

I can hear sounds that seem to suggest that we're underwater. Maybe that's the effect of the river that must be rushing around nearby, or maybe it's just the way sound travels down beneath the earth. Still, when the tunnel opens up some and I see a flicker of light, I'm more thankful than I can remember being in a long while.

Since that first night, maybe, when Gran and Augie and I huddled in the basement, said very little, and waited to see if we would make it to morning. Then did.

I don't like being thrown back into those memories. I don't like how clear they are, how crisp.

I try to breathe as deeply and as quietly as I can to get rid of them.

We're in what seems like a wider sort of subterranean corridor now. It suggests that we're in a more populated area, though I'm happy not to see crowds of vampires waiting. But there are torches in the walls, actual fires burning on sconces like some medieval castle. Thanks to them, I can see that we're in some kind of cave.

The vampire doesn't look back at me. I assume she can hear me just fine, and I already know she can scent me too. I don't particularly want to focus on what it is she can scent on me tonight.

Or what she thinks it means. Ariel's *sacrifices*.

Luckily, I have images from visions and nightmares to keep me entertained as we keep walking. A long walk in the pitch blackness of the tunnel is, it turns out, an excellent way to enhance the visuals. I see beaked things and slithering, and hear that vile voice inside me. The Goddess of Filth like a corrosion in my head. I also see a clearing on the side of a mountain, high up. I see cloaked things whirling and a woman on an altar. I taste blood and fear.

I sneak a hand up to wipe at my face, and I'm not sure if I'm surprised or relieved when it comes away clean.

No blood. No terrible wounds. Just copper in my mouth and all those horrible screams trapped inside me.

I think of the stupid vision that comes to me every night now, weaving its way in and out of too many nightmares of that Vinča bitch. In my nightmares, the vision expands. I get smells, tastes, touch—so viscerally that when I wake up in my bed, I'm shocked to find myself there.

I usually have only a breath or two before the headache kicks in.

Last night, I dreamed that I stood on that mountainside in the cold, my feet bare, because that's how I went to bed. When I woke up in my bedroom, the damned cards were fanned out all around me and my foot hurt. A sharp pain, and I looked down to find a shallow cut on the sole of my right foot as if a rock's jagged edge sliced it open.

I could ask Gran about this kind of thing, I know. But I haven't.

I haven't actively sought out those cards again, either, but that doesn't keep them from turning up. I lock them away and find them in my pockets. I reach for a gun and find them tucked into my holsters. I wake up with them all over me, like they're either protecting me in my sleep—or trying to smother me.

Despite what I said to my grandmother about sentient cards, and how I scoffed, I already know better.

I can feel them calling me all the time. It's not a voice like the horror of Vinča in my head, not really. But it's a call just the same, and it tugs at me. Even now, all the way across the valley floor from my family's house, I can hear them clamoring for my attention.

If Ariel hadn't stripped me, I'd expect to find them tucked away in my clothes again.

One night I woke up to find myself clutching them as if I got up at some point, went to pick them up, and crawled back into bed to cuddle with them.

I threw them across my bedroom and they hit the far wall, then spilled all over the floor.

Yet when I got back from a very hot shower to chase away another rough night on a bloody mountain, they were waiting for me in a neat pile on my desk. Right next to the guns I cleaned and oiled before bed.

"Panic" isn't the right word to describe how *that* felt. It's not the wrong word either.

I've stopped throwing the deck at things.

Now, as I walk through these dark underground corridors that I'll never find my way out of—either to see my brother at last or possibly meet my own death—it occurs to me that I've turned out like everyone else in my family after all.

I spent all these years certain that if they just decided they wanted it enough, they could kick these addictions of theirs. These compulsions. The drugs, the cards.

Yet here I am, covered in a vampire's mark and jonesing for the very same deck of cards I always thought Gran was unreasonably attached to.

Not quite the moral high ground I'm used to inhabiting.

The vampire turns abruptly and pushes through an archway hung with what I decide to believe is fabric. Though what I think it might actually be is skin. Once I clear the skin curtain and manage not to scream, I look in both directions. To one side, I see another long, cavernous hall like the one we came from. To the other, I can see figures moving in the distance, as if they are coming together for a grand old subterranean vampire party.

"You can go that way if you like," says the woman in her arch, unpleasant voice. "I'm sure that they would love nothing more than to treat you like a buffet."

I swallow down the response I'd like to make—because the time for unwise moves seems past—and smile at her. Guilelessly, I can only hope.

She sniffs, then jerks her head in a demand to follow her as she leads me to a door that looks exactly the way anyone who's ever seen a scary movie would expect a dungeon door to look, only this one is real. I hear her murmur a few words in a language I don't understand at all, and the door swings open.

I follow her down a set of stairs, when I would have said it was impossible to go any deeper. The steps themselves are roughly hewn stone. The walls are cold and damp.

Colder and *damper*, that is.

When we get to the bottom of the stairs, I see that she's taken me to a row of cells.

I immediately expect her to laugh and toss me into one, and I wonder if that was Ariel's plan all along. Maybe I really am a fool who fell for age-old vampire tricks, just like everyone else. After all, why wouldn't I? I'm nothing special. I'm just a twenty-five-year-old barista who somehow didn't die three years ago like most of the people in this valley.

How could I possibly stand a chance next to vampires and werewolves and *sorceresses*? And everything else that goes bump in the night—or any other time of day they damn well please.

I brace myself for getting flung behind bars, which is at least not *immediate* death. Anything that's not *immediate* death is a chance to fight. I tell myself that once or twice or maybe twenty-five times, but she makes no move toward me.

She leads me down the row of cells, and I dart anxious glances into each one as we pass. The first two look empty, but when we pass the third and I see a hint of movement, I realize that probably, the people—or creatures—are pressed back against the farthest wall, where the shadows are deepest.

There's the sound of moaning. The air is thick with despair and the scent of something foul beneath it. As we pass the fourth cell, I see that the moaning is coming from one of the Kind. It's chained to one of the near walls, a huge being that looks half beetle and half man and is covered in a green goo that it takes me a second to realize is probably its own blood.

It makes me feel like a monster that I look away.

I don't look back at the cells again as we pass a few more. I can't bear it.

But then, at the end of the row, my vampire guide abruptly stops.

She sniffs at me. It occurs to me that she's literally taking in my scent, and Ariel's mark, which must come with some kind of instructions, because she wheels around again and starts walking back the way she came.

And it takes me what feels like a vast, inordinate amount of time to turn my head and look inside the cell in front of me. So long that I have what feels like several eternities to understand how terrified I am to see what might be waiting for me there.

I pivot slowly.

I can't breathe.

And I see him.

It's Augie. It's really Augie.

An earthquake of relief rattles through me, shaking my bones and the teeth inside my head and making my eyeballs hurt.

Only now that I'm looking at him right here in front of me do I let myself think about how long it's been since I last laid eyes on him. This has been the longest stretch yet. And here, in this dank and vile place, I can admit to myself that it's been brutal.

It's October now, but it was still winter when I glimpsed him from afar, in a huddle down by the river, looking deeply unhealthy. He'd been wearing clothes that didn't fit him, his always impressive cheekbones looking like switchblades, smoking cigarettes with people who looked just like him. Desperate and twitchy.

He looked gaunt then. Weathered in that way addicts get when they live outside, one with the elements but not in a good way, and have given up worrying about things like laundry. I watched him as long as I could—until a nasty-looking thing that looked like it wanted to be a great bird but got stuck shifting ran at the truck, then started squawking loudly when I brandished my weapons at it, which drew way too much attention.

I pounded the steering wheel so hard all the way home that my hands were bruised for weeks.

I remember going up to my room and lying there, breathing too fast. I remember thinking, *We're really going to lose him.*

Part of me thought we had, it's been so long.

And this isn't better, these circumstances we're now both in, but he's not dead.

He's not dead.

Though I wait a moment, holding my breath, until I see his chest move. Proof of life.

Only then can I take in the rest of it. He's been stripped naked. There's an iron manacle around his ankle, connected by a tough-looking chain to an iron clamp in the center of the cell. There are no facilities to speak of—not even the minimal toilet and sink that used to be the only amenities in prison cells, according to the weird docudramas Augie and I used to watch while our parents were fighting.

I don't really like what any of this suggests about the way he's been treated here, but it does allow me to see the full state of his health.

And I . . . don't know what to make of it, because he's lying there spread out on the floor like a starfish, his phoenix tattoo gleaming in what light filters in from the torches on the walls, but that's not the wild part. The wild part is that he looks . . .

It can't be. He can't look this *healthy*. He looks like *my* Augie, my twin. He looks like he's taking a peaceful nap, possibly on the couch in the study like he used to do when we were in high school and Gran wanted us to do yard work. His hair is blonder than I remember, but then it's been a long time since I've seen it clean. He has a full beard, though it no longer looks scraggly.

He looks *clean* in more than one sense of the word.

He looks like the brother I had, not the tense stranger I lost.

"If you've come to taunt me some more," he drawls, though he's still lying there with his eyes closed and his limbs outstretched like maybe he's on a lovely beach instead of a cold stone floor in a cell somewhere deep underground in a vampire lair, "I still don't know anything. You're still wasting your time. I don't know how many times I can tell you that."

And for a fierce, jagged sort of moment, I'm glad he hasn't looked over yet. Because that means he won't see me cry. The tears spill over even though I don't want them to, because he sounds . . . normal. He sounds like *him* again.

My twin. The other half of me.

My broken heart beats hard. Painfully hard.

I wipe my cheeks ferociously because I know better than to let him see me cry over him.

Few things make him angrier, probably because few things make him *feel* when clearly, what he's wanted all this time is to stay numb.

He heaves a sigh, lying there on the ground. Then he jackknifes up, turning his head and opening his eyes.

And then it's another eternity, both of us frozen in place. The two of us on either side of a set of bars, identical indigo eyes locked together.

"Augie," I whisper, "what have you gotten yourself into?"

But his reaction is bigger.

He leaps to his feet and slams himself against the bars, reaching out a hand—

Though it's not clear if he wants to grab me or try to bend one of those bars before him.

"Winter," he growls, and he doesn't sound the least bit *beachy* any longer. He sounds pissed—which I know is Augie's first sign of terror. "What the fuck are you doing here?"

15.

This is definitely not the tender reunion I might secretly have hoped for, but at least that part feels a little more normal. It's still an upgrade from no contact.

"It's good to see you too," I say. Pretty sharply for someone who definitely wasn't crying a moment ago. "After all, the last time I saw you, you were wearing a tarp like a jacket."

"You can't be here," he's muttering, like I didn't speak. Or like he's hallucinating me. "How did this . . . ?"

Augie jerks his head around, peering down the long row of cells. Then he whips his head back at me, looking something like panicked.

I'm not afraid of getting into range of his hands through the bars. I'm not afraid of *him*. I never have been, even when he was at his most erratic and out of his mind. I would go and stand there, right in his face, and dare him to hurt me.

Gran used to warn me that just because he never did that didn't mean he *wouldn't*.

But I didn't believe it then. I don't believe it now.

I step closer, pushing myself up against the bars so that I can reach through and touch him, to make sure he's real and this isn't some vampire trick. I put my hand on his arm and he's warm. Real. *Alive.*

Once again, I have to fight back the urge to cry. This time I succeed.

It's not until this moment that I understand that I didn't know which thing to be more terrified about. That maybe they had already turned him into a vampire, and this is all a sick little game, so he would be cold. Or maybe that this is some mask or something and he'll still feel sickly and fragile, strung out and leathery like he used to.

But what he feels like is Augie.

I never thought I'd get to feel him like this again. The circumstances might not be ideal, sure, but he's *him*. For this brief moment, anyway, he's *him* and he's *here*.

"Why do you seem *normal*?" I demand, pitching my voice to stay lower than that moaning beetle thing.

"I'm not fucking *normal*," my twin tells me. He's blinking down at my hand on him as if he's not sure how he feels about this either. But I know him. So I know that what he's feeling matches what I feel. He's just spent years doing his best not to feel anything at all. "I'm chained to a floor, bare-ass naked in a vampire cell. In case you missed that."

"An upsetting situation," I agree, still with my hand on him, like he's a battery and I need his energy. Oh, how I need it. "But also a bit of an upgrade from some of your previous circumstances. I'm just saying."

I expect him to shake off my hand, but he doesn't. He stares at it. Then lifts his gaze to mine again, and I'm pretty sure he's going to yell. Tell me to fuck off, like he has a thousand times. Say hurtful, hateful things to drive me away.

I've heard them all.

I brace myself, but he doesn't do it. Instead, he blows out a breath and then he moves closer, leaning his head against the bars.

I don't think. I do the same thing. When our foreheads touch, I feel his free hand move to my other arm.

Once again, we are one.

And I never thought that I would feel this again. I never thought I'd find him. I never thought he'd *live*. I was sure that either the drugs or the monsters got him, and all I've wanted, all this time, was simply what peace there might be in knowing how he left us.

I have no place to put what's happening now. His warm hand gripping me. Mine gripping him.

Our foreheads touching the way we used to do when we were little, to soothe each other.

"You can't be here, Winter." His voice is barely a whisper.

"We're past that," I tell him in the same voice. "Way past that. What I need to know is why you're here. What they want."

He pulls his head back, and again, he's him. My beautiful, sensitive marvel of a twin brother. My best friend. My heart.

"You're still wearing the medallion." He reaches over and touches it. "That's good. Don't take it off."

"If it's some kind of talisman, maybe you should be wearing it." I frown at him when he shakes his head. "You're the one in vampire jail."

"You have to know there's almost no way you're walking out of here." He's looking at me in a way I can read too easily. Greedy for the sight of his twin, but scared. Delighted to see me, but furious it's *here*. "I don't understand how you got in."

"I don't think you want to know."

His eyes are indigo like mine and clearer than I've seen them in years. But wary now. "It's not safe."

"What is?" I counter.

"Take whatever you think is happening and amp it up by about a million," he tells me, and his voice is as serious as his gaze now. "That's what's happening here, and believe me, you want no part of it. If you can leave, you need to leave."

I drink him in. His face looks filled out again. His body isn't too skinny and bruised everywhere. He doesn't have that gaunt, haunted look about him. He's not hunched over or twitching. He doesn't look like he's been living rough at all. Even naked in a cell, he looks *bright*, the way he used to.

I don't know what to make of it.

"You look good," I say, and I don't do a good job of keeping the emotion out of my voice. I don't really try. "I didn't think I'd ever see you look like this again. Healthy, I mean."

His hand snakes out and grabs my arm again. "I'm not healthy," he grits out at me. "I'm very fucking far from healthy, do you get me? What I am, Winter—and I need you to hear me on this—is fucked."

"Welcome to life in the Reveal." I study his face. The one I know better than my own and always have. "What do we have to do to get you unfucked?"

He only shakes his head, something much too close to despair on his face for my liking.

For a moment, we just . . . breathe together, and I almost think we'll be okay. Almost.

I hear sounds from down the line of cells and I don't turn, but he does. When he looks back at me, there's nothing to see but panic. It's all over his face.

"You shouldn't be here." He sounds anguished. "Winter, I wish . . ."

But he stops, and he moves away from me, deeper into the cell. I move too, stepping back to press myself against the slimy wall that marks the end of this terrible corridor. Because at least that way nothing can come up behind me.

What's coming toward my face, however, is not exactly great. I'd almost prefer to get jumped from behind so I'd have less time to contemplate the horror.

Vampires pour down into the dank little corridor we're in. There appear to be hundreds of them, but that's the hysteria and panic talking. There are at least ten, which is no small number of vampires in these tight and creepy quarters, but that's not *hundreds*.

Small mercies, really. They're all beautiful and terrible, not least because they look like they're flooding into a club for a party. It's disconcerting. It makes my head hurt, like my brain can't process what I'm seeing when I'm standing in an actual dungeon where my twin brother is in literal chains.

At first, I think they're coming for me and I can't believe that Ariel threw me to them like this, like table scraps out the back door to feed a little wildlife. If I survive, I intend to excise that *thing* in me that apparently cares whether or not the scary vampire king who probably sees me as little more than a sex toy *likes me*—

I realize in the next heartbeat that they're not here for me.

Or not all of them anyway.

One by one, they peel off to go into the cells along the way. Immediately, I hear various cries. Sounds I can't quite make sense of, chains against stone, laughter.

So much laughter.

Until there are only two, the vampire bitch who brought me here and one of her buddies, this one an absurdly pretty man. They stop at the cell before Augie's. The male vampire flashes his fangs at me before he opens the cell, and then I see the woman inside. A human woman, I think, until I see that her ears are pointed. She sobs when she sees him, and I think he's going to beat her, and I don't know if I can stand here and *watch* a woman get beaten no matter if she's not my species—

Instead, she crawls toward him, making sounds it takes me long moments of disbelief to understand are her *begging*.

The vampire laughs, because this is clearly high comedy for bloodsuckers, and then slices open his own arm with a fingernail. He stands over her, letting the blood swell up, pool, and then drip down into her face.

But she's not lying there passively, letting him splash blood on her.

She's writhing on the floor, her mouth wide open and desperate, whining a little as she tries to get each drop of blood into her mouth.

My stomach turns and I gag. I try to shrink into the wall, but my favorite vampire bitch is strolling toward me, a smirk on her face.

"Feeding time," she purrs at me.

She opens the cell door with a wave of her hand, no keys required. Showy vampire tricks, but I have to admit they're effective. My stomach twists again, but this time when I cramp up, it's fear.

I expect my brother to do something when she saunters toward him, but he doesn't. He looks at me with anguish all over his face—

But then he looks back at her.

And I understand, even though it makes me want to heave. Or scream. Or maybe sob.

She's his fix.

Augie has never been able to turn down a fix.

"Kneel," the woman orders him.

And he does. I can see by the set of his shoulders that he's embarrassed, but that doesn't stop him. He doesn't look back at me, either.

She does.

Making sure I'm watching, she pulls up the skirt she's wearing and slices a long, deep cut into her inner thigh.

There's no way for me to *not* see what she's doing. And better yet, how my brother tilts himself forward and eagerly begins lapping at the cut she made. I can hear the sounds he makes as he does it. I can see the way he grips her leg as if there's nothing more precious on this earth.

I feel my own gorge rise like a battering ram.

I don't know how I manage not to be sick right there on the floor.

The vampire woman stands there, her legs spread wide, one taloned hand on my brother's head as if he's in need of guidance.

She wants me to look at him like this, I know it. Kneeling down, lapping at her, looking a lot like he's licking her pussy. And maybe he does that, too. I don't know. I don't *want* to know. When I lift my gaze to the vampire's, she stares at me.

"When you've seen enough," she tells me, spite and malice all over her face and loud in her voice, "he wants to see you again. If I were you, I wouldn't keep him waiting."

And added to the long list of reasons I hate myself is this: I don't simply walk away.

I bolt.

I leave my brother in the thrall of that bitch, and I sprint down that hallway of damp despair.

I don't look into the cells as I go, but the things that I see anyway from the corner of my eye will stay with me for a long, long time.

I make it to the stairs and start to climb, making a kind of wheezing noise that might suggest I've been struck down with some kind of dungeon-inspired pneumonia, but it's not that. It's the only sobs I'll allow myself.

I run up those cold stone steps, making my legs move faster than they want to go, and I hurtle myself through that barricaded door and throw myself through that revolting curtain that is definitely skin—

Then I slam straight into another cold wall.

But this time, it's Ariel.

And for one long, wild, impossible moment, I feel a sense of relief so intense and so profound that I almost want to call it *joy*.

I would, maybe, if he were . . . anyone else.

He sets me back on my heels but keeps hold of me, gripping me just above my elbows. It's all too chaotic. His touch is setting off the same explosions despite the terror and anguish and horror inside me. It shifts so suddenly and without warning to that shocking punch of lust and need that it makes me feel sick again.

"I'm going to throw up," I warn him.

His face is stern. Sure. "I would not do that if I were you."

So . . . I don't.

I pull in a breath. That sick feeling inside me stretches wide, then—slowly—starts to subside.

I tell myself to pull away from him.

I don't.

"What do you want with my brother?" I ask him. "I thought you needed him to pay you or something. But apparently he's still happily addicted to vampire blood." I shove that awful image of him on his knees from my head. Or I try. Then I dare ask the next question. "Are you turning him into one? Is that the point of all of this?"

His head tilts slightly to one side as if I said something that actually hit him like some kind of blow. I should be happy about that.

Too bad that right now I very much doubt I'll ever feel *happy* again.

Ariel sighs, but it strikes me as too studied. As if he's holding back his actual reaction. "Contrary to popular opinion, becoming a vampire isn't like catching a virus. It isn't like werewolves and their *bitten* minions." He makes his opinion of that clear without lowering himself to a full roll of his eyes. "Becoming a vampire requires an invitation. The mortal in question must ask. The vampire in question must also ask, because vampires cannot be made without the permission of the king."

"That's very hands-on, isn't it? I thought the whole point was the maiming and the turning and the undead armies."

"You are thinking of fictional television shows made by humans." Again, that *almost* eye roll. "All new vampires become my problem, forever. So, no, your brother will not become a vampire because he's drinking blood from Marbella, because he does not *want* to. He is *compelled* to. He'll become high. But vampire blood does not have the same effect on the human body that your nasty street drugs do. You should thank us."

"I don't want to *thank you*. Are you *insane*?"

That this is not how a person should speak to a vampire king only occurs to me when his silver eyes darken, and his grip on me tenses. Just enough.

"The more he drinks, the healthier he gets." Ariel's voice is cold. "Though I don't suppose it's truly healthy. After all, if he doesn't get his top-up twice a day, well." He shakes his head, and I decide that now is a good time to remember how powerful he is and how powerful I . . . am not. "I'm told the pain is agonizing. Like knives flaying every square inch of his skin."

All I can see is Augie's panicked, anguished face and I want to die, but that would be easy.

"And what is it that you think I can do about this situation?" I grit out.

I don't care that he's gripping me the way he is. I don't even look around to see if anyone's watching this interchange. I shove myself forward a little, like I'm tough. Like he couldn't snap me in half like a twig if he felt like it.

If he could be *bothered.*

"How exactly do you want me to pay?" I demand, since making demands is clearly not what I should be doing. "You're going to fuck the price out of me? Take it out in ass? Great. Sounds awesome." I'm obviously high on bravado, so I keep going. "Tell me, exactly how long do I have to be your sex slave to get my brother the hell out of here?"

"It's not sex that will pay off his debt." Ariel lowers his face to mine, and I have the uncanny suspicion that he's actually . . . pissed. Genuinely mad, like I've managed to get under his skin somehow, and I really should worry about that.

What I shouldn't do is take it like a victory. But then, I've never been as wise as I ought to be.

"Sex is just the cherry on top. And make no mistake. You're going to beg me for that, too."

"Over my dead body," I say.

Foolishly.

His hand shifts from my bicep so fast it's a blur, and I only realize it even happens when he grips my throat.

Then lifts me, just slightly.

This should terrify me. I know it should. But that's not what I feel.

I feel it like light and heat, blazing a path through my body to pool in my pussy. I feel want and need all over me.

And most of all, I feel a kick of temper, like fire.

"Do you really think that can't be arranged?" he asks me in a low, furious voice, that beautiful face so close to mine. "What autonomy you have now exists because you are not my subject, Winter. You should think about what that means before you tempt me to change it."

"I think it means I can tell you to go fuck yourself," I bite out at him.

His hand around my throat tightens. I laugh, not because I think this is funny, but because, somehow, it's all part and parcel of the same rushing mess inside me. Bravado, I guess.

Or maybe I just don't have it in me to give a shit anymore. About anything. Maybe this is nihilism.

Maybe I've finally reached the point where I just can't care what happens any longer.

"It's not that I don't want to fuck you, Winter," Ariel seethes at me, and all I can see in his eyes is a storm. "Because despite myself, I do. And I will. But what I want as payment for your brother's bullshit?"

I'm breathing too fast. He knows it as well as I do.

Ariel lets go of my throat and slides his hand up against my temple. A cool press against my flushed skin and it makes me tremble. I'm sure he can feel that too.

"I want your visions, little seer," he growls at me. "I want to know what's coming and when. And I'm the only one who's going to ask you straight out. You should be significantly more respectful." I stare up at him blankly, my pulse going haywire. He laughs, that stark and hollow sound. "All the others playing their little games, hiding in plain sight. The difference between them and me is that I want you walking into what comes next with your eyes wide open. I want you knowing exactly what you're signing up for."

"*I* don't know what you're talking about."

"I'm talking about prophecy," he belts out at me, and I can't imagine that the knives against skin he mentioned can cut any deeper than the blades of his words. "I'm talking about the fact that you, Winter, are the new oracle. Everyone knows it. The cards have chosen. What I don't understand is why you're bothering to pretend otherwise. It is as clear to everyone as the mark I left on you myself."

I feel cold. I don't know how I could have felt that sense of relief just moments before, or why I can stand here so calmly while this man—not a man, a predator, and I need to remember that—keeps that hand on me as if he's being gentle when we both know how easily he could kill me.

I'm not sure why he hasn't.

Surely, there are other avenues toward whatever prophecies he wants without getting this involved with one fractured little family here in a rural valley in Oregon.

I feel colder. At the same time, that same shivery heat is making its way through me with a certain inevitability. I think of my brother, kneeling before that terrible vampire bitch. I think about the susceptibility to addiction that clearly runs in our bloodstream.

I wish I could believe that I was being compelled too.

"I hate you," I tell the vampire king, and I say it starkly. Without drama. Without heat. A simple statement of fact.

Ariel only smiles. That cruel mouth of his succumbs to a curve, and he shifts that hand from the side of my head to my throat again, but only for an instant. He keeps moving, tracing a path down my neck, and then stays there a moment, fiddling with Augie's medallion.

I should slap his hand away.

I don't do that. I tell myself I'm only imagining the burst of sudden heat I feel, just for a moment, but it's gone again too quickly to mention.

"I know it doesn't matter," I tell him, holding his gaze, though it makes every part of me ache. "But I do. I truly hate you. I think it's important that you know that."

I wouldn't describe that smile of his as sad, exactly. But it's no expression of joy, especially when it deepens.

"Little seer," he says, and even his voice sounds bittersweet, "that won't help you either."

16.

I let myself into the house, the heavy door falling closed behind me. I throw all the locks, then test them by rote.

It's late again. Very late.

I should be used to these late nights since Ariel came into my life, but I'm not. I can't say I've slept well over the past three years, but at least I spent most of those nights actually lying down. *Resting my bones,* as Gran would say, even with all the nightmares.

There's been very little resting lately. Of my bones or anything else.

The moon lit my path all the way home, only the faintest sliver away from the fullness it will achieve tomorrow. But everything felt weird already. I was convinced I could see shadows acting of their own accord from the corner of my eye.

When I drove into Jacksonville, I felt so separate from the group of humans I saw congregating on the sidewalk, in clear violation of curfew, that I felt like I might as well be a different species already.

I swallow hard and stand there in the front hall, my forehead against the front door.

Like I can't decide if I want to pound my head against it until I think a little less loudly, or open it back up and run screaming into the forest to see what might become of me. I consider both options.

For a while.

The pounding in my head would likely bring unwanted attention from my tenants and possibly even require explanations to Gran, all of which would defeat the purpose of it. And running off into the forest would almost certainly lead to my death, when I have things to do. Some of those things involve continuing to take care of my spicy grandmother, whether she wants me to or not.

Whether we talk about visions and prophecies, goddesses and lies, or not.

I turn around, but I don't move away from the door. I think about Augie. I don't want to sob, or scream, or throw up. I kind of want to do all three. I can almost envision it. It feels like relief, me on my hands and knees in my own bathroom, purging my body of . . . everything. Starting with the past three years, my parents' disappearance, my brother's slow slide into addiction preceding it. All the way back to high school, when we would both sneak out to parties but he was the one who got obliterated and I was the one who got him home.

I could start with all that and end with everything I saw tonight, and from far too close.

I'm tempted to indulge in a full-on fit, but I'm not sure I'd ever stop.

I push away from the door, my whole body feeling jerky and strange. Like the hangover I had the day after our twenty-first birthday that inspired me to never, ever drink that much again, no matter how many times Augie called me a lightweight.

I think of him looking healthy. I think of him being able to focus on me, to talk to me. I think of our foreheads pressed together, and even the memory of it is soothing. Maybe in time I'll stop remembering where we were. Or the bars between us.

I head toward the kitchen, thinking I'll make myself a nice snack and try to quiet down my feelings with a hefty dose of sugar.

But when I open all the locks and make it into the kitchen, I stop short.

The lights are all off, but Maddox is standing there. She's staring out between the bars and the planks over the window toward the moon up above.

She looks back over her shoulder when I walk in, and for a moment, we stare at each other.

I don't have to ask where she's been. I can see the usual marks on her shoulder since her sweatshirt is drooping halfway down her arm. Her smoky-quartz gaze sharpens and traces over me, and I know immediately that she can scent Ariel's mark, but when her gaze meets mine again, she doesn't ask.

There are more similarities between us than differences, at least in this moment. Sure, she's a whole werewolf as well as being *her*, but we both look a little rumpled. A little shaky. More than a little off our game.

Something passes between us that feels like communion. She nods. I smile. Then we set about making ourselves more of that decadent hot chocolate, and when it's done, we go and settle outside on the back porch again.

It's already significantly colder than it was last time we did this. I don't even remember when that was. It seems like a lifetime ago. Another life I lived before Ariel, but I think that really, it was a week.

Just a week.

We sit there for a while. It feels much better than being sick and sad on an impervious floor.

Maddox keeps looking at the moon, so I do too. I try to imagine what it must be like to live a life that's consciously arranged around moon phases. Maybe we all follow the moon, in the end, and only some of us know it.

As I think that, I shift where I'm sitting and realize that the cards have found me again. I can feel the weight of them, pressing there between my breasts like they're aiming to press deep into my heart.

That's not the kind of creepy I'm in the mood to share, so I don't. I think about what Ariel said. That I'm the next oracle. That *the cards have chosen.*

I'm pretty sure I don't want to know what that means. On the other hand, the cards pressing into me feels almost soothing, so maybe I know more than I want to admit.

"You good?" I ask her, eventually.

She laughs a little, or maybe it's more of a sigh that the night breeze twists into something new. "You know. Ty gets a little cranky around the full moon. It's not unexpected."

"Your ritual."

"To be honest, though, I don't really mind it from him. I get where he's coming from. My whole family, on the other hand." Maddox shakes her head. "Anyway, it's been a long night."

"Apparently, it's a big night for family drama," I mutter.

I feel her gaze on me, but I'm still looking at that moon.

That horrible vision takes the opportunity to pummel me again, like it's offended I might find a little solace in the night sky. It's not a jumble of vision and nightmare this time. It's crisp. It *hurts*.

I could ask my grandmother for guidance, but I still don't want to. That feels like surrendering, and I'm full up on surrender at the minute. I have to interpret these things on my own.

I breathe through it, telling myself I'm in charge. That I'm looking for clues, so it's not so much a surrender as a deliberate immersion.

It sucks me in, hard.

I get the distinct and immediate impression that the vision feels like I'm not taking it seriously enough. This time, I'm less an observer of the ritualistic slaughter and more a participant. Not just any participant—this time, it's me on that altar.

And I can feel everything.

The ropes on my wrists and ankles, so tight that they're sawing into my skin, leaving a bloody mess. I can feel how shredded my throat feels from the screaming, and how much every part of me hurts. I can feel the burn of the cold against my naked body.

I can feel, too well, every sickening blow from the cloaked figures who swirl and chant around me, and the blades that tear me apart.

Everything is blood and agony, tiny and overwhelming at once.

I shudder back into myself, and for a moment, I'm standing there on that frigid mountainside, watching from afar. I see the trees all around, the moon up above, and rock formations in the mountainside that look like goblins frozen into place—goblins who sneer and snarl at me like only they know I'm there—

In the next breath, I'm back.

I'm on the steps outside my house with Maddox, a surprisingly comforting presence next to me. I glance at her, but she doesn't appear to have noticed that I was outside my own body for who knows how long.

I tell myself that's good news. I can quietly have visions without alerting everyone around me. It doesn't have to be me frothing on the ground, foaming at the mouth, or rolling my eyes in the back of my head while moaning about messages from the great beyond.

Where that impression of oracles came from, I don't know, as I've never seen Gran do anything of the kind.

I blow out a breath. I can't get the full moon tomorrow out of my head—especially the view of it I keep having from the same blood-soaked mountainside—and looking at it nearly full now doesn't exactly help with that. I can't seem to get the claws of that vision out of me.

That's not even getting to Augie and all the vampires.

Or all the things my grandmother never told me.

Somehow, a werewolf seems like the safest space around right now. "What if I know something bad is going to happen and I want to stop it before it does?" I ask.

Maddox doesn't laugh. She doesn't ask me what the hell I'm talking about. She doesn't question how I could know something is going to happen before it does.

What she does is tilt her head a little, like she's considering it.

"Are you certain that you can stop it?" she asks.

Something about her reaction is poking at me, but I put that aside. "If I don't try, I know that I can't. Do you really think it matters if I *know* I can stop it?"

When she looks at me, there's something in her gaze I can't quite place. It's not pity. But it hits me in a similar way. "I think that if something is so huge that involving yourself, or revealing yourself, will only harm you and do nothing to change what's coming . . . there's no point."

That sets off a soft little chime deep inside me. A kind of alarm, maybe. I tell myself it's simple recognition of the enormity of what I'm about to do. The knowledge that I should keep this secret is like a hand around my throat—

But that only makes me think of Ariel, and I flush.

I frown hard to sober myself up. "A woman is going to be murdered horribly on a mountaintop tomorrow night." My voice sounds sharper than expected.

Again, Maddox doesn't react the way I expect her to. She doesn't question the murder part. She holds my gaze. "Do you know which mountain?"

"I have an idea," I say. "A vague idea." I gesture in the approximate direction of the distant mountain range on the far side of the valley, not that it can be seen from this porch.

She makes a low noise like she's mulling it over.

Those alarms in me get louder, and suddenly all I can think about is what Ariel said about those who hide in plain sight. I think about how strange it is that either version of Maddox should be here at all. The popular girl from high school or the future queen of the werewolf pack.

I want to believe that she really does want that space she told me she craved, from Ty and the rest of what sounds like a very fraught powder keg of a family dynamic, and I know from powder kegs.

But.

But.

I turn to face her, thunking my mug down between us on the porch step. "Did you move in here because you knew?" I think about that night when Ty Ceridwen came to the door, that thing he said to me. That I *better be worth it.* "Did you know that I was the new oracle?"

The cards have chosen, I hear Ariel say again.

Maddox lets out a sound then. A hollow little noise. "Yes." I suppose it's to her credit that she doesn't prevaricate. "I did know." She looks at me. "But, in fairness, you weren't the new oracle *yet.*"

I laugh, and it's another bit of hollowness. "I guess the joke's on me that I thought I could actually be friends with *the* Maddox Hemming."

I don't know that I actually meant to say that, but there it is, hanging between us. She blinks, very slowly, and there's something almost stricken in her smoky-quartz gaze.

"What the fuck is that?" she asks, her voice a little hoarse, like there's emotion there.

I start to answer her. "You know—"

But she's on a roll. "What in the high school bullshit do you think that even means?" She's still gripping her mug, and for a moment I think she might actually crumple it between her hands. She seems to notice that too and sets it down. Carefully, I think. And her voice is even hoarser when she speaks. "I was a *literal wolf* walking around pretending to be a teenage human girl. And let me tell you, contrary to what you might imagine if you watched a lot of stupid television shows, secret identities suck. It's hard enough being fourteen. Fifteen. Try policing yourself constantly for any possible slip, any possible hint you might have inadvertently given away that could lead to the extermination of your entire family and species."

She takes a sudden, sharp breath that makes me think she was holding it. When she blows it out again, she sounds tired. Bone-deep tired. "It's exhausting. Now try doing it when you're just a kid and you don't understand that everyone will think you're a monster if they know."

I start to say something else, but she lifts her hand. "In case you wondered, Ty takes a dim view of mistakes. Back then, showing ourselves to outsiders was forbidden. By pack law. And trust me when I tell you that you do not want to break pack law. It isn't a question of whether or not you will be punished, but how badly, and will you survive it. Harsh but true."

"That sounds shitty," I say, feeling off-balance, because it never occurred to me to think about Maddox Hemming's actual, personal feelings, and I fear that says some things about me. "But that doesn't have anything to do with—"

"I wasn't popular, Winter," Maddox says flatly. "I was mysterious. Unknowable. People like to tell stories about mysteries they can't solve, that's all. So in the end, I probably did break pack law. Because they always treated me like a werewolf, even then."

"Maybe," I say after some moments spent stewing in my own obliviousness, "high school is a curse upon everyone it touches, simple as that."

"Everyone knows who you are, Winter," she says after a while, and she picks up her mug again. "Your grandmother has been around for a long time, and she's always been accurate in her predictions. Not like some, who just want attention. Her kind of sight runs in families. Everyone in the . . . supernatural community, I guess you could call it, knows that too."

"You mean the Kind?" I ask.

Something else gleams in that gaze of hers. "You're learning all kinds of things down at the MMA school, aren't you."

Maddox very deliberately—and exaggeratedly—looks from my face to the sweep of my back, then returns her gaze to mine. Letting me know that she does, absolutely, know that mark is there. I can't decide if the embarrassment is actually life-threatening or not.

Yet.

"Yes," she says when she's done making her point. "The Kind. The way we see it, there's humankind and then the regular Kind. There have been other points in history when the Kind have ruled. Humans just don't remember it. They call it things like the Dark Ages. Or the quote 'barbarian horde,' unquote. Whatever. We've all been here forever." She takes a pull of her hot chocolate. "Oracles aren't exactly human or Kind. They're . . . somewhere between."

"Even more good news," I say, though really, what's a little species confusion at a time like this. "It just keeps coming and coming." I make myself look at her, and I hope she can't see anything on my face, because I'm not sure that I'm controlling my expressions the way I wish I were. "Is that it? You came to live here so you could cozy up to the next generation of oracles?"

"The thing is that big-time ancient goddesses don't do anything simply," Maddox tells me quietly. Matter-of-factly. "This particular one was put down a long time ago, for general shadiness."

"Vinča," I say, though naming her tastes sour. And suddenly my nightmare is in my head again, foul and vile. I can feel her breath on me, filled with dead things. My headache pricks to life all over again.

Maddox nods, her gaze becoming something more assessing. "Yes. The infamous Vinča. Goddess of Filth."

That she uses a term my grandmother has used makes me go cold. Because I understand immediately that Gran has been telling me about Vinča all along. I don't know where to put that.

"And when we talk about goddesses being shady, we're not talking about the odd war or even wiping out a city or two," Maddox says. "We're talking about widespread pestilence. Famine. Aspirations to take over the whole world and make it into her personal playground, which usually means excessive exterminations and that sort of thing. Goddesses like that are powerful, and the things they find entertaining tend to make people sit up and take notice."

I remember what Ariel said about her that first night. Carnage. A rabid cult. Centuries of mayhem.

But in my head I see a ripple at the bottom of blue water. A disturbance in the smoothness, like a warning. A whisper.

Maddox is still talking. "But because they like to be worshipped and feared, they also like to herald their comings and goings. That's where you come in."

"And you think that a goddess has something to do with a woman being murdered on the mountaintop."

"I think it could," Maddox replies. Evenly. "In a situation like this, when a big event has already happened—that being the Reveal—you're basically looking for weird shit. Because weird shit tends to come in threes, and usually, when it does, it fucks everything else up. That's how you know." She lets out one of those short little laughs again. "Consider that Apocalypse 101."

"So what you're telling me is that I have vampires after me. And werewolves after me. And everybody wants to know if I know about any upcoming weird shit, is that it?"

"See? You were born for it."

I want to be furious. Maybe I am. But I can't help thinking that she didn't have to tell me any of this. It clearly would have been easier to just lie, like everyone else.

What I can't decide is if it's pathetic that I want that to mean that we really are friends.

The thing is, I just like her. And liking her is not complicated by her holding my twin brother naked in a prison cell under the river. Or by my wanting to fuck her. That's strictly a vampire thing, it seems.

It also doesn't escape me that there's no one else in the world who can understand my situation the way she can. For a variety of reasons.

"Maybe if we can find this woman on her mountaintop, we can save her," I say after a few more moments roll by and the moon is already looking toward the horizon. "But I'm not sure that we can. I'm not sure if a vision is set in stone or if it can be changed."

"Nobody is," Maddox replies. "There are a lot of theories, but really? Nobody knows anything. No matter what they might tell you."

"That's what I like about you. Filled with platitudes and easy comfort."

Maddox smiles at that. She looks up at that nearly full moon.

"Tomorrow the moon will be full and bright," she says softly. "Great hiking weather. And if you're climbing up mountains, you might need someone with a very good nose and an excellent sense of direction."

When she looks at me and smiles, I don't think I'm a fool that I smile back.

Because this is the other side of the Reveal, and everything is complicated, sure. But that doesn't make it fake.

Still, when I finally go to rest my bones in my bed upstairs, what I think about is Ariel. His hand on my throat and that look in his silver eyes.

As if maybe, just maybe, I'm more than just a pawn to him, too.

17.

And this is how I find myself agreeing to hike up Mount McLoughlin on the third of October—much too late into fall to attempt this trail, by all accounts—under a full moon and in the company of a werewolf.

McLoughlin is a supposedly dormant volcano, though I'm not sure I ever trust claims of dormancy no matter how many eras it's been. On clear days, you can stand in certain places in the Rogue Valley and see all the way down to Mount Shasta in California, and then look north to McLoughlin, too. They're like a matched pair, since McLoughlin is the southernmost volcano in the state. The next in line is Crater Lake.

There's no part of the valley where McLoughlin isn't waiting to peek out all year long. The peak is snowcapped for much of the year, sometimes wreathed in clouds, and only clear enough to climb toward the end of summer. After September—and sometimes during—the snow comes back, making the trailhead impossible to reach, and the trail itself a mess.

It's ninety-five hundred feet high, though the trail is only about five miles long. With, sadly, four thousand feet of elevation gain. I have never felt the slightest inclination to climb it before, mostly because my quads hurt just thinking about even attempting it. Some things are better looked at from afar.

I knew people, however, who went ahead and made the climb every year. They would set out before dawn, because the climb takes a minimum of six hours *if you're in excellent hiking shape.* And there's a scramble at the top once you pass the tree line and have nothing but lava rock and other rubble to clamber over to get to the summit. The reward for all that effort, naturally, is the view that might or might not be cloudy, and then you get to turn around and make your way back down again. Hopefully faster.

No, thank you. I'm capable of coming up with pointless exercises on my own without potentially falling off the side of dangerous mountains in pursuit of nasty rituals involving very sharp knives.

But Maddox and I agree to set out before dawn all the same.

I dig out my old hiking boots, which of course I have even though I've never been a serious hiker, because what I am instead is a native Oregonian. We are prepared, at all times, for any potential hikes and all hiking-associated issues, and we always have the relevant gear on hand. Like water filtration and a pop-up tent, if needed. I don't bring those things. I do pack a first aid kit, even though it seems a little bit ridiculous if I think about the amount of blood I keep seeing in those visions. Do I think I'll combat the ritualistic killing with some cotton swabs and medical tape?

I also pack snacks. Far more useful.

Maddox, on the other hand, flits into the kitchen in jeans, flip-flops, and a sweatshirt that has the name of a coffee shop that no longer exists emblazoned on its front.

We gaze at each other. She looks like she's going for a stroll, possibly on a beach. I look like I'm about to climb Everest.

"You're going to . . . hike McLoughlin in flip-flops?" I ask.

She gazes back at me. Blandly. "Don't you worry about *my* hiking. I'll be just fine."

I discover pretty quickly that *just fine* is an understatement.

We get to the trailhead, after surviving Maddox's reckless driving for some thirty-five miles into the wilderness. Then up the old Forest Service access road that no one's touched in years. I settle in for what I anticipate will be a fairly arduous hike, but Maddox just . . . lilts along. She doesn't have to stop to catch her breath. She doesn't have to choose between talking and living. She doesn't even seem to notice as we start gaining elevation. The fact that she's wearing flip-flops on questionable terrain doesn't seem to slow her down at all.

The only thing slowing her down is me.

I'm not sure why it takes me so long to realize that if she wanted to, Maddox could simply lope her way up the side of the mountain without a care in the world—and probably without breathing heavily while she's at it—but is holding back.

For me.

I have a lot of time to think about that, especially when I stop trying to chat with her as we go.

"You seem a little broody," she says at one point.

I wave that off, while panting. "Oh, I'm just contemplating my fitness level compared to your fitness level, wondering why anyone thinks hiking is fun, and in between all that, I'm focusing on the great many people who have decided to lie to me over the past few years. You know. Light and easy stuff."

She laughs. "I mean, part of that is that I'm not a human," she reminds me. "You're doing great for a human who also hasn't trained for this."

"I was born here. What training could I possibly need?"

That bravado lasts about three steps.

We hike on through the morning. We stop to eat lunch, though it's pretty clear that I'm the only one who requires calories to go on. Maddox is lounging around as if she's in a bar. Or perhaps on a poolside recliner somewhere. That's how little this hike requires of her.

I eat what I can, hoping that it gives me more energy, because I'm going to need it.

We set out again. And it's worse. Slower, steeper.

I know that I must look wretched when Maddox takes my backpack.

"I'll take a turn." She sounds so cheerful, complete with a smile. "It's only fair."

I know perfectly well she's taking it out of pity, but I remind myself that there's absolutely no point in attempting to prove my strength to an actual supernatural creature, so I don't.

We climb. Everything hurts, then hurts some more, and still we trudge on.

I think about how I sneaked into Gran's room early this morning, leaving her some breakfast and her coffee in an insulated mug.

Careful, child, she whispered, when I thought she was asleep. *Fate does not look kindly on those who seek to thwart it.*

I wanted to sink down onto the side of her bed. I wanted to crawl up and curl myself into her and let her hold me the way she did when I was little. When my mother had broken off another piece of my heart and smashed it on the ground. When I believed she could fix everything with a hand on my forehead and a few soothing sounds.

I wanted to tell her about Augie. About all the things I saw. About the things that are happening to me.

About this terrible pull I feel toward Ariel and how I wish it were as simple as sex.

How I can't get past that moment when I ran up the stairs and out of that dungeon, and felt sheer relief that he was there. Waiting.

Like *he* could fix everything, even me.

I wanted to tell her that I don't know what this makes me and I don't know who I am.

But I already know that if I said something like that to my grandmother, she would very likely tell me to snap out of it. And not soothingly.

You can't be anyone but you, try though you might, she would say, the way she did when I was in seventh grade and was sure that everyone only pretended to tolerate me because they loved Augie so much, and I was their consolation prize. *That's your only power in any given situation, so it's best to come to terms with it.*

That's what I tell myself now as my calves complain and my hamstrings scream and my feet swell up in these boots I haven't worn in years.

I keep going.

But as the day wears on, it gets harder. Not just because it's steep and relentless, but because the vision keeps pounding at me, more with every step.

By afternoon it begins to feel as if the vision itself is pummeling me with nasty psychic fists. As if the vision wants me off this mountain and away from the scene of the crimes that will be committed here.

I figure that can only mean I'm in the right place.

Maddox starts telling me stories. Silly tales of inconsequential things, like episodes of long-ago television shows we watched when we were kids. I understand at once that she's distracting me, and I'm grateful. Though I can't really concentrate on what she's saying, that's okay, because for a while it seems as if the sound of her cheerful commentary alone might keep the worst of the visions away.

Sadly, this doesn't last.

What does last is the headache, the worst one yet.

As it starts to get dark, I slow down even more, from a crawl to something slugs could beat without trying hard, because all I can see is blood.

Not the trail before me. Not the trees all around.

Those wicked blades piercing flesh. The grotesque dancing and that flickering flame and that blood, everywhere.

As if the point of the whole thing is a wholesale exsanguination.

As if they want to paint the forest, and the mountain, and the whole damn valley with the fruits of their bloodletting.

I have to say, it feels a lot like the sort of Goddess of Filth carnage I've heard about and seen too much of in my nightmares. The moment I think it, I know.

It's her. It's been her all along.

And it's grisly, this coming sacrifice. I can feel the weight of it. There's a sour copper taste in my mouth, and I'm moving slower and slower, as if I'm the one who's been stabbed.

I have to force myself to keep moving anyway.

"We can stop," Maddox says. More than once. "I can always run on ahead and scope things out."

I want that to be the solution. I collapse, maybe at the notion that there can be any solution that isn't this pounding in my head. She crouches next to me, and when I look at her, I can see that there's worry there.

Not just for me.

I'm afraid I know why. "You don't think that you can find it, do you? That only I can."

Maddox doesn't look all that cheerful now. "What I'm betting is that it's the kind of thing that we'll only be able to find afterward. I think you're probably the only one who can find it ahead of time. Because to you, it's already happened."

Every time I sit down it's harder to get up, but I keep doing it.

It gets darker and darker and I think, *It's okay. I can fight through this. All I have to do is put one foot in front of the next until I get there—*

But then the moon begins to rise.

And the moment I see it, I'm done.

A blinding, nauseating pain shoots through me, a headache so vile it takes my knees out. I crumple, and the pain swells. I'm heaving, emptying my stomach, clutching my head, and thinking that a better idea might be to pick up any rock I can find and bash these fucking *things* right out of my head—

"Okay, then," Maddox says, with a quiet finality in her voice, "I think we're done."

"I can keep going," I manage to moan, though I'm not even remotely certain that's true. "I just need a minute."

"You can take that minute," Maddox tells me. "You can take fifteen. I'm going to call in reinforcements."

She shrugs out of my pack and slings it down to the ground.

The headache hasn't exactly eased, but I'm getting used to breathing through that bright, vicious clamp of agony. Tears are streaming down my face, yet somehow I don't care about that. Not even when I can feel them start to get too cold on my cheeks, because it's already winter up this way and we haven't even crossed the timberline.

I watch blearily as Maddox stands up again and walks a little bit farther up the trail. Then she stretches, dipping her head back and seeming to almost sigh, as if she's arching into the moon itself, and then—

It's like there's a burst of light—though I think it's more the suggestion of it—and then she *changes*.

She shifts right there before me. One moment she's the girl I've always known, the mystery no one has ever been able to solve, and the next—

It's like for a split second, I can see the human and the wolf tangled up together, superimposed, one over the next, but then it's just her again.

Only now she's a wolf.

Wolf Maddox has those same smoky-quartz eyes and a beautiful coat, multicolored like her hair. She's much bigger than I expected, yet somehow manages to keep that lithe, easy athleticism she's always had.

"Wow," I whisper, because even through the horror of this headache, she's amazing. "It's kind of a shame you ever have to be human."

I can see a wolfy sort of smile.

Then she tilts back her head and howls.

It's a long, exquisitely wild, desolate, and exultant sound.

It seems to expand inside of me, like its own tide. As long as it goes on, I feel no pain. There is only that song of hers, spilling out into the night. Dancing with the moon.

Filling not only me, but the valley all around us.

Maybe the whole world.

I remember the first time I heard the wolves howl I was hiding in the house with Gran and Augie and thinking we wouldn't last the night. This is the same sound, and it's not that it isn't scary, because it is. It makes all the hair on my body seem to prickle, and some of it is surely standing up straight.

But it's different when the wolf making that sound is directly in front of me.

And is also my friend.

She stops and cocks her head slightly.

Then she howls again, longer this time, and I want to say it feels lonely inside me—but that's not quite right. It's more that it reminds me how lonely I am, which isn't the same thing.

It seems to wind its way into my heart and burrow in deep.

This time, when the last note of her song fades away, there is a deep, expectant pause.

I think even the fir trees that stand watch are waiting. Listening.

And then, far off in the distance, I hear an answering howl.

I'm pretty sure that what I'm hearing is coming from the Coastal Range, over on the other side of the valley, though we are currently in a different mountain range altogether, the High Cascades. It makes me want to cry a little, and not from the pain, but because this is how the wolves keep track of each other.

It's beautiful. More than beautiful, it's distinctly untamed and wonderful, but it also reminds me that there are whole worlds operating all around me all the time that I know nothing about.

I'm still on the ground. Maddox pads over and nudges me with her muzzle, and I take that to mean that she's encouraging me to actually sit and rest. To lean back against the nearest tree instead of crouching on my hands and knees like I'm about to leap up and keep grinding.

When I gingerly arrange myself against the tree and even let the trunk hold my head up, she whines in approval.

Then she sits, her head cocked, and waits.

I'm not entirely surprised when my eyes drift closed, as if my body can't bear another moment of using any energy that isn't focused on fighting the pain like spikes in my temples and an iron crown welded onto my head.

I don't nap. I don't think I fall asleep, because my head hurts too much for that, but I drift.

The good thing about this terrible headache—assuming there is one—is that it keeps the vision at bay. I can feel it pressing in at me. It feels imperative. Like a rude stranger pounding on the door—

But at least there's still that door.

I tell myself that's something.

High up on this mountain, I hear only the wind moving through the trees. It smells like snow. The ground I'm sitting on is frigid already, and I expect that as the night wears on, it will be colder. It might even snow on us. If I could move, I suspect that it wouldn't take long to cross out of what little protection the trees offer and scramble around toward the summit, fully exposed to the moon and the elements alike.

But I don't move. I sit. I wait.

Only when I hear Maddox let out what sounds like a bark do I open my eyes.

Then immediately wish that I kept them closed, because the biggest wolf I've ever seen comes loping up the trail, all fangs and claws and a head that looks large enough to gulp down the two of us like a couple of pieces of candy. If that.

He's enormous. I'm pretty sure he's as big as my truck, but he moves like fear and dread. Silent and focused, death on four massive paws.

And when he sees us waiting there on the trail in front of him, he bares his ferocious teeth.

Then growls.

18.

I don't see Maddox change this time because I'm too busy gaping in awe and wonder—and what feels like an appropriate level of sheer terror—at what can only be the werewolf alpha in his natural form. When I thought his human form was over the top.

But when Maddox moves to put herself between him and me, she's human. And wearing clothes. The same clothes she was wearing before, which strikes me as fascinating even with the headache from hell. How do they change in and out of clothes while shifting from one form to the other? Where do they put the clothes while gallivanting about as wolves? I assume this is all part of the magic.

It's also pretty clear to me that I'm deliberately thinking of anything but the giant wolf prowling toward me with what looks like a lot of sharp-toothed, furry murder on his face.

"Calm down." Maddox talks to him like he's a cute little dachshund puppy instead of a monster straight out of a nightmare. "I need your help."

There's a flash, and something I feel like a thunderclap deep in my bones, as if the marrow is on fire. Then he's standing there before us in his slightly less terrifying human form.

I would hide, like any sane person would when faced with *anything* his size—much less a *werewolf*—but I can't move. All I can do is sit propped up against the tree while death in numerous forms swirls all around me.

"What fucking games do you think you're playing?" Ty Ceridwen, the fierce and formidable werewolf alpha, demands.

Happily, not of me.

"I keep telling you that I'm not playing games." Maddox still sounds like she's talking to a sweet, domesticated pet, and I wonder if Ty can see that she's pissed, because I can. Though I sense that probably, he doesn't care. "Maybe you didn't notice that it's a full moon."

"I notice every fucking full moon, asshole, and guess why? Because every time the full moon rises and there's no ritual, the more you look like a problem I'm going to have to deal with. And the more I look like a little bitch for not handling you."

"Nobody thinks you're a bitch, Ty," she replies. So sweetly that I wince in anticipation. "They don't know you as well as I do."

I expect him to blow up at that, but he laughs. He swaggers closer. Like Maddox, he's not remotely dressed for running around mountainsides. He's wearing something very similar to what he was wearing last time I saw him. Jeans. Motorcycle boots. And a black T-shirt because obviously, the cold does not dare mess with Ty Ceridwen.

Apparently, only Maddox dares.

He reaches over and hooks a finger in the collar of the shirt Maddox is wearing and yanks her to him. "I'm sick of this," he growls at her. "How many times do I have to say that? When are you going to listen?"

"I always listen. Maybe you could try it for a change." She throws out an arm and points at me. "Winter," she says, though she doesn't look in my direction. Because I guess even she isn't foolish enough to take her eyes off the danger that is Ty. "Where are those cards of yours?"

I would very much like to know how she knows anything about those cards, but I don't have the strength to ask. I obediently tap the front of my chest, where the cards lodged themselves a few hours back, tucked in tight to my sports bra.

Ty's laugh this time is lower. Meaner. "Bullshit."

Maddox keeps holding his gaze, even after he belts that word out. "Show him, Winter."

I feel profoundly lucid, which is odd, because I also feel weak as fuck. I'm still seriously contemplating taking the nearest rock to the side of my skull. Yet what occurs to me then is that my insistence on trying to understand everything that is happening around me is a hindrance more than anything else. Why would I understand?

I'm surrounded by dynamics, rules, and agreements that have nothing to do with me. All I can do is follow my own gut, and I know that's not an entirely foolish endeavor, because I'm still alive. Still alive, if not currently kicking, despite my numerous skirmishes with the king of the vampires. Not to mention my current predicament, which involves what feels like a near-death experience some eight thousand feet above sea level, in the company of werewolves.

While the full moon beams down on all of us and Vinča's disgusting ritual is about to begin.

So obviously, I reach into my shirt and pull out my deck.

I realize as I hold it that it's the first time I've thought of it that way. *My* deck. Not my grandmother's. *Mine.*

In my hand, the cards warm. I interpret that as approval.

Like they really did choose me.

Shit.

Ty stares down at me, huddled there against a tree. I try to imagine what I could possibly look like to a creature like him. Small. Chewable.

But something about the fact I have the cards in my hands changes him. He shoves a hand through his hair, throwing Maddox a look that I would describe as vicious.

However, it only seems to relax her.

"Tell me," he growls.

There's something different about him when he says that. Or maybe the way he looks at Maddox shifts. As soon as I think that, it hits me. It's that authority of his that's always obvious but has always been filtered through their relationship when I've seen them together.

He is speaking now as a leader, not as her lover.

"I already told you. The cards have chosen. She's the oracle," Maddox says, sounding exactly the same. "And in case you think I'm bullshitting you, everybody knows that only the chosen oracle can carry those cards. Meanwhile, this full moon is bringing with it the gift of a nasty little ritual."

Ty doesn't like that. "Another lock."

She nods. "Unless you stop it."

Ty looks at her, and something passes between them, wordlessly. Then he cuts his gaze to me. "You look like shit, oracle."

"That's good news," I manage to say, "because I also feel like shit, and I really hate when I don't match."

"Cute." I think we're both thinking about how easily he could eat me, a quick little snack. "Doesn't look like you can stand. What's your plan? You going to make it up this mountain and do what, exactly? I'm guessing that whoever's throwing a full moon ritual that has Maddox worried enough to go hiking isn't going to welcome you with open arms. You plan to fight them?"

"Hadn't really thought that far ahead." I try to smile, and my head feels like it might explode. I have to breathe out, hard, to keep it at a roaring ache instead. "But now that we're discussing it, I'm kind of hoping that the presence of werewolves might work in my favor."

"Have you pinpointed the location?" Ty asks Maddox. She shakes her head. "So . . . what? We wander around playing grab ass all night while we hope that your weak-ass friend can stand on her own two feet and make it happen somehow?"

I want to be offended, except I agree with him.

"Do you have a better option in mind?" Maddox demands.

But I've had enough. It takes an enormous effort on my part, but I manage to climb to my feet. I mean that literally. I have to use the tree behind me to launch myself painfully upright, and none of what's happening inside me is good. I stagger forward, not unaware of the way Ty stares at me. In what I'm pretty sure is disbelief.

"Let's go," I manage to get out past that clamping-iron agony pressing into my skull, worse with every breath, every step, every beat of my heart. "I've had a rest. I'm great. Let's do it."

And then I somehow force one foot in front of the other and start up the trail again.

I hear Ty swear under his breath. I hear Maddox say something to him in a low voice.

The next thing I know, there's that thunderclap, and then that huge, massive wolf is beside me. He's looking at me with what I can only describe as a deeply challenging expression.

"Go on," Maddox says.

I turn back and stare at her in confusion. The wolf beside me growls.

Maddox's gaze is locked on mine. "Ty is going to carry you."

I know several things simultaneously then. One, that no human should be touching a werewolf. Two, that this particular werewolf does not want me touching him. And three, that to refuse this offer would be an insult.

A biteable offense, I'm pretty sure.

I stare at him. He stares back. I feel frozen until he makes a huffing sort of sound and lowers himself closer to the ground.

Only then, gingerly, carefully, perfectly prepared for him to turn and bite my head off—literally—do I climb onto Ty Ceridwen's back.

And then . . . I'm riding the werewolf alpha.

Like a goddamn horse.

Maybe it's lucky that the pain in my head is so intense that I can't really concentrate on that. Not for long.

I grip his thick fur in my fists as he begins to move. I wonder if a headache can actually make a whole head implode from the inside out or if I only wish it would so the pain would stop. I try to ignore the complaints from my stomach, a parade of queasy uncertainties that movement certainly doesn't help.

But riding a werewolf is a whole lot better than trudging up this mountainside by myself. Step by brutal step, each one a new stabbing pain that only builds on the one before.

I hold on and hope that not forcing myself to keep climbing will soothe the pain even a little.

I'm not sure it does. It just shifts. Or time flattens out.

Maybe it's me that's gone flat. I notice things and file them away, but I can't seem to lace them together to make any kind of sense. It's like a drawn-out fever dream, though I don't think there's anything going on inside me tonight but this killer headache.

Maddox, back in her wolf form, is quick and capable, keeping up with Ty's pace with what looks like not much effort. Sometimes she loops ahead or roams off to check things on either side of the trail. Once or twice I see her tipping her head back, like she's taking in whatever secrets the trees want to tell her.

I don't know how werewolves communicate in their wolf forms, but I can see that they're doing it. It even looks like they make an excellent team. There's no doubt Ty is in charge, but he looks to Maddox all the time and seems to pay attention to her suggestions.

Or maybe I'm making all this up to entertain myself as my brain eats itself alive, hard to tell.

The moon gets higher. The air gets thinner. Eventually, we stop, so far up the mountain that I can taste snowstorms in the air. I can hear wolf paws against the earth, meaning there's something to crunch on. Ice. Frost. Whatever it is, it's cold.

Maddox shifts, then smiles at me. "You good?"

I nod, then wince because the movement makes my head feel swimmy and sick. The pain doesn't even throb anymore—it's constant. An endless piercing, lacerating me straight through and *expanding* as it goes.

Like it wants to consume me whole.

But in the tendrils of it, I see different views of that same damn clearing.

Like Google Images has resurrected itself in my head.

When I realize that Ty is glaring over his furry shoulder at me, I mutter something like an apology and slide off. My knees don't do their work, so I topple onto the ground, but it's a slow-motion topple, and I'm so boneless already that I can't really bring myself to care.

Then I decide I'll just lie there a minute, my face in the frigid dirt.

This is as close as I've been to feeling good in quite a while, so I stay there.

I feel that thunderclap again, all through me, and I don't have to look up to know that Ty has changed again.

"She's wearing his fucking mark," he growls.

"She sure is." Maddox's response, though I didn't sense her shifting, is so bland that even in my state I can tell it's pointedly so.

"This is bullshit," he growls at her. "Running around on Mount McLoughlin under a full moon like assholes. Just more of your stupid games."

"You calling my legitimate feelings about *my life* 'stupid games' is a real good way to make sure I keep playing them," she drawls, like he's not the least bit scary at all.

But then, I know now that scary and *scary* depend a whole lot on a body's response to the person in question. I know that better than I'd like.

"Keep it up," he suggests, his voice a soft threat. "You think I don't know that you keep shifting into human form because you think I'll behave better when your oracle buddy can understand me?"

"Not everything is about you," Maddox retorts loftily. "It's rude to talk about things that affect someone in languages they don't speak. Common courtesy, babe."

"Babe," he repeats, as if he can't believe she dared call him that.

I decide that at this point, the two of them squabbling is like a lullaby. Even if it's not, there's nothing I can do about it when even listening hurts.

I let my eyes drift shut. I let my face stay in the dirt, because it's cold and that feels fantastic against my aching head. It's like an ice pack provided by the earth itself, and I am eternally grateful.

I feel a weight pressing into me, digging into my side, and I don't have to reach over to know that the cards have wedged themselves there in the vicinity of my hip. Just in case I want to reach over and grab them from this ridiculous position.

In my current state, I have to admire the cards' continuing optimism that if they keep on presenting themselves, I'll surrender to them.

Right now I feel like I'd surrender to anything, but it takes too much energy to reach for the deck.

Ty and Maddox are still sparking at each other. They're probably touching, too, because they usually are. I find myself thinking about hands on throats, and I wonder what's happened to me that I now unambiguously find that hot. Both when I saw it and when it happened to me.

Surely someone concerned with her own longevity would think better of responding the way I did to a grip like that.

Though the fact that Ty mentioned Ariel's mark floats up then, dancing around in what little mind I have left that's not taken over by the searing pain. I spent a very long time in the shower before I finally went to bed last night, scrubbing myself everywhere. Wishing I could reach inside my brain and scrub out some of the images in my head, but in lieu of that, I did the best I could with what I had.

But apparently the damn mark stayed put.

I should probably feel grosser about that than I do. This is becoming a tired theme. I should feel a lot of things, yet I don't.

What I don't know is if that means I'm already too far gone.

Face down in the dirt on Mount McLoughlin, chasing a nasty ritual sacrifice under an ominously full moon, it feels a little late to be worrying about such things.

The pain in my head seems to bloom then, brighter and hotter.

It takes over everything. It blots out any other line of thought I could possibly have, until I'm scrabbling around for a rock to start bashing my own face in—

And then I see it.

It's like an entire map suddenly drops, fully formed, into my head.

I sit up, even though it makes everything seem to lurch, and wipe dirt from my face. I'm vaguely aware of Ty and Maddox off to the side of me, clearly testing the limits of that push-and-pull thing they have going on.

"Hey," comes Ty's voice when I start to move, "where the hell do you think you're going?"

"Winter? Are you okay?"

But I don't answer Maddox either.

Maybe I think that attempting to speak will take more energy than I have left. Maybe I'm not thinking anymore.

I walk. I leave the trail and start picking my way across the mountainside. I can hear that they're following me, thunderclaps and all, though I don't turn around to check.

After a while, I start climbing again, and the great part of the continuing headache is that I don't really pay any attention to how my quads scream at me or how tender my feet feel in the damn hiking boots. I just keep going.

And it's not too long before I see those rock formations that look like goblins, leering down at me as if, if it were up to them, they'd devour me here and now.

I stagger past the rocks and then, finally, I see the trees that have been haunting me for what feels like a brand-new forever.

I hear a growl from behind me and know that it's Ty. It's so deep it sounds like a Harley engine, which maybe explains the whole werewolf/biker connection, but I'm too messed up to follow that or any other line of thought.

Besides, he's not growling at me.

I don't know how I know that—I just do.

"Blood," Maddox says, like she's agreeing with something he said. I'm surprised that she's not in her wolf form, not that I turn back to confirm that. Her speaking *is* the confirmation. "I smell it too."

I make myself keep going, putting one foot in front of the other until the pounding in my head nearly knocks me over. I sag against the nearest tree in despair, until I realize I've made it to the clearing.

The clearing that's been haunting me.

I made it. We're here. I force myself to look around and see . . .

Exactly the scene I saw laid out in my head.

"Winter," Maddox murmurs, urgently. She's crouching next to me, but her eyes are on the scene in front of us. The scene I've seen so many times in my head that seeing it in living color, scent, and sound feels unreal. "Stay here."

"No problem," I assure her.

Ty growls at her, and I have no trouble interpreting it. *Hurry up.*

I try to stay upright, gripping on to that tree, as she lunges forward and shifts in midair—

Then she's a blur of teeth and fur, and she and Ty streak straight into the dark heart of the ritual.

At first it seems like there are too many cloaked figures to count. I get the overwhelming sense that they are not quite human, though they are shaped as if maybe they were. Once. I force myself to focus and try to count them, whatever they are. At some point I realize my vision is doubling and that there are only thirteen.

This is not excellent, but it's a far cry better than twenty-six.

There's a split second when the werewolves move in like death while the figures dance and chant, waving those nasty-looking blades in the air, entirely unaware.

I have the feeling that moment is burned into me, that splayed-out instant only I see.

Then the next moment comes, and it seems that there are suddenly werewolves everywhere.

I know there are only two of them, but I have to keep reminding myself of that. Because if I didn't know not only how many there are, but *who* they are, I would think there were a great many more.

A whole damn pack.

Ty is astonishing. It's amazing to me that anything that large could move the way he does, sleek and too fast to believe, like a terrifying wave of singular mayhem.

He's all claws and teeth, tearing through the cloaked figures with a vengeance.

Maddox is no slouch herself.

She smaller, so she's faster and, to my eye, more vicious. She goes for the throat every time, and she doesn't miss.

The pain in my head shifts somehow, or maybe I'm finally used to it.

Then again, it could be something else.

It sounds like a whisper at first, though I don't get the sense that I'm *hearing* it. Not with my ears.

Yet I know what it is. A beckoning. An invitation.

I look around, blinking against the clamp of pain—however dull in comparison—and I see the figure, bound and still on that flat stone altar.

Then I suck in a sudden, ragged breath, because she's looking right at me.

Not dead.

Not yet.

Her eyes are wide and glazed, there's blood all over her face, and her mouth is open wide like she's panting.

Or screaming.

I force myself to my feet. I make my way toward her, doing my best to stay out of the way of the cloaked figures and the furious werewolves battling it out before me. I figure they're giving the cloaks and blades a lot more to worry about than I could.

Besides, it seems to me as if the moon itself is leading me along, guiding me.

Making sure I keep going, no matter how much every step hurts.

I fall more than once, but I still keep going, crawling if necessary, puking when I can't *not*, until I make it around that fire. Once I do, I kneel right there beside the altar.

I confirm that she's not dead. Not yet, though that seems like a foregone conclusion, and I can remember feeling the marks that I see all over her gouged deep into my own skin. I feel them again now.

The woman reaches out her bound hands to me, and I don't think. I take them in mine.

I think that I ought to say something beautiful or comforting or *something*—

Her hands are bloody and mangled, and she shouldn't be able to grip me as hard as she does. So hard that she jerks me toward her. Much too close, as a matter of fact, though I question my empathy that I should have a problem with a poor, sacrificed woman getting what comfort she can—

She croaks at me.

"What?" I ask, my head swimming again, though I try to give this dying soul my attention—and what tattered empathy I have in me—in her last moments.

She grabs my hand even harder, painfully hard, grinning at me through teeth soaked in blood.

I know I'm not making that up, because she laughs.

"She's coming," the woman tells me, a terrible echo of words I've heard before.

Then her mouth goes wide, her eyes go dark and opaque, and when she opens her mouth it's like I'm being sucked inside, lost forever—

And everything I am, everything there is, goes black.

19.

I know I'm awake again because I hurt. Everything hurts.

Hurt barely covers it.

I feel foggy and strange. It seems to take an enormous, Herculean effort to open my eyes. When I do, I rub them as if that might make what I'm looking at begin to make sense.

But it doesn't, no matter how much I rub, so I stop.

When I look at my hands, I see blood. Then I remember that woman—and I'm pretty sure I just rubbed her blood all over me.

I start to turn, maybe a little wildly. I wonder what happened to her, and to me, and to all those terrible cloaked figures—

"Settle down," says a voice close beside me, and I recognize it immediately.

I do as I'm told. I settle, and only then look to see Maddox there beside me. It seems to take me much too long to process the fact that her arm is around me—a lot like she was cradling my form while I . . . lay about unconscious?

Because I'm pretty sure I passed out. I'm actually a little shocked I'm not dead.

It's an incredibly disconcerting thing to consider—the image of me, entirely defenseless and unaware, just . . . laid out for any of the dark and terrible things here to do whatever they want with.

It's more than disconcerting. It makes my back curl where I sit, or would, if that sort of movement didn't make everything hurt *more*. It also makes my stomach start to act up again when, surely, there can be nothing left inside me to throw up.

I try not to think about it. I look back to the center of the clearing, past the choking black smoke and a charred, sweet scent I opt not to think about too closely. There are cloaked bodies lying all around, many of them ravaged and in pieces. I've seen a lot of dead bodies in the past three years, and I'm weirdly glad about it now, because otherwise I think I would simply lapse off into shock at what I'm seeing.

Instead, I know to let my gaze skim right over the details without letting them land. I do that, and find myself squinting at the two upright figures in the center of the clearing, surrounded by bodies.

One is Ty, as expected.

The other one is Ariel. This is not expected at all.

And they are not having a quiet, civil conversation.

"How could you risk her?" Ariel is shouting, and he's angrier and scarier than I've ever seen him. For one thing, there's the *shouting* when I think of him as still and quietly terrifying. For another, I can see his fangs. For yet another thing, the silver of his eyes has gone dark and mean.

He also has his hands spread in a way that makes me wonder if he might sprout claws at any second. He looks like he's considering it.

This is the moment when I should find him repulsive. This is the moment when I should remind myself that these little fantasies I've been toying with will be the death of me. The actual death of me.

It will look like this. Like this monster most reasonable people have nightmares about.

Yet . . . I do not find him repulsive at all.

Even now, when I'm not entirely convinced my internal organs are in the right place.

"Now you're concerned about risking her?" Ty grits back, and I'm fascinated. "That's fucking hilarious. You're so concerned that you send her off to wander around the valley with your mark all over her but no protection?"

Ariel seems to expand, silver gone dark. "My mark is, by definition, protection."

"It's only protection against those who give a shit if they piss you off." Ty belts that at him like a punch from one of his massive fists. "It's stupid as fuck. What it's not is *concern*."

Ariel's eyes seem to glow a dark, tarnished, scary sort of silver now. "At the very least you should have called in reinforcements the moment you knew what was happening here. We all made these agreements for a reason."

"I've never much believed in oracles, asshole," Ty shoots back. "It's you undead fuckers who like messages and signs. Werewolves don't need magic. We don't get our paws read. We have teeth and claws, and we take care of ourselves."

Ariel leans in, looking more like a walking, talking nightmare than ever. And I can't seem to look away. "And when you say you take care of yourselves, is that how you would describe installing your lover in the oracle's yard?"

Ty growls. They close in on each other. Two night terrors in a field of blood and broken bodies who look a lot like they're about to start tearing each other into pieces.

"My *fated mate*," Ty corrects him in a deadly tone, "is not *installed* anywhere. She makes her own choices and her own rules. I know you bloodsuckers hate that shit. You like them messed up on blood, too fucked in the head to do anything but worship at your feet."

Beside me, I feel Maddox stiffen, but I can't tell if it's because she liked what Ty said . . . or didn't.

Then I don't wonder about anything. I think maybe I pass out. Everything seems to swirl around and around in a drunken sort of narrow circle, and then there's nothing.

Until there is again.

Mostly pain.

Through the haze of that, I remember where I am. And who's talking.

"There are treaties in place," Ariel is saying, his voice a whole dark, cold winter. "Are you declaring them null and void with this stunt? You know what will happen."

Ty only laughs. "You want to go back to how it used to be? I was under the impression your creepy little leech boys like their heads on their necks, but I can always—"

"Hey."

Both of them look over at Maddox, as if surprised to find she's still there. Ariel's dark gaze finds me, and holds, and I really should question why I have the urge to run *toward* him—

Though I can't do any such thing. The pain is like a tide, the waves are getting higher, and I have the terrible suspicion that I am not okay.

Like . . . *really* not okay.

"If you two want to burn down the valley tonight, be my guest," Maddox is saying in her best bored tone. Like they're nothing but dumb boys in the high school parking lot, pretending they're fighters. Clearly, neither one of them enjoys her tone, but that doesn't stop her. "But please remember that the treaties you're talking about don't mean just the two of you and your cute little bromance. You want to change things up? You know who else needs to be here."

"I fucking hate sorcery," Ty growls.

Ariel looks like he agrees, but he only inclines his head at Maddox. His eyes flash silver, and I realize that what I'm watching is that vampire magic. Or vampire tricks. Whatever you call it, he's doing it.

I struggle to sit up again, shaking Maddox's hand off me when she tries to keep me from doing it, but I only manage to move a little. It's enough to make me wheeze in agony, as everything inside me seems to revolt.

The night goes gray around me. My ears ring, loud.

"You're very weak," Maddox tells me, her gaze smoky and direct.

"Yeah, yeah," I mutter, though even my lips feel weird and my voice sounds like a death rattle. "Humanity is fragile, inside and out. Tell me something I don't know."

But she doesn't seem to find me funny.

"Here's something you don't know," she says, and there's more wolf in her glare now. "That bitch did something to you. I don't know what. She took you down and knocked you out, flat. All tied up to a stone slab in the middle of her own sacrifice. So, I don't know, maybe take a breather?"

I don't have time to think about whether or not I'm deeply chastened—or maybe a little bit scared—by that.

All around us, suddenly, there's a kind of humming that seems to come from the earth itself. It sounds oddly familiar, though I can't quite place it. I hear scraps of voices in the breeze, up so high on this mountain that I never forget is a volcano.

Then, out of nowhere, there is a column of light.

It beams down into the clearing, blinding gold, and when the brightness dims enough so we can look at it directly . . . she's there.

I can see who it is, but my brain refuses to make sense of it.

It's like I *can't* accept what I'm seeing.

I feel my teeth chattering, that's how wild and total my reaction is. The nearly dying part didn't send me into shock, or not yet, but this is making it happen.

"I'm so sorry," the figure drenched in light says. "This is not how I expected to reveal myself."

I expect her to smile at me in that serene, calming way, but her gaze stays on me too long. She frowns, and the sound I thought I recognized gets louder. It's chanting, I realize. The same chanting I hear almost every night from her cottage.

I have to accept that this really is Savi.

"Why are you letting her bleed out internally?" she asks, but I don't think she's speaking to me. I think she's speaking to Ariel and Ty and maybe even Maddox, but once again, everything is dimming to that worrying gray around me.

I don't want to fade away. Instead, I try to concentrate on Savi, who I last saw in my kitchen, and the fact that she is standing on a mountaintop bathed in a light of her own making. I watch as she moves her hand through the air in a gesture that feels ancient and timeless, graceful and powerful, and murmurs words I don't pretend to understand as she does it.

More of that chanting fills the air.

As she speaks, the tight, harsh grip of the cold seeping into me . . . eases.

Even my headache dissipates enough so that I can take what feels like the first deep breath I've had since the moon rose.

Only then, only after she's looked me over with a critical eye and exchanged one of those too-long looks with Maddox, does she deign to turn her notice to the two men standing before her.

She is not scared of either of them. She makes this very clear.

"I don't like being summoned," she informs Ariel. "You are too free and easy with your demands, vampire."

And whether or not I can comprehend that Savi is *the sorceress* I've already heard about, the way she says that makes it inarguable that whatever else she is, she is a creature of intense power.

Sorceress fits.

"You must have mistaken me for one of your lost acolytes," Ariel returns, sounding so deadly it makes *me* want to hide, and he's not talking to me. "I bend a knee to no one. Your parlor tricks do not impress me."

"How about we stop measuring dicks?" Ty interjects. "We all know I'll win."

I still haven't managed to sit all the way up, but for the moment, I decide that's okay. I lean against Maddox and watch the scene before me as the three of them face off, standing in their little triangle of power.

The vampire king. The werewolf alpha.

And Savi, who seems impervious to the weather and the raw power emanating from the two of them.

"There seem to be failures of communication all around," Savi says. She sounds tranquil, as usual, but her words still send a shiver of apprehension down my spine.

"Do you mean like your decision to move into Jacksonville, conceal your true identity, and insinuate yourself into the life of two oracles?" Ariel asks her, each word a different bite, sharp and deep. "All without calling a summit?"

Ty snorts at that. "You're just bitching because you know she wouldn't let a vampire into her house."

Savi smiles at Ariel. "It seems as if you found a way to create a more intimate connection, didn't you?"

I am still woozy, and I'm not sure that whatever Savi did healed me so much as numbed me, but I get that she means Ariel and me. And probably his mark that everyone can see. And there are a lot of things I'd probably want to say about that if I felt better, but I don't.

Because now that Savi has given me a shot of a sorcerer's painkiller, I'm remembering other things.

The way that woman held on to me. Her blood-drenched teeth.

And the fact that I think she was *smiling*, not afraid.

I shudder, and my attention is drawn back to the center of the clearing again. Now that I'm warmer, it's easier to focus, but it also means that I'm aware of all the things the pain blocked out. Not just that woman and her face and what she said to me, but the state of me. All the clothes I'm wearing are soaking wet, no doubt because of all the crawling and collapsing and flinging myself on the damp earth. I know better than to get wet on a mountain in the cold, but then again, I wasn't expecting the crippling headaches.

That my head isn't currently trying to kill me feels like a miracle.

But I'm beginning to think I might need more than one.

The three of them are standing there, venting their tempers at each other in highly charged yet ferociously careful words. What I see is this trinity of power who—unbeknownst to me until right now—are responsible for everything that's happened here over the past three years.

Everything.

That tide comes for me again, this time a different kind of pain.

Because there we were, staggering around with no idea what was happening to us, watching friends and neighbors die horrible deaths, and all the while these creatures were . . . playing power games?

I feel like I'm having some kind of seizure.

But it must be emotional, because there's too much wrapped up in it that I can feel. And because I retain consciousness.

There's the fact that Savi, unlike my other two tenants, is the one Gran talked to. And clearly already knew. That makes more sense now, but I didn't have to know who Savi really was to understand that she made my grandmother a little calmer. Just by being there. I can't discount that.

There's the werewolf alpha himself, who I'm pretty sure is responsible for the fact there have been no zombies in my trash since Maddox moved in. No stray banshees in the trees, no tunneling goblins. He might not have approved of what Maddox was doing, or even signed off on it, but he supported her. He supports her and therefore me.

That makes everything complicated enough before I even get to Ariel.

I think of that rush of relief I felt when I found him again in that subterranean hell and how that's really not something I should feel in his presence, ever. Yet I'm honest enough with myself to admit that the sight of him here has the same effect on me.

I don't know if I can walk, but I want to *run* to him.

I'm not willing to look too closely at what that is. Much less what it might mean.

I'm afraid I know. And I don't accept it.

I *won't* accept it.

I pull in a breath. I glance behind me, and I can see the body of that woman on the altar, the still-smoking remains of the fire making her seem to flicker and shift when she isn't actually moving at all. Nor ever will again.

Looking at her makes me shudder, and the medallion around my neck seems to burn again in commiseration. I remember that terrible blankness in her eyes. I see her mouth wide open, her bloodstained teeth. I can feel, once more, that spiral into darkness.

Even the memory makes me feel cold all over.

She is coming, the woman says in my head once more, but it's mixed in with too many echoes of that same phrase. Gran's dark words. That sickening voice in my nightmares.

The world starts to spin again, dark and drunken, and I try as hard as I can not to make the connection that's right there in front of me—

But there's no pretending I can't see it. That it hasn't been the point of all of this.

Vinča.

Vinča is coming.

A dying woman used her last breath to tell me so, and I don't have to know all the ins and outs of this gruesome monster world to understand that means something.

Almost certainly something bad.

A lot like what's already happening inside me, because I can feel all my organs again, and not in a good way. It's more that I'm beginning to feel like I might actually be falling apart from the inside out.

I don't want to think about that.

Augie's medallion is so hot that I ought to worry about it scorching my skin and raising welts, but I find I like the reminder. Of him. Of me. Of the fact that if it hurts, I'm still alive.

Though I'm beginning to wonder if I'm getting off this mountain tonight. Or if that vision was leading me to my own high-country grave.

My medallion burns even hotter and my head starts to feel fuzzy again. I'm having trouble tracking the conversation between the three of them as they stand there, carefully equidistant, as if the harmony they represent can only exist if each of them maintains their own distinct space.

I think that's pretty funny, but when I have the urge to laugh out loud it comes on so fast that I suspect I'm actually hysterical. That's no good.

No one wants to be the laughing maniac in the middle of a crime scene.

Though I'm not sure this will ever be a crime scene, since I very much doubt anyone here is going to call in whoever or whatever qualifies as the creepy police. For awful things that happen on mountaintops because of the full moon and ancient death goddesses and all the rest of this shit that I've accepted on one level—that level being that I have no choice and am plagued by terrible visions—but haven't really thought through.

I also think that I'm losing my shit.

"Here's the thing," Ty is saying in that growl of his. "I don't think the situation is contained."

"That's easily enough done." Ariel inclines his head at Ty. In an exaggerated fashion. "Isn't that what your bitten minions are for?"

"I'm not talking about cleanup." Ty jerks his chin at me. "I'm pretty sure that bitch left a little parting gift when she went."

All three of them turn to look at me then. I can feel Maddox's gaze on the side of my face.

I respond to all this scrutiny by going very, very still. Like any wise creature would when she suddenly looks out and sees the equivalent of three terrifying birds of prey peering down at her from . . . not that far away.

"I don't need any more gifts," I protest. "I can barely deal with the visions."

I decide that it's imperative that I prove I'm fine, and fast.

Nothing happened tonight, not to me. Despite the fact that I'm wet and tired, headachy, and almost certainly covered in sacrificial blood, I'm basically at the top of my game. Reports of my own death have been greatly exaggerated, no matter that my insides currently feel pureed, and I just need to show them this. I need them all to know that I am *perfectly fine*.

I shift forward and slap my hand on the ground, the very same hand that the woman grabbed, thinking I'll just vault on up to standing—

And despite all the warnings since I woke up, the grays and the spins and all the terrible pain, I'm completely unprepared for the agony that shoots through me, somehow bright and hot and dark and sick all at once—

I hear Ariel, very clearly, as he says—and loudly—"Fuck this."

But then everything swirls around, and it doesn't mess with any gray. It goes black once again, sucking me in fast and hard and deep.

Too fast and too hard to do anything but let it kill me.

Maybe this time for real.

20.

I wake up surrounded by warmth and softness, like I'm stretched out on a happy cloud, safe and sweet in a way I haven't felt since I was very young. Too young to know better. Too young to understand what life was going to do to me, like it or not, even before the Reveal.

At first I don't even open my eyes.

I surface into awareness. I have the sense that I'm coming out of a deep, restorative sleep, not the usual head too full of bloody visions all night long and the pain in my temples to match. Or the driving anxiety of wondering if the house was breached in the night, if Gran is still alive, if there are zombies snuffling around and dripping body parts out back—or worse threats.

Usually, I wake up hard and fast, my blood pressure already jacked up high because I have to be ready to fight.

Today I'm lying face down on a bed that I know isn't mine, but I can't summon up any concern about that. Not yet.

This bed is too remarkably soft for any dramatic cardiac responses. The pillow beneath my head smells faintly of herbs, or maybe I do for some reason. I stretch, wiggling my toes, and I'm so warm and so cozy that it takes me a moment to remember that really, I shouldn't feel this good.

I open my eyes then, reluctantly. Then I turn over and try to make sense of my surroundings.

The room I'm in is shadowy and cool. I sit up, gingerly, waiting for the usual aches and that awful headache to settle in, but still nothing hurts.

Around me, there's exposed brick, and very little else. The bed I'm in is all white linens, wide and high off the ground. It's the paintings on the far wall—actual paintings in serious frames, not prints and posters stuck to the wall—that click.

I'm in Ariel's apartment. This has to be what this is. It reeks of sophistication in a way nothing else in this valley does.

As I think that, flashes start to come back to me.

The mountain. The blood.

That fight I'd watched and even crawled through, those terrible cloaked figures—I still don't know what they were, and I'm not sure I want to know—the flashing knives, and that creepy chanting as they slashed and fought.

Werewolves in the midst of all those cloaks, full monsters in every sense of the term—but it's hard to hold on to the fear I ought to feel, because they saved me.

That woman with blood all over her mouth and the way those hands of hers that should have been weak grabbed on to me. Hard. I frown down at my hands, flipping them this way and that, looking for marks. Looking for wounds or broken bones or *something* to indicate why it was that I reacted like that.

She's coming, the woman said, and something about the way she said it knocked me out, tore me up, and—I'm pretty sure—almost killed me.

But what else can you expect when the *she* in question is a death goddess?

Fucking Vinča, I think now. *The asshole goddess of filth and pain.*

But more flashes of memory are hitting me now.

I see myself in Ariel's arms, something fierce and stark on that gorgeous face of his as he carries me into a bathroom that I know I haven't seen before. I look to my right from the bed I'm in and am certain that the bathroom in question is there. Just behind that door.

It's not so much that I remember it. It's that I know it.

I have a flash of being in a bath filled with hot water that turned red as I sat there, as the vampire king himself washed me. Then rinsed out my hair, making me smell like him. He took his time and, when he was done, wrapped me in the softest towel I've ever felt against my skin.

"Bullshit," I whisper to myself.

I must be having those dreams again. Not visions, just fantasies.

Yet even as I think that, they keep coming.

And they get weirder.

Silver eyes on mine that I would have thrown myself into, if I could. A question and my answer, *Yes.*

As if I would have shouted it out, if I were able.

His mouth on my neck, licking my pulse, and then those fangs I saw on the mountain piercing my skin.

I can feel the pressure, the pain. Then the way the pain . . . *blooms* into something else, something sensual and *good.*

Even the memory is a lush, marvelous sensation, washing all over and through my body.

I remember that sharp pain fading, and then a pleasure almost as intense as the orgasms he's given me.

That's not all. I have flashes of him running his nail along his own neck, then guiding my head there, holding me in place until I began to lick.

Until I could gulp him down, warm and bright and thick on my tongue.

I'm breathing heavy now and I look around again, wildly, and that's when I see the still figure standing over by the tall windows that make up the wall above the street, staring out.

It's just a dream, I tell myself. *Just a crazy dream after a crazy day . . .*

My hand moves of its own accord, up to my neck, where I can feel what ought to be a terrible, open wound or nothing but the smooth bit of skin it was yesterday—

But what I feel instead is a faint, raised scar.

Like a wound that's already healed.

I'm scrambling out of bed before I know what I'm doing, and it's only when my feet hit the hardwood floor that I realize I'm naked.

I should probably care about that, but I don't. That phoenix tattoo on his back is like some kind of homing beacon and I move toward him, not sure why I'm running directly toward the very creature who made me *drink his blood.*

I don't know what I might have said when I get to the window where he's standing, but the rain stops me.

Because I remember, then, that Savi makes it rain. That she's doing this right now.

I remember that clearing, how it was soaked with blood. This must be her way of washing it all away.

It's suddenly clear to me then. This ecosystem I've lived in for years now without knowing it. How they work together—vampire games, werewolf brawn, and a sorceress to tie it all together and sometimes make it pretty.

I put my palms on the glass and let the chill seep into them. I have the urge to press my forehead against the glass, but that makes me think about Augie belowground, and that's another spiral of shame and fury.

"How long have I been out?" I manage to ask.

He doesn't look at me. "You slept all night once I brought you here."

I shut my eyes. "What did you do to me?"

It takes Ariel so long to answer that I open my eyes again, then turn to look at him. He's staring out toward the rain, out over the buildings across Main Street, and I find it . . . odd.

All our other interactions were heavy on contact and intensity.

Now I'm naked and in his bedroom, and he won't even look at me. If even half of what's in my head happened last night, doesn't that mean . . . ?

"Ariel." I make my voice as stern as I can. But maybe what comes out is scared. "What did you do to me?"

"I saved you." He says it quietly. As if he is saying it to himself. Or maybe to the rain. "I *saved* you, Winter, when what I could have done, more easily and without your input, was simply help myself to whatever gift you received from last night's sacrifice."

Ty called it a gift too, I remember. And clearly not a happy one. I decide I can't focus on that. My heart pounds, but I remember the taste of his blood, and I don't know if it's his or mine I feel rushing too hard inside me. "What do you mean, help yourself?"

He turns to me then, his silver eyes blazing, though his mouth is stern.

"If I take your life, I get your life." There's a starkness in his voice that I don't understand. A bleakness. "That means all your visions. All your memories. All your hopes and dreams, everything you carry in your blood and bones, all mine."

I don't know why that makes me . . . not as upset as he looks. "Thanks for showing restraint, I guess?"

He does not look restrained at the moment. He looks . . . bothered. Furious. Confused, even—though it seems ridiculous to imagine that a twenty-five-hundred-year-old vampire could be *confused* about anything.

On him it looks a lot like temper.

Yet I don't flinch when he reaches over and runs his fingers over that very same mark on my neck that I found myself. "I could have simply helped myself to the gift you received from last night's sacrifice. It would have been so easy. Of course, if I had, even if I'd showed restraint, you would be little more than a vegetable now."

I lift my hand as if to push his away, but it doesn't end up that way. Instead, the two of us stand there, rain beating against the windowpanes, both of us holding tight to that bite mark on my neck.

"You bit me," I say.

In my head, this comes out as an accusation. Stark and short.

That's not how it sounds here in this room, though. The gloom all around us seems almost seductive, whispering secrets whether I wish to hear them or not.

Ariel's mouth curves, though his gaze remains stark. "I did much more than that, I'm afraid."

He moves his hand beneath mine, his thumb sweeping over the bite mark, making it feel . . . bright.

Bright like blood, I think.

I can't seem to think of much besides that. Besides him. His silver gaze. His body, so big around mine, blocking out the world. The fact that the terrible headache that plagued me yesterday is gone. The fact that there's a part of me that wishes that scar on my neck would stay there forever, a mark even humans could see.

"What exactly did you do?" I dare ask again.

His mouth curves, but again, it's bittersweet. It makes a low ache start in me, and I don't know how to combat it. It sweeps all through me like a fever, and it feels far more dangerous than any bite.

Because it has *emotion* written all over it.

It's almost as if I already know what he's going to say.

"I bound you to me." The way he says it, I can hear that it has meaning. That it's something more than his mark. Or maybe even more than his sacrifices of days gone by. *I bound you to me,* he said, and it echoes inside of me, like a vow written in blood and pressed deep into my bones. "I gave you my blood and you accepted it. According to the ancient laws, Winter, that makes you mine."

Something hitches in me, and while it's not as simple as fear, it does the same work.

"Or, alternatively, you and your ancient laws can fuck right off."

That half smile of his hurts a little less, now. "Somehow I thought that might be your reaction to this extraordinary honor I have bestowed upon you. Never fear. The laws hold regardless of your feelings about them."

His hand moves to cup my face, and I don't push it away. I should push it away. I really should. I *know* I should.

I still don't.

I can hear my heart pounding and pounding and pounding in my chest, as if it's looking for ways to break free. The way I ought to be right now, but am not.

"Am I . . . ?" My mouth feels ridiculously dry. I try to swallow. "Am I a vampire?"

His eyes are so silver they hurt. "I did not make you like me, little seer. I saved you."

I shake my head, though there's not much shaking to do when he's still holding on to me, the coolness of his skin making my own seem to burn all the hotter in response. "I don't know what that means."

"I healed you." He tilts his head slightly as he regards me, his gaze so serious. "Could you not feel it? You were dying. That vision in your head was killing you, and then that woman nearly finished the job. I believe that was her plan."

"That woman was a victim," I say, and fast, like if I let what he said sit on me it might wound me even more. The confusion is mounting in me, so I step back.

Then I put even more space between us, though it feels foolish. Foolish, maybe, but necessary. I turn back to the bed, but I don't see anything that even resembles clothing, so I pull the snow-white blanket off and wrap it around me. As if my naked body will betray me by simple virtue of its exposure.

Or maybe because he can already read me too well with clothes on.

He stays by the window and I watch his gaze drop, as if he's tracing the place where my phoenix tattoo claims my abdomen, even through the barrier of the blanket. As if he feels that link the same way I do.

A greater link now, if he's telling me the truth. Now that my resurrections aren't entirely figurative.

"She was tied up and brutally killed," I say, still too fast. "A victim in every sense of the word."

Ariel looks as if he would rather not disappoint me, and I can't decide if the warmth I feel at that is temper or a kind of melting sweetness at the idea that anyone might want to protect me from the harsh realities of life. It's so . . . novel.

"That woman was an acolyte," he says after a long while. "She was a sacrifice, yes, but she chose her role. Fought for the glory of it, I would imagine. And the goddess she serves likes blood and fear, pain and suffering, so that is what she delivered."

I think about that painful climb up the mountainside. About that last, terrible, stumbling half crawl across the clearing to get to her. I remember—vividly—taking her hands in mine and trying to think what comfort I could offer someone in her position.

"Vinča is coming," I whisper. Ariel shifts, stiffening, and I shake my head. "That's what she told me. That's why she was there. And I'm not sure that makes her less of a victim, in the end."

"She wanted to be there, and was tasked with delivering a specific gift," Ariel says with a certain gentleness. "It was not a gift for you. It was a gift to her goddess. A further demonstration of her faith. If you hadn't had the questionable sense to go there in the company of wolves, you would be dead. They were expecting you, Winter."

I clutch that blanket closer to my chest. "That's impossible."

"Don't you understand? You are an oracle. Visions are not supposed to tear you apart, and yet the one that got you up that mountain was deliberately designed to do just that."

"To what end?" I demand. "Nothing you're saying even make sense. How did a woman on an altar even know who I was?"

His gaze seems to sharpen, to get more brilliant and more pointed. "Everybody knows who you are."

"If they have a coffee addiction, maybe."

"Your family has always been known," he tells me, almost impatiently, as if I'm being deliberately obtuse. "And another thing that everyone knows is that your grandmother could easily contact you across the veil if you died. It's why oracles are so popular with the longer-lived of the Kind. They make the burden of outliving everyone you know, over and over again, a little lighter." The look on his face is forbidding, so I don't ask him who he misses. "The goddess knew that her message would come through no matter what happened. That was the plan. That is the gift she left with you, and she didn't care if you received it dead or alive."

My head is reeling, and I'm tired of reeling. I'm exhausted, and I feel certain, somehow, that this is his fault. Because it has to be his fault. If it's his fault, he can stop it. He can fix what he did and we can go back to—

But where do I think there is to go?

"One option I had was to let you die, then negotiate with your grieving grandmother for whatever message might have been sent through you," Ariel says, very deliberate and intent. "Another was to do what I did."

He's standing there, so austere. So far apart from me when I still have those images in my head, those flashes. When I can *feel* how close we were when he was biting into me. When I was sucking his blood deep into my mouth.

"Or you could have killed me yourself," I say.

He inclines his head, those silver eyes gleaming. "Or that."

It shouldn't be this hard to breathe. "But you didn't do that, Ariel. Why didn't you do that?"

I keep coming up hard against this thing I don't want to admit. I don't want to feel it. It doesn't make sense to feel it. I go around and around—

It's too soon. It can't be real. I can't discount the fact that he's a vampire—in many ways, *the* vampire—and anything I might be feeling he could have planted in me for his own amusement.

Except there's this: the way he's looking at me in this unlit room with only the rain outside. It feels like it's inside both of us. As if the downpour is washing us clean, too, not only that clearing high up on McLoughlin. As if it's washing away all the excuses.

I desperately want them back. I want to hide in them.

But I can't seem to make myself say the things that could make that happen.

All Ariel does is gaze at me much too long. Until, finally, when I think there will be no more words between us, he shifts slightly where he stands.

"I found the notion of your death, with no hope of resurrection, unappealing."

He says it so stiffly. As if he's perplexed and somewhat outraged that he feels such a thing at all.

As declarations go, you might think it anemic.

But inside of me, it catches hold. It lights a spark.

And inexplicably, impossibly, it begins to burn.

"Careful," I say, though my voice hardly sounds like mine. "Be very careful, Your Bloody Highness. Don't go soft on me."

I'm shaken. I'm shaken straight through, but there is that flickering flame inside me and it's growing by the moment. He found it *unappealing*. This creature, who traffics in death as a matter of fact and preference and no doubt no small personal delight, found my death *unappealing*.

I pull in a ragged breath. "I hope you got what you wanted, anyway."

But if that's an attempt to change this conversation or lighten the mood, it fails.

Ariel does not change his expression or his stance at all. "You kept lapsing off into a coma, and for reasons I still cannot explain, you're one of the only creatures I have ever encountered who appears to be entirely capable of keeping me out of your head."

I try to digest that. I don't think I'm understanding him. I can't be understanding him.

"So none of this is you . . . doing that thing? That song inside of me that makes me think . . . ?"

"Most people can't even tell that I would like them to start singing," he says dryly. "And when I say *most people*, I mean none. Only you, Winter. If I had to describe it, I would say that I saw the door, opened it as I always do, and you slammed it back in my face. Trust me when I tell you this has never occurred before."

I have to make myself breathe. I don't really want to. What I want to do is . . . I don't even know. Disappear. Lie down.

Scream?

"I'm sorry," I say, very carefully, almost warily, "that my mind is my own, I guess?"

He starts toward me, and even though there's a large part of me that screams at me to run, I don't.

This would all be so much easier if he truly terrified me like that.

Even from the start, he fascinated me more than he scared me.

He comes closer, and then he's too close, so I have to tilt my head back up to look at him. And he helps me, putting his hands on either side of my head as if he's still trying to find his way between my temples.

"I am not a merciful creature," he tells me. "I am not soft. If I had done what I would have done to any other human in your position, I would already have the answers I need. Instead, what I have is—"

But I don't want to hear what he wants to call me. I don't want to know what I am to him.

If I do know, it's too much. It's too overwhelming.

I am *bound to him*, that's what he said.

"How did you find me up there anyway?" I ask him, interrupting him.

Ariel reaches over and runs his finger down my back. I feel his hand moving along my spine, then flaring out over my hip. "Why do you think I marked you?"

"One of your vampire minions suggested it was what you always do with your sacrifices," I say, the flare of temper that comes with it bubbling up from a place inside me I didn't even know was there.

"I have always liked a sacrifice." He sounds somewhere between sardonic and nostalgic. "But in your case, it was strategy. Marks are like flares. They make you easy to find, even on the top of a mountain in the middle of the woods."

"So why bother binding me?" I snap at him, because I feel vulnerable. Wide open. Naked in more ways than one. "You just wanted an extra charge on that flare?"

"As I said, the mark was strategy. As for binding you to me . . ." He pauses then. His hands on me almost feel warm, as if I'm giving him my heat. As if it's enough for the both of us. Again, the way his mouth curves makes me want to cry. "I don't know what this is."

The admission sounds torn from him. I can hear it. I can feel it. I just *know* it.

But I don't want it. That's what I tell myself.

"What this is," I say with as much bravado as I can summon, "is over, because I have to go sling coffee in a drive-through shack on Stage Road—"

Ariel shifts. He sighs a little, then strokes my temples.

It's then that I realize there are lingering bits of a headache remaining, and he's soothing them away. Stroking the sides of my face as if he knows exactly where to touch me to make all the pain simply . . . disappear.

"You are an oracle," he tells me. "And oracles are not built to keep their visions to themselves. It's time to share what you've seen, Winter. What you know."

I can feel the truth of what he's saying. It pulls at me, but I don't want to go there. I can't bear how *real* this feels, and if I feel terror in his presence at last, it's not because of what he might *do* to me.

It's because of how he makes me feel already when he's barely done anything at all. When he's protected me. When he's cared for me. When he has at no point tossed me in the dungeons I know all too well he has at the ready.

But I don't have it in me to worry about Augie right now, not when I am *bound* by blood to a vampire king and an ancient goddess left her shit *in me* and I have no idea what any of this means or what it makes me—

I take a breath.

Part of me would prefer all of this to be one big mind game. That way, everything I'm feeling would be fake and I could happily move on, secure in the knowledge that he never *really* got to me and I never *really* felt like I might—

I refuse to admit it, even to myself.

"The only thing I see is my paycheck disappearing if I don't get to work," I begin, because the coffee stand is just about the only normal thing I have left, the last relic remaining from life before monsters.

I need it.

But Ariel leans forward then and presses his hard, cruel, beautiful mouth to mine.

He kisses me like I am something precious to him.

And he sets the whole world on fire.

21.

Burning alive feels better than it should.

I can feel flame lick over every part of me, curling deep into my legs, igniting me inside and out.

Ariel keeps kissing me, slow and sure. When I try to make it more intense, when I try to go deeper and wilder, he doesn't let me.

He cups his hands around my face and holds me there, making us both marinate in the way our mouths fuse together and the demands I try to make that he meets, parries, then ignores. He continues to do precisely as he pleases.

And what he pleases is this kiss.

Is it one kiss or is it a thousand? Is it one long, complicated, life-altering kiss—or one after the next, on and on into a raw, hot, dizzying infinity?

I don't know when I let go of the blanket, but soon enough I'm pressing the whole of my body against his.

Needy. Insistent. Desperate.

My arms wrap around his back and my fingers press deep into his cold muscles as he moves, ripples, stretches. By now I could trace that phoenix tattoo of his from memory, and I do.

He pulls away, looking down at me with his silver eyes gleaming bright.

So bright it makes me shiver.

Or . . . shiver even more.

"A phoenix tattoo for a vampire is practically a cliché," he says, and I realize that note I don't recognize in his voice is warmth. Maybe even amusement. "What about you, little seer? How many lives have you lived that you require a phoenix to mark them all?"

My mouth feels bruised, but it's the kind of ache I want to lean into. I let my hands move down that sculpted back of his and run my palms over the marble flare of his buttocks, his powerful thighs.

"I think I'm on at least my third life," I tell him, and there's a teasing note in my voice, though I'm not kidding at all. I'm matching him. "There is the life I had before my mother and father left. There is the life we all had before the Reveal. And I don't know what you did to me last night, but I don't feel the same, so maybe this is a new life too."

"I told you what I did."

His voice sounds almost harsh now, but there's something about the way he looks at me that makes me think it's something more than that. That it's that deep, unfathomable feeling that echoes in me, too. I just . . . know it.

I have the strangest certainty that it works in me, too.

As if we feel the same, this immortal vampire and me.

Then again, what we do feels like *this*.

This wildfire with no beginning and no end. This shattering that only goes on and on and on. Of all the things he's said to me, all the games he's played since we met, I take this as truth.

He never expected to feel the things he does when he's with me.

This makes me feel bold. I step back but grip his wrists as I go and then tug him with me, away from the window and deeper into the room. He lets me do it. He lets me move him across his own floor and then push him back down on his own bed.

Then I stand there before him, stripped naked, bathed by his hands, made new.

I have the strangest thought. That this is a kind of baptism. That there is something holy in his gaze, something sacred in the space between us.

I shouldn't let this happen. I open my mouth to slap it back, the growing intensity between us, but I don't.

The words sit there on my tongue, unspoken.

Worse, I let them.

Instead of defusing this, I move toward him. I put my knee on the mattress and crawl up his body to press my mouth to the place where a pulse would be if he lived, there at the base of his neck. I suck a little on the spot I find, the place where my own pulse thunders, until he makes a sound like breath.

But it's only *like* breath.

He pulls me over him and settles me on his lap. We stay like that for another eternity or two, me sprawled over him so I can rock myself gently against the thick shaft of his cock and drive myself quietly—or maybe not so quietly—over the edge.

Still, I know, with a kind of dawning awareness that feels like a revelation, that we are no longer playing games. That the games we've been playing all this time, little as they may have done their job, are over now.

That all of this is new territory.

I've dared him to fuck me more times than I can count. He's responded by making certain that the things we do get us both off, but me significantly more than him.

These have all been power games. I understood this the whole time and still presented myself before him every night.

I was beginning to think that playing such games was no more and no less than what vampires *do*. That they don't have it in them to simply *have sex*.

Now I'm beginning to understand, by the way he holds me, that I've been wrong about that, too.

I feel as if I'm hovering on the edge of another understanding. Something glimmering. Something made up of white-hot heat and that stark emotion I don't want to read all over his face.

It isn't that this is without power. His stern hands are all over my body. The way he moves me up and down against the thick shaft of his cock—always so close and yet not quite there—is hypnotic. Only hotter.

Especially when, with the rain outside and a different storm within, he lifts me higher than before. And then lowers me, shifting the angle so he can notch the thick head of his cock in the entrance to my pussy at last.

I must make a noise, because he freezes. Or maybe time simply slows like that.

There's nothing between us now. There's nothing holding us apart. It's like he's daring me to understand what's happening, on all the levels it's happening. As if he's daring me to acknowledge what this is.

What I think to myself is that I will never be the same.

Yet right at this moment, arched up above him with his hands tight around my hips, I don't *want* to be the same.

I want this.

I want *him*, no matter how dangerous this is.

I want this new thing we're becoming more than I want any of the things I've lost. Even though I suspect that later, I will find that shameful.

Right now, I understand that I'm poised on the verge of yet another brand-new life.

And he's a vampire, through and through. He's cold, immortal, and he will wait forever for me to beg him. To *invite him*.

To sign myself up for my own ice-cold immolation.

"Please, Ariel," I whisper. "Please. You told me I would beg, and this is me. Begging. *Please.*"

He mutters something in a language that sounds old and foreign, or possibly the words to a spell, and then he smiles.

It's like its own explosion inside me, that smile. It's a marvel. It's terrible. It's like nothing I've seen on his face before. It fills me up inside until I am full to bursting—

And then he simply slams me down on his cock.

I shatter completely.

The person I wanted to be, the person I remember being once, is gone that easily. That fast.

I feel the orgasm in my fingertips and my toes. There's nothing sweet or soft about it, no lovely uncurling or breaking waves.

It's as close to violence as an orgasm can get.

And I love it.

He keeps moving my hips, kissing me as he shifts me against him. He uses me like some kind of fuck toy on his own cock, and I reward him by screaming.

Whether for *mercy* or *more* I can't tell.

I'm limp in his grasp, his cock so deep and so wide, a near unbearable intensity inside of me. He is holding me up and his grip feels like iron, so what I do is arch back. I let my arms go wide, my head falling back while my breasts graze the hard sculpture of his chest.

His cock is enormous. I've had it in my mouth, and halfway down my throat. I've ridden it from all sides. I've had his thick cock head butt up against my clit over and over, and all of that pales into insignificance next to this.

I can't believe how deep he goes, how much he fills me. Every thrust is like the first. Every time, it seems as if I'm too small, too tight, too shallow—

But he makes room.

If it were anyone else with a cock like that, there would be no possible way. It would take forever for him to work his way inside.

Luckily, even thinking about Ariel makes me wet.

Near him, I'm hovering on the verge of an orgasm all the time. I woke up halfway there, even though I nearly died last night.

My body wants him. Constantly. This must be why it works like this. There's no pain, only an intensity of sensation. It feels so good that I want to believe this has to be some kind of magic. Some vampire trick.

If it is, I don't care. I want him to trick me forever.

His hands move from my hips to grip my ass, then he's rolling us with a speed that is itself a kind of spellbinding. I hold my breath, and then he's moving over me in the bed, his cock deep inside my body.

Then he sits back, kneeling up and shifting my legs so that they hang around his neck.

"Acrobatic," I manage to pant out.

"The trouble is that I dreamed about this for far too long," he tells me, his voice rough and his gaze bright. "In a thousand different positions."

He pulls out and then thrusts in hard and I come again—a long, hard ripple of delirious greed and heat.

He does this again and again, and when I'm incapable of more than a few wild sounds, he flips me over. Face down on the bed, I can feel him crawl down the length of me.

Leaving a trail of bite marks as he goes.

My breasts are pressed into the bed, so when he slides his hand beneath my belly to lift up my hips so he can slam into me from behind, the abrasion against my nipples skyrockets me right back up into that quivering *almost*—

He stays behind me like that for a while. He's so big and so *hard*. His perfect body is all over mine, one hand between me and the bed. And he plays with my clit until I'm screaming once again.

But he still won't let himself come.

"Why are you holding back?" I manage to ask him, though it feels like work to speak. To form words and let them out.

"Because I want everything," he tells me, his voice so intense that a bolt of *something* moves through me, cold and hot at once.

Once again, being with this man is an education. Things I didn't know my body could do. Things I would have said couldn't possibly feel good. It can and they do, and he never has the slightest doubt.

I think to myself what a marvel it is to be with someone who knows bodies *this well*. Who knows exactly where to stroke and when to press. When to be slow and when to go hard and fast. Someone who has done everything, and well, and at a volume so high it's dizzying to contemplate.

Even if, at a conservative estimate, he had one lover a year. Or even every ten years.

Thinking of all the bodies he must have touched and tasted, tempted and torn apart, sends me off into another orgasm so hard and so long that I almost think it might kill me.

That maybe it does.

The rain is beating against the windowpanes. Inside, the room stays shadowy and cool, but I am the inferno he's made me. Every time he does something new, I let off enough heat to ward off the coming winter.

I don't know how many lifetimes come and go before I find him rolling me over once more. I can still feel the pulse of that last orgasm throbbing in my earlobes. The tip of my tongue. My eyelids.

Ariel gathers me to him and pulls me over his lap once more, my back to his chest. He settles me, and I feel the press of his cock against my back, hot now because he's been inside me.

Then he lifts me high and lowers me to thrust in deep once more.

I let out a groan. My head falls back of its own accord. He has one arm around my abdomen, holding me in place, and once again I think that if this was anyone else or any other scenario, this would be nothing but awkward.

With him, however, I am boneless. It's the easiest thing in the world to simply tip myself back into his arms and shift to get as much of his cock inside me as possible.

Because the moment he moves, it doesn't matter what position I'm in.

All there is here, in this room and across our ruined little world, is our own wildfire. The one we keep fueling and building until it blazes up to the sky.

This time, he moves differently. I feel his mouth on my neck.

"You need my blood?" I ask. I don't even know where the question comes from. My voice doesn't sound like mine, it's so hoarse and rough. "You can have it."

"I accept your invitation," he says, and it's that formal language that shivers through me, a key into a lock.

I whisper his name, not certain if it's a curse or a prayer.

"I do not *need* your blood, little seer." His voice is a low murmur against the skin of my neck. He's on the other side from last night, and when I raise a boneless hand to feel my scar, it's gone. "But I will take it. And I will give you some of mine in return."

"Do I need it?" I ask. Not that it matters, because I want it.

I can already taste it, rich on my tongue.

"Oracles are meant to interpret signs the deities put out, not to speak with them directly. Oracles are mostly human. Very breakable, in other words."

Ariel licks my neck, his cock still so enormous and hard inside of me. I can feel another orgasm lurking, curling toward me, and when the hand on my abdomen moves lower and presses there, just at the top of my pussy, it takes everything I have to hold it off.

I don't even know why I try.

"I don't want to be a vampire," I tell him.

"I don't want you to be a vampire," he replies, as if what I said is amusing. "But I need you a little less breakable, Winter. I healed you. Now I want you tougher."

"So I can tell you things I see in visions."

I'm just saying stuff. It's hard to really think beyond his fingers playing with my clit, that hard and heavy cock like marble so deep inside of me, and his mouth on my neck.

He grips my chin with his free hand and swivels my face until I'm looking straight at him.

"So that you *live*, Winter," he says forbiddingly. "Through whatever comes."

Like he's affronted I don't get that.

It makes a new kind of sensation wind its way through me, until I wonder if I'm ever going to breathe right again.

"Ariel . . ." I whisper.

"It is the only thing I must insist upon." His voice is dark even though his eyes glow. "You must live."

Then, hiding nothing, he tips his head back and I watch as his fangs elongate. They are sharp and long. Terrifying.

Yet I want to lick them.

He is a monster, and he's making sure I see his true face. Not just his marble beauty but this, the reality of him.

I should scream.

And I do, but only because another orgasm slams into me, like a punch.

Even as I'm shaking my way into it, I watch him lower his head. I assume he's going to slam those fangs deep into my neck.

And there must be something wrong with me, because I want him to.

I want to feel those fangs deep in my body, so he's penetrating me in as many ways as he can.

But he doesn't bite me. He bites himself, ripping open the inside of his own wrist.

"This time when you come, I will come too," he tells me with a stern certainty that has my clit throbbing. "And this time, you will not pass out the way you did again and again last night."

"Did we have sex last night?" I'm outraged at the idea, fighting to get my breath back so I can truly be furious about this unbelievably intense and stunning thing happening and me somehow missing it—

"Don't be ridiculous." His voice is so dark. His gaze is so *hot*.

He doesn't say, *You would know.*

I would know.

"Ariel," I say again, but my gaze is on the place where his blood wells in the cut he's made on the inside of his wrist. "Ariel, please. *Please*—"

His silver eyes flash like a thunderstorm.

I feel it inside me, that high wind and the sudden shock of cold.

His cock seems to swell as he presses his wrist to my lips.

I taste flesh and copper, and I have the split-second urge to recoil, but then the flavor hits me.

Rich and textured. Coppery, yes, but layered with complicated notes of spice and wonder, something like rosemary, and him.

All him.

Ariel's cock seems larger still, pressing against the walls of my pussy to make the already astonishing sensation that much *more*. That much wilder, that much more impossible, that much more astonishingly *good*, like my body was made entirely for him to play with as he pleases—

I can't *say* please, so I suck on his wrist even harder, circling my hips to work his cock even deeper into me.

He lowers his head and opens his mouth wide against my neck. Then he bites down, sinking those fangs deep into my skin the same way he slammed his cock into my body.

So hard and so deep it ought to split me in half.

22.

The pain is astonishing, a sucker punch—

But this is also the moment when he begins to move inside me, that huge cock finding every sensitive part of me and setting it on fire.

It's not fast, it's deliberate. It's slow, deep, and sure.

I drink him in. He drinks me too, and it's a different kind of spell. A wildfire alchemy made more intense by how deep inside me he is.

I feel my entire body . . . shift.

Not my bones and my ligaments, no thunderclap into a wolf form. This is something else. Something deeper.

Something I might call my soul, if I believed in things like that.

I feel as if I'm flying, soaring somewhere high in a clear sky, and it's all blood and sex, hunger and joy.

A joy so intense it actually hurts, but not enough to stop.

A deep, hard joy I've never experienced before.

I feel him go harder and tighter, this stone statue of a beautiful man. I feel him clench me tighter and bite down harder, and I want to cry out in the mad whirl and wild *joy* of this.

Instead, I suck harder on his wrist, like I want to consume him the way he's devouring me.

Not *like* I do. I do.

If I could, I would bite him too.

He stiffens, then comes. In a flood so cold it almost feels scalding.

As he lets himself go, I feel the mark he left on my back light up. I feel certain that if I were to look, I would see myself glowing.

I think, *No wonder everyone knew. They could see exactly what he did.*

Right now it feels like a different, better, dirtier tattoo.

He pours himself into me. On and on he goes, and as he does, it triggers something that I understand on some level is another orgasm.

But this one is different.

This one feels like I'm suddenly taking flight.

For real this time.

I soar high, up and up into the cosmos. I am part of the stars and the Milky Way itself, a whirl of planets and asteroids and mysteries that feel both entirely beyond me and a part of me in ways I never understood before.

I grow. I expand. I am everything all at once, I know every atom and every speck of it all, and every last part of it is as simple and as wondrous as me, too.

I want to ride this forever. It feels like I do.

And then everything changes.

I'm no longer a body. Or I am so far removed from mine that it's like I've lost my way back. I'm no longer me at all, even though, somehow, I'm more me than I've ever been.

There's a part of me, some little bit of consciousness, that can still feel that enormous vampire cock lodged deep inside my mortal body far below.

I know that Ariel is the reason why this is happening.

Or it is more accurate to say that I'm *aware* of him and the fact he's made this happen, if deeply uninterested in it at the moment. Immortal or not, he is still only a man.

Meanwhile, I am made of galaxies old and new, dancing to and fro. Solar systems glide in and around me.

I feel no draw to ever go back. No need to ever return to the confines of blood and bone and all that useless flesh.

I am made of stars. I am kin to the moon. There are tides at my disposal, and in my fingertips I feel the pulsing power of too many lives to count, mine to play with as if they are nothing but random little thoughts.

Thoughts that scry across my consciousness and disappear as easily, leaving no ripples behind, no rearranging of the universe, no sign they ever were.

What I crave is an immensity, a life so large it can never be taken without planets collapsing all around it, like bowling pins, like scattering insects, all consciousness and matter an afterthought next to my incomprehensible glory—

Wait, some small voice inside me protests, sounding tinny and far away. *That's not me. That's not who I am at all—*

And when I turn, I see her.

I *behold* her.

She is wondrous and fearsome beyond measure.

One moment the universe is only me. Then she is there, and she puts me and my universe to shame. I am instantly aware that I am nothing more than the head of a discarded pin she cannot be bothered to pick up.

That is how small and insignificant I am.

She changes as I look at her, too vast to settle on one thing. One face. One enormity.

Instead, I see a flicker of a woman, round and fertile, her features a complicated mix of deep beauty one moment . . . then something slithery and rotten the next.

And I know her.

She has been in my nightmares for a long time. Last night she stopped being a nightmare and became something else, something that very nearly killed me on Mount McLoughlin.

I am in the presence of the Goddess of Filth, the death goddess of old, at last.

Vinča, I think. But I am an immensity all my own, however puny next to her. Maybe I make my tiny heavens shake with such a thought. Maybe I roar her name until new constellations form.

Here, it is all the same.

There's another flicker and then she has a new head, this time that of some kind of bird. A bird of prey, I know without having to ask, or having ever seen something like it before—because I have felt what this bird can do. It has rent me apart more times than I can count, night after night. There's that long, malicious-looking beak and that round body of hers wrapped in something that looks like feathers, with a glossy sheen on the wing tips. As if she is made of colors so impossible and blinding that my mind can't process them or even identify them.

Yet I understand at the same time that none of this is the truth of her.

I'm seeing only what little I can comprehend.

My mortal eyes might imagine themselves whole universes, but in the end, it's simply the blissed-out and blood-high eyes of a twenty-five-year-old barista who might have let herself be eaten whole by a vampire king.

I can't be expected to approach the vastness of who she is. That part is abundantly clear.

And yet . . .

"Hey, Vinča," I say. "Nice to finally meet you."

I think of that woman on the altar in those cold, high woods. I think of that bloody-toothed smile and the way she gripped my hands too hard. Much too hard.

How she looked for a moment as if she were laughing.

I felt this—*her*, Vinča, this immensity before me—then. She brushed me, and the world went dark.

I understand immediately what Ariel was trying to tell me.

It was *supposed* to kill me.

They lured me there to crush me like the bug I am to them. To her.

"You should be dead," says this creature, this magnificent and hideous *idea* too huge to be contained in a normal body. What bones or flesh could hold her?

I realize the word I'm looking for is "goddess."

I've never had occasion to think about what a god *means* before. How a god *feels* when it is standing before you, as capable of erasing the totality of your existence—and all existence—as it is in creating new galaxies to orbit the ones it's already wrecked.

Even thinking these things in the expansive form I'm in hurts me. It makes my head pound—a lot like it did on the mountain last night.

When she speaks, it's as if the voice rings out from inside my own bones. If she has a mouth at all, I cannot see it move.

"Why are you not dead?" she asks. Demands, more like.

"I'm not sure that I'm *not* dead," I manage to reply.

She moves toward me, and I have the sense then that I'm not so much out among the stars any longer. I am in a different sort of enclosed space. It's another prison, a dungeon without walls.

Yet I also have the distinct impression that I'm standing in a temple.

Her temple.

"You dare to speak to me like this?" comes the voice, from everywhere. From inside me. "You should not dare to speak to me at all. Oracles come to me with humility, cutting their own throats and waiting upon my pleasure to see if I might let them live."

"Tempting," I choke out, overwhelm like a thick lump in my throat. "Really."

"You will scream it soon enough," comes that terrible voice, swelling up inside me like the urge to be sick. Like every nightmare I've had of her already, combined. "It will be the only prayer you know, for mine is a worship that requires total and complete attention. If there is one morsel of food before you and it will rot if you do not eat it immediately, you should cast it aside. Better to sing my praises and wait upon my mercy."

I swallow hard, tamping down that rising horror inside. "I'm sure you will understand if I suspect that your mercy is a bit out of reach."

What with the trying to kill me and all.

I don't say that part, but I feel as if she hears it anyway.

"You can think of me as fate," the voice tells me. In front of me, all around me, possibly even inside me, she flickers back and forth between visages. Until it is all rotted beak, slick feathers, and a terrible goddess who makes the bones she is speaking through—the ones inside my own limbs—so brittle and sharp that I worry that if I tremble, they will crack and crumble into dust.

I understand then that if Ariel was not pouring his blood into me, I would not survive this encounter.

I'm not meant to live through this. Vinča is about death, not life.

I try to pull myself together to make the most of this meeting. I think about all the scraps of things I've heard about this goddess, locks and keys, and all the rest.

"You are coming." I try to pronounce that with some drama, the way Gran did. The way it echoes inside me. "That's what I keep hearing. I believe my grandmother saw it herself."

"Soon I will rise," she agrees. Her head moves to an unnatural angle, and I feel as if that long, pointed beak is pressed hard against my solar plexus. And she digs it in, all without touching me. "I will rise, and when I do, this world you consider ruined will be my playground. I will feast. I will play. Immortals will worship before me, mortals will cower, and I will kill them all as I please. I will build this world in my image, as I have always meant to do."

It's difficult to know where I am in a space that feels like death on all sides, a 360-degree sphere of that same intensifying horror. It grows and grows. I remind myself that it doesn't matter where *I* am. It matters where *she* is.

I do my best. "Where are you now? Where have you been all this time?"

"I have been looking out through the eyes of the faithful for a very long time." She flickers into the sacrificed woman's face, but it's wormy and foul. "I have ordered them to find me, and time and again, they have failed."

Another flicker, and there is something malevolent staring out at me from behind that dark beak. I don't ask what became of those who failed her. I figure I can guess, and I definitely don't want any details.

"There was a priest, in the old days. He was meant to protect me, but he did not." Again, I see things on her face and in it as she shifts between them all, things I already wish I could scrub out of my head. "He brought in his sorcerer to cast nasty little spells. The last thing I did before they sunk me in my hole and locked me up tight was to make sure that every follower I ever had, any of my faithful, need only look upon him and know him. Then tear him to pieces, with their own dull fingernails if necessary."

She drip-feeds images to me as she tells me these things, so that instead of making some quip about dull fingernails versus a set of sharp knives, I can see it. I see shadowy images of people dressed in styles of clothing I can't make sense of, converging on a single man. I see a pack of them all over him, grunting in satisfaction as he screams. Shoving their hands against him to bruise him, then digging their way into him with their bare hands. Tearing him apart by the fistful, tossing chunks of flesh and gristle to the dark earth.

I want to throw up.

I'm not sure how I don't.

"Your fate will be similar," Vinča tells me. I feel her beak against one temple. I feel her smile, terrible and vast, against the nape of my neck. "You dare to defy me, tiny human? It will not bode well for you. I will see you torn into pieces, shredded and peeled, and I will make certain that you live through most of it."

It's hard to swallow. It actually hurts, but it's that or start puking. "I don't think I deserve that. I don't know anything. I'm supposed to see futures, but you're the past."

"You smell like night leeches and wolves who cheat the moon," she tells me, that sickening swell of her words from inside my own body. "It is only a matter of time before I rise. The steps have already been taken. Only one lock remains. When the chains fall, you will know my wrath. I will make sure of it."

"Tell me where you are and I will tend to you sooner," I tell her.

I feel something hit me, but I don't know if it's merely the force of her or some separate blow.

Once again, I'm entirely too aware that even here, on some astral plane, or whatever the hell this is, she would kill me easily if it weren't for Ariel. That it is his borrowed power, his immortal blood, that is making this possible.

Another blow slams into me, and though I waver and feel weak, I'm still here. In one piece. In whatever strange space this is.

With Vinča the killer death goddess.

"They sunk me deep into the earth so that no one would ever find me," comes her hideous voice, inevitable and corrosive, like hot oil choking me from the inside out. "But faith always seeks its own level."

She laughs then, a terrible wind. And then she is a new storm that howls and destroys, sucking in stars and planets as she swirls all around me. I can feel death pressing in. I can feel the history and the sweep of centuries, all of it a kind of cyclone that leaves me off-balance and fighting to keep my footing as she rages on and on.

There's a scream inside me. There's that searing pain in my head. My poor bones shake and rattle, and I don't know how they don't snap.

Until, at last, she's there before me. "I will rise," comes that voice, tearing through me.

I can hear it inside me. I can see it on all of her faces at once, a terrible rippling all over her as if she's about to explode.

Then she does, straight at me—

23.

I wake up in Ariel's arms.

I move carefully, gingerly, not sure whether or not I really did break my bones. Or possibly ingested whatever she was, like a deified chemical spill. I expect to feel fuzzy and hungover again at the very least, but I don't.

On the contrary, I feel remarkably clear.

Even good.

I move to sit up, but Ariel's big hand moves to the back of my neck. There's not much I can do to keep him from swinging my gaze to his.

Maybe I don't try.

Our eyes meet. They hold.

I can feel every single thing that's ever happened between us. The depth of his cock inside me. The taste of his blood.

How very much I wanted him to sink those fangs into my neck.

How much I still do.

"What did you do to me this time?" I ask.

"Last time, I healed you," he says, and he sounds faintly reproving. "By now you must realize that you would have died if you looked upon a being like Vinča without any interventions. She likes killing. She has managed, for centuries, to maintain a small but highly motivated cult of diehards who are only too happy to murder in her name. But she really does prefer to do it herself. She's always had a grandiose idea of her own greatness."

"You know her," I say, following a hunch that comes over me in a rush. Then again, I'm the oracle. Maybe it's not a *hunch*. "Personally, I mean."

His silver gaze is brighter than before. I can feel it everywhere. "If you're asking if I fucked an ancient death goddess, I did. She wanted a pet vampire and picked me for the role, thinking she could control me because I was new. Only a few hundred years old. She was wrong."

My imagination is too vivid for this. I can conjure up entirely too many scenarios to fit in and around what few words he actually said. I can come up with timelines and storylines and entire bedroom scenes between a vampire and that long-beaked horror—

This is not healthy. I know this is nothing close to healthy.

More importantly, I have other things to do.

"I have to go," I tell him.

And I do. I can feel it like an itch, deep in these bones of mine that she tried so hard to snap. I have to find some kind of touchstone, something as close to normal as I can in all of this, or I'm not going to make it.

But he still hasn't told me what he did to me this time.

Maybe that's written all over my face, because one of his brows lifts, as if he needs to look *more* arrogant. "I gave you some armor, that's all. You're not undead. You are not precisely mortal any longer, not in the way most humans are. You can be killed, but it will take effort. Even for her."

"I don't know if I should thank you for that or not."

He moves so fast I don't even see it. I only really know that he does it after the fact, when my brain tries to reconstruct the split second it took for him to go from lying down on his back to crouching over me, holding my face between his hands.

While my body tries to convince me that what I should do is melt against him, *I* try to convince myself I should be mad at him.

"If I hadn't done it, you would have died." He growls this at me, his eyes dark the way they were on Mount McLoughlin. "For the second or third time now. I can't have that. I told you, Winter. I need you alive."

"Everyone needs me alive. For their own purposes. I get it."

"I don't think that you do," Ariel says, his voice little more than a dark thread.

And his kiss lights me on fire all over again, but this time, I'm the one who pulls away.

I think of immensities and galaxies. I think of Augie.

"I didn't ask for this," I grit out at him. "I didn't ask for any of this. Not you, not a sorceress and a werewolf playing games on my land, not the entire fucking Reveal in the first place—*none of this*. But I'm handling it. What I need from you—"

"Do you truly believe that I don't know what you need by now?"

"I'm not talking about sex."

I move away from him and see the glint of gold on the simple nightstand beside his bed. Augie's medallion. I don't want to touch it. I feel actively repelled by it, actually—

But I tell myself that's just shame. That I'm embarrassed—as I should be—because I certainly understand my twin's vampire blood thing now, don't I? I took a deep dive into it and didn't exactly come away with the desire to be a teetotaler.

I feel like a fraud.

I make myself scoop up the necklace and drop the chain over my neck, and it feels like a harder blow than it should when the medallion thuds against my chest.

Ariel scowls at the sight of it. "As if anything that's happened between us is as simple as sex. That's not the kind of need I mean."

The tide that rises in me at that statement, not to mention the look on his face, terrifies me in a completely different way than death goddesses and monsters do. I lean into the temper that hurries along after it instead. I lean in hard.

"If you had the slightest idea what I need," I bite out at him, "my twin brother would not be languishing in a cold, damp *dungeon,* forced to feed from a vampire bitch with a chain around his ankle." That feels both good and terrible to say. It feels risky. But I keep going. "You've been holding him over my head since you demanded I come see you in the first place. I thought he was dead, Ariel. Actually, permanently dead, not whatever dead means to you. That's what families of addicts do. We assume they're dead and pray they're clean while you just *use it*—"

I cut myself off. The medallion is in my fist, and that's where Ariel is staring.

I didn't mean to say any of that. It doesn't feel like I'm telling him anything he needs to know. It feels like guilt—mine, for wasting time with him that isn't actually rescuing Augie, not that I could do that without him anyway.

It feels like I'm baring my neck and my soft belly and daring him to sink his fangs in deep.

And not in a fun way.

I can still taste the layers of his blood on my tongue. The complexities of his kiss.

I am bright with shame and disaster.

"I have to go," I tell him when he raises his gaze, very slowly, from that medallion to me. "There are things that have to be done, and we don't have much time."

"You sound like her," he says, in a very measured tone that I find I don't like at all. "I tried to tell her that she had all the time in the world, that being the curse of eternity. But she could never hear it."

I drop my hand from the medallion. I decide that, actually, I don't want to imagine Ariel with that bird-faced goddess. I certainly don't want him to fill me in on how things went for them, way back when.

I might have more masochistic tendencies than I thought I did, and I certainly proved that last night, but it turns out I have a line after all.

"I'm going to take a shower," I tell him, and I try my best to match that measured tone he seems to use so easily. "I live with a werewolf, in case you missed that. I don't need to smell more like you than I already do."

That's not even getting into whatever the sorceress and the other oracle—*Gran*—might know, simply by looking at me. Or reading my aura. Or whatever it is either one of them does.

Something is changed now. I can feel his power all around me, as always, but it's like I'm inside of it now. Not like it's pressing into me, but like it's part of me. Or I'm a part of it.

It's different, and it feels intimate.

Too intimate.

If I think about it too closely, I can feel that tide start to rise inside of me again, and it's already too big, too unwieldy. Too fucking intimate to bear.

But if I think about naming it—really looking at it and calling it what it is—I think it might take me down to my knees. So hard I won't get up again.

I can't let that happen.

I walk across his bedroom, let myself into his bathroom, and stay in his marvelously expansive shower until I'm a pickle.

When I get out, I use one of his absurdly fancy towels that feels like a cloud against my skin. I look at myself in the clearly unnecessary mirror—here in a vampire's lair—and turn so I can see my ass and a swath of my back.

Obviously I don't *actually* expect to see anything.

But I do.

His mark is all over me. It looks like gold.

Like he has made me something precious, and the gold not only gleams, it holds me. Like he gave me a place to rest and—

"You have to stop," I order myself in a voice that's barely above a whisper.

I come out of the bathroom expecting to have to fight him some more, but he's not in the bedroom. My clothes are, though—washed clean of blood and dirt and laid out on his nicely made bed, and I spend a lot longer than necessary thinking through his domestic arrangements.

Do vampires do their own laundry? Is this just that magic he seems to use as he pleases? Does he actually *make his own bed*—but if not, does that mean there are invisible servants scuttling around in here?

Obviously, I'm putting off having to face him.

When he was kind enough to lay out all my weapons, too, arranged next to my clothes in a way that makes it clear he knows exactly where and how I wear them all.

Even though I never wear them here.

For no reason at all that I choose to entertain or acknowledge, that makes me want to cry.

Instead of indulging such a strange and dangerously soft urge, I dress quickly and make myself walk out into his living room, where I find the vampire king lounging in a chair in a gloomy room with only a small lamp switched on beside him and a book in his hands that I can't identify. When he sets it aside to look at me, I see that it's in a foreign language. It makes me wonder how many he speaks, but I don't ask.

I remind myself that I'm not building a relationship here. I'm not *getting to know* him.

I'm negotiating my brother's release and, apparently, I'm neck-deep in saving the world that I don't even like that much from a beaked bitch who wants to make it even worse.

If I tell myself that enough, maybe it will make that soft part inside me that feels the gold of his mark and wants to *know him* settle down.

"I'm calling a meeting," I tell him. "Tonight, sundown. My house."

"Are you asking me on a date?" he asks sardonically.

Or I think he's being sardonic. I don't want to think what else he could be, sounding intense like that.

I belt out a laugh. It's too loud, too telling. "You wish."

I don't know what makes me say that, but the moment I do, I can feel electricity crackle between us. I think that he probably does wish we were going on a date.

If I'm honest, though, so do I.

I expected to feel better once I put on my clothes and strapped all my weapons into place. *Me again,* I want to think. That's what I want—desperately—to feel.

I really don't.

"I want all three big powers in this valley at this meeting," I tell him. "I'm going to talk about your adorable and not-at-all-apocalyptic ex, and I'm only going to do it once."

His eyes take on a darker sort of gleam then, and the silver only emphasizes it. "Will you order us all around now? Do you imagine this will get you what you want?"

"Nothing has yet." I say that with entirely too much bitterness for someone who wants to avoid feeling anything. "I have to assume nothing ever will. So I guess that means I might as well do what I know I need to do instead and stop worrying about it."

I don't know what I expect from him. Speeches. Impassioned monologues. Another rush of movement, then him suddenly holding me when, moments ago, he was across the room—

Nothing happens.

Whatever I expect, all he does is study me as if he can see every single star I encountered out there—every last galaxy, comet, and constellation. And while I can see a complicated kaleidoscope of what I'm pretty sure is emotion in his gaze, all he does is nod.

"Sundown," he agrees.

It's not until I make it down from his apartment and out to the parking lot behind the MMA school that I remember. I didn't actually come here last night.

I didn't drive here, I mean.

I blow out a breath, and then Ariel is there at my shoulder.

Annoying vampire tricks, I think crossly, when the real truth is that I'm relieved to see him. Again. I'm something a little too close to pleased that he followed me out here.

That he remembered I didn't drive here when I didn't.

That he cares—

I stop myself right there.

"Would you like me to take you home?" he asks in such a calm way that it makes me want to scream.

I have to clear my throat so that I don't.

"Yes, thank you." I say this so politely it hurts.

The rain is coming down all around us, all over us. I must be soaking wet, though I hardly notice. Or maybe what I mean is that I don't care.

Ariel's gaze is too silver to bear, and I can feel his power all around me while what I remember is his bite and his cock and all the ways he made me come apart—I remember every single touch, every single shift of his body and mine—and I go to lift my hand.

Like maybe I want to reach over and put my hand on him, all that marble and power.

His lips nearly curve. Not quite. The rain is relentless. And all he does is reach over and brush his cool, hard thumb over my lips.

Once. Again.

Then, in a flash, I'm standing on my own doorstep.

I'm there on the porch, and Ariel is nowhere to be seen.

I'm wet. It's cold. I could go inside and get warm, and even though I frown at the door as if I might do just that, I don't. I dig in my pockets for my keys and go to my truck instead. I start the engine and am halfway down the drive before I realize that I didn't spend a single second looking around the yard.

Because I don't want to see my usually powerful tenants? A werewolf queen, a fucking sorceress, and whatever the hell Briar is—a born-again goth? Or because I'm afraid that what I actually want is to go to them and tell them everything that's happened to me since I last saw them, like we're *girlfriends* on one of those old sitcoms?

I don't know. Instead of worrying over it, I sneak around the side of the house and put my ear to Gran's window. When I hear her snoring, I know she's okay, so I drive down to Jacksonville and then up over the next hill on Stage Road, making my way out to the coffee stand. When I pull up, there's no one around, and I have a terrible, sinking feeling—

But then Birdie appears at the drive-up window and laughs when she sees me.

"I got here at ten," she tells me. "And people were *het up*. There was a crowd, recriminations aplenty, and *several* claw marks on the back door."

"I hiked McLoughlin yesterday," I tell her. "I don't know what I was thinking, but I slept in."

"I hiked McLoughlin once," she says. "It sucked, and not only because I was pretending I might be straight. Don't do that again."

I think of those cloaked figures in the clearing, the rise and fall of those terrible blades. That laughing, bloody mouth that sucked me in and wanted me dead.

"I won't," I promise her. "But I did want to check in here and make sure the stand was still . . ."

"Standing?" She laughs again. "Barely. There was a weird message when I got in, though."

She ducks back behind the counter and comes out with a piece of paper, then passes it out to me through the window. "Supposedly from good old Doug. Who I, personally, haven't laid eyes on in a very long time."

"Not since May," I agree. "I only remember because he was here talking about *managerial training* like we have to worry about corporate dropping by and then made a May the Fourth joke."

"Hey, as long as we get paid, right?" Birdie sighs a little, but what else is there to say? Disappearances rarely have happy endings. That was true back in the before times too. "Just don't make me have to step up and manage this place. I shirk responsibility as a matter of course. The best part of the Reveal is that no one's around to lecture me on my wasted potential."

I don't think she's serious, having known her all our lives, but I don't challenge her. I frown at the message instead.

It doesn't really make sense. There's something about protected space and how we should all prepare ourselves for new hours.

"I guess we wait and see what the new hours are," I say, shrugging.

"Living the dream," Birdie replies with fake cheer.

But she also hands me my paycheck, so when I wave goodbye to her, I drive back into Jacksonville and park in front of the historic old bank.

I might recently have been bigger than the galaxy, a goddess in scope if not ambition, but there are still small, venal men and their pet goons who need their money. Somehow I doubt Franklin Hendry will care that I had a face-to-face with a vicious death goddess out on an astral plane. I doubt he would even know what those words mean.

I get out of my truck and dash for the bank's door, because it's still pouring—something I'll have to chat with Savi about—and wish I really was a devourer of worlds when I push my way inside to find Franklin Hendry and a couple of his dead-eyed thugs inside.

I've met monsters I like better than these actual humans.

A *lot* better.

It doesn't say great things about me and what I've become that I find myself hoping that last night with Ariel rearranged enough stuff in me that I'm coming down on the nonhuman side of that equation. I shake off the rain, run my hands over my wet hair, and walk in like I'm thinking about having them all as a snack.

I might not be a vampire, but I know how to play one.

The men, who usually leer and make vile remarks—supposedly under their breath but always *just* loud enough to hear—are shockingly silent.

I take this to mean I'm giving them a show that's too close to *vampire* for comfort.

I do nothing to make them feel any better about it.

I look each one of them full in the face, like I'm memorizing them. There's the moon-faced one, who I heard likes to beat up women. And the rat-faced one, who the rumor mill claims lit his mother's house on fire. Whether she died before that in a wraith attack or during the fire, thanks to her loser son, nobody knows.

I used to be a lot more wary of them than I am now.

I'd like to see any of them go down into a vampire dungeon and emerge unscathed. To say nothing of a little girl talk with a death goddess who calls herself *fate*.

I have to remind myself that this isn't about me. It's about Gran, who might have turned out to be an oracle and not as impaired as I thought she was, but is still an elderly woman I can't watch all the time.

I have to remind myself of that repeatedly as I come to a stop in front of Franklin Hendry's desk and can't really bring myself to do much but stare at him like the worm he is. And I know from worms today, having seen far too many in a bird goddess's grotesquely changing face.

"I hear you've taken up with the monsters, Winter," Franklin says, like he's on close and chatty terms with people who know people and is privy to my private information.

"Everyone's heard that," I say, like he's dumb. "I'm pretty sure it was all around town and the talk of what's left of the Pacific Northwest. I'm sure I told you I was taking in renters."

He doesn't like being talked back to, or any suggestion that he's a dimwit. His eyes go flat. "I told you it's a lost cause."

"It's not Halloween yet," I say merrily. "It's barely October." I pull my paycheck out of my pocket and slide it onto the desk. "Here's a little more. I'll need a receipt on that too, of course."

The rat-faced one moves, slinking in much too close. The old me wouldn't have moved any more than the new me does.

But the new me looks him square in the eye. Hard.

And he mutters something I *actually* can't hear for once, then retreats.

I decide I like it.

I ride that high through the rest of the unpleasant encounter and take it with me when I head outside again. The rain has let up a little, so I stand there a moment and breathe it all in.

It doesn't feel as if I've seen much daylight lately.

I decide to walk around, the way I used to do all the time. I go down one side of the cute old town and back up the other, almost *too aware* of how human I'm acting. Out here on the streets of Jacksonville, smiling at my neighbors and the people I wouldn't necessarily call friends but like seeing and would miss if they disappeared.

On a day like this, that feels like love.

I swing down one of the side streets, smiling at the yellow, gold, and orange leaves already carpeting the sidewalk. I'm thinking about the fact that I never made it back east to see the famous New England leaves turn and now probably never will.

When Samuel steps out of a little white house that has been many different shops and a few spas in my lifetime but is now where he and his sister spend their days doing town and human sanctuary things, I'm already smiling.

He is not.

And he doesn't start when he sees me.

"Where have you been?" he demands.

It takes me an extra-long beat or two to realize that he's talking to me.

And that's when I realize something else, too. Something that's shocking, or should be, given the past few years.

I haven't thought about him at all.

24.

"Hey, Samuel," I say, and I wait for that melting feeling to wash over me the way it usually does when I see him.

It doesn't happen.

He's staring right at me, and I look back at him and wait for my nervous system to react, but it doesn't. I try to drink him in the way I used to, but instead all I see is . . . a guy. A good-looking one, sure. He still has those shoulders and those green eyes. They are *very green*, and they look particularly good set against the black of his brows and his hair.

But he's just a guy.

I'm not sure I understand until this very moment *how* wrapped up in Ariel I am. How deep I've fallen down that rabbit hole.

Or how little I want to come back up for air.

That's the thought I try to push away before it takes hold, but I don't quite get there. I have the urge to put my hand up and fit it over that tender place on my neck that only I know is where he bit me, but I don't.

Still, the very idea of fangs deep in my body makes me heat up enough that I'm surprised I'm not letting off steam into the cool air.

Samuel strikes me as more of a memory than anything else as he comes off the porch of the little house to meet me on the sidewalk. A memory, but not one that has me feeling nostalgic.

It's always nice to see old friends, I tell myself. Mostly because if I don't, I assume they're dead.

"I asked you where you've been," he says as he draws closer.

I'm certain I misheard that. "What?"

"I saw your truck the other night," he says in that same confrontational way. I'm so floored by this that I don't do anything but stare. "Had to be three o'clock in the morning. Where the hell were you coming from at that hour?"

"Samuel." I keep looking for the Samuel I've spent all this time admiring on his face, but he's just glaring at me. Maybe it wasn't him I admired. Maybe it was just something to do while the world was ending. *That* makes me feel something, but it's still not nostalgia. "Curfew is a suggestion, not a law. Even if it was a law, you're not the police. The only thing you can do is encourage people to behave in their own best interest. I don't recall agreeing to file itineraries with you."

"So you are consorting with monsters." He says that like he caught me out. Then he shakes his head at me. "Unbelievable."

"If I am consorting with monsters, I would have learned that from you." I'm nodding at him, encouraging him to stop doing whatever this is. "You're the one who built bridges with them in the first place. It seems to me that we should all do the same. Or all we are here in Jacksonville is a petting zoo."

I'm over my little walk and start to turn back but stop when he grabs my wrist.

There was a time, and not long ago, when a single touch from Samuel would have had me giddy for days. It was never the touch itself. It was that I would obsess about it. And it was nice to be touched by someone, especially after Augie disappeared. It's not like Gran is tactile.

Now I find myself staring down at his fingers wrapped around my wrist, wondering what on earth gives him the audacity to think he can wander around grabbing people like this.

"Let go of me," I tell him.

I don't know what's in my voice, or what he sees on my face, but he lets go.

I pull my hand back and grip my wrist myself, like I need to restore my equilibrium or wipe his touch away.

"You've changed," Samuel tells me in a low voice, and this is clearly an insult.

"I don't think I have." What I think is that he doesn't know me well enough to discern whether or not I've changed, but I don't say that.

"I knew it was a bad idea for you to let those people live up there with you. Those *things*."

"It could have been a terrible idea," I agree. "But it doesn't really matter, because they pay me money. I have to have money, Samuel, or Franklin Hendry will throw me on the street, which can't happen. Not because I couldn't figure it out, but because my grandmother needs her house. So what I don't need is your commentary on the practical solution I took to solve my problem."

"You need to be careful." He's scowling at me as if I've defied him, or betrayed him, and I have to remind myself that this is the same person I banged in my living room *one time*, and neither one of us mentioned it again. And this didn't happen last week—it was a year and a half ago, or more. "There are more important things than money, Winter."

"Spoken by someone who isn't going to lose the roof over his head anytime soon." I shake my head. "Listen. Things are a little tense right now. I know that you made yourself the liaison between the humans here and the powers in this valley, so you've undoubtedly seen things the rest of us haven't."

"It was a position that needed to be filled. I was willing to fill it."

I think he sounds defensive, but I don't trust any of the things I'm feeling around him today. Or what I'm feeling in general. Maybe I really shouldn't be out here interacting with anyone. Maybe I'm still processing what happened to me. What Ariel did to me.

What he made me, because I can feel that I'm different now.

"No one's arguing that," I tell him, and I'm not placating him. I can't see any point in fighting with him. "There's a big meeting tonight. Sundown. My house."

He stares at me for far too long, until it's like I'm looking at a stranger. "What are you talking about?"

"The werewolf alpha, the vampire king, and the sorceress," I say, slowly, watching him take that in like it's further evidence of me betraying him. "Everyone will be there. It would be nice if you came to represent the human voice."

"And what are *you* exactly, Winter?"

His eyes are so green, but I don't find them mesmerizing. Not anymore. "I think you know. I've taken over for my grandmother." And he doesn't deserve to know how stating something like that, so matter-of-factly when I've been trying so hard not to accept it, hits me. Or how the cards that are wedged inside my shirt seem to hum. I make myself smile. Sort of. "Anyway, I hope to see you tonight?"

For the first time I can remember since the Reveal started and I spent more time with Samuel—only once not in public—I can't wait to get away from him. I keep that smile on my face, back away, then turn and walk briskly back toward my truck.

I feel good about myself for extending that olive branch.

It's not his fault that the crush I had on him has disappeared like it never existed. There's no reason for me to treat him any differently. After all, *he* is exactly the same.

I'm the one who's changed.

When I make it home, I tell myself that I should probably get something to eat since I can't remember the last time I put food in my body—

But I stop dead before I make it to the front door, because Savi's there.

She's sitting on the front step and looks a lot like she's sitting on a throne, though that could be because I know who she is now.

Once again, the sweep of her dark hair is so glossy it defies description. Her eyes are luminous and direct. Her skin is *dewy*, and I'm not even the kind of person who notices things like *skin*. Today she's wearing what looks like a simple pair of trousers and a sweater, but this is Savi.

So of course she looks like a magazine spread.

She gazes at me for a long while. I return the favor.

"Sorcery," I say. Eventually. "You're *a sorceress*."

"I'm afraid so."

"That would explain the chanting I always hear from your room. Not a happy little meditation practice, I'm guessing."

"I find spell work can be very meditative." Her lips curve slightly. "But no, I'm not much for yoga."

"And almost everyone in this house knew who you were. Everyone but me."

"I wasn't hiding." Savi says that very matter-of-factly. "Though I am also not in the habit of illuminating those who seem perfectly happy in the dark."

"What about people who don't know they're in the dark because they're being manipulated by the sorceress who plays with the weather?"

She inclines her head. "I have been in this valley for a long time. Long by your standards, anyway. You wouldn't think it would be hard to find, especially when there's an interstate that runs right through it, but even before the Reveal it was something of a forgotten place."

Five hours to the Bay Area, five hours to Portland—not that either place is likely standing these days. "Is that something you did deliberately?"

"It's true that I don't wish to be found." Savi does not answer the question. Not directly. "I've been on the run for some time."

"From your family," I say, remembering something Ariel said.

"From my own family, yes. And also from my husband." I work hard not to react to that. I get the feeling she's doing the same. "It's hard to say, century to century, if they're still looking. Sorcerers love nothing more than an epic grudge, however. So I imagine they are."

I think about the cards that follow me wherever I go. I think about Gran. About the inevitability who is Ariel. "I didn't have any choice about the things that chase me. Did you?"

Her smile widens. "I see you're stepping into your role." But her expression shifts. "Very few of us do. You do your best to survive, and if there's space, you do what you can to thrive a little, too. Whether your life is short or long, that's really all there is to it."

"Great pep talk," I tell her, and I'm surprised to find I feel like laughing. "In case no one told you, I'm calling a meeting. Right here at sundown. I'll need you there. I'm tired of playing games, and maybe you haven't heard in between making the rain and the smoke, but there's a death goddess with a major attitude problem on the loose. Might make sense for the big, bad supernatural creatures to focus on that."

"We are all tired of playing games." She laughs, but when she tilts her head slightly, her gaze is assessing. "Though it is not my experience that anyone or anything cares if you're tired. You still have to play."

"Noted," I say. "That sounds like an order, not a pep talk."

"Who am I to tell an oracle what her future holds?" Savi replies, lightly. Very, very lightly.

I can feel the cards nestled against my heart, pressing in hard.

I forget about getting food, because the truth is, I'm not that hungry any longer. When I let myself into the house, I go to Gran's room. I don't let myself look out the windows to see what Savi might be doing.

I'm not sure what I'm expecting. I haven't left Gran here for this long in years, and I have no idea what state I'll find her in. I'm already mad at myself, though I know I couldn't have done anything differently.

But when I walk in, she's sitting up in her chair by the window looking clean and well kempt.

"I was beginning to think you died out there," she says with a sniff.

"I'm sorry I left you for so long, Gran." I decide not to play the game of *does she know me* today. "I figured you would understand. But I'm glad you seem to have managed."

"Savi helped me." Gran lifts her brow at the expression on my face then. "I might not be on death's door, but I'm no spring chicken. As I've said. Besides." She looks at me gravely. "I've known Savi for some time."

I refuse to ask how Savi got in. I'm sure I don't want to know. "The sorceress, you mean."

We stare at each other. I realize I'm standing just inside the door, my arms crossed belligerently, so I move farther into the room and go to sit on the edge of her bed. So we can face each other.

"The fact that you're not overwhelmed with joy that you are the oracle is a good thing," Gran tells me. Slowly. "It's those who are a little too pleased to find they have the sight that end up blinded. It's appropriate to be apprehensive. Seeing what is to come is a heavy load to carry."

Her gaze doesn't waver. "There is a large part of me that was pleased that Lilianne was spared. She could never have held up to the demands of the cards, let alone the visions themselves."

"I saw Augie." I blurt that out. "I actually talked to him. He's not well in the sense of being clean, but he looks well. I'm not sure which is worse."

"When I see him, I see him in despair," Gran says quietly. "Buried somewhere in the earth, not dead but not quite alive, either."

"Yes," I say. "More or less that."

We sit there for what feels like far too long, and I hope Augie feels it, down there in his cell. I hope he *knows* that there are people here who still love him.

"I need you to listen to me." Gran surprises me by leaning forward and taking my hand in hers. "I have always known that this gift would be yours. I have always understood that you would be the one to take my place. I waited for you to step into the role and accept it as only you can, but I want you to know that I never had any doubt. Not the way I did when I wondered if it would be your mother. I knew she couldn't handle it. But you're something else. You're stronger in every possible way."

I think about the things that Ariel did to me. The things I let him do. The things I begged him to do. The things I am pretty sure I would do again, if he asked, no matter how I might have left him earlier.

"I don't think I'm stronger at all," I say quietly.

"It's not a question of opinion." Again, she looks at me in that intense way of hers, as if she's looking straight into me, right past all my defenses. "Remember, child, I have always known where this is going. And you are the only one strong enough to survive it."

"I met Vinča," I tell her. "The Goddess of Filth herself, in a vision. At least, I think it was a vision."

"But to look upon her face is to die," Gran says softly. "For such is the terror and wonder of her bearing. So it has been foretold."

"The funny thing is that I think I did die," I say after a moment. "I just didn't realize it at the time. But it turns out I had a secret weapon."

Once again, we take the measure of each other, my grandmother and me. We have gazed at each other too many times to count over the course of my life. But this time, maybe for the first time, we're truly seeing who we are.

Indigo eyes and all.

"Do you still have a pulse?" she asks quietly.

"I have a pulse." I can't tell if she looks relieved or disappointed. "But between you and me, I'm not entirely certain I qualify as one hundred percent human any longer."

"You are the oracle." Gran says that with a little nod that tells me that whatever else she is, she's deeply proud. I plan to think about that later, when I'm alone and don't have to worry that what I feel shows on my face. "You can and should be whatever you wish."

First there are chores to catch up on. I start with the laundry, and when I bring mine down into the laundry room I see that Maddox left me my hiking pack by the door. It amazes me how long ago that hike feels to me now. It seems like a whole different lifetime when I thought I could charge up a mountainside and outwit a death goddess, when it was only yesterday.

Like that Winter was very different from the one who called the most powerful monsters in the valley over for a meeting tonight.

By the time sundown rolls around, I'm more than ready.

"You want to do this outside?" Savi asks, sounding faintly scandalized when she comes down to find me settling Gran on the bench out on the porch.

"I sure hope it doesn't keep raining," I murmur. "That would suck."

Sure enough, the rain tapers off and slides into a lovely, pretty evening. The clouds are stacked high into the sky. The sun plays through them, and Gran and I both sigh a little as we watch it, because it's so typically Oregon. And because we normally don't stop to appreciate such things—mostly because they are usually wreathed in smoke.

As the sun cools and the sky darkens, we hear the sound of revving motorcycle engines in the distance.

"Here come the wolves," Gran mutters.

They come roaring up the drive. Ty is first on a big-ass Harley, with Maddox sitting behind him. Two other men flank him, and they all pull up dramatically by the side of the house, in perfect formation.

I want to ask them if they practice their choreography. I think better of it.

Maddox swings off the back of Ty's bike with her usual lazy grace. She comes sauntering over to the porch, sweeps a look over Savi and my grandmother, then settles on me.

"'Sundown in the front yard,'" she says, but not in her own voice. It takes me a second to realize she's quoting the note I left her. "'Bring your alpha.'" Maddox shakes her head. "When did you get so butch, Winter?"

"Winter is the consort of the vampire king," Savi reminds her. I'm not sure I like that word or feel that it describes my whole thing with Ariel, but she keeps going. "That would be a powerful position even if she wasn't the oracle. Empires have been built on less."

Maddox shoots me a speculative look. "You building empires, Winter?"

"Sure." I have to make myself laugh. "I'll get right on that."

I realize I'm tense as the last of the light spills all around us in the last few moments of proper daylight before the sun disappears behind the mountains.

I'm tense—but then I see it. A sudden bit of mist when there was none there a moment ago, undulating up from the ground.

I know it's him.

Sure enough, the mist resolves into a man, and it's Ariel.

He looks around the clearing, taking in the group of us on the porch and the werewolves to the side. Then he does something with one hand, some kind of peremptory gesture, and a pair of vampires appear. I haven't seen either one of them before, but I forget about them the minute I see them.

Because they're holding Augie between them.

Ariel issues an order in a language I don't understand. His vampire minions bow their heads slightly and disappear again, leaving Augie behind. Standing there in the cold, wet grass in the middle of our yard.

For a moment, everything is frozen.

Augie sways a little, and while I see they managed to give him a pair of pants and a T-shirt, he's still in bare feet. He looks unsteady on those feet, but he doesn't fall over—and I wonder if it's physical or emotional. He glances at Ariel, who remains unreadable. His gaze moves to Ty, who stares back at him unflinchingly.

He straightens when he sees Maddox and Savi over by the porch. He looks at me.

"Augie," I whisper.

When he moves, it's toward Gran.

It takes everything I have not to run to his side, to help him, to guide him. Yet somehow, I know better.

My brother walks haltingly at first, as if he expects vampires to appear and drag him back to that dungeon. A valid concern. When they don't, he moves quicker, until he's practically running.

He keeps going until he makes it to Gran's chair, then he goes down to his knees in front of her.

"I'm so sorry," he whispers. "Gran, I'm so sorry."

And my grandmother, who was always so strict and so unforgiving to our parents and to Augie before, opens up her arms and hugs him tight.

I have to blink to make sure I don't cry.

It's a very close call.

"It's time for us all to work together," I say, forcing the words past the lump in my throat before there can be any other surprises. "Some of you have been working together already. Congratulations. But as far as I can tell, I'm the one with a connection to Vinča, the very-much-more-than-foul bitch who wants to kill us all. So maybe it's time to stop keeping me in the dark."

"The oracle was never in the dark—you just took your time taking her place," Ty says with a drawl. "If you want to be in the loop, you have to step up and face the responsibilities of your role. That's just the way it is."

Up near the porch, Maddox laughs. "That's not pointed at all."

The look he tosses her way is so ferocious that I almost lose my train of thought.

Then I really do, because Samuel's truck comes bumping up the drive.

I realize I forgot about him again.

I immediately feel guilty. But a look around at everyone gathered here makes it obvious that Samuel inspires a lot of different reactions.

None of them positive.

It makes sense to me that monsters might not love the human agitating to not be treated like food. It also makes sense that Samuel is a little wary of everyone in this clearing.

As he gets out of his truck and joins the gathering, I decide the best thing to do is ignore him and focus on actual issues.

"Some of you were around when she was causing trouble the first time." I lift a brow at Ariel. "Maybe you have some insight into how you got rid of her then."

"Even goddesses can be stopped," he replies. "Anything can be stopped, with the right combination of war and magic. The trouble with Vinča is that no one has been able to discover where she is."

"We've been looking," Ty contributes. "Nothing fits the description."

"The goddess was sunk deep," Savi says in an odd tone, as if she's reciting a poem from memory. "She was given her temple to remind her of her narcissism and the faithful now lost to her, and she was left to her eternity in the watery deep."

"That sounds like an ocean," Samuel says, sounding both confident and impatient.

I watch the three most powerful creatures in this valley turn, slowly, to regard him in varying degrees of arrogant astonishment.

"Thanks, dipshit," Ty growls. "No one thought of that. You're a fucking genius."

"We examined the possibility, obviously," Savi says coolly. "Some of us have been looking for her for a long time. There's never been a hint of her in any of the oceans, not for centuries."

I feel something stirring me, and the cards start poking at me once again, like they can feel it too. When I put my hand down to press against them and hopefully convince them to quit it, one of the cards seems to flash across my vision, as if I turned it over out in the open.

Once it does, it's like there's a *click* deep inside of me.

"Why are you all here?" I ask them. These monsters who stand here in the yard an ancestor of mine cleared with his hands. "Once the Reveal happened, surely you could've rampaged across the continent at will, then taken the party to Europe. Asia. Wherever. Why didn't you?"

"There have always been wolves in the Pacific Northwest," Maddox tells me, and something in the way she says it makes me wonder if there were a lot of politics around this very issue. "Even when the humans tried to kill off the domestic wolf population, we were still here. It's easier to do pack things in a place where we can run around at night without being seen."

The other wolves make growling noises of approval. At least, I think it's approval.

"My people don't think much of the New World," Savi says, and I know, somehow, she's not planning to share even what little she told me about her husband. Or her family. Though surely everyone here already knows. "They prefer the power they have in the Old World, and so they stay there, hiding away in their ancient castles on hills no one dares climb and becoming ever more irrelevant."

"I find Old World conventions irritating," Ariel says when all eyes turn to him where he stands, dressed entirely in black, yet with short sleeves, as if impervious to the vagaries of weather. "I also don't like being told what to do."

I sigh. "I don't know what that means."

"It means that when he won the crown there was great commotion all across Europe, because everyone supposed he would take its rightful place in the usual way," Savi says. "There is a vampire court, many ancient traditions, and all the rest. But he didn't do it."

I study Ariel. This beautiful man. This impossible lover. This creature who has changed me, irrevocably.

"Transylvania didn't do it for you?" I ask.

Ariel's eyes gleam. "A vampire king cannot inherit the crown, they must fight for it. The life of a traditional vampire king involves endless challenges from hopefuls."

"You didn't want to be challenged?" Samuel asks. He makes it sound like Ariel is too cowardly for that, and I'm not the only one who frowns at him. I think I hear Ty growl. "Makes sense you'd take off."

"It wouldn't be fair to them," Ariel corrects him, with a certain menace I can feel beneath my own skin. "I have lost one fight in my entire life, living or dead. So I decided that, instead, I would find myself a remote spot of no particular interest to anyone, and any young hopefuls who came my way I would train, not kill. Because I would have the opportunity to talk to them outside the din and nonsense of court."

"Of course," I breathe. "That's why you have the school. And you were a Spartan."

"I am always a Spartan," he says, correcting me this time, but with far less menace. "Since those days, I have studied every martial art there is." He tosses a scathing look Samuel's way. "I don't have to fight."

"Don't you know?" Savi asks quietly, and while she seems to be speaking to me, I think her real target is Samuel. "Ariel did not seek the crown. The previous vampire king challenged him and in such a way that he couldn't refuse."

"I decided that I'll be the last vampire king," Ariel says, and I feel the cards hum, suggesting that what he's saying carries far more weight than is evident here in the yard in the growing dark. "In the hundred and fifty years since, I have had no serious challengers."

I can't be the only one who hears the threat in that. The promise.

"I was born here," Augie drawls from behind me. "Less exciting, I know."

The fact that he's *here* and sounds like *him* and is now sitting on the steps of the porch looking like I dreamed him here—healthy and normal and him—makes me want to break down and sob.

I don't have time for that. I smile at him, but then I look back out at the raggedy group of people in my front yard. Well. Maybe they're not all that raggedy, but this is a far cry from any other gathering that's ever taken place here.

"I don't think it's coincidental that the ritual happened here." I see Augie's gaze sharpen when I say that, but he doesn't ask questions. I'm sure he'll save them for later. My brother, when not high, was always a master of timing. One of those childhood trauma gifts that keeps on giving. "I think that if the goddess wasn't nearby, the ritual wouldn't have been here either."

"Agreed," Ty says impatiently. "Got any ideas? Or are you all headaches and fainting spells?" I'm pretty sure he mutters something like "weak-ass human" under his breath to his buddies, who growl low in obvious approval.

Luckily, I don't care if Ty Ceridwen thinks I'm weak. Compared to him, I am.

"I think she's here," I say, but I don't think it. I know it. I see it, clear as day, in my head. "I think they stuck her at the bottom of the deepest lake around, and I think that's why she keeps reaching out, stirring shit up. She knows exactly where to go when she gets out. She's practically in the neighborhood."

"What the hell are you talking about?" Samuel says then, sounding annoyed. Like I've lost it completely.

But if I don't care what the wolf who hauled me up the steepest part of McLoughlin thinks, I *really* don't care what Samuel the Human thinks, so much so that not caring about him isn't even a revelation.

I can hardly remember who the version of me was that did care about him.

Tonight my gaze is on Ariel. He nods, either because he's come to the same conclusion I have, or because he trusts me.

Either one is heady enough.

"She's in Crater Lake," I tell the gathering. "I'm sure of it. What we have to do is keep her there."

25.

After my announcement, Ty, Ariel, and Savi all look at each other.

No one else speaks.

Beside me, Gran nods her approval. It feels less like my grandmother supporting me and more like the blessing of a powerful oracle, and I think I'll hold on to that. It feels like validation when I would have said I had no need of any such thing.

As the powerful staredown continues, I have the urge to leap in and defend myself, or make further arguments, but I don't.

There's no need to oversell this. I *know* where Vinča is the same way I know where I am right now. I am absolutely certain. Beyond any possible doubt.

When the three-way stare ends, I can feel the air seem to shift in the yard. I stand straighter. Maybe we all do.

Savi is the one who speaks, likely because she can make anything sound like a welcome speech in a spa retreat.

"After the Reveal," she begins, and though she sounds as serene as ever, I also think she sounds careful. Maybe "diplomatic" is the word I mean. "After the first wave of it was over and there was a settling—"

"She means after the initial bloodbath, when everyone collected themselves and it was time to think about restoring order," Ariel says coolly.

"After the party, in other words," Ty chimes in, and his lieutenants all laugh.

Even I have to bite back a laugh at that, which horrifies me immediately. How far have I fallen if I'm laughing at a werewolf calling a massacre a party?

It's a relief when Savi keeps talking.

"After a few rules were established and cooler heads prevailed, we went looking for her," Savi tells us. "And not just for Vinča, specifically. It wasn't clear, then, which god was responsible. Or if it was any god at all."

"Most gods are dicks," Ty says.

Samuel sputters at that, but I'm pretty sure it's the confused look on my face that gets Maddox to pipe up.

"The Reveal was foretold forever." She tells me this, then rolls her eyes. "'For there will come a day when the black rot of humanity will be peeled back and the Kind shall rise. They will reclaim what is theirs and wash the world clean with blood. Once this earth is cleansed, so too shall the Kind be free.'"

She intones that in such a way that I'm certain I see every other supernatural creature in the yard stand a little straighter.

"That sounds like something you'd say in church," I say.

Augie nods. "An evil church."

Specifically like Christmas and Easter, when Gran would drag us in and make us stand too straight, exuding politeness, or she would make us wish we had.

"Some religious sects arranged themselves around that prophecy, yes," Savi says. "But it has been around as long as I have." She cuts her gaze to Ariel. "As long as he has, even."

"Longer," Ariel agrees, his arms still folded and that forbidding look on his face.

One I should not find attractive. Especially not at a time like this.

I order myself to concentrate.

"Once the Reveal happened, we all felt that same . . ." For the first time since I've met her, Savi looks . . . uncertain. As if she doesn't know what words to choose.

"An unlocking," Ariel says, the way he did to me.

"A locked gate flung wide open," Ty growls.

"And about damn time," one of the bikers flanking him throws in.

It's in this moment that it occurs to me that if I view some of these monsters in my yard as friends or a lover, I also have to take onboard the possibility that they lived in some version of their own Reveal for a whole lot longer than I have. If people are people, but some of them have claws or powers, then none of those people should be hiding away in fear.

I'm going to have to sit with that, and this is no time for *sitting*.

"There are two further prophecies that follow on from that one," Savi tells me. And everyone else. "Two locks to open. And two different keys. The first, a living sacrifice, as painful as possible beneath a full moon. The second, a terrible betrayal and an unwilling sacrifice. You'll notice those are both quite vague."

"The bigger the prophecy, the more likely you can claim it came true no matter what happens," Maddox murmurs. "It's all in the marketing."

Savi nods. "All over the world, there are different cults and sects and communities claiming that they felt that first lock open wide last night. What I haven't heard reported or whispered about in any capacity is what happened to you, Winter."

I try my best to catch up. "But you knew it was going to happen. That she was going to come for me. Specifically me."

"We knew that it would *eventually* happen," Savi says, which sounds like splitting hairs to me. "The details were fuzzy."

"The cards could not make up their minds," Gran chimes in, with a wave of her hand.

That was exactly the sort of thing I would have taken as confirmation of dementia a month ago. No one in this clearing blinks.

Aside from Samuel, that is.

"We explored this entire territory looking to see if there was anything we should worry about," Ty said gruffly. "Most gods are narcissistic fucks and like to flash it all up with the douchey temple and all the trimmings. There's none of that around here. There's a very dramatic collection of vampires in Grants Pass who claim they see a temple every time they turn around, but I've never taken Grants Pass vampires seriously. I'm not starting now."

Ariel inclines his head as if to say, *Fair enough*.

"Where does this leave us?" I ask, instead of tossing myself down a rabbit hole into heretofore unknown-to-me vampire politics.

"It leaves me intrigued," Savi says at once. "I think we have some research to do."

Ty nods. "I'm going to lead a team up to Crater Lake myself. Get a sense of what we're walking into. Last time I was up there, last night hadn't happened. She'll be stronger now. We should be able to feel her."

"We," Ariel says, indicating Savi, "will examine the lore. We will do well to reacquaint ourselves with the specifics involving Vinča and her cult."

"Which specifics are those?" I can't keep myself from asking, unable to stop thinking of him as her *pet*.

Ariel's gaze is bright and silver. I feel it inside me, and all over me, and that mark I wear hums a little. Like the gold is a musical instrument only he knows how to play.

"Her preferred form of a reign of terror," he tells me coolly. "Better yet, her aspirations. Some gods live for worship, others prefer to destroy all they touch. It's different forms of power and obedience, that's all."

"That's all," Augie says under his breath.

"If you think about it," Maddox says quietly, "a god is only a god because they say so. Everyone else who has a power or two has a community. Not gods. They want to be the one and only, they're big on killing their own families, and they're constantly rising here, rising there, fucking everything up. They're never just living or minding their own business. Honestly, it's exhausting."

"We will gather more details in places you can't access," Savi tells me when no one else jumps in. It made me think about the place I met

Vinča and wonder if that's the sort of place I shouldn't have been able to access—way out there in the midst of too many galaxies to count, out on some plane of existence I can't even name. "We'll come up with a plan of action from there."

"Can I ask the obvious question?" Samuel says then, with a short little laugh. Instead of being rapt and attentive the way I've traditionally been with him, all I want to do now is point out that he is already asking a question. I hold myself back. "What the hell do you think you're all going to do against a god?"

Ty laughs at that. "I like to start by shoving their religion up their ass," he grunts. "But then, I like to make a good first impression."

After that, the conversation seems to fizzle out—or maybe some people are communicating by other means. I tell myself I don't care when Ariel simply disappears, leaving only mist behind. I tell myself I can't feel that golden glow of his mark all over me, and that even if I can, I'm not taking any comfort in it.

Ty and his men roar away. Savi and Maddox walk off toward the cottages.

"All things considered, it could have been much tenser than it was," I say brightly to the humans who remain. "The last time I saw the three great powers of the Rogue Valley in one place, there was significantly more blood."

"We need to talk, Winter," Samuel says, frowning at me.

I probably would have entertained his request, not because I'm interested in anything he has to say but because I feel a kind of secondhand embarrassment for him. All this time I've believed—and he'd made sure all the humans in Jacksonville believed, if I really think about it—that he has some kind of power around here. Now I know otherwise.

But Augie is shaking his head. "We're going to have some family time, man," he says, with all that charm he somehow got at birth that allows him to tell people to fuck off and get them to leave smiling.

It has the same effect now. Almost. Samuel doesn't smile. But he leaves.

Then we go back into the house. Gran and me and, for the first time in a long, long while, Augie.

"I can't believe you actually rented out those cottages," Augie says as we make our way into the kitchen and settle Gran into a chair. I'm still thinking about tense creatures and a far tenser Samuel, but I stop when he laughs. "I didn't realize you were so enterprising. Way to go."

"We talked about doing this for years, even before the Reveal," I remind my twin, trying so hard not to act like it's weird that he's back home and in the house and standing here in the kitchen like when things were normal that I . . . am clearly making it weird anyway. "Mortgages need to be paid."

"There are still banks?"

I can't tell if that's a dry little joke on his part or if he's acknowledging how little he knows about the life that passed him by while he was out there letting it run him right over.

Though when I think about the contents of said life, I'm not sure why I would want anyone I love to share that experience. Maybe he's had the right idea all along. Oblivion sounds fantastic right around now.

Though if I were oblivious, off in my own little world, I would miss this. Gran beaming at the kitchen table. Augie leaning against the counter as if he's never been away. If I squint my eyes and think only about the here and now—and, at all costs, do not ask myself when, exactly, things were *really* ever normal—everything feels right.

I decide to believe in it. Because nothing has felt *right* in a long, long while.

"I'll make dinner," I say, and I don't wait for either one of them to respond to that. I need to do something with my hands. I need to perform some kind of task, because the alternative is succumbing to the feelings inside of me, and I can't do that.

If I start letting all these feelings win, who knows where it will end?

I feel Augie's gaze on the side of my head, but I don't look at him. I don't ask anyone what they want to eat, I just bustle around like it's one of those nights back before. When there were still too many things no one wanted to talk about hanging heavily in the air, but we would gather around the kitchen table, determined not to fight, and figure out how to enjoy each other for a while.

I break out the eggs that I buy in bulk from one of my neighbors on the hill who figured out a way to enclose a chicken coop in her house to keep the predators out, now that it's not foxes she worries about. I whip up golden, fluffy scrambled eggs, get some cheese on there too, and I find a fresh loaf of bread in the freezer that a previous version of me cut into slices so I could make toast whenever I pleased.

If I could high-five previous me, I would.

I find some sausages and a rasher of bacon, and when I'm done, I've created the breakfast-for-dinner feast of my dreams.

"Now it feels like a homecoming," Augie says when I start ferrying the plates over to the table, where he and Gran have been talking intently, but only about easy topics. Her health. His take on the state of the house. The weather.

Breakfast for dinner was how Gran made it fun when our mother was too high to take care of us after school, or up and disappeared altogether. She would gather us in the kitchen, act like it was a holiday, and then we would pull out all the breakfast food we could find.

Sometimes we even forgot to be sad that our mom wasn't there.

Even Gran cackles with glee when I slide her plate in front of her, piled high with eggs and buttered toast. She spears a few sausages and tucks in, acting as if she hasn't been fed in months.

I sit down with my plate, and I see Augie studying his eggs as if he thinks they might bite him. It occurs to me that he might not eat food in his current state.

But when he catches me looking, he digs in.

And because I'm pretending tonight, I let him do it too. I don't ask about the ghosts in his eyes. I don't mention our last meeting or what I saw there. I don't look too closely at the watchfulness he wears too easily, then hides too quickly.

For a while, then, the only sound is the three of us not only eating but seemingly taking pleasure in it as we do.

There weren't a lot of safe spaces for me growing up, and I understand now, finally, that this quiet sort of moment—when there was family together with no yelling, no dramatics, no upset or acrimony—is the only thing that got me through.

Once again, I feel tears pricking at the back of my eyes, because I couldn't possibly have imagined that this would ever happen. It wasn't that I'd given up on Augie, because I never did. I never will. I can't, physically. Unless and until he's dead, it's like the very cells in my body refuse.

But I'd long ago given up on *this*.

On ever feeling anything like happy with my family again.

For a long while, all I do is bask in it. In them. In *us*.

"So you're the oracle now," Augie says when we've all finished eating and have all gone back for seconds, too. When he looks at me, and I see Gran doing the same, I think about the fact that all three of us have the same indigo eyes.

"Mom's eyes were blue," I say. When both of them blink at me, I make a face. "Am I remembering that wrong? A pretty blue, but just blue. Not like ours."

"You're remembering it right," Augie says.

"The indigo eye has always indicated that the sight can or could be evident," Gran says. "It has been handed down for centuries, with little attention paid to scientists and their recessive genes."

Augie laughs that delightful, infectious laugh of his, and I tell myself I can't hear the strain in it. I pretend I can't see that he's acting the part, maybe partly because that's a major upgrade from some of his visits home in a lot of dark years. "I guess I'm the exception that proves the rule."

"I'm not sure even you know what visions might have come to you in the state you've been in the past few years," our grandmother says tartly.

Ordinarily, this would set Augie off. Even when he'd come back claiming he was balanced and good and ready to change, a comment like that would send him off into a spiral. I brace myself, but all he does is smile wider while he fidgets around with his fork.

Maybe we're all onstage tonight, but I can't bring myself to hate it.

"Yes," I say, jumping back to the original question before this shifts and that twitch I'm sure I see in his eye makes him explode. "I'm the oracle, I guess. Fun fact—not only did I not sign up for the honor, you apparently can't opt out, either."

"It's a gift." Gran eyes me, but I'm sure I can see the rare hint of her smile on her lips. "Surely, I raised you to know that returning a gift is rude. As is refusing it outright."

"I have no choice. The cards never leave me alone." I don't give them the satisfaction of moving them from where they're pressing hard against my solar plexus. "That vision didn't ask me if I was in the mood either. It came for me, no consent, like it or not."

"That's a goddess for you," Gran says matter-of-factly, as if she has spent her life—born at home in the tiny town of Ruch out in the Applegate, then come all of eight miles into Jacksonville, where she's remained ever since—neck-deep in too many pantheons to name. "They always think that all the world is their shrine, and woe betide you if you don't worship them precisely the way they like. Wearisome, every one of them."

She spears herself the third sausage while Augie and I sneak a look at each other. There might have been a time when he would make a circular motion next to his temple after a statement like that, quietly confirming that she was over there losing her marbles.

But that's not the world we live in anymore.

"Was all of that really supposed to kill me?" I ask her. "Because it felt like I was dying for part of it. For most of it, really. But I don't see why she would go to the trouble of telling me something if she was going to kill me with it."

"Gods of every description are deeply fickle and pride themselves on being unknowable. They never wish to be understood, theirs is the mystery of faith, and so on." Gran rolls her eyes. "In this case, she had the great comfort of knowing that the bloodline continues whether she killed you or not. I'm still drawing breath. Augie is still with us. For all we know, so is your mother. She knew if you were killed, sooner or later, one of us would try to contact you on the other side."

I remember Ariel saying something very much like that. I don't particularly want to think about it any more now than I did then. "So you're a medium, too?"

"Mediums channel spirits around Ouija boards, in headdresses, while brandishing crystal balls, because they are actually con women," my grandmother says with a sniff. "It's more accurate to say that what I do is . . . look through a window. Just as you do to see the present day. You open a window, something is either there or not there. That's all there is to it."

"That sounds like a long way to say yes, you're a medium," Augie says after a moment. In that deadpan way of his that makes me want to laugh and cry and maybe smack him upside his head.

"I'm glad to see you've retained what passes for your humor after your trials and tribulations," Gran tells him.

And for a moment, I think we're actually going to talk about this. Drugs. Vampire blood. What actually happened to Augie, how he went from the open-air prison of despair on the banks of the river with all the other addicts into an actual stone dungeon to feed an even worse master. Or mistress, in his case.

For a breathless moment, I think we're actually going to have the kind of conversation that we should have been having all along.

But instead, he grins at Gran like the happy golden boy he never quite was. "What I want to know is, do you really think that we're going to be able to do this?"

What I think is that we have to, but I don't say that.

"I do think it will work," I say, with enough uncharacteristic enthusiasm that Augie's brow lifts. "We have a good team."

"I'm not sure I'd call it a team," Augie says mildly. "There's a pretty strict hierarchy. And a food chain."

He's not wrong. And yet . . . I keep reminding myself that they could have just killed me at any point. They could have let me die last night. *He* could have.

"You're the one who came face-to-face with Vinča herself," Gran says, and I wonder how long I've been sitting there without answering. "That can't have been fun."

I have a flash of that terrible face and the way it changed, the rot and the beak and the worms that I can suddenly feel as if they're *on me*—

But I push all that away.

"She was horrifying," I say, as calmly as I can manage. "But I was fine."

I don't have to tell them *how* I was fine. I don't have to explain that somewhere between Ariel's cock and his cold come and his fangs deep in my neck, I had the strength to keep taking his blood. Or that because of those things, I survived.

I suspect that Gran might already know. Augie can certainly guess, especially given where he's been lately.

"Your man Samuel had a point," Augie says, still fiddling with the silverware. "You can't just roll up to a god and think you're going to get them to do what you want. If you could, they wouldn't need to be gods, would they?"

"Both you and I managed to survive vampires," I point out. "That's not supposed to happen either. I like our odds."

When I get up to clear the table because I can't sit still, Augie helps me. It keeps feeling like a dream, the fact that he's here. Not just *here*, but here as the version of my brother who wasn't around much even when he physically was. I keep thinking I'll wake up, but I don't.

He helps me clean up, and then, together, we go with Gran into her room.

And for once I have the very thing I kept wishing might happen. For years now. All three of us together. Both Augie and me carrying the load, caring for Gran in a way she'll accept.

All of us happy to just *be* with each other after all the things we've lost.

I get her ready for bed. He settles in to talk with her some more, and I kiss her on the forehead, then hug him too before I leave them on their own.

They deserve their own time together.

He stays in there a long while. I go upstairs to the linen closet and pull out what I need to make up the bed in his old room for him to use. When I take the old bedspread down to the laundry room to wash it, because it's abundantly floral and I don't think Augie would appreciate it, I get the creepy feeling that I'm being watched.

Sure enough, when I look up, Briar is there in the doorway.

Scowling, obviously, with that hat jammed down on her head, as always. Tonight she's wearing a sweatshirt, I assume in deference to the October weather outside. Everything is black, so that she looks like a shroud, and I remind myself that she pays to live here. I can't demand to know what the hell she's doing, lurking around like that in the communal kitchen area.

Though I do wonder what the hell she's been doing while all this has been going on.

Something pokes at me as I think that. Maybe the fact that I don't know what she is. Human or something else, I have no idea. I remember the weird way she and Savi seemed to face off that first day they showed up here. It seems impossible that she's not *something*.

If she knows what's been happening, though, it's weird that none of them indicated that she should be involved in the gathering earlier tonight. It's tempting to consider it a simple oversight, and I almost ask her, but some odd reluctance inside me keeps me from it.

"Do you need something?" I ask instead.

"A man is moving in?" she demands. "I didn't sign up to live on this property with some *man*."

"Briar," I say, in my best imitation of Savi's endless serenity, "you don't interact with anyone. You barely leave your cottage."

"But I could," she retorts.

I have no idea how to reply to that, so I don't. I walk toward her so that she'll have to back up and let me out of the laundry room, though it seems to take her a beat too long to do that. She moves back into the kitchen, still glaring at me sullenly.

"Anyway, my brother's home. He'll be staying here, in the house he grew up in, obviously. If you happen to run into him in the kitchen, no worries. He doesn't bite." Though as I say that, I have to wonder why I'm assuming *she* doesn't. "Since you don't seem to be even remotely trepidatious about walking in the woods, you might also enjoy sitting out on the back porch. Or the front porch. Knock yourself out."

"This place is bullshit," she growls at me. Briar puts a hand up while she says it, then rests it against her own chest. Just below her clavicle. It makes me do the same, though it makes me realize that I'm not wearing Augie's medallion. "This place is bullshit, you're bullshit, and your brother is *fucking* bullshit."

"I'll pass that on," I assure her. I even smile.

I go back into the main part of the house and sit in the living room. I hear Briar crash around in the kitchen, and though I'm flipping through a book when she storms back outside and circles around the house, I manage to catch her filthy glare from between the boards on the windows all the same. Maybe I just feel it, but it lands either way. I can even hear her cottage door slam shut across the yard.

Everything around me is still, then. Quiet.

There are so many things that I could think about, now that I'm alone. Everything involving Ariel. The whole death goddess situation. The fact that Ariel returned Augie to me with very little fanfare and no further talk of debt—and I'm not sure if I should celebrate that yet, because maybe it's coming. My grandmother, whose condition seems pretty stable these days. Maybe even better now that I know that a lot of her strangest statements are because she's an oracle.

Instead of any of those things, I entertain myself by thinking about my one asshole tenant, like a normal person.

And the more I do that, the more I can almost convince myself that everything really is normal. Just for a little while. Augie's fine. I'm fine. No vampires, no werewolves, no supernatural shenanigans. We have a mortgage to pay, so we took in renters. Augie's in with Gran, and I can hear him making her laugh.

I wish more than anything that our problems were no worse than these.

Bills to pay. Family complications.

Honestly, looking back, it all seems a lot more peaceful than I remember it being at the time.

When Augie comes out of Gran's room, I'm still sitting there. He walks over without a word and throws himself down beside me, and then we sit there for a long while.

His shoulder presses into mine, like our foreheads down in that dungeon.

There are so many things to say that neither one of us says anything.

It feels a lot like peace.

Gradually, however, I realize that he's tense. Getting tenser by the moment, though he still doesn't say anything.

I know what it is immediately, and I wonder why I didn't think of this before. Did I want to believe that Augie could magically be cured of his addictions? If there were a magical way to make him clean, surely, someone would have mentioned it by now.

But . . . I don't want to end this moment. The closest thing to peace I think we've ever had. Reveal or no Reveal.

I think he feels the same. I can see when he starts to sweat, but he doesn't say anything then, either. Probably because he doesn't want to lie to me, the way he's done too many times to count. Like we both want to believe that part—the lying part—is all in the past no matter what we're pretending tonight.

But addiction never has given one shit about anyone's *feelings.*

"Augie," I begin, determined to help him, whatever that looks like—

Before I can finish, there's a knock at the door.

I'm up immediately, drawing one of my guns. I don't mind when Augie comes up hard beside me and helps himself to the second gun I carry in my harness. We go to the door, like the well-oiled machine we were, once. Because we taught each other how to do this, back at the beginning of what the werewolf alpha called *a party.*

Augie goes to the door and waits for me to get into position. He reaches over to swipe open up the peephole and I pause, just barely, then look.

Big mistake if anyone was going to attack immediately.

But when I see who it is, I'm not exactly happy. I'd prefer an attack.

"Go away," I tell the door.

Ariel is even beautiful through a peephole, damn him, and he doesn't argue. He steps aside so I can see that there's another vampire with him.

It's another female vampire. Mercifully, not the one I saw belowground before.

I open my mouth to tell them both to fuck off, but I catch myself.

He's not here for me. Or he might be, but that's not why he brought this woman.

I open the door, and I swear I can see how relieved Augie is when he sees who's there. He lowers his weapon. He swallows hard.

Then the look he gives me is anguished.

"Not inside," I manage to say. "No vampires in the house where Gran is. That's all I ask."

"Understood."

His voice sounds too thick, and he can't meet my eyes. I can see him in that cell again, covered in the terrible shame that I saw him like that. He's not happy about it now, either.

But addiction is addiction. We both know that entirely too well.

He steps outside and walks with that vampire into the dark. He doesn't look back.

It hurts to breathe. I do it anyway.

"I assume I can trust you not to kill him?" I ask Ariel.

I stay inside. He stays on the porch.

I don't invite him in.

"I could have had your brother killed at any time," he reminds me, softly. "And you, and your grandmother. Why would I bother with the rest of this?"

"Because you're a monster."

"Aren't we all," he says quietly.

"Did you really give him back to me?" I can barely get that out, and it's barely a whisper. "Or is this some sick little game?"

The look he shoots at me then is . . . arrested. As if I've *wounded* him somehow.

As if *I* should apologize to *him*.

I nearly do.

When I don't, he looks away again, and that feels even worse.

And once again, I expect . . . something. I expect him to mount an argument. I expect to feel that song of his rise in me, whether he thinks I'll fall for it or not.

Instead, I feel that silver gaze of his move all over me. Instead, he looks at me as if he is committing me to memory, and then I'm left standing there with the mist he leaves behind.

I wait until Augie comes back inside, the tension gone from his body. He looks completely restored.

Though he doesn't quite look at me. There were times when I would have lit into him. I would have demanded to know what he was doing, what he was thinking, and most of all, why he couldn't stop.

Tonight, I do none of those things. I walk to my brother, my twin, and hug him.

Hard.

"I made up your bed," I tell him as he hugs me back. "Otherwise, you know where everything is. Just remember, there could be other people in the kitchen at any time." I see he's tucked the gun he commandeered into the waistband of his pants. Though he's still barefoot. "I didn't throw your stuff out. Most of it is packed up in the closet off the laundry room, yours to reclaim. I'll see you in the morning."

"Winter." He hugs me again. "I love you. You know that."

"It is my curse," I reply, the way I always did way back when.

"You wish it was your curse," he replies, as is tradition.

His voice is hoarse. I'm not the only one having a hard time with this.

I tell myself that's something. It's more than I ever thought we'd get.

When I climb upstairs and lock myself in my bedroom, I reach in and pull the cards out from the pocket they chose to fill. Usually I take them and toss them. Try to hide them, to see if they'll stay where I put them.

Tonight, I decide to stop fucking around.

I sit down cross-legged on the floor, and I fan the cards out in front of me the way I've seen my grandmother do a million times. I run my fingers over them, tracing the runic shapes I see there. I think about tonight, all this hope.

All this wild, foolish, marvelous *hope.*

Slowly, carefully, deliberately, I pick a few cards out, turn them over, and then surrender myself to the message.

The vision comes immediately, and the good news is, it doesn't take me over like that last one. It doesn't slam into me, making me feel like my head might explode. It blooms there inside, like it's a part of me. Like it's just another way to see.

The bad news is, all I see is death.

26.

While the supernatural among us do their research, I look at the cards every day. When I take Gran her coffee in the morning, I show her what I'm doing, what I pulled, and how I interpret what I saw.

She listens. She gives advice. Sometimes she offers an alternate interpretation.

Most of all, she teaches me. She shows me how she does things, and why she chose the particular methods she uses.

"Everything you need is already inside you," she tells me, leveling that stern look of hers on me. "All you need to do is access it. Let your blood lead the way."

I try.

Every day, I try.

I don't get used to having Augie home, I revel in it. Every day, I feel as excited to see him emerge from his old room as if it's the first time. Ariel's vampire shows up regularly, every evening, but it takes me a solid week to realize that what she's doing is keeping him going along on the same even keel. No ups, no downs. Just Augie.

"I'm not a big drug person," I say, out of nowhere one day.

"Jesus fucking Christ," my brother mutters.

We're in the truck, headed down the hill to pick up various supplies. Eggs. Cheese. With him around again, we have more things to barter—like his labor—and that makes me feel rich. It's the cash money I have trouble getting a hold of.

"I just mean that it used to be really obvious when you were high, and now . . ."

He goes quiet, but I take it as a good sign that he doesn't freak out. He doesn't start yelling, jump out of the truck, or come at me swinging—verbally, that is—all things that have happened before.

"The high is euphoric," he tells me after a fraught sort of silence that I think is him wishing I would start talking about something else. "But they decide whether or not you get high. It's about intention."

That echoes unpleasantly inside me, because Ariel said much the same thing. "Seems like heroin would be a better bet, then."

"With heroin, you're playing Russian roulette with the fentanyl situation," he says shortly. And a little too matter-of-factly, if I'm honest. "With this, part of the game is seeing if you can convince them to give it to you the way you want. But it doesn't matter, because once you taste it, you're done. Nothing else will do."

I want, desperately, to ask him if that's why all I do is dream about that night in Ariel's bed—but I don't.

I drank quite a lot of Ariel's blood, and the craving I have isn't for that. Or not only for that. It's for him. All of him.

I can't distinguish between the longing for the best sex I've ever had or that simple, whole-body relief I feel every time I see him.

Happily, this isn't about me. "So they're keeping you even. Not getting you high."

"They are." He looks at me then, his gaze intense. "It's not a punishment, or whatever you're thinking. I asked for this. I keep waiting for them to fuck with me, but it hasn't happened yet. If they do, and they probably will, I want you to know it's *not* what I wanted. I want to be here, Winter. I do."

I'm glad we make it down the hill then, because it's hard to discuss this without crying. When he gets out of the truck to go move a few things for our neighbor so we can get those eggs, I let my eyes go a little damp.

Just a little.

The hours change in the coffee stand. Birdie is on early-morning shifts. My hours are cut down significantly, but my pay is higher. I assume that this is a mistake, but there's no one to talk to about it. Doug, wherever he is, can't be reached.

Assuming Doug is the person who's doing this, which I don't.

On the fifteenth of October, twelve days since the full moon on Mount McLoughlin, I collect all the rent payments. I then take great pleasure in presenting them to Franklin Hendry, who gets less and less polite each time I see him. I take this to mean that he is no longer so certain that he's going to win this battle of his.

It occurs to me that I should worry about that.

But there are so many other things to worry about that I forget to bother.

We don't have a full gathering again, but information flows pretty freely between us. Maddox reports back from the werewolves. Savi spends time with Gran, and with me, talking about the things she discovered and what she thinks they mean.

"She's looking for a spell," Gran tells me a couple of nights later, once Savi goes back to her cottage, that chanting floating in the air outside the slightly cracked window shortly after. "It will be a complicated one, to handle such an ancient threat. It will need to happen on a full moon, and now that the second-to-last lock has been opened, it will need to be the *next* full moon."

"The next full moon is Halloween," I point out. "That means we have exactly fourteen days to figure this out."

"Yes." Gran nods. "It's unlikely that she will have the chance to do it but the once."

It gets colder. Darker. Wetter. At night, I stare up at the moon and watch it get larger, rounder.

I think about Halloweens when I was a kid, when I would creep myself out. Every year, without fail. Our parents certainly never monitored what Augie and I watched, so we glutted ourselves on scary movies, which always seemed like fun while we were doing it.

On Halloween, wandering around the neighborhoods in the valley that catered to trick-or-treaters—specific, denser neighborhoods in Jacksonville and Medford, because it's too hard to walk from house to house farther out in the country—I would regret those movies.

Augie and I would compete to see who could pretend to be the least spooked all night. We would even scare each other when we could, hiding in shadows and leaping out of bushes. We would pretend we weren't *really scared.*

But I was happier than most when we got too old to wander around dark streets in unfamiliar neighborhoods, masked-up monsters all around.

Anyway, it's different now. No one's dressing up as a monster for Halloween. There are too many real ones just . . . around.

The nearer we get to the end of the month, the less certain I am that I want to see a death goddess up close and personal on the night that creeped me out the most as a kid. I'd rather skulk into Franklin Hendry's office and beg for more time I already know he won't give me.

Good thing it doesn't matter what I *want*, only what I'm going to *do.*

I keep telling myself that, hoping it sticks.

"So," Maddox says on the last Saturday before Halloween, while I'm sitting at the kitchen table with my cards spread out before me, conducting what Gran called a *getting to know you* reading.

They already know me, I argued when she told me I needed to do this. *They know too much.*

It's not about what they know, Gran retorted with a roll of her eyes. *It's about what you know, and what you can pick up, and the relationship you have to build with them.*

I stared at her, dead-eyed.

Yes, Winter, she said after a moment, still sounding impatient—but a bit softer with it. *You have to build a relationship with the cards. With everything in your life. With life itself, and death too.*

Death can take care of itself, I protested.

Death is a gift, she replied. *Think of all the other things that could happen that are much worse.*

She has a point.

I'm only too happy to look away from the bright gold images on their dark backgrounds with frayed edges, all of them oddly evocative, though half the time I don't have any clue what they mean. I only know the messages they send. Gran is certain that if I get to know them better, I'll understand the deeper meanings in the images on the cards themselves.

I'm happy for a break.

"So what?" I ask Maddox.

"So . . . the vampire king situation." She eyes me. "Haven't met up with you sneaking back into the house in the middle of the night in a while."

"I haven't invited him into the house." It sounds ridiculous when I say it out loud, but we all have to pick our hills to die on.

"Trouble in undead paradise?"

I sit back, contemplating what to say. How to say it. The house feels cavernous around us. Gran's in bed. I haven't seen Savi in days. She's off doing sorcery shit, as far as I can tell. Briar was lurking around earlier, but whether she's hidden in her cottage or off in the woods, I couldn't say.

Augie told me he was going down into Jacksonville to have a beer at the tavern.

I couldn't help myself. I made a face.

He laughed, though it was a bitter sort of sound. *Oh, how I wish that a beer was the problem,* he said. *I would be fucking delighted to be a goddamn alcoholic.*

Somehow, after he left, I was the one who felt ashamed. I could have *not* made a face. Why did I?

"Ariel and I were never *together,*" I tell Maddox after a moment. "If that's what you mean by 'undead paradise,' I don't qualify."

She laughs. When she sees I'm not laughing with her, she sobers. "Oh. Sorry. You're being serious?"

"He released my brother, which is great. But he also imprisoned my brother to pressure me into giving him access to my visions, so we have no other reason to interact." I sigh. "Aside from the whole saving the world thing."

"Winter." Maddox looks like she can't decide whether she wants to laugh, shake her head, or maybe shake me. Or possibly all of the above. "His mark is upon you. More than that, you're bound to him."

She waits, as if she expects to see a light bulb literally burst into its brightest shine above my head.

"I don't know what that means." I cross my arms and glare at her, mostly because she's the one in the room and this is an enduring frustration. "You all know exactly what's going on all the time. *I don't.* In case you've forgotten, I thought you were just a girl in high school. I don't know how vampires operate. I don't know what it means—"

"You know what it means." Maddox's voice is quiet, but with a certain steel in it that reminds me, against my will, that she is another alpha of the werewolf pack. That soon enough, she will be considered its queen, and that she, too, will rule. She nods at whatever expression shows on my face. "Yes. It means that. You're his, end of discussion."

"What? Like he put a dog tag on me?"

"It's more like he put a brand on you." Maddox frowns as she studies me, as if she's looking for clues. "If he's *giving you space*, if I were you?" She shakes her head. "I'd worry more about that."

"Maybe he's being respectful."

She laughs. "Sure. That sounds like the vampire king we all know to love and fear. He's definitely known for being *respectful*."

I sit with that long after she heads back out into the night, lit up by a chunky half-moon a little too close to three-quarters full. It reminds me how little time we have left.

"Did you have fun in town?" I ask Augie the next day. He and I are doing a perimeter check, though that duty has shifted, too. It used to be that I was looking for holes in our defenses or evidence that monsters have been sniffing around. These days, I'm not that worried about defending us. If the monsters want us, most of them have a key.

But I still need to know what's going on with our property, because the alternative feels like being willfully blind.

"Jacksonville was exactly the same," Augie says. "And completely different. It was trippy."

It's a chilly morning. There's frost on the ground, and the mist is thick and wet and decidedly unvampiric. The leaves on the trees are shades of gold. The pine trees stand green and tall. It's October 26.

"It's a small town," I remind him as we check the woods behind the cottages. "Give or take a few apocalypses, that is."

"What I want to know is how so many people got eaten, but the same pack of middle-aged barflies are still there. Not a hair on any of their heads harmed."

"Maybe they're too pickled to eat," I theorize. "Not everybody likes a pickle. Hard as that might be for you or me to believe, I know."

"I had Samuel in my face," Augie says as we keep to the tree line, looking for tracks or tells, checking out angles and potential surveillance spots. "He thinks the monsters got to you."

"He's obsessed with monsters. It's so weird. You would think that of all people, he would be the least wound up by the presence of them since he works with them. But I swear, after spending all this time negotiating with them, he's just . . ."

I don't even know what he is. I do know that once again, out of sight is out of mind with him, and I still feel strange about it.

"I don't think he's obsessed with monsters, Winter." Augie looks at me like I'm being dumb on purpose. "I think he's obsessed with you."

I laugh, and my voice startles a little cluster of wild turkeys. They flutter a bit, then saunter away, eternally unfazed.

"I can't tell you how much I wish that were true. How much I would have loved that to be true about a year ago, but it's not. You know we hooked up one time."

"You hooked up? With Samuel Ruiz?"

I ignore the way he asks that, a little *too* surprised for my liking. "It was a long time ago, it never happened again, and honestly? I don't even know if he remembers it happened in the first place. If he does, he didn't care enough about it to discuss it, much less get moody about it years later. He's not obsessed with me. Really."

"Whether he is or isn't, that's how he acts." Augie sniffs. "I told him to get it together. You're the goddamn oracle. He's beneath you." He glares at me. "Which was also true before you were the oracle."

I don't know if he actually said that to Samuel or not, but I'll admit that I choose to believe he did. Makes me feel warm and happy.

I try to hold on to that feeling as the last week of October begins, slinking in all ice and gloom, and Savi announces that it will be go time on Friday. Halloween.

Because, of course, it's not only a full moon, but a blue moon. Sounds like exactly the kind of thing a self-obsessed bitch goddess like Vinča would like.

The plan is that we'll go by day. Savi has a spell ready. She and the other powers have put their heads together and determined a strategy.

We go over this at sundown on Thursday, though it seems a lot colder and grimmer out in the yard now. Once again, Briar is nowhere to be seen. I'm relieved. I might not know who she is or why she's here—or even if she's human—but she's not exactly a force for good.

Even on a simple tenant level.

This time, Ty comes without his lieutenants, and both he and Ariel crowd onto the porch.

It makes for a tight little group.

If Samuel's nursing his obsession for me, he hides it well. He's much too busy glaring at Ariel, then Ty, and then back again.

"Usually, these things are done at moonrise, in the dark," Savi says for the human contingent, since I assume everyone else already knows this. "That's why we're not doing it that way. If we do it in daylight, it gives us an advantage."

"Is this goddess a creature of the night?" Augie asks.

"Not at all," Ariel replies. "It's nothing but habit. It is easier to be scary in the dark, perhaps."

I absolutely do not look over at him.

"If everything goes according to plan," Savi says, "we'll get up there easily enough. Winter, you and your grandmother and Augie will all go. We'll see if that much oracle blood in one place helps boost the visions and keep us on track. I'll make sure it's nice and cloudy. We'll have werewolves and vampires ready to fight, but hopefully none of that will be necessary. I'll cast the spell, she'll be trapped anew, and we'll get back to our lives."

"That sounds simple enough," I say optimistically.

Ty belts out a laugh. "That's if it goes well. It won't. Nothing ever does."

"She was put away once," Savi reminds him. "It can be done. It gives us an edge to know that it not only *can* be done, it *was* done before."

We talk about a few other details. Samuel volunteers to drive up in his truck, transporting the humans.

Augie and I exchange a look, but it seems easy enough to agree.

The meeting breaks up. Augie's vampire lady appears, and they wander around the side of the house. Ty and Maddox lope off into the woods. He throws that big arm over her shoulders, and I catch the way she looks at him, like he's all the galaxies she needs.

When I look back, Samuel has followed Savi over to where she parks her SUV and appears to be making a case for . . . something.

I don't care enough to try to eavesdrop.

Ariel simply waits. He's wearing dark trousers, which I know aren't his gi pants only because they cling to his form that much better, and another black T-shirt. In case I was having withdrawal from the sight of his biceps.

"What do you think our chances are?" I ask him.

"You could mean that question any number of ways. Pick one."

I don't really like his tone, so dark and edgy, but I don't argue about it. "You're the one who knew her. Do you think we can keep her trapped?"

"Can we? Yes. Without question. Will we?" He shrugs. "That very much depends. Some wars are won by superior strength and strategy. Others by trickery. And still others because one side simply would not fall. I cannot say what this particular group will do. We are not an army."

"Thank you. What a stellar pep talk that was. You should consider becoming a motivational speaker."

He regards me for too long, and I have no doubt that it's deliberate. It's meant to make me feel . . . unwieldy in my own skin. It does.

Or maybe it's the memory of him moving me up and down on his cock, like his own little fuck toy, that makes me feel as close to twitchy as I get.

"I am a fighter," he tells me in a low voice. "All I have ever known is war. I'm good at it. Give me a battlefield and I don't need any oracle to predict what will happen."

He reaches over and brushes his cool fingers over my cheek. What I want to feel is that it's too cold for vampire nonsense. What I *want* to feel is that anything that cold on a chilly fall night is too frigid for me.

But I'm not cold at all. And when he touches me, I ignite.

It would be so easy to let him in. Take him by the hand and invite him inside, then lead him up into my attic, where I could lock us both away until tomorrow.

It would be so, so easy.

"Tell me what war I'm fighting here," he urges me in that same low voice, his silver eyes on mine.

All I want to do is melt.

Instead, I step back, as if I hear something. For a moment, I think I only *wish* that I heard something, but then I see Samuel's truck head down the drive.

I can't tell what he might have seen from where he was.

Was he standing there, watching us? That's creepy, but I shake it off.

"Sounds like we have a big day tomorrow," I say, far more brightly than the situation warrants. Or I feel. "You're not used to daytimes, are you?" I smile, then I haul the door open, and I think we're both completely aware that I'm deliberately putting that gate between us. "You probably want to get your beauty sleep before you run into your ex."

Ariel only smiles. He reaches around the gate between us and pulls me toward him, gently enough. But there's no possibility that I won't do exactly what he wants me to. There's no room to do anything but what he wants.

I tell myself that's why I do it.

He backs me up into that gate and then leans in, his hands fisting around the iron bars on either side of my head.

"If you are going to react this way every time you encounter a former lover of mine, you are going to exhaust yourself quickly," he tells me, and his voice has some of his own iron in it. "Besides, it's boring."

"A happy solution would be to not spend any time with me, then."

"That's even more boring."

Then he leans in and sets his mouth to mine.

I expect the spike of flaming heat. I expect my body to shudder, practically at its flashpoint that easily.

What I don't expect is the way he kisses me. Soft. Knowing. Easy.

Sweet, I might even say, if I didn't feel—every now and then—the hint of his fangs.

He kisses me until I'm limp against him, melted down like candle wax, clinging to his T-shirt like I want to climb him.

He kisses me until I betray myself so completely that I don't even protest when he sets me back against the gate, fixes me with one of those dark, searching looks he loves so much, and then leaves me there.

With nothing but regret and an ache inside me, so deep and so wide it won't let me sleep.

27.

Samuel picks us up before first light.

I sit with Gran in the back seat so that Augie can bro it up in the front.

What that looks like initially is a monosyllabic exchange that peters out long before we make it down the hill into Jacksonville.

"I can't even think when I was last at Crater Lake," Gran says, musingly, gazing out the window. "Years ago. I think I went with your grandfather."

"Neither one of you liked snow that much," I say, remembering. "So it would have to have been in summer."

"That lake is bitter cold at the height of August." Gran laughs, but there's something almost wistful in her expression, I think. Maybe even sad. She catches me looking and nods. "This will be quite an adventure, child."

It already is. We drive out of Medford, heading north through communities I haven't been to in well over three years. Most of them are in ruins. White City is little more than rubble, with the Table Rocks standing sentry. Created millions of years ago, the two volcanic mesas were popular hiking destinations throughout my childhood and are now the aeries of harpies, gorgons, and other terrifying winged things. Eagle Point is nothing but empty houses and the packs of wildlife that inhabit them until some other enterprising creature decides to have a buffet.

Shady Cove, a hardscrabble little river town that was always a bit on the scruffy side, is filled with goblins. They chatter at us as we drive by, and I get my guns ready because I expect them to chase the car, but they don't.

"That's weird," I mutter. "Since when do goblins sit by and let anything roll on through?"

Gran taps her fingers against the window. "We have an escort."

That's when I see that there are wolves trailing Samuel's truck. Easily keeping up with it when they like, but also falling back to teach a few lessons to the creatures who fail to keep their distance.

I feel a warmth I really shouldn't. All through me.

We wind our way deeper into the wild countryside of Oregon, heading east into the Cascades. Up by Lost Creek Lake, it's so pretty on this gray morning that I can't seem to think about anything but long-ago camping trips. Augie and me and our high school friends would come up here and get silly with only the stars as witness.

We had no idea how innocent we were. Or how quickly everything would change, even before the Reveal.

I can't decide if the nostalgia feels good or if it hurts.

At least Augie's right here, in the same truck, and if he's not exactly clean, well. He's more *him* than he's been since back in our camping trip days, and that feels like a circle well closed.

Samuel navigates around a gaping hole in the side of the bridge we need to cross that's eaten up most of one lane, and we keep going. It's green and cold, and the farther we go, the higher we climb, the more the bit of frost on the ground turns to snow. The drive takes us through what has to be the prettiest stretch of forest I know. Douglas firs stand tall and let the light peek through, here and there, like hints of faraway hope filtered through trees that are some seven hundred years old.

Still younger than Ariel, I can't help but think.

There are pockets of mist and fog, small-animal tracks, and waterfalls in all directions. Beside me, Gran is humming to herself.

In front, Samuel and Augie are talking in low voices about old football games played by long-since-eaten teams.

Just substitute my grandfather for Samuel, or even my dad in one of his rare family moods, and this could be any sweet Saturday from our childhood. The kind of day that would make me imagine that really, it wasn't all *so* bad. It has the same effect now.

By the time we get to Union Creek—where there was once a very small community, my favorite campground in Oregon, and a diner that made the best pie in the Pacific Northwest—I'm almost ready to pretend everything really is normal. To get out of the car, go into the still-standing diner building, and ask if they have a slice of homemade marionberry they can heat up for me. And go heavy on the vanilla ice cream.

When we drive by, there are signs of life, but none of us knows what to make of it. Snow has been cleared from the main road. There are trucks parked all around and lights on inside the diner and the general store across the way. I can see smoke coming from some of the buildings.

It looks beautiful and bucolic, and we know better than to stop.

"Do you think they're human?" I ask. Maybe a little bit wistfully.

"I haven't heard one way or the other," Samuel says, frowning out his window. "I suppose they could be. This is out of the way."

Gran sniffs. "Not for wolves."

Augie says nothing.

Samuel keeps driving. "Humans really have to stick together. That's such an important part of keeping Jacksonville on the map. If we're together, we have strength. I believe that. Don't you, Winter?"

Only half listening, I jolt to attention when he says my name.

"I've been to every one of your meetings, Samuel," I remind him. "As you know."

Augie glances over his shoulder but doesn't have to say a word. I'm just glad that both of us find Samuel annoying.

"I appreciate this notion you have," Samuel continues as he navigates his way to the turn—where there used to be signs—that leads to Crater Lake. "It's a very interesting experiment you're doing, Winter. Really. And I know that everyone in school had a thing about Maddox Hemming. I get it."

"I have a thing about rent money, Samuel," I say, making sure to use his name in the same way he's using mine. Irritatingly. "Maddox Hemming is just icing on the rent cake."

"Humans should stick together," Samuel says again and darkly, to my ear, and I swear he deliberately wiggles the steering wheel so I crash into the window next to me.

"Hey," Augie says, sounding deceptively relaxed when I can see that he's tense. "My grandmother is in the back seat. Be careful."

The look that passes between him and Samuel then does not seem friendly and *up with humans*, but Samuel has more to concentrate on. This road is covered in snow, no hint of any plowing, and we have to bump along as best we can.

It's actually a relief when we finally make it up the winding road and into the park. Or what used to be a national park and is now . . . just here, though likely better off with the lack of annual tourists.

We make our way up to where the visitors' center used to sit—and still does, I see, though it was gutted long ago. There used to be a gift shop, a cafeteria, a small museum. A little farther down the road is the lodge, where I always wanted to stay but never did.

But if anyone is staying there now, I don't want to know.

We climb out of the truck into significant snow on the ground. I'm comforted by the fact that there are no tracks or footprints anywhere to be seen, and also that we all dressed appropriately. The sky above is still gray, with no snow flurries. At least not now.

All good news for our little gang, I think.

Augie and I each offer Gran an elbow, and she holds on to us with a surprisingly tight grip as we walk over to the rim and one of the overlooks.

There's a wall there, still. And without meaning to, I catch my breath as we look out. Because Crater Lake is stunning, no matter why I might have come here today. Considered one of the seven great wonders of Oregon, I always thought it had its place on any list of wonders of the world. It's the deepest lake in America. It has always been the sort of place that lends itself to myths and legends. Some claim that the natives feared this place and would not come here. The Klamath told of a monster who lived in its depths and asserted that the hills surrounding it were ripe with all manner of demons.

A trip to the abandoned library in Jacksonville also told me that there are other stories of those who came here to find their power, to risk whatever lurks in the lake, and to harness the magic here.

I find I believe all of the above, and more than that, I know *exactly* who is at the bottom of this lake.

I've swum in it myself. Some summers, I've hiked down the trail that leads to the water's edge to put my feet in. Sometimes I've even gone swimming, jumping off rocks to submerge myself in the lake's icy grip.

I always left exhilarated.

Like it was preparing you to be a vampire's lover, something in me whispers.

I'd like to ignore that, but even here, in the midst of all this natural beauty and without the faintest hint around me that he exists or vampires even *could* exist, I can't stop thinking about him.

That and the way he kissed me last night.

I scowl at the water, so blue it seems to bleed into me. As if looking at it makes you a part of it.

Samuel makes a low noise. I look up, blink the blue away, and see that our wolf guards are with us still. Now they're sitting on either side of the little knot of us at the wall. They do not change into human form so they can communicate with us. This seems significant.

I recognize them as the lieutenants Ty brought with him to my house that time, but I can see that Samuel doesn't.

I don't identify them to him.

Especially because I get the distinct impression that they know that staying in their wolf form bothers him and are therefore doing it deliberately.

Ariel appears then, flickering into view in the middle of a thick tangle of conifers, high on the little swell of hill that juts out beyond the wall. He's dressed differently today, or maybe it's that I finally realize he's been wearing different forms of combat attire this whole time. Today he's pulled it all together. Those combat pants and the typical black T-shirt, though this one looks like it's made of a more technical fabric. I can see every mouthwatering ridge on his abdomen. He wears a harness like mine, with wicked-looking blades attached to it and shotguns at his back.

He looks around, his gaze cool and assessing as he takes in the scene, and I have no choice but to think about what twenty-five hundred years of fighting *really is*. It's this. It's him. He's a weapon. From head to toe, one carved muscle to the next. Every inch of him is deadly.

I know that better than most.

I can't let myself look at him beyond that initial first glance. I'm afraid that if I do, my own grandmother will see the longing on my face. And then, obviously, I will have to immediately die of embarrassment. Nobody wants that.

Gran moves forward to brace herself against the wall looking out over the lake. Augie and I stay back, watching—or in my case, not watching—as Ariel moves around in the gray morning, clearly performing tactical objectives he does not share with the group.

The cold gets to me and I shiver, then zip up my coat now that we're out of the warm cab of Samuel's truck. Augie's gaze cuts to me and he lifts his chin. "Where's that medallion?"

I stop mid-zip and feel around for it. "I think I took it off last time I showered. Must have left it on my bedside table."

The truth is, I don't remember the last time I had it on. Ariel's apartment, maybe. But it burned. For some reason, I think of that weirdo Briar standing there in the kitchen, scowling at me with her hand in the same place mine is now.

"You should find it and wear it," Augie tells me. "It's supposed to deal with evil spirits and that kind of shit."

"Again, I think maybe you should wear it, then."

He looks at me for a moment, then over at Ariel, who is studying the lake down below us now as if he expects an eruption at any moment. "Because your evil spirits are hot?"

I do not deign to answer that.

Also, my brother is right. Ariel is hot.

And I was up for most of the night drowning in that kiss of his. Reliving it again and again and again, and imagining it going further. I'm glad that our twin bond doesn't allow for *actually* reading minds.

There's a sudden golden light, and when Ariel doesn't react to it, I know it's Savi's dramatic appearance. Sure enough, she arrives in an all-white ensemble that makes her look like a dream, and she seems to float above the snow when she moves. Maybe she really is floating.

Soon after, two wolves I recognize, one of them enormous and the other much sleeker than either of the lieutenants, lope over to take their place beside us.

There's that thunderclap and flash, and then we're all together again.

Ariel comes down from the little rise he's walked all over so he's closer to the group. "It seems very on the nose, but I can't help thinking that they call it Wizard Island for a reason."

"I do like the symmetry," Savi says. "It's not hard to imagine that another sorcerer would as well."

We all gaze out at the little island that sits there. So named, as far as I have ever been aware, because it actually looks like a wizard's hat.

"I know we're all here for a serious reason," Samuel says, and he has a big, sappy kind of grin on his face as he walks toward the end of the wall, near where Ariel is standing beneath the last tree. It makes me feel guilty for finding him so . . . Well. For finding him less hot than I used to. Less . . . *everything*, and how is that fair? I'm comparing him to an immortal Spartan vampire warrior. Who could measure up? "But it's only a serious reason that would get me to drive up this way, and probably, if I did it myself, I would've been eaten by goblins. Or whatever's living in Union Creek."

"You don't want to know," Ty assures him with an ominous-sounding laugh.

"Do they get to eat Beckie's pie, though?" Augie asks me in an undertone.

"The first serious question of the day," I reply in the same tone.

When Gran glares at the pair of us, I feel like we're little kids again. Being chastised in a public place, like the grocery store or our biannual church appearance, and I find myself grinning too.

"I used to come up to Crater Lake all the time," Samuel tells us, and he seems more relaxed than he has lately. Maybe things are changing for the better after all. Maybe today really will solve our problems. Maybe this lake really is magic. "That's one of the things I miss the most. It's not safe to go hiking anymore. It's certainly not wise to leave the valley and come all the way up here. No telling what lurks in the hills around a place as powerful as this."

"It's beautiful here," Savi murmurs, looking out over the water. The rim of the crater is impressive, with mountains all around and cliffs that drop steeply and insistently into that wild blue water. "But dangerous. In many ways."

"I wish it was sunny," Samuel says, then sighs happily.

He keeps his gaze out on the water, and we all watch as he goes over and climbs up the bank a little bit, on the small rise that turns into the steep walls of the caldera, and slides all the way down into that unreal blue. He stops to stand beneath the trees like Ariel, still looking out across the crater.

I see the way Ariel looks at him, the way he would look at a pet that was acting out. Someone else's pet, obviously. His are better behaved, and I flush when I think about *how* well behaved I'd like to be for him.

Beside me, Augie shifts. "I can't remember the last time I was up here. It was definitely sunny, though."

"It was after we graduated from high school," I say, because I remember all too well. I remember the good things. I collect them. "Late that summer. It was hot until we hit the water."

Savi smiles. "I'm not opposed to a little bit of light," she says. "To remind us what we're fighting for."

She looks over at Ariel as she speaks, and I realize why when he nods. He's the vampire. He's the one who has to worry about sunlight—and when his eyes go a bit unfocused and he does something with his hand, I assume he's warning all his minions to take cover.

Savi chants, then seems to paint in the air. For a moment I see symbols on the breeze that remind me of the ones on my cards, but they're gone before I can tell if I know them.

Her chant gets louder, and the gloom falls away. The sun beams down from its spot in the sky across the lake, and everything is suddenly *dazzling*.

Perfect.

The blues are impossible. The greens are glorious. The snow glitters and gleams like crushed diamonds. I can *feel* all this light inside me, like it's lifting me up and changing all my molecules as it goes. Like it's infusing us all with joy, right here where we stand.

It wouldn't surprise me at all if there were more than one god or goddess stuck down there beneath all that unearthly blue, because the other thing that's unmistakable about this place is the power that seems to sing out of the rocks themselves.

McLoughlin was the same. Volcanoes make themselves known, that much is for sure.

The sun feels good on my face. It's been a long time since I've seen it for more than a few sunrise or sunset moments, and longer still since I've had the time or felt safe enough to feel it all over me. I let my eyes drift shut. I bask.

When I open my eyes, I see Samuel still standing at the top of that little rise. He's staring out at the sun with a smile on his face. He stands a little ways above Ariel, who is not gazing hopelessly at the sun as a person who's watched too many vampire shows might imagine, but is instead looking down at the water with a strange expression I can't quite place.

All of this feels like grief and love, hope and despair. All of it, from the sun on my face to the blue of the water so far below. The exquisite price of living, and maybe it's always been this way. Maybe life has always been, like that song my mom used to play when I was little, so precious and so cruel.

Maybe monsters aren't the only thing that's been revealed in these last few years. Maybe the truth about the Reveal is that it's a mirror, where we see who we really are.

I'm going to have to think about that, and now is not the time.

I wish that this moment of sunshine could last forever, but I can already sense the impatience coming in hot from Ty. And if there are spells to cast and goddesses to chain up tight, I'm for doing it quicker.

After all, I'm the one who had to talk to that bitch. I'd prefer to never do *that* again.

I turn to say something and see that Samuel is making his way down the hill. I think that it was sweet of him to suggest this and sweeter still of Savi to give the humans a moment. I decide to tell him so as he moves behind Ariel, who stands so still he might as well be one of the pines.

And then everything happens in slow motion. And almost cinematically.

Samuel lunges forward. Then Ariel is falling. Over the side of the cliff, out of the shadows and into the light.

The sunlight that immediately begins to burn him.

Everything in me screams *no*—

I hear the werewolves howl—

Samuel is hurtling down that hill toward us, so fast it's hard to tell if he is falling or if he's running—

Until he stops, sudden and hard. I stare without comprehension at the bloom of red on the front of his chest.

Then I look behind me and see the gun in my grandmother's hand.

I hear Augie's voice. I hear all kinds of noises, loud and probably terrifying, but Ariel is in the sunshine, completely exposed in midair, no shade, no help.

I swear I hear him begin to sizzle, and then he disappears.

Just like that, he's gone.

He's gone.

It is only then that everything seems to speed up again. Too fast. Too bright. Too loud. Savi shouts something into the air and everything is plunged into darkness, thunderclouds rolling in at high speed.

Everyone is lunging toward Samuel, but he is howling out in pain and rage. He's also closer, and he throws himself toward Gran.

They both hit the ground, hard. Too hard.

For a long beat of my broken, disbelieving heart, neither one of them moves.

So I do instead.

I throw myself toward them—and the wall that's the only thing keeping them from sliding off the cliff and down the slick sides of the crater to their deaths.

28.

Augie clotheslines me.

One moment I'm lunging for Samuel with every intention of landing on him or in him or whatever works to get him *off* Gran—

"Stop," Augie orders me when I slam to a halt and start coughing because he threw that arm across my chest so hard.

I'm lucky it wasn't my throat.

"You can't die," my twin grits out at me. "*You* can't fucking *die*, Winter."

I recognize that look on his face. I know exactly how he feels. I can see, in this shitty little moment, that he finally gets it. What these years have been like. How many times I've had to say goodbye to him, always certain that the next time I saw him it would be on a funeral pyre or in a box.

He gets it, and I wish he didn't, but I can't deny that there's a part of me, deep inside, that's glad.

But there's no time for our stuff. Not now.

We both throw ourselves on our knees next to the pile of Samuel and Gran, then pull Samuel off her roughly.

Samuel is dead. His eyes are wide open and vacant. The little bloom of red on his shirt has spread.

It turns out Gran hit the bull's-eye.

"I always was a straight shooter," she says, weakly, and even laughs, and it feels for a moment like Savi brought the sun out again.

Good riddance, I think, still looking at Samuel. Fucking Samuel, who I thought was so special and then stopped thinking about at all, then felt sorry for, and who turned out to be another human monster. Might as well have joined up with Franklin Hendry's team of thugs.

For all I know, he did.

I feel Ariel's mark begin to . . . *shimmer*, and I have to gulp back the sob that wants to escape me. It's a full-body sob, and I know, somehow, that if I indulge it I won't stop until it tears me in two, and there is still a whole death goddess to handle.

I feel the mark throb a little, all along my back, and I think, *Is this how I know he's dead?*

But *how* can he be dead? He's twenty-five hundred years old and three seconds of sun does him in?

I can't bear it. I have survived far too many things, but this one might kill me.

This one I don't *want* to survive.

Maddox whines, still in her wolf form, and when I look up, I follow her gaze.

I see mist between the trees, rising slowly.

I hold my breath.

Then he's there. Silver eyes blazing.

And burns. Nasty, awful-looking burns all across his face, down his neck, and all over his arms.

But he's here. He's not gone. He's *here*.

The relief that courses through me is so profound that it feels like a blow. Like another whole body landed on me, too, and knocked all the air out of mine.

Who needs air if he's not dead? I'm happy to keel over if it's for a good reason instead of the worst—

"Gran." Augie's voice is intense. *"Shit."*

I stop worrying about whether or not I can breathe and return my attention to my grandmother. She's covered in blood, and it can't be Samuel's blood, because new blood is still welling out of her. She's panting, heavily, and the hands that held her handgun in front of her have fallen to her sides.

Revealing the hilt of a knife sticking straight out of her chest.

"No," I say, or maybe I scream it.

Savi starts chanting again. The wolves are howling.

Everything is terrible, but then Gran opens her eyes. She looks between Augie and me, and she smiles.

"I'm an oracle," she croaks out at us. "I came here today knowing this would happen, precisely like this. I was not betrayed. This is a willing sacrifice. He wanted this to be the key that unlocks her, but it's not."

"He did not betray me either," comes Ariel's dark, furious voice. "I always thought he was a two-faced fool."

Ty roars, and I think we all know it's in agreement.

Everything feels charged and slow and terrible, but I remember what Savi said at our first gathering. *Two locks to open. And two different keys. The first, a living sacrifice, as painful as possible beneath a full moon. The second, a terrible betrayal and an unwilling sacrifice.*

"You would have to have trusted him to be betrayed by him," I manage to say, looking at Ariel. I look back down at Gran. "And you knew what he would do. That means you sacrificed yourself. *Willingly.*"

Though my voice cracks when I say that word. *Willingly.*

"Why else would I bring your grandfather's gun?" Gran asks with a rough approximation of her usual saltiness.

"There will be a different betrayal, a different sacrifice," Savi says, her eyes blazing gold. "And there is nothing to say it will be amongst us."

"It wasn't last time," Ariel points out. "It was all entirely triggered by Vinča's acolytes."

Gran nods. Her breathing is getting shallower. "Remember," she says, though she has to struggle to get her words out, "I walked into my death with my eyes open. I chose it. I didn't hide from it, I didn't try to change it. I want the two of you to *live.*"

"It should be me," Augie grits out, his voice thick with the same fury and disbelief that I can feel eating me up inside. "I'm the fuckup. I'm the disappointment. *It should be me.*"

"I'm a seventy-five-year-old woman," Gran tells him, her indigo gaze bright. "Death and I are no strangers to each other. And you, August, would do well to remember that it will come for you when it's ready. No matter how you court it. No matter how you chase it. *You* don't get to decide your time."

"Gran," I whisper.

Augie is sobbing, gripping one of her hands. I only know that I am too, because I see my tears splash on her coat.

"If I had to choose the perfect way to go, it would be exactly like this," Gran says, her voice getting weaker. We have to lean in to hear her. "All of us together. The way it should be."

We hold on to each other for as long as we can. Until, no matter how many times I try to plead or bargain, her grip goes slack.

And she is no vampire. She is not supernatural, only a gateway to the supernatural. There is no possibility that she will come back in the mist, or at all.

The finality of this beats down on me, a weight too great to bear.

I feel the rain begin. It's warmer than it should be on Halloween this high in the mountains, courtesy of Savi, I imagine.

The wolves howl, though the sound is changed from the howls I've heard before, and I understand that it's a tribute. A lamentation to fill the air, and it's beautiful. It's lonely. It's one of the most mournful and lovely things I've ever heard.

It breaks my heart again and again and again.

Augie sits up first. He wipes at his face, then begins arranging Gran's body so she looks the way she did when she was alive. Perfect. Unruffled.

Ready to cut everyone down to size with a few well-chosen words.

I sit back too. I feel . . . dazed. Hollowed out with this new grief that's like the sharp edge of that knife stuck deep into my own chest.

And while I know that it's sliced into me good, I also know that the real pain hasn't hit yet.

There will be a lifetime for that.

I look around blindly, but Ariel is already there. He crouches down and wraps me in his arms. His burns are already gone, only the faintest shadows over his skin to show that he was ever marked or marred.

I find I can revel in that, and find it desperately unfair, all at the same time.

He holds me there, tucked against his body. His strong arms wrap tight around me, like he's holding me together. I don't just feel that mark on me glow.

I glow straight through.

And this is the scariest thing that's happened with him yet, because it isn't sexual at all.

He gives me pure comfort. And I take it. I sink into it and feel that deep, resonating *relief.* Not that his hug takes away the pain. But somehow, because he shares it, the pain is slightly more bearable.

I think that *maybe* I won't just die right here after all.

"I hate to interrupt," comes Ty's low, furious voice after a thunderclap I barely register. "She was a decent lady. But we have bigger problems."

That's when I hear it. The shouting in the distance, a terrible din.

Ariel stands, bringing me with him. We all move back up toward the place where the road that lazily circles the crater would be, if there was no snow.

But I can't focus on the snow or the road in my memories.

They're coming in fast.

It's those same figures in their creepy cloaks and horrifying masks, looking like plague doctors from another time, only far more ominous and terrible.

And it's clear that they're heading straight for us.

"What the fuck are *those*?" Augie demands.

"The Goddess of Filth has many species of acolyte in her cult," Ariel says. "Orcs. Ghouls. Harpies. Every creature you can imagine.

She collects them. I'd suspect this lot are not human, however. Too easily broken."

Augie makes a low, anguished noise. "Not easily enough."

I can feel something in me sit up and take notice, even though every other part of me wants to lie down and let grief do what it will. I want to let the grief eat me whole. I might not want to *die* the way I did a few moments ago, but living holds no appeal at all.

Too bad I don't get to choose to avoid it, and not only because my grandmother's dying wish was that Augie and I live. It feels like a commandment.

I can't succumb to that urge to simply fall down until the weight of this lessens, because there's that *thing* inside me.

Gran would call it my gift.

I call it fucked up.

Because I know what this is, and what's coming.

I've already seen it.

29.

Seeing another vision of mine come to life, starring the same fuckheads, is clarifying.

It's not that I stop grieving, it's that I feel that grief shift. Become fuel.

It helps to know that Gran would have bitten my head off, then told me to wipe my face clean and get to work.

Not sentimental, our Gran.

I do what I know she would want me to do. I retreat to the place where she's lying, much too still. I pull the cards out from the pocket they chose today and shuffle them, humming a little in the back of my throat. It isn't a tune. It's more the suggestion of one, and I let it play through me and into the cards.

Beside me, Augie finishes arranging Gran and turns to handling Samuel. He goes through his pockets. He finds the other weapons Samuel had stashed away on his body. He turns him over and pulls open the pack he was wearing on his back.

Ariel is moving too. I hear him bark out orders, and I realize I've heard him do this before. I've watched him do it, and watched his vampire minions respond to his commands with their brutal poetry.

When I look up, I see the vampires appearing. They go from mist to corporeal form, then into those same perfect lines I saw in the MMA studio.

It was his army all along.

They melt into formation, Ariel at the helm.

Ty has shifted again, and he lets out a new roar. It isn't a howl, not that sound.

It's another call to arms, I realize in the next moment as the wolves begin to pour in, coming from all directions, some of them from behind—like they've been hiding out in the hills.

They flank the cloaked figures, the vampires advance, and the battle begins on a much larger scale than the one I barely survived on Mount McLoughlin.

Savi steps over the retaining wall and floats out onto the little spit of cliff on the other side. Maddox goes with her, a sleek and terrible wolf bodyguard.

I keep shuffling my cards. I keep humming. I wait for the sight to take hold.

Augie makes a noise as he digs around in Samuel's pack. When I frown at him, he pulls out one of those cloaks. I could try to explain that away, but he follows it with a beaked mask.

It's another blow I didn't see coming.

I stop humming. I find myself holding the cards to my heart. "He was one of them?"

Was he there that night on the mountain? Did he know what would happen to me?

But even as I wonder these things, I release them. Samuel is dead. I'm not. That's all that matters.

Augie's mouth twists as he looks down at the mask in his hand. "Everyone wants power," my twin tells me in a low voice. "Maybe especially the ones who pretend they don't. You should know that by now."

His gaze meets mine. We're looking at each other, but we *are* each other. It feels right. It feels like a much-needed return to form.

But it's also so new that it aches.

"What do you want, then?" I ask.

His mouth twists even more. "Power, obviously. But I want it over *me*, Winter. I want power over *myself*."

He doesn't say *for once*, but I hear it.

I reach out my hand, and I don't know what I'm about to say, but there's a calamitous noise so loud it makes the air itself seem to shake.

When we turn, the smooth surface of the lake now looks like it's . . . boiling.

"She is coming," I belt out, in a voice that is not mine. I feel it echo not just in me, but in Augie. In everyone around us.

In the tall trees that stretch for the stormy sky.

Out in the blue water of the lake, Wizard Island trembles.

And then, as it shakes, it begins to rise.

Savi is still chanting. Now she catapults herself straight up into the air, then out over the water so that she's hovering over the intense blue of the lake, and the island seems as if it's rising to meet her.

She stretches out her arms, as if crucifying herself in midair. Then, as her hair whips around her and her eyes blaze like fire, she begins again.

The counterspell rains down all around her, like more weather.

I shuffle the cards, but I don't need to look at them. They tell me what I need to know. They pour into me, and I need—

I need *something*—

I reach out, stretching along the lines of magic that I can suddenly see spooling out of me, and Augie, and every creature here. Lines of brilliant color that dance into the sky and need only to be pulled to lead me to the person in question.

That's how I find Ariel. I look for the thickest cool-blue line, the one that whispers of age and time, and I pull it.

Hard.

Little seer, he says, but he's inside me. He's speaking inside my head, that rich, dark voice like a caress. *How clever of you to find me this way.*

I whip my head around, and I think I see him, deep in the center of that swirling, deadly mass of cloaks and creatures, fangs and claws. They fight and fight, they stain the snow red below their feet, and still they keep going.

And as the cards pour into me, I pour into him.

I watch as he follows my predictions. He doesn't ask. He doesn't question. I don't have to prove to him the things I see.

He treats my visions like cold, hard facts, and because he does, the tide begins to turn.

The cards are shuffling so fast in my hands I can barely keep up, and my fingers ache, but they would need to be cut off before I stopped.

I won't stop.

Not until we all do.

The priests, I tell Ariel down the line that chains us to each other now. Maybe it's magic. Maybe it's our bond. I don't know what it is, but I know it's ours. I know it's permanent.

And there's not one part of me that wants to fight it.

I hate priests, he replies, and his voice in my head is so cool, so calm.

Then I can see what he's doing, with my own eyes, and in my head, too. I see the fight before me as if the battle is on a movie screen. I glimpse it occasionally through his eyes, and on top of this, the cards show me different views as they please.

It's a whole kaleidoscope, ever shifting, but I understand each view and where it fits.

And I keep telling him. Showing him.

It's her priests who presented her with a key to her lock, I tell him. *They didn't trust Samuel's claim that he could do it. They took care of it themselves. Worst-case scenario,* I say in a voice that doesn't feel like mine—too ancient and wise—*she has unwilling sacrifices to choose from.*

I can hear his laugh *inside* me. *That sounds like every death cult I've ever encountered.*

Then I see him in the air again, this time with no sun to burn him. He leaps up as if he wants the fighters from both sides to track him. They do—all the cloaked figures watch him go—but his own warriors attack them in the next second, taking advantage of their momentary distraction.

Ariel doesn't fly. He doesn't hang in the air like Savi. He leaps far higher and farther than any human could, and when he goes down again, he lands where I can't see him. Not with my eyes.

In my head, I follow along.

"It's the priests," I say out loud so Maddox and Augie can hear me, and maybe Savi too, though it's hard to tell while she's still in midair, making it storm.

Making that island tremble all the more.

"This can't end as long as those priests remain." I say it out loud. In my head.

To everyone.

"Don't worry," Maddox says from behind me when I didn't see her change. "Ty is on it."

I don't think about what I'm doing. I want them to see what I see, so I make it happen. I pull on each thread, indigo for Augie, smoky quartz for Maddox, and then we're all there.

We're all connected, and we're *in it.*

Ty and Ariel have both left their armies to fight the goddess's acolytes up above as they chase the priests down the old trail that leads to the water's edge. On one of the switchbacks, the priests turn back to face them, knives out.

It's a bloodbath, brutal and cruel.

Up at the rim, the three of us sit with our backs pressed together, Gran and Samuel laid out before us, Savi in the air behind us, and these battles in our heads.

Savi's voice rises. The storm intensifies.

There's something worse than thunder, more electrifying than lightning.

Then there's a great and terrible scream.

It seems to erupt out of the crater itself. We all duck as if there's something shooting straight at us, when there isn't.

The scream goes on and on, and when my head starts to ache—that sharp pain in my temples that I know too well—I understand.

It's her.

I have to think that a sound like that, rage and fury and a deep bewilderment, can only be a good thing for us.

But I retract that thought immediately, because suddenly, she's *here.*

Wizard Island shakes, Savi is in the thick of it, but there's a seven-thousand-year-old death goddess of filth and fury in my head. Not just my head. She's swelling into being down each and every colored thread of magic, blackening them as she goes.

Vinča is here.

And she's pissed.

"You!" she bellows, and she is a mess of black, slithering worms and beaks red with blood. She is all things and nothing. "Pestilent human, do you believe that you can stand before me? Do you *dare*?"

"No," I tell her, though I can feel her all around me, like a wind. And inside me, like some horrific parasite that intends to consume me from within. "Not me. I'm nothing but an oracle."

The oracle, I think.

And the cards are like fire in my hands, their images and symbols scrolling through me, and I don't need to get to know them anymore.

I am them. They are me.

I see what I have to do, and I do it.

I see everything. Savi up above the lake. The wolves and the vampires. Augie beside me, anchoring me, keeping his vigil over Gran.

I gather up all the threads I found and I pull them, hard.

Vinča is smoke and maggots, fury and blood.

But she is *in my head.*

If she could hurt me, I would already be dead.

I pull on the threads of magic for strength, I call down the constellations she uses as her stepping stones, and I tie them into knots.

Then I stare the bird-faced bitch who used Ariel as a pet straight in her face while I shove them in my mouth and swallow them whole.

Like I'm a goddess myself, devouring her destruction the way she has eaten entire civilizations whole.

Not this time.

"I don't see you rising," I tell her, my mouth full of galaxies. "And maybe go fuck yourself, too."

And this time when she screams, I can feel the mountains tremble all around us.

The threads of magic find their colors once again.

Vinča is no longer in my head.

Out above the lake, Savi is getting louder, the chanting more insistent.

Inside me, I can *feel* Vinča scream, on and on and on, but I know somehow that she can't get to me from there.

I watch the battle instead. With everyone else.

In my head, we watch Ty rip an orc priest in half, then leap on another one—a wraith this time.

Ariel fights his way into the scrum.

And I can see it, I think. All twenty-five hundred years of peak physical prowess, because he moves like poetry, though his verses are deadly and profoundly disturbing.

But . . . not unhot.

Maybe swallowing a death goddess has made me callous. Maybe he's just that beautiful.

Maybe I need us all to live.

The two of them take the pack of priests apart with focused precision, and when they converge on the final one, Ariel throws his head back, lets his fangs grow, and waits as the last priest cowers.

Until Ty rips his head off.

That scream inside me, inside Wizard Island, gets louder and then louder still—

Until it is nothing but a howl of anguish.

And then it's gone.

Everything is quiet, except the wind. We can hear it snaking through the trees, almost whistling, as if it's made of ghosts. When we look down the rim road, there are only bodies and blood.

The wolves move to the fallen, sniffing them out. The vampires come behind them, pulling off the masks and looking at each face.

They are making sure we know who to thank for today's events, Ariel says. Right there in my head, as intimate as it is possible to be.

Almost.

Because the only thing I can think about that would be more so would be to have his voice in my head, his cock buried inside me, and his teeth sunk deep in my neck.

I don't need the cards to tell me that will certainly happen. And soon.

I hear the thread of amusement and need in his voice when he responds, and I know he knows it too. *I like to know who tries to kill me. And all of their associates. And anyone else who might think the way that they do.*

I support this completely, I reply.

"Hey," Augie says then, "I think you better look."

Maddox is standing on that wall, hands on her hips as she looks out over the lake. I'm afraid that what she's looking at is Savi's dead body, but as I get to my feet, Savi herself lands.

But she lands hard and doesn't quite stick the landing, the first sign of anything but perfection from her that I've seen. She sags against the wall, and I don't think. I put my arm around her.

She leans against me. "Thank you," she murmurs.

I only nod.

And together, we all stand there and look out at the temple that hovers, frozen in midair, high above Crater Lake and Wizard Island, where it must have been hidden all these thousands of years.

The goddess, interrupted.

I don't know how long we stand there. I only know that we did it.

We beat that awful, rotten-faced bitch. I can't feel her inside me any longer, and I know that the threads of magic from all these supernatural creatures and the constellations dissolved her and shot whatever's left of her straight back into her prison.

I feel the cards hum in triumph.

Only then, when I tuck them away this time and nestle them of my own volition right next to my heart, do I turn back around, kneel next to my grandmother, and tell her that I love her.

That she is the best parent I ever had, and I wish I'd accepted the gift a lot sooner so I could have known her better.

I tell her all of this, but I think she knows.

Wherever she is now, wherever her soul has taken root, I think she's known it all along.

We say our farewells to Gran up there in those beautiful mountains where she made her sacrifice, making her funeral pyre and honoring her by letting her burn there, alone, beneath the Halloween blue moon.

We sit in a circle around her. No one speaks. We let her return to the magic she came from.

No one puts bodies in the ground, not anymore. One of the first things the monsters did was dig up the graveyards. The freshly dead are even more of a draw.

So we let her burn. And I promise the flames that carry her onward that I'll make a monument to this woman, out of materials that monsters won't care about, but she would. I will.

And I will honor her in as many ways as possible for as long as I live.

When we get home from Crater Lake much later that night, I invite Ariel in.

It's not the momentous thing it would have been before, because now there are too many momentous things to count, and all I want is him near me. When his vampire friend turns up for Augie, I go to invite her inside too, but Ariel shakes his head.

"There is no need to be too familiar," he tells me in his stern way, and Augie follows her out into the dark.

I show the man whose head I've been in, whose body I know so well, up to my room. When he pulls me into his arms, I kiss him like he's a fever and all I want to do is burn up with him.

But then I pull away. "There's something I have to do."

He nods, his gaze so silver it hurts. "These first deaths are the hardest," he tells me. "They are the ones that scar."

Someday he will tell me who it is he misses. All of those he lost who scarred him.

Tonight, I sit there, right on the floor in my bedroom. I pull out the cards.

And I find her.

In my head she's young again. Her eyes are sharp. She smiles at me, though she shakes her head too. "You don't need me, child. You have everything you need, right there with you."

"But . . ." I begin.

"I will always be here for you when you need me," she says. "That's a promise. But it's your time now, Winter. And there is still so much to do."

She leaves me there to sit on the floor a long while, letting tears fall down until they make puddles on the cards themselves.

I let them.

When Ariel comes out of the shower, he finds me there. On the floor, still covered in mud and blood and all the rest of the things that happened today. And I think that if I learned one thing up in the snow today, it's this: There can only be love. That's the only thing we really have, no matter what it looks like.

Even though it makes me feel panicked and dizzy to even think such a thing, given the fates of everyone I've ever loved.

Still. That doesn't change anything. Hiding from love is like hiding from the dark, pretending the stars aren't shining all the while. Hiding from love is breaking your own heart, then wondering why it hurts.

Love turns into grief, I know that part, but love is why it matters to lose someone.

If I'm going to lose everyone and everything I love—and isn't that the deal? Isn't that how this always worked, even before the world ended?—then I better love them hard while I'm here.

That's really all there is.

I look at Ariel, like a marble statue before me. I feel my heart ache inside my chest, telling me what I already know.

"I love you," I tell him, like I'm confessing a terrible sin. "You should know that."

He comes over and he lifts me, straight up from the floor without so much as a grunt to indicate he feels my weight. Then he holds me in his arms.

I lock my legs around his waist. I wrap my arms around his neck.

I revel in his perfect, unburned skin.

"You are my heart, little seer," says this twenty-five-hundred-year-old vampire king. Out loud and inside me, at once. "I don't have my own. I have only yours, and so you will have to let it beat for the both of us. I will insist upon it."

"You can just say it," I whisper, there against his mouth. "You love me too. And you should know better."

"I do," he growls, and then his mouth is on mine and his hands are gripping my hair, and then everything is heat and madness.

I can't get enough. Too much death, too much blood, but then blood is the basis of all of this.

Blood is what keeps us all alive. Blood and love are tangled up in each other, and so are we.

Soon enough, he's inside me. His cock so deep I can barely breathe. His fangs sunk into my neck.

This time, he opens up the vein on the side of his own neck, and that's where I drink from him.

I love you, he tells me as he thrusts inside me, making me come and come and come. *When I say forever, Winter, I mean it. You'll see.*

I decide, then and there, that I will.

No matter what.

30.

There's another gathering the next evening, All Saints' Day, or maybe it's a kind of wake for the woman we all lost.

We sit around in the living room of the house, and these powerful supernatural creatures tell me stories about my grandmother. The oracle they knew, like it or not.

How imperious she was in the face of creatures who could eat her in two bites. How happy she was to lecture a werewolf or vampire on how they should clean up their act.

How certain she was that they would not dare hurt her . . . and she was right.

"She was a terror," Ty growls, but I'm beginning to understand the werewolf alpha now. I can tell the difference between his bark and his bite. He catches my gaze and holds it. "She will be missed."

We talk about Gran for a long while.

Later, we turn to other topics, now that we're all showered and fed and recovered. Or as close to recovered as we're going to get.

"Do we think that the goddess will stay like that?" Maddox asks from where she sits on Ty's lap. "My vote is no."

"Almost certainly not, though the magic was good," Savi agrees. She is a bit tired and pale, and she sits in the armchair in the living room, a poultice of unidentifiable herbs pressed to one temple. Though she smiles a little. "I think we have to assume that we only scratched the surface of her followers. Hopefully the last of that particular type. All those nasty priests and people consumed with religious fervor. There are other ways. Other kinds of interest in death goddesses. It's not all cults and bird masks." She laughs. "I hope."

When the knock comes on the door, we all know what it is without having to look. Ariel confirms it, inclining his head to indicate to Augie and all the rest of us that it's his delivery.

My twin brother stands. He looks around the room, and he seems . . .

Not defeated. Not exactly.

"I hate this," he says, baldly. Matter-of-factly. No self-pity discernible at all in his voice. "I can't function without it, but I fucking hate vampire blood. And I don't want to leave Winter with all of this again, which I feel is inevitable if I need something like this." He shakes his head, and he looks at me . . . but he's not talking *to* me. "I need to detox. I need to kick this."

There's a small silence. I'm holding my breath. I'm also certain that no one here understands the importance of what just happened.

I've heard Augie talk about quitting things before, but it was always couched in maybes. It was never statements to groups. It was never without drama and emotion, because he was never matter-of-fact about it.

Because he never meant it.

"*Can* you kick vampire blood?" Savi asks. She's looking at Ariel.

He lifts a shoulder and drops it. It is not reassuring. "I have heard that it can happen, though it is rare," he says. That silver gaze is too knowing. He moves it to Augie. "It is a long, arduous process. There is no guarantee that you will survive it."

Augie is still standing in the middle of the room. He still looks *so good* to me. He looks healthy, happy. I have to remind myself that he's not. That it's the blood doing this to him.

"Most blood addicts don't last as long as I have." His voice is quiet. "They either try to ingest too much and it kills them, or they get drained and discarded by their dealers while they're still pretty. I spent a lot of time in that dungeon, wondering what made me so lucky."

The way he says *lucky* makes my eyes tear up. I blink the moisture away.

"Blood," Augie says. "It's always blood, isn't it?" He's looking straight at Ariel now. "You wanted that oracle bloodline, and if Winter, the chosen heir, didn't work out, you wanted to have the spare on hand."

My heart skips a beat, though I had already gotten there. And Ariel doesn't deny it. Instead, he nods.

"We are, all of us, controlled by our weaknesses," he says. "Your sister's weakness is you. Yours are your addictions. There is no possible way you do not know this already. If you can't control yourself, anyone can control you. And therefore her."

I want to slug him. I want to kiss him. I hate him for saying something like that to my twin.

I love him for saying it so plainly, no dancing around it at all.

The kind of no-bullshit intervention we never gave Augie, I'm ashamed to say.

I expect my brother to freak out, but he doesn't. He nods. Then again. He swallows, hard.

"This is why I want to get clean," he says in a low voice, and while there's an anger in it, it doesn't seem to be focused on anyone but him. "I'm sick and tired of being a fucking bargaining chip."

Ty eyes him. "I can dry you out. But you won't like it."

"It's my understanding that it's excruciating," Augie says. "And it goes on forever. And most people kill themselves rather than face it."

"Uh. No. That's not okay," I say immediately.

"I want to live, Winter," Augie tells me. He's standing in a room full of people, but he's telling me. Just me. I think everyone knows it. "I want to be *alive*. And I don't know how."

That takes my breath away. All I can do is nod.

Not giving him permission. But maybe that's my blessing.

He turns back to Ty. "I'll do it. I need to do it. One way or another."

Ty nods, very slowly. I think there's something close enough to respect in his gaze, and I don't need Maddox to tell me that this is unusual.

"We'll find out who you are on the other side," Ty says, and it sounds like a promise. "But I'm warning you, the journey will change you."

"It already has," my brother says.

He doesn't go with the vampire who waits for him outside. He lets the wolves take him, meaning he's diving straight in.

He doesn't look back. He doesn't hug me goodbye.

But he doesn't need to.

You've got this, I think at him. I don't need to be in his head.

I know he hears me.

Deep in his bones, in the cells we once shared, he knows.

Later that night, in Ariel's bed, I don't cry. I don't discuss Augie at all.

I move in the dark, biting him, scratching him, leaving my marks as best I can.

Because no one ever said that forever wouldn't sting.

He lets me do it, and laughs while I do, then fucks me so good and so long that I couldn't mount an argument if my life depended on it.

Or sob out my grief when he's so good at making it into this other song we only sing together.

In the morning, I wake up and go to the roof to see Savi's hint of sunrise because I missed it yesterday. I know by now that Ariel's apartment has no eastern exposures, and that's how he gets away with all that glass.

Outside, it's All Souls' Day. November is here, Gran is dead, and I'm looking forward to Franklin Hendry trying to take what's mine. I really am.

I think of Augie, wherever he is. I turn and look over at the hills in the distance, the ones that rise above Jacksonville, where the werewolves roam along the old mining trails and make their own paths into the old-growth forests so ancient and so impenetrable that people who've seen all the monsters the Reveal has offered still think Bigfoot is out there.

"It's a new day," I whisper. "It's a new dawn."

And we're all going to be okay.

I drive back through Jacksonville later that morning, where the details of what Samuel did keep coming out. Not just what he did to Gran, though that's shocked the whole community. But all the rest of the things he was up to on the side.

His sister, Jenny, is shocked, but not as shocked as might be expected.

"I knew something was up with him," she tells me, sitting out on the porch of that little white house. "I knew it. At first, I thought all his organizing saved him, and then I thought maybe he was trying a little too hard. He liked the power more than the people. I think he became what he always said he hated."

"Maybe we all do," I say. "If we're not careful."

The cards hum a little at that, whether to support me or warn me, it's hard to tell.

November keeps chugging along, more winter than fall most days. Samuel doesn't leave the vacuum that folks initially expect, because people step up. They decide to expand into what happened instead of shrinking because of it.

"I loved your grandmother," Birdie tells me the night she leads the community meeting. Her wife, Miriam, is in the front row, a huge smile on her face. "She knew I was gay all along, and when my parents needed to pray on it for a little too long, she was there for me. And to be perfectly honest, I always thought Samuel was a turd."

"Well. He was."

"Maddox Hemming, on the other hand . . ." Birdie says leadingly, and both she and Miriam laugh.

I decide it's possible that the human contingent of the Rogue Valley is going to do just fine. Maybe better now that there are more hands on deck.

It also doesn't hurt that some of us have an in with the monsters.

In the middle of all this good stuff, something better happens. Franklin Hendry never comes for me. He disappears.

As far as I can tell, he was there the day before Halloween, smug and vile. But the next morning, the bank was empty. His ledger remained, however, and all the people in it received their money back. It appeared on doorsteps or was shoved through windows.

His thugs disappeared too. A lot like someone went and cleaned house, and I have a few ideas about who that could be. Several *whos*, in fact.

But I don't ask. I take it as an early Thanksgiving present.

I assume that everyone will move out of the cottages now that there are no more false pretenses, but no one wants to leave.

Savi wants to stay close as she works on the spell to get rid of Vinča for good.

Maddox claims she still isn't ready to take her place at Ty's side, and she has the bruises she loves so much to prove it.

Even Briar seems friendlier, though it doesn't seem like she has the slightest idea what happened.

"It's like a monster sorority," I tell Ariel. "I kind of like it."

"I like it too," he tells me, in a much more serious tone. "They can protect you when I can't."

We are up in my room then, there beneath the eaves. We have just spent a very long time experimenting with each other, scratching at the surface of the time that spools before us.

Of the small bit of this journey I'll get to share with him before I become another one of his scars.

Something I should think is sad, but I don't. I think it's beautiful.

And besides, he has no intention of letting me die.

"I've already changed your hours at the coffee stand," he tells me. When I blink at him in astonishment, he continues. "People know you're the oracle, Winter. It's not only cards and visions, it's a vocation. They will come by that stand and ask you to see things for them. Just as they used to come here and ask your grandmother at her window, and I don't want them at this house, not anymore. I want you safer than that."

"Wait." I'm hung up on the first part of all that. "You changed my hours? What happened to Doug?"

Ariel rolls me beneath him and hikes my knees up wide, then thrusts deep into me once more, that cool, enormous cock nearly making me come that easily.

"Doug," he tells me in a deeply casual tone, as if this is a tea party, "was an unfortunate casualty. But the people like coffee, and I, as a benevolent king, wanted to make sure they got it."

"And you," I say, as he sets a slow, deliriously deep pace, "got your in with the new oracle without having to move house. How clever you are."

"All's fair this side of the Reveal, my love," he tells me, his mouth against my neck, his tongue on my pulse. "I didn't need a vision to tell me that you would be a problem for me. Though your grandmother took great pleasure in delivering it. All I had to do was look at you, one risen phoenix to another, and I understood that I would never be the same."

"And while you're at it, you could be sneaky and underhanded like everyone else," I say, grinning at him. "No moral high ground after all. I can't wait to tell everyone."

"You won't, little seer," he tells me. "You wouldn't dare."

And then he shows me why.

Over and over and over again.

31.

I fall asleep like that, wrapped up with him, no part of me left that isn't entirely his.

No part of him that isn't mine.

You know exactly what it means, Maddox said once, and I do.

Bound is what it sounds like. Tied up and tangled into one, forever.

Asleep, wrapped up in his cool embrace, I fall into a dream.

Moonlight. Starshine.

I am outside, maybe in the yard here, twirling around and around.

But the dream becomes a vision in the middle of a happy spin.

I find myself in the woods, following a path, until I realize there are footsteps ahead of me.

I feel the urge to hurry, so I do, and I see Briar.

Not like I've ever seen Briar before. She's not wearing a hat, and I see that her ears are long and pointed, sticking up through her black hair.

Also, she's wearing Augie's medallion.

She turns back as if she hears me, when that shouldn't be possible in a vision.

And when she sees me, she laughs.

As I watch, she becomes Vinča.

I watch her face as it melts, one into the next. I see the worms as they slither through her eyes, and I can feel them all over me, too.

I want to scream, but find I can't.

"Sleep while you can," the goddess sneers, so close to my face that I can feel the brimstone heat of her rotted breath. "Rut with your little leech. I know where you live. And I'm only just getting started."

ACKNOWLEDGMENTS

Thank you to everyone at Montlake, especially Selena James, for letting me write this book I've always dreamed of writing. To Holly Root for always encouraging my various flights of fancy so I can make them into stories that you get to read. And to all my usual loves for the advice, suggestions, and many, many years of listening to me rant extensively about *Buffy*, *Supernatural*, and every paranormal romance I could get my hands on. Especially Jeff.

ABOUT THE AUTHOR

USA Today bestselling, multi-award-nominated, and critically acclaimed author Megan Crane has written more than 150 books and shows no sign of slowing down.

Megan has a master's and PhD in English literature. She has taught many creative writing classes, including through UCLA Extension's prestigious Writers' Program and in a great many workshops. She has a black belt in Krav Maga and a blue belt in jiujitsu, and spends more time in martial arts studios than she ever imagined possible. She lives in the Pacific Northwest with her comic book artist husband, though, at any given time, she is likely to be either huddled in a coffee shop somewhere or off traveling the world. Preferably both.

You can find out more than you ever wanted to know about her at www.megancrane.com.